W9-BDL-360

WITHDRAWN
No longer the property of the
Boston Public Library.
Sale of this material benefits the Library.

Boston Public Library

STORME FRONT

ALSO BY W. L. RIPLEY

Dreamsicle

STORME FRONT

A Wyatt Storme Mystery

W. L. RIPLEY

Henry Holt and Company
New York

Henry Holt and Company, Inc.
Publishers since 1866
115 West 18th Street
New York, New York 10011

Henry Holt ® is a registered
trademark of Henry Holt and Company, Inc.

Published in Canada by Fitzhenry & Whiteside Ltd.,
195 Allstate Parkway, Markham, Ontario L3R 4T8.

Library of Congress Cataloging-in-Publication Data
Ripley, W. L. (Warren L.)
Storme front : a Wyatt Storme mystery /
W.L. Ripley. — 1st ed.
p.   cm.
1. Private investigators—Colorado—Fiction.   I. Title.
PS3568.I64S76   1995   94-21891
813'.54—dc20   CIP

ISBN 0-8050-3601-6

Henry Holt books are available for special promotions
and premiums. For details contact: Director, Special Markets.

First Edition—1995

Designed by Betty Lew

Printed in the United States of America
All first editions are printed on acid-free paper.∞

1 3 5 7 9 10 8 6 4 2

*Grateful acknowledgment is made to reprint lyrics from
"Bad Moon Rising," words and music by John C. Fogerty of
Creedence Clearwater Revival, © 1969 Jondora Music,
courtesy of Fantasy, Inc.*

For Robynn Leigh,
and Mason Cole,
and Jared Cain,
and Logan James.
The best and brightest.
And for Linda Diane,
their beautiful mother.

ACKNOWLEDGMENTS

Special thanks go to the following:

Special Agent Larry Scott of Alcohol, Tobacco, and Firearms. Larry is one of the country's leading authorities on guns and illegal weapons trade. His contribution was considerable and lent authenticity to this fictionalized account.

Jan McRoberts in Boulder, who provided housing and real estate information about the Boulder–Denver area and the nearby mountains. The Colorado Division of Wildlife was helpful in establishing the Elk range and weather patterns for the Boulder area and the surrounding mountains.

My brother, Jim, for researching the law enforcement hierarchies in Colorado.

My sister, Janet, for her constant encouragement and unwavering belief in my ability.

Gary L. for his comments on the manuscript and his friendship.

*"Everyone is a moon, and has a
dark side which he never shows
to anybody."*

—*Mark Twain*

*I see the bad moon arising.
I see trouble on the way.
I see earthquakes and lightnin'.
I see bad times today.
Don't go around tonight,
well, it's bound to take your life,
there's a bad moon on the rise.*

—*John Fogerty, "Bad Moon Rising"*

I wasn't happy to see Jackie Burlingame. Hadn't asked him to come. I don't like drop-in company much. Besides, I don't like nervous people and Jackie was nervous.

And I don't like Jackie.

But I don't turn people away, though I like my privacy, which is why I live away from what passes for civilization and particularly away from the city and its concrete canyons and gray towers and antiseptic lifestyle. Some people call me reclusive, a hermit. Mostly, I'm just private.

So I let him in. He stood there, surveying my mountain home with quick, furtive glances, as if he was in an alien environment, which he was. Stone fireplace, huge area rug, hardwood floor, large window wall that looks down on the Little Silver River as it cuts through the Colorado Rockies. Walnut gun cabinet, comfort-worn furniture. Country simplicity. Nothing Jackie B. would be familiar with. He tugged at his wispy hair and chain-smoked Pall Malls. His eyes were raw and watery. Not used to being awake before lunch.

"You got anything to drink?" he asked, squinting through cigarette smoke.

"Coffee," I said, sipping mine and watching him over the rim of the cup.

"Any hard stuff?"

"Coffee's what I got." I sat on a barstool by the counter.

"You're not much of a host."

"Wouldn't have you as a guest. What do you want, Burlingame?"

"Hire you to help me with a little . . . a . . . errand, I'd guess you'd call it."

I smiled. "Like I'd do you a favor."

"I'll pay."

"I don't need the money."

"Everybody needs the money." He said it as if it were a philosophical certainty. "Buy yourself some new furniture." His brow wrinkled in thought, then he asked, "What is it you do anyway?" Wasn't an original question.

"Little of this, little of that."

"You getting rich?"

"I'm not starving," I said. "Can't see money's done anything special for you."

He laughed a short, staccato burst. "You never change, do you?"

"Not much," I said. "What do you want?"

"I need you to help me. All you gotta do is come with me on a delivery."

"Why me?"

"You're big enough to make people think twice about messing with me while I deliver something."

"I'm not for hire. Call Rent-a-Thug. I don't like drugs and I don't like you."

"It ain't drugs."

"Bet it isn't Muppet Babies, either."

He scratched his throat, a raspy sound. He had a three-day growth of stubble. "The smart shit ever stop around here?"

"I don't get many visitors."

"It's not that good a show."

"I'm giving you my early morning performance. I save it for wasted pukes."

He swallowed, dryly, and wet his lips. "I need a drink."

"This isn't the Holiday Inn," I said, standing. "I'll get you some coffee. You tell me what you have in mind. Then you leave. And I don't want the abridged version. Shoot me straight or I'll toss you. Which, incidentally, I'll enjoy."

"I get a drink or not?"

"Telling the truth make you nervous?"

He glared at me. He was wearing a leather jacket over a hand-stitched silk shirt. Diamond ring, heavy gold chain around his throat. European boots. Ransomed from the weak-willed and the soul-sick.

"Think you're bad, don'tcha?"

I shrugged.

"Big shot ex-pro. Big playboy. You ain't shit. Thought I had something for you, but I was wrong. Too big-time for you."

"I say something offends you, Jackie?"

"I got more important things to do than sit around talking to has-beens. See you around, hotshot—"

I saw it coming way ahead of it actually happening. Partly because I expected it from a weasel like Jackie. Partly because he wasn't any good at it and I'd seen better guys do it. Sucker punch. Play it like you're walking away, then let the victim have it. It probably worked on the zombies and teen dopers he was used to dealing with.

Always watch the shoulders. They rise slightly before a punch. Jackie started a roundhouse from his thigh—tried to hide it, but it was slow-motion. As his bony fist came at my face, I stepped inside the arc of his swing, caught his wrist with my left hand and twisted. At the same time I kicked him in the shin with the hard edge of my Dunham hiking boots. He yelped like a scalded coyote. I squeezed his arm and forced him into a chair.

Kids. You gotta teach 'em everything.

"Shit!" he said, bellowing in pain. "Son of a bitch!"

"Watch your language," I said. I released his wrist. "I'm at the age where I pick things up." I stepped back and watched him rub his leg. "Okay, Jackie. You're on a pass now. You try that again and I'll bounce you around the room."

"You broke my fuckin' leg," Jackie said, whining.

"Not yet. It's a thought, though. Quit being a baby." He retreated to the corner of the chair, looking up at me with defeated eyes, the snarl still on his lips. I picked up the cup I'd dropped and poured myself more coffee. "Soon as you can walk, you leave. Sorry I can't play anymore, but us has-beens tire easily."

Jackie rubbed his ankle and grimaced, rocking back and forth in the chair. He was stalling, looking for the right angle. I could almost hear his mind whirring. "Okay. Whoa. Back up a minute, buddy."

"I'm not your buddy."

"Hey, sorry I swung on you." He was chuckling and shaking his head. All a mistake. "Shoulda known better. But I need you to hear me out. Money in it for you. For both of us. Easy money. Couple hours out of your life, that's all. What's it cost you to listen, huh?"

"If you're involved, I know it stinks. And there's no such thing as easy money. But I'll listen. No promises. Go ahead and talk. Meter's running."

He lifted his head and indicated the barkwood bar behind me. "Really need that drink, first."

"There are glasses in the cabinet behind the bar," I said, giving in. Nine A.M. and he wants a drink. The thought made my stomach draw up. "Get it yourself."

He limped to the bar. I walked back to my stool and sat. He took inventory with delight. "Chivas, Beefeater's, Jack D., Glenfiddich, Wild Turkey . . . You don't mind I open a new bottle, do ya? Hey, they're all new." Producing a fifth of Wild Turkey, he cracked the seal and poured four fingers into a tumbler. "That's weird. All this booze and none of it open. And only the best stuff. Want some of this?"

I shook my head. Bourbon for breakfast? Jackie threw back a large swallow of the whiskey and set the glass down. He sloshed more bourbon into the glass, the bottle gurgled, and then he added water from the tap. "Much better," he said. He limped to a chair like a man with a rock in his shoe. "So, what're you doing up here in the mountains? Figured you for the executive suite when you quit. You know, big decisions, golf on the weekends. Gold card and room service." He took another knock of the autumn-gold liquid. He was becoming expansive now. My buddy. A cold breeze wafted through the window. Might have to build a fire later.

"But then, you always had a different way of looking at things," he said. "Went to Nam, didn't you?"

"I was there."

"Kill anybody?"

"I conquered Indochina while I was there, but the press covered it up," I said. His voice was like Styrofoam scraping against concrete at the outer edge of my patience. He was a hustler and a doper and I was tired of him. "Get to it, Jackie."

"Hey. Relax. This is right up your alley." He gestured with his glass. "I gotta make a delivery and I need an escort. All you gotta do is be there and flex your muscles."

"My muscles don't flex like they used to." It sounded too easy. Guys like Jackie always had an angle. Why me? He didn't like me any better than I liked him. "Not my thing anyway."

"You've done stuff like it before. I heard you took down a leg-breaker from Denver. Some people say you took out a couple guys in Missouri, last year."

"Wasn't me." It was, but I didn't need to keep Jackie B. updated. So he thought I was for hire. He should have known better, but he had wires loose in his head. Needed to quit sampling the product. Still, I wanted to know more about what Jackie was up to. Naturally curious, I guess.

"Pay you two hundred dollars."

"Charge that just to let you hang out with me. When?"

"Tomorrow. Around four."

"What are we delivering?"

"I'll pay you three hundred."

"I want five and you'll tell me what you're delivering."

"Five hundred! For that much, you don't need to know. Maybe I can get someone else."

"But will they have steel-gray eyes and a Dentyne smile?" I knew there was some reason he'd picked me. Somebody else wouldn't do, or he couldn't trust anyone else. Made me wonder how much money was involved. "My price goes up as we go along."

His eyes narrowed. Guys like Burlingame harbor the suspicion that everybody is on the make just like them. A necessary defense mechanism when you deal in other people's miseries and greeds.

"You shouldn't mess around, Storme. You really shouldn't. There are some major-leaguers involved. People I don't want to piss off."

"Heavy hitters don't mess with juicers if it's anything important."

"Yeah?" He wanted to impress me, shut me up. Let me know he was somebody. His ego, artificially propped up by bootlicker substance abusers, was fragile. "What if it was guns? Aut-o-matics. Rat-a-tat-tat, baby. Explosives? Big-ticket handguns? Steady market for more?"

When had Jackie graduated from pharmaceuticals to guns? Why would anyone trust him on a deal like this? Something was wrong. The Sicilians and the Colombians pulled their own strings. Who then?

"Why me?" I asked.

"Told you why. You're big enough and the delivery is out in the damn woods. You know your way around out there and I don't." He pulled a cigarette from his shirt pocket and lighted it with a disposable lighter. "Besides, these are not normal people. Real space cowboys. Twitchy, ya know? Want me to make the— Hey, you in or out?"

"Who's buying them?"

"Hunh-uh. No way, baby. You get no more until you're in."

"I need more if I'm to make an informed decision."

He considered a moment, and I knew the panel was slamming down. He took a long pull on the cigarette, exhaled a blue-gray cloud of pollution, and said, "In or out?"

"I'm thinking about it. Who are you selling to and how much are you going to get?"

"I'll tell you this much. I'll pay you a grand to go with me." It was going to be tough to get any more information out of him. He was going to make a big score and was afraid of the people he was selling to. I didn't want anything to do with this, but the last thing I wanted was a shipment of illegal weapons floating around the countryside. "You going or not?"

"Not until I know more about it."

"Not even if your buddy Matt Jenkins is involved?" he said.

"What's Matt got to do with this?"

"Go with me tomorrow and I'll tell you." He smiled and downed the rest of the Wild Turkey.

"I want to know now."

"Want in one hand and shit in the other. See which weighs the most."

"I don't think he has anything to do with this."

"Believe what you want. Call me if you change your mind. Have to be soon. I'm in the book." He rose from his seat, handed me the empty glass, then walked to the door. "Oh, yeah. It'd be a major mistake to mention this to anybody."

"Made 'em before."

"Not like this one." He forgot to shut the door when he left.

I washed out his glass and thought about what he'd said. How could Matt be involved in something like this? He was a good man. I'd known Matt since Vietnam, then later when he was a

Dallas Cowboys fan. He'd been a Cowboys fan because I played wide receiver for them. Possession receiver. That's what they call the white guys, even though I could turn a ten-flat hundred on my best days. Matt had made money in land speculation and the stock market. Had a cattle ranch outside Boulder. Despite his success, Matt was the kind of guy who could hang out in small-town coffee shops and never get a second look.

I dialed Matt's number from memory. His wife, Kelly, answered on the third ring. We made small talk. I asked to speak to Matt. She told me he was out. I asked if she knew Jackie Burlingame.

She was quiet, then said, "Is he a creepy-looking guy that chain-smokes and smells like a distillery?"

"That's him."

She was quiet for a moment, then said, "I don't like him. He's . . . greasy. Unclean, even with the expensive clothes and fancy car. That make sense?"

"You're a good judge of character. How do you know him?"

"He's been here twice. Matt didn't seem glad to see him, but they went into his office. Closed the door. Later, he wouldn't tell me what he was here for. 'Business,' he said."

"Look, I'll try to get by and talk to both of you. I don't think there's anything to worry about."

"Wyatt?"

"Yeah."

"He frightens me."

"Don't worry about Jackie," I said. "I'll take care of him. You won't see him again."

I hung up the phone and thought about it.

I didn't like Jackie sniffing around Jenkins's place. Decided he needed a partner, after all. I wanted to find out what Jackie was up to. Before I did anything else, though, I decided to call Chick Easton. I might need a little help. Good to have friends.

Chick Easton was a good friend.

And more than a little help.

The Tumbleweed Connection is a quiet restaurant in Largo where they serve the best coffee in Colorado. One of my favorite places.

Chick Easton was leaning back in his chair, drinking coffee and smoking Camel cigarettes when I opened the door to the restaurant. There was gingham cloth on the table and blueberry muffins, a house specialty, in a wicker basket as a centerpiece. A sturdy-looking blond waitress bustled up and poured me a cup of coffee and freshened Chick's cup. He thanked her and I sat down in a sturdy wooden chair.

"What's up?" he said.

"My expectations."

"Any time you offer to buy dinner I know you want something. What's it this time?"

I peeled back the napkin from the basket. The generous aroma of hot muffins rose from it. I selected one from the basket and juggled it hand-to-hand to my plate. "Sure are suspicious. Bad for the heart. You've got to learn to enjoy the little things." I broke open the muffin and steam rose in a warm little cloud. "The dew glistening in the morning. Good cup of coffee. Stimulating conversation with an intellectual giant."

He cocked his head, squinted at me. "You didn't promise some of your football buddies we'd take them hunting again, did you? Never again. They have no appreciation for the mountains or the animals. They're loud and—"

"That was Broedeholt. I didn't invite him, he just showed up. Anyway, that's not what I need—"

"I knew it." He smiled. When Chick smiles, the hard eyes soften and he looks younger, with a twinkle in them to remind you of the good times, not the eyes of a man who has seen too much and didn't look away. His age is indeterminate. Somewhere between thirty-five and fifty. There are lines at the corners of his mouth and eyes, but he has a thirty-one-inch waist and can jump up and kick the top of a door frame. He is a couple inches shorter than me and the muscles in his shoulders are like steel cable, but don't show in street clothes. You wouldn't pick him out in a crowd as a tough guy, but that is a mistake many have made. And regretted. "What is it this time?"

I explained the situation to him over lunch. Told him about Jackie's visit that morning. About talking to Kelly Jenkins.

"Can't figure Jenks on something like this," he said. "Not his style. Something's happened he hadn't figured on. Or, they got him in a bind. Sounds like you're being set up for something. What do you need?"

"Backup. I need your broad shoulders and powerfully manly ways in case we're attacked by Indians. I'm not sure what we're up against, but it doesn't feel right."

"What do I get out of this?"

"The usual deal. No money up front and none forthcoming. You get to hang around with me and soak up charm."

"Good," he said. "I was afraid I was gonna get screwed again." Then he ordered Canadian Club whiskey and a Dunhill cigar for dessert since it was on my tab. I didn't mind, since I knew he'd be there where I needed him and when I needed him.

The next afternoon I drove into Boulder. Chick with me. I'd been unable to get hold of Matt, and that bothered me. He hadn't come home last night. Under my jacket was a Browning nine-millimeter pistol with a full clip. Chick, the romantic, carried a Colt Peacemaker .45. Not stainless steel. Blued. With walnut grip. "You've seen too many John Wayne movies," I said, when I saw it.

"Impossible to see too many John Wayne movies," he said, spinning the cylinder on the atavistic weapon.

We were on our way to see our old buddy and local gunrunner, Jackie Burlingame. I drove the Bronco, its sides splashed with mud, the tape player spilling Bob Dylan. I nosed the truck into the suburbs and then toward some upscale apartments. Corning Estates. The kind of place where few questions were asked if you came up with the fifteen hundred a month extortion money. Like most guys in Jackie's line of work, they never have enough, something I never understood. Like the guys in the NFL who spent their money on luxury cars, condos they only used once and forgot, alligator shoes, jewelry they rarely wore, and women they couldn't keep. Never understood the procurement urge, the fever to possess and impress.

My temptations ran along a different path.

I found a pay phone outside a nearby convenience store and dialed Burlingame's number. He picked it up on the ninth ring. I'm nothing if not persistent.

"Yeah," he growled.

"Hey, Jackie babe. It's Wyatt. I'm in town. Remember me? The has-been with the great smile. How you doin'?"

"What do you want?" he said. I got the feeling the question lacked sincerity.

"I've been thinking it over and decided to take you up on your offer."

"Forget it. I got somebody else. Cheaper too."

"Cheaply gained is cheaply prized, Burly."

Silence at the other end, then, "Where are you now, Storme?"

I lied. "I'm at a supermarket on the north end across from the Golden Saddle motel." Which would have placed me thirty minutes from where I was, which was in view of Corning Estates.

"You know where I live?"

"No." I felt ashamed, lying to a great guy like Jackie. Probably wouldn't sell me any cocaine now.

"Well, you're not very far from it." He then gave me directions which would have taken me several miles from his apartment at Corning Estates. I felt vindicated. What a world. It's getting where you can't trust your friendly neighborhood dope pusher. "I'll wait till you get here," he promised.

"Be right there," I said. I looked at my watch. Three thirty. I bought a tabloid in the liquor store. ELVIS ALIVE AND PERFORMING COUNTRY-WESTERN IN PHOENIX BAR. BOY MEETS PLUTONIANS. I also bought a can of honey-roast peanuts, a six-pack of Michelob, and a pint of Canadian Club.

"You're a good man, Storme," Chick said, when I got back into the Bronco and handed him the items. "I'll need my vitamins if we're gonna surround the bad guys."

"You know Elvis was alive and singing country in Phoenix?"

"Everybody knows that," he said, cracking the seal on the Canadian whiskey. "Where've you been?"

"Always the last to know." I drove the Bronco around to the side lot. Chick got out of the truck, and took a bottle of beer and the tabloid with him. He set the beer on top of a Dumpster and opened the paper, as if waiting for a ride. I sat in the Bronco and waited. The sign on the gates of Corning Estates said LUXURY AND SOLITUDE, OUR DUTY. I unwrapped a Macanudo cigar and listened to Bob Dylan sing "Tonight, I'll Be Staying Here with You," which made me think of Sandy.

Sandra Collingsworth. My fiancée. Every night I watched her on the Channel Seven news, saw her perfect smile, and listened to her easy, bubbling-stream voice. We were back together, but problems remained. Lifestyles, for one. Hers was not mine. And mine was not hers. Hers was lights and events. Glitzy company and sequined nights. Mine was misty mornings and starry nights. Pine trees and long distance sights. The smell of damp forest and the dazzle of sunny meadows. Never saw the skyscraper I'd trade the smallest mountain for. Sandy liked the outdoors, but her dream was in the city. At one time, I'd thought mine was too.

But one morning, I'd awakened with its taste in my mouth and knew there was nothing for me there. So I left all that air-conditioned nonsense behind.

We had agreed to try. To overcome the barriers. To find out. Neither of us wanted to live without the other, and we would find a way to bridge the gap in expectations and geography.

I'd been ruminating twenty minutes when they came out of the apartment building—Jackie B. and a big guy in a plaid mackinaw and a rust-colored cowboy hat. Snakeskin boots.

"Too flashy, Jackie," I said to myself. I looked in Chick's direction. He gave no indication he'd seen them. But I knew he had. Like I knew tomorrow was coming.

Jackie and the big man got into a nondescript Ford Cargo van. Probably a rental. Or stolen. Be easier to follow them, since they had the rear window covered. I didn't want him to sell those guns. But I had to know what Matt's part in this was before I blew it up.

I started the Bronco, drove through the gates and into the parking lot, and pulled up behind the van to block it. I felt the bulge of the Browning hidden under the tail of my jacket. I looked back to the convenience-store Dumpster. The paper was lying on top of it, but Chick had disappeared. Jackie and the large human in the snakeskin boots and feathered Stetson got out on opposite sides of the van. They weren't smiling or anything. If I didn't know better I'd have thought they weren't happy to see me.

I got out of the Bronco. "Hey, Jackie," I said. Cheerful, friendly, glad to be here. "Got here as soon as I could. The instructions were perfect. Didn't have any trouble finding it at all."

Jackie had a pained expression on his face. Snakeskins came around the truck. He had a big face, crooked nose. About thirty. A little overweight. Too many Coors in cowboy bars. Blond mustache, untrimmed, and a diamond stud in one ear. His hands were immense.

"How did you . . . ," began Burlingame. "Shit!"

"Did I come at a bad time?"

"You want me to get rid of him, Mr. Burlingame?" said snakeskins.

"Mr. Burlingame?" I said. "Ego-stroking, Jackie? It diminishes you."

"This ain't none of your business, asshole," said the giant.

"Has brains, too. He walks, he talks, he grovels and wears reptiles on his feet. Just what everyone is looking for in gorillas this year." I winked at the big guy and made a kissing motion. "Love the earring, hon."

"You muthafu—"

"Take it easy, Turk," Jackie said, looking around, nervously. He didn't need the attention, with illegal weapons in the van. Something Turk hadn't thought about.

"Turk?" I said. "Is that short for 'turkey'?"

"Keep pushin', fuckhead," said Turk, face red, "and I'll stomp you."

"But not here, Einstein. Jackie's got too much to lose if you make a scene. A fight in the parking lot of Corning Estates? It isn't done."

"What do you want, Storme?" Jackie asked.

"Take you up on your offer."

"I got Turk."

"Yeah? But he dresses bad. And he has a weird nickname. Besides, have you thought this out? I'll bet Turk here hasn't thought of anything during the past month. How were you going to make the drop?"

"What's it to you?" said Turk. "You ain't going."

"That's real good, Turkey," I said. "Didn't know you did impressions. Glen Campbell, right? *True Grit?* Now, I don't want to hear your voice anymore. You got it?"

He wasn't used to being talked to like this. They never are. He grunted and started toward me. In the NFL I learned two things about fighting—first, never take off your helmet, and second, never let the moat monsters that live in the pit get their hands on you.

Reaching behind me I jerked out the Browning and swung it level on Turk's face. When I snapped back the hammer he stopped in his tracks. "Besides," I said, "I've got this pretty gun here and you don't. See, Jackie?" I kept my eyes on Turk, who was keeping his eyes on the black gun. "He's stupid. Doesn't size up the opposition. Bigger ain't always better. Smarter is. Bad things could happen to you while he's being a tough guy."

"You won't shoot," said Turk. "Too many people around."

"Wrong again, Turkey. Didn't they teach you anything at the thug academy? Jackie can't afford to be connected with these guns in any way. I blow you away and Jackie and I become best friends. You've got some oversize shooter under your coat and from the way you're favoring your left leg, you've got one in your boot. I shoot you, you have guns. I've got a permit for mine. Jackie and I tell the police you were forcing Jackie to run guns. We caught you and I shot you in self-defense. His story'll be same as mine. I'm a hero and you're dead from the neck down, too. The police will annoy me for a while, but they'll let me go eventually. Tell me if I've left anything out."

"Pretty good, Storme," said Jackie. He was quiet for a moment, then said, "Okay, you're in. Back off, Turk."

I eased the hammer down on the Browning and put it back

under my jacket, keeping my eyes on Turk. I was safe, anyway. Right now, Chick Easton was sighting on Turk with his Colt. Didn't have to see it. Knew it.

"When this is over, I'm gonna kick your ass, smart guy," Turk said. Same tune, over and over.

"Maybe you can't do it. Ever think of that? You're overweight and slow. Me? I'm in good shape and the force is with me. I'll wear you out, fatso. You even dream it and you better wake up and apologize."

"Okay, okay," Jackie said, looking around again. "Let's get out of here."

"I get paid up front," I said. "Right now. One thousand dollars. And I don't take American Express."

"A grand!?" said Turk. "I only got—"

"More than you're worth," I said, interrupting. "It's a wonder they just don't come in and take the guns, dumb as you are. Pay up, Jackie, or I'll flatten your tires and saddle up."

"Dammit, Storme," said Burlingame, gritting his teeth. "Not here."

"Right here. Right now."

He reached into his jacket and produced a fat wallet. He gave me ten crisp hundreds. How do I claim this on my 1040? What a dilemma. I folded the bills and put them in my pocket. Then he counted out two more and gave them to the boy genius.

"Where's the rest?" said Turk.

"Get in the fuckin' truck, wouldja?"

I moved the Bronco, leaving it unlocked for Chick, and walked back to the van, slid the side door open and sat in the back where I could keep my eye on Jackie and Cuddles the Wonderthug. When I got in I saw the tarp-covered boxes. I sat back in my seat. Placed my Browning in my lap. Kept it ready.

Turk drove, while Jackie smoked cigarettes and drank from a pint bottle of Jack Daniel's, then passed it to Turk. They didn't offer me a swallow. Wouldn't drink after them, anyway.

"You know," said Jackie, pausing from imbibing, "I just had

a thought. I keep getting this feeling I'm being watched. Where's your buddy Easton?"

"He has the sniffles," I said.

"I'll bet."

"Who's Easton?" asked Turk.

"Nasty fucker with mean eyes," said Jackie. "Badass from Nam, some kind of Special Forces guy or something, wasn't he?"

"Something."

"I don't like not knowing where he is."

"All the more reason for you to be nice," I said. "And deal the cards face up."

I thought about the situation. I didn't think the buyers would queer things since Jackie was only delivering part of the shipment, which was smart. There had to be some reason he'd survived and prospered all these years, in spite of the booze. Where were the rest of the weapons, though?

"Who are the buyers?" I said.

"I'm not sure," said Jackie, his cigarette bouncing up and down as he spoke. "And that's straight. They call me. Use tape-recorded messages through the mail, which I'm supposed to destroy like it was fuckin' *Mission: Impossible,* or something. Only met with one guy. Calls himself Captain Marvel, wears dark glasses like Roy Orbison, and a green stocking cap. Stood in the shadows. Spooky-acting."

"You ask what the guns were for?"

"Just the price, man. Just the price."

"You're a humanitarian, Jackie. No doubt about that."

"Somebody's gonna sell 'em to them. Might as well be me. Why're you along if you're so squeamish?"

"What's Matt's part in this?"

"So that's it," he said, laughing. "I shoulda known. Captain America only stands for good, right?"

"You forgot truth, justice, and the American way."

"You ain't Superman."

"And you're not somebody I'd go to the beach with. Tell me about Matt."

"One of Jenkins's ranch hands . . . young guy, Billy McCall, that's it. McCall's into me for some big dough. He's got the coke greeds so I give him some on the cuff because I'm a humanitarian, like you said. He ran a big bill. Anyway, McCall's engaged to Jenkins's niece's best friend, or some shit, I don't remember. McCall ain't got the jack, so Jenkins finds out and comes around to 'straighten me out,' he puts it. Was gonna break my neck. Looked like maybe he could do it, too. But Turk had a talk with him." I saw Turk's smile in the rearview mirror. "But your buddy wasn't scared of him. Stupid. I don't understand people anymore. They don't make good business decisions. Anyway, Turk bounced him a little."

I got a handful of Burlingame's hair and jerked his head back and down where I could see his face. "Hey! Owwch! C'mon, don't—" Turk looked around and slowed the van. Using my free hand, I stuck the Browning in Turk's face.

"Drive," I said. "Or I'll shoot your ears off." Turk kept driving. I turned my attention to Jackie. "You listen to this. Something, anything, happens to Matt or his wife and I'll drop-kick you around the entire state."

"Hey, hey. Don't get upset. After this deal, Jenkins is square. Promise. Jenkins offered to pay off McCall's debt. How long I be in business if I just forgot when someone owed me?" I twisted his hair and he yelped. For two Cheerios boxtops I'd stick the Browning in his mouth and do the state of Colorado a big favor. Instead, I let him go.

He rubbed his scalp. "You didn't have to do that."

"What's the rest of it?"

He lighted another cigarette and took a long pull from the whiskey, which he spilled into a little puddle on his seat. "The amount McCall owed was more than your friend wanted to pay. Anyway, he knew somebody, some old army buddy who knew about this gun deal. He had the connections and I could get the guns. Simple as that. He introduces me, he gets McCall off the shit list."

"How much do you get?"

"Enough. Plenty, in fact, when you figure they'll be steady customers."

I took the gun out of the back of Turk's head. "Something for you, double-ugly," I said. Anger bubbled and worked its way up my back. "You touch Matt again and you're going down. If not me, there'll be somebody else."

"I ain't afraid of you."

"You've been told," I said, putting the gun back on my lap. "How are you going to make the exchange?"

"We hand 'em the stuff, they give us the money. Simple. I still got the balance of the shipment."

"Where are the rest?"

"Get serious, Storme."

"Maybe they don't need the others," I said. "What if this is all they need? They take you out, keep the guns and the money."

He took a final drag on the Pall Mall, then lit another one. Vonnegut says only legitimate suicides smoke Pall Malls. "So, what do we do?"

I was improvising. He didn't know the people he was dealing with. People who want guns have plans to use them. And usually don't mind using them.

"We keep the clips," I said. "I stay in the van with a loaded one. You and Turk meet with them. I'll stay out of sight."

"How do we know we can trust him?" asked Turk.

"You have no choice," I said. "Don't give them the clips until the deal is done and we leave. Tell them they can pick the clips up down the road. Make sure you see the money before you make the deal."

"Hey," said Jackie. "You don't have to tell me how to collect the rent. What do you think I am?"

I let that go. I am a paragon of restraint.

We took Highway 117 west to Ryland. We drove to a telephone booth on Arapahoe Street. Waited. Rylanders drove by, going home from work, to the grocery store, never thinking about three thugs standing around a phone booth waiting to make connection on an armaments deal. I caught a glimpse of the Bronco, turning off on a side street. Chick was on the job. Turk stood around, tugging on his calfskin gloves and trying to look unobtrusive. Well, as unobtrusive as a 250-pound man in a feathered Stetson and snakeskin boots can look. Jackie did what he did best, which was fidget, chain-smoke, and act like a Martian. I felt like I was stuck in a cartoon.

At 5:03 the phone rang. Both men jumped at the sound. It was Captain Marvel. He told Jackie to drive fifteen miles north and turn west, where we would be met by a man who would direct us the rest of the way—directions which would place us mere seconds from the middle of nowhere.

During the drive, Jackie and Turk continued to drink whiskey while I sat in the back of the van, which was loaded with illegal ordnance, heading for a rendezvous with an unknown man with a comic-book pseudonym. What was I doing here?

Years before, I couldn't wait to get back from overseas and the noisy, steamy, muddy, murky madness of war. Then, later, couldn't wait to get away from the NFL with its airports, motels, team meetings, pregame meetings, postgame meetings, game films, game plans, depth charts, contract negotiations, smarmy journalists, coaches who stepped on your chest to get to the top, referees who melted when tossed into the maw of the home beast, and the taste of your own blood in your mouth . . . and yet . . .

And yet I remember the comet-streak rush of spiraled leather on fingertips, then against chest, while the beast howled, echoing in your helmet. And the adrenal surge when the tracer bullets zipped by, ripping elephant grass and trees, blood-spiking your heart and brain, making you hyper-alert to the sensations of life, fear, and survival. And later, the drained, guilty peace that came from surviving. Having been there and back, where few ever go, knowing the monster had taken a bite, but hadn't swallowed you yet. Glad it had taken someone else, not you. A dark, uncomfortable thing to learn about yourself.

We met the camouflaged contact man, who waved us over to a side road. I hadn't figured how to stop the shipment and get out. Couldn't hijack it. The buyers would just find another jobber, and I wanted to know who they were. I wanted to know what Matt's involvement was, and if they could come back on him. Besides, anybody who wanted two dozen automatic weapons has impure thoughts.

And I'm the quality control supervisor for central Colorado.

We drove on. About a mile down the rutted road, seven men stepped from the woods, all camouflaged, faces smudged. I hunkered down in the back and peered over the seat.

"Hey, look," said Turk. "Rambo impersonators."

But Turk missed the hard edges. They were a mixed lot but

a few of them weren't playing soldier. They didn't look like rummies or trigger-happy survivalists. They looked hard and lean. Five of them carried M-16s, or what looked like 16s, could be semiautomatic Colt AR-15s. Two others carried sidearms. One of the sidearm-bearers, by attitude and stance, appeared to be the leader. He was positioned at the forefront, arms folded across his chest, occasionally turning his head to speak to the others. His face was covered with a bow-hunter's camo-hood, which lent a sinister, mysterious aura to his appearance.

One man seemed to be out of place with his comrades. He was the shortest of the seven, slender of build, but the kind of slender one associates with shortstops, point guards, and rodeo cowboys—lean, spare, and quick. And his stance, unlike the others, was relaxed, loose, with hips canted, head cocked, one thumb tucked in his belt, the other hand dangling and occasionally caressing a tooled leather holster, worn western gunslinger style, low on the hip. The butt of a revolver, similar to Chick's, protruded from its lip. His eyes were bright, and a faint smirk played at the corners of his mouth. He wore kidskin gloves turned back at the cuffs and he smelled of reckless danger and sudden violence—a counterpoint to the more controlled threat posed by his mates.

"Watch yourselves," I said. "Keep your eye on the short guy, he's looking for it."

"Who?" said Turk, snorting. "The shrimp? Fuck him. He ain't nothin'."

"Jackie," I said, "if you want to get out of here with the money and your head, you'd better muzzle your pet."

"Yeah." Jackie nodded absently. He wasn't ready for what he was seeing. "Turk, you keep your head shut, let me do the talkin'."

Turk turned to me. "We finish it when we're through here." I plain forgot to register terror. What a boring guy. Burlingame and Turk got out of the van. The truck listed when Turk stepped down.

Jackie and Turk were in trouble. Jackie was smart enough to realize it, but Turk wasn't. There was no reason the quasi-soldiers couldn't overpower Jackie and take the weapons. But not having the whole shipment, and having no clips, should give them pause. If they were ex-military, they would assess the situation before acting.

I watched Turk and Jackie walk toward them, Turk with an exaggerated swagger. Turk didn't have tough down right. Tough is indifferent. Tough is attitude. One of the camo guys had it down. He was a hard 235, no fat. A block of sinew with a head like a water buffalo's. Slitted eyes in dark-smudged face.

As quietly as possible, mindful not to rock the van, I pushed a loaded clip into a Mac-10. Perspiration formed on my forehead.

The sidearmed leader stepped forward and did most of the talking. I could only make out snatches of the conversation. Then Turk forgot to shut up. The slender guy with the cowboy rig stepped forward, spun his nickel-plated revolver Roy Rogers–style from its holster in a flash of silver, placed the business end within millimeters of Turk's nose, then just as suddenly spun the gun back to its resting place on his hip. That done, he folded his arms across his chest, rolled his shoulders and smiled, his head cocked back, chin raised.

He was quick. Lizard-tongue quick. The kind of quick you get from doing something over and over. Strange talent for a nuclear age.

I was in a bad situation and didn't like it. I looked at the keys dangling in the ignition. Get out of here, Storme. Crank this thing and head for the barn. You don't owe Jackie Burlingame. The money he paid was squeezed from some yuppie's appetite for buzzing membranes. But I stayed. Not for the money, not because I felt any commitment. Because . . .

I didn't know why. I was hypnotized by the danger, the electric tension.

Turk recovered from the snake-strike gunplay and began talking trash again. The leader snapped something and I heard

Jackie tell Turk to shut up. Then the leader said something I couldn't make out, but I heard the word "unacceptable." Jackie said something else, then turned and started walking back to the truck. I sunk down further in the truck, pulled the Browning out and cocked it. It made a *snick* sound. There I sat, armed to the teeth like Pancho Villa, pistol in one hand, machine gun in the other, and no idea what to do next. I tried to will myself invisible but it didn't work. So much for my psychic powers. I'll bet Mannix never spent one second trying to turn invisible. At least I was open to new experiences.

One of the soldiers followed Jackie, stopping halfway to the truck, rifle pointed at the van. The side door slid open and Jackie looked in. His hands were shaking.

I put down the Mac-10 and placed a finger to my lips.

"Fucking Turk is gonna get me killed," he hissed through pale lips. His chest was heaving, as if he'd been running. "You were right about the cowboy." He took a deep breath. "They want to see the product. I need a clip. They're pissed off about not havin' 'em."

"Only reason you're alive now," I said. I handed him a clip. "Load five shells. Tell them this is the only clip you have. Tell them you want to see the money. If you can, get the money, then get back in the van."

He swallowed and wet his lips.

"What's the holdup?" said the rifleman nearest the van.

"Be right with you," Jackie said; then to me, "I'm hating this shit. I'm about to dump my bladder, man."

"Should have stuck to pot."

"Thanks a lot."

"Leave the door open."

He frowned and stepped away from the van, clip in hand. He walked back to the knot of men. I could hear the conversation now that the door was open. The leader had moved closer to the van and I could see him. He held out his hand for the weapon.

"I wanta see the money," Jackie said. The leader nodded and snapped his finger. The linebacker stepped back to a Jeep and pulled a large gym bag from the back. He walked back and handed it to the leader, who zipped it open and showed the money to Jackie. Jackie reached for it, but the camouflaged man shook his head.

"First we test the guns."

Jackie was nobody's fool on these things. "First, the money. I wanna see green in my hand. There's a bunch of you and only two of us. How I know you won't stiff me?"

"Number Four," said the leader. The rifleman by the truck stepped back toward the group. The leader handed him the bag. "Take this and put it in the van and wait there."

There was no place to hide in the truck. He was sure to see me. Number Four had the satchel and was walking to the van. I was trapped in a small area with few options. Number Four walked into view.

"Hi," I said, pointing the Browning at a strategic point in the middle of his face. He grew silver-dollar eyes and his mouth fell open. "Nice to see you. I'm the governor of Colorado and I'm counting on your vote this November. Put the bag in the van and do exactly as I tell you or there'll be this really loud noise which you'll never hear." He put the bag in the van. "Now, get your finger out of the trigger guard and tell them you need Jackie—that's the short, nervous guy—to come over here."

He looked back over his shoulder. "Number One."

"What?"

"I need to see the short guy for a minute."

The leader said something and Jackie came walking over.

"Aw shit, man," said Jackie, when he came into view. "Now what?"

"We got the money," I said. "Let's split."

Jackie's eyes widened. "You lost your fuckin' mind, man? They'll blow us away."

I shrugged. "There's that," I admitted. Number Four was

getting nervous eyes so I gave him the attention he deserved. "Hold on there, hoss. Don't get heroic. I am deadly adroit at this range and will not hesitate to snap the hammer on you."

"Shit," said Jackie.

"Always wanted to use *adroit* in a sentence," I said.

Jackie said, "Shit," again. He was in a rut. "You're crazier than shit," said Jackie, shaking his head. "I brought a fuckin' crazy man with me. Man, we deal with these guys or they're going to waste us."

"Always looking on the negative side of things," I said. "We've got the money. We've got the product. And we'll have clear consciences to go with it if we burn these guys like you said." I said it loud enough for Number Four to hear. I was planting a seed, trying to drive a wedge between Jackie and the shadow soldiers. Jackie didn't like it.

"What? Like I what? What are you doing to me?"

"What's going on, Four?" asked the hooded leader.

"You want in?" I asked the soldier.

Realization spread across his painted face, mixed with surprise and fear. "No. You won't get away with this."

"Now you sound like a cop."

"Do you see the weapons, Number Four?" asked the leader.

I nodded at my guest. He could see them anyway. However, I could no longer see what was happening outside the van.

"Yes, sir."

"How much is there."

"About half what we agreed on."

I nodded at Jackie.

Jackie said, "Half now, half when we're clear."

The leader laughed. "You're suspicious, man."

"Just careful," said Jackie.

"This won't work."

I was considering options when I heard Turk say something you don't say to people carrying guns. I heard a deep voice say, "You need to have a little more respect."

"Perhaps this will help you to understand it better," said another voice.

Then I heard the bark of a gun and Jackie pitched forward. He lay on the running board like a beached fish. There was another crack and there was the sound of something falling on the road. Number Four swung his rifle up, but not before I snapped off a round from the Browning. He was jerked back into the dirt, quivering, but he never felt it. I dropped the Browning, pulled Jackie into the van and jumped into the driver's seat, smacking my knee against the steering wheel, but managing to hold on to the Mac-10. I cranked the starter and slammed the shift lever into first and pulled the wheel hard left, hoping the turning radius was sharp enough to turn in the road. If not, I was in big trouble. I heard Jackie yell something at me.

"Hang on, Jackie," I yelled. The tires bit into the dirt and chat. I heard the reports of a handgun and a rifle. Jackie grunted again.

I pointed the Mac-10 at the passenger window and squeezed off a burst at the group of soldiers. Glass shattered and they threw themselves to the ground. I saw a body lying in the dirt. Turk's. I felt a dull pain in my wrist from the kick of the Ingram. The van bounced hard in the ditch, gouging a chunk of embankment before bounding out and onto the washboard road.

I buried the pedal, but there wasn't much response at first. The engine was beginning to stretch its muscles when I heard the ping of metal followed by the crack of rifle fire. The rectangular sideview mirror exploded into a shower of silver fragments.

Intermittently, I could hear the moans and sobs of Jackie Burlingame. Each bump elicited a cry of pain from him. Couldn't be helped. I cranked the steering wheel hard, right and left, to make it difficult to shoot out the tires. Bullets slapped against the walls of the van and into the back of the passenger seat. I pulled the wheel too hard and the van gave a sickening lurch and began to swerve. The rear end fishtailed in the gravel and dirt while I fought to keep it from racing the front. I managed to get it under control before I reached the corner. The corner was safety. Once around it, they wouldn't be able to shoot at me, though there was still the matter of the front-door man we met coming in.

Just as I was coming out of the corner it happened. A loud pop and then the flubbedy-rubber sound of ruptured tire. The left rear. The steering wheel tried to take over and pull me left. I let up on the accelerator and regained control. Once we straightened, I gave it more throttle. I couldn't afford to lose momentum, as it would be difficult to regain it with a tire gone. The metal rim screamed and the van shuddered violently when it struck potholes. Boxes bounced and slid across the van floor, spilling weapons.

I knew they were starting Jeeps and would be after me. No way to outdistance them with a bad tire. I would have to abandon the vehicle or make a stand. I couldn't leave Jackie and the weapons behind. I had a good lead and an automatic weapon. But if they had a military background, they would merely flank me and take me out.

It was then I saw my Bronco bumping up the road. Chick! I slid to a halt, turning the wheel to leave the van blocking the road. Chick cranked the Bronco hard and spun around 180 degrees, pointing the truck back in the direction he'd come from. No sooner had the truck come to a rest than he jumped from the cab with a pump shotgun in his hands.

"Taxi?" he said.

I vaulted into the back of the van and threw open the side door. Jackie was lying in a pool of blood. His legs were lifeless noodles that swept the ground as I tried to drag him to the Bronco. There was no need to drag him anywhere, ever again. I let him down slowly to the ground, though it made no difference to him.

Chick had the door open for me. I threw an armload of weapons into the truck and ran back to the van for more as Chick took up a position at the front bumper of the van to cover me.

I jumped into the van, grabbed as much as I could carry and ran for the Bronco. I heard the high-pitched whine of taxed engines as the Jeeps pounded up the road.

Tossing the load into the Bronco, I ran back to the van and grabbed three more guns and the money, leaving several weapons behind, some of which had been damaged by rifle fire.

The nose of the first Jeep appeared. Chick pumped three rounds of double-aught buckshot into the front of it. The heavy shot slammed into the vehicle and ripped the driver from his seat. The driverless vehicle then banged across the ditch and into the woods. The passengers were thrown or jumped from it before it rammed a tree. One of the passengers jumped up and ran into the woods.

I heard the other Jeep bumping up the road. By the time it made the corner, I was behind the wheel of the Bronco and headed for the highway.

"We've still got to do something about the front-door man," I said.

"He's taking a nap," said Chick.

"About time you did something," I said.

"Arrived in the nick of time, didn't I?"

"You call that the nick of time? It was a few seconds after the nick of time."

"See, you know nothing about the hero business. The cavalry always arrives in the nick of time. No sooner. How many times I have to tell you that? How many guns you get?"

"I don't know. Had to leave some. Some were shot up. Something feels wrong."

"Why do you say that?"

"Felt like a setup. Why? Jackie said they were a steady market. More to come. He only gave them half the guns. Doesn't make sense they killed him."

Chick had the gym bag open and was counting the money. He whistled in appreciation. "How much you think they paid for those weapons?"

"I don't know," I said. "Twenty-five, maybe thirty thousand."

"Yeah. What I figured, too."

"So how much is there?"

"Couldn't be more'n two hundred grand here give or take twenty thou."

"How can that be?"

"Maybe they were really nice guns."

When I hit the highway, I pointed the Bronco opposite the direction we'd come in. After three miles of white-knuckle driving Chick mentioned it might not be a great idea to get stopped with a load of illegal weapons in the back and blood on my jacket.

I slowed the Ford. They only had one Jeep and by the time they could've gotten around the van we had a good head start. They wouldn't have known which way we turned when we hit the highway and they would have stopped to pick up the guns we left behind.

"Two hundred thousand dollars," I said.

"We hit the jackpot, man."

"Why so much? Why kill Burlingame and Turk?"

"Coulda been you, y'know?"

"Yeah. I thought about that."

"No way the guns're worth this much," said Chick.

"And they surrendered the money too easily. Without getting

the whole shipment. They just put the money in the van like it was no big deal."

"They knew they were going to whack Jackie."

"Why take a chance with that much money?"

"Makes you think somebody's jacking somebody else."

"And where'd the money come from in the first place?" I said. "They won't let go, now. They'll be looking for us. We need to see Matt."

"Okay. Let's get something to eat first. Busting up gunrunning rings always makes me hungry," Chick said. He patted the gym bag. "I'll buy. But I'm on a budget. We can only eat two hundred grand's worth."

Reaching Aspencliffe, I stopped and covered the guns with a tarp I kept under the backseat. That done, I drove to a convenience store, bought some ice, four chicken salad sandwiches, a bag of Chee-tos, and a large cup of coffee. Chick poured the ice over the Michelob in the console cooler and I drank the coffee.

"Who do you think those guys were?" Chick asked.

"I don't know. Couple of them looked hard. Military. Smelled like marines. No names on the pockets."

"*Semper fi.* Jenks was a Marine, wasn't he?"

I nodded. "Maybe that's the connection." I didn't say anything for a while. I sipped the coffee. It was hot and burned my tongue. Jackie's death was working on me. Also the fact that I'd had to kill someone. I'd killed in Nam. I'd killed two hit men in Missouri last year. Them or me. But the residue of death clings to you long after the fact. I could still see the man reaching for his gun. Still feel the triggers tripping on the sawed-off. The sudden stillness, the finality of death. It reaches into your nostrils, into the back of your brain. Invades your dreams. Your peace.

It was quiet for a few minutes.

Chick said, "No other way to do it."

"I screwed up."

"No loss. Jackie was headed for it anyway. Sooner or later."
My tongue felt raw. "Still don't like it."

"The Lone Ranger thing, huh? Shoot the guns outta their hands and ride into the sunset? This ain't the NFL. You don't line up and run another play."

"I should've stayed out."

"And let the guns circulate," Chick said. "There's an idea." He unscrewed the lid on the Canadian, took a small swallow and chased it with the beer.

"Should've called the police," I said.

"Which would've implicated Matt, which we could not do without hearing his side. Besides, guys like Burlingame smell cop a mile away. He'd have gone to ground until the heat was off and delivered the guns later. This way we stopped half the shipment, they don't know where the rest of the guns are, and the world is better for not having Jackie B. around. No," he said, settling back. "It was the only way to play it. Your instincts were good."

"You hit anybody in the Jeep?"

"I try not to think about it," he said, throwing his head back and taking a swallow of whiskey. "Got too much to think about as it is. The hell with it."

"I can't do that, you know."

"Yeah," Chick said, reclining the seat and pulling his cap down over his eyes. "I know."

It was twilight when we got back to my place. We buried the weapons under a blowdown at the back of my property, using the lights of the Bronco to see what we were doing. There were two Uzis, a half dozen nine-millimeter Berettas, three Mac-10s, and a street-sweeper shotgun with a twelve-round drum. That done, we drove back to the cabin.

I grilled a couple steaks and baked potatoes. Chick opened a bottle of Amstel Light and I drank coffee. We ate. Chick's appetite was unaffected by our adventure. I left half of mine.

After we ate I called Matt Jenkins. This time he was home. I told him we were coming to see him.

We were getting ready to go out the door when Sandy called. Sandra Collingsworth of Channel Seven news in Denver. The beautiful Sandra Collingsworth.

"Good evening, you gorgeous hunk of masculinity," she said. "You miss me?"

"This isn't that smart-aleck anchorwoman on that news show I never watch?"

"Maybe. Is this that broken down has-been I love?"

"Broken down has-been?" I said.

"Dead giveaway, isn't it? Can you come by the station tomorrow afternoon? The weekend anchor has the weekend off so I'm filling in. Father's in town. He'd like to see you. I'll be done at seven tomorrow evening. We could go to dinner and then, who knows?"

"This sounds like a thinly veiled ruse to get me alone and molest me. I'm wise to the ways of you modern women."

"Will you resist?"

"Will it make any difference?" I asked.

"None."

"Okay, then. I'll give my harem the afternoon off and drop by."

"I'm the only girl for you and you know it."

"You'll remain oppressed if you refer to yourself as a girl."

"You can take me out to dinner after work. I hope you've been saving your money. I'm in the mood to spend your money at a pricey restaurant."

"No problem. I've been collecting aluminum cans. Very lucrative. That and I found several thousand dollars in a gym bag." I explained, peripherally, leaving out the shooting and the possible danger.

"How did you get involved?" she said. "Why not just leave it alone? I need you intact."

"It isn't like that. It involves Matt." We talked about it, back and forth. She worried about me. I didn't want to worry her, but was glad she cared. Hearing her voice was good. Seeing her would be better.

I told her I loved her and hung up.

Thought about the distance between us.

It was good to see Matt and Kelly. Kelly smiled and kissed my cheek, but was apprehensive. Matt led us into a den with a window wall offering a view of the foothills. The den's furniture was wood and leather. Thick nut-brown carpet. Hardback books on walnut shelves. We sat in overstuffed wing chairs. The stars over the dark purple mountains sparkled like sequins on velvet.

Kelly left after offering food, which we declined. Matt served drinks from a bar. Chick drank Chivas, Matt Jack Daniel's. I had a Dr Pepper.

"Not drinking, Wyatt?" asked Matt as he handed me the bruised-purple can.

"Not selling guns, either," I said.

The smile fell from his face. He sat down heavily, looked at me. Chick's expression showed nothing. "That's not fair."

"Jackie Burlingame's dead. Also some low-rent muscle named Turk. Talk to me about fair, Matt. I've got enough weapons hidden out on my place to outfit a platoon." And I may have killed a man and wounded others, I thought. "This isn't your type of deal. I know you. I want to hear why."

His mouth worked dryly. He swiveled in his chair to look out into the great dark mountains, and said, "I didn't know it would be like that. But that's no excuse." He swiveled back to face me. "I should've known that Burlingame was . . . well, it doesn't matter now, does it? He's dead. I'm not sorry about that."

He got up and shut the double doors to the large room, then returned to his seat. He swirled the ice in his drink, looking into the glass as if the answer were somehow circling around inside it. I waited.

"I can't tell you all of it," he said. "You'll just have to trust me on some things. There are . . . there are things you don't know about . . . things nobody can know. Can you allow that?"

I nodded. Chick said nothing.

"How much do you know?" he asked.

I related what Jackie had told me about Billy McCall's drug bill. About Matt trying to pay it off.

"I went to Burlingame, offered to pay Billy's debt, but he wasn't interested. I was mad. I went there, first to smack him in the mouth, but he had that gorilla, Turk, there to keep me off him. I'm getting old. Time was I could've held my own, but not now. Too soft." His eyes looked tired.

"I thought I could scare him off. Didn't know how deep Billy was in. Hell, the kid goes with my niece. They're engaged. Had to do something. We talked and finally Burlingame offered to deal."

"Burly had a heart of gold," said Chick, pouring himself more Scotch.

"What was the deal?"

"Wanted me to introduce him to Crispin Purvis."

"Who's Purvis? And why him?"

"Entrepreneur. One of the biggest in Colorado. Owns a logging company, a dude ranch, some funeral homes and a few other businesses. Invests in movies. Hangs out with movie stars and politicians. He's pushing Joring Braden for U.S. Senate. But he's a shadowy guy. Everything he does is offstage. When Burlingame wanted to meet him it seemed like a simple thing. At least that's what I wanted to believe. Fooling myself, I guess." He looked at Chick, then at me. "I make the introduction and McCall's debt is forgiven. That's what I was told. Stupid. I knew Burlingame was scum."

He poured more bourbon into his glass. "Purvis is a weird guy. Keeps to himself except when he has one of his notorious blowouts at his place. Has a big house outside Boulder. Has a helicopter and a private jet. Flies up to his logging camps in Oregon and Washington about once a week to check on things. Knows how to get things done. Leans on people in the right places. Knows how hard to push, when to back off."

"Why did Burlingame want to meet him?"

Matt shook his head. "Don't know. But I knew it had to be something dirty."

"You know anything else about him? Education? Military service? Anything like that?"

He thought for a moment. Shook his head. "No. He's not really a friend. Just an acquaintance. Never heard anyone speak of any military background or college. But he's intelligent. Actually, he's more wily and calculating than anything. Not really an intellectual but he likes to give that impression. No close friends, but people jump when he says. Wouldn't surprise me to find out he'd served in the military, though."

"Why do you say that?"

He shrugged. "Feel it more than anything. He's never really relaxed. Never nervous though. More like wary. Alert. Cool and on top of things. Nothing gets to him. His clothes immaculate, knife crease in his trousers. The guy has a presence. The kind of guy who assumes he's running things. I've heard he carries a gun. I've never seen it, but a friend of mine swears he does." He looked uncomfortable. "I'm sorry for all this. I didn't mean to cause trouble for you."

"You say Congressman Braden's running for the Senate?" Chick asked. "Why would Braden give up his power in the House? He's a big dog there."

Matt seemed to lose his concentration, momentarily. "Huh?" he said. "Oh. His party is in danger of losing their majority in the Senate. They figure he has the best chance of picking up the senate seat. The party prevailed upon him, so he's agreed to run."

I filed that tidbit away. Must remember to ask Sandy about Braden. A U.S. representative with ties to a shady business-man who may have links with a gun-running operation? Interesting.

"Why did you go to all this trouble for McCall? Why not just fire the guy?"

Matt reached into a round leather humidor and plucked a cigar from it. He offered me and Chick one. I shook my head. "I told you," he said. "McCall goes with my niece."

"I'm not buying that," I said. "Sorry."

"Didn't figure you would. That's one of the things I can't answer. Can you accept that?"

"If you can," I said, "then so can I."

He looked at Chick. "What about you?"

"Good Scotch, old buddy," Chick said. "Good company, too. Doubt if either of those things'll change."

Matt smiled for the first time. "Appreciate that. So, what do we do now? Do I go to the police?"

"No," I said. "Not yet. Maybe not ever. You'll just implicate yourself, and maybe us, for no good reason." I didn't tell him I was worried for his safety. Kelly's too. I hadn't told him about the money. We'd burned somebody. Badly. Right now, the only link the shadow soldiers had was Matt, if Jackie had told them of his involvement, and Billy McCall. "The bad guys aren't going to tell anybody in authority. They can't."

"Will you look into it? You've done things like it before. Be glad to pay you."

"No. No need to pay us."

"Why? Think I can't afford it?" His pride was injured. Not my intention. His pride had already taken a beating. "I'll be damned if—"

I held up a hand. "I don't work for friends. However, I might do it for free. Besides, we've already been compensated by an unusual benefactor."

"Well, at least let me pay you, Chick."

"Sorry, Jenks. Feel the same way. Just came into some money, anyway. Inherited it, kind of."

"If you need anything," said Matt. "Money, contacts, you'll let me know, won't you?"

I nodded. "I'll need to talk to Billy McCall."

He gave me McCall's address and phone number. "I don't know how receptive he'll be. I docked his pay the other day. Drunk on the job." Again I thought it interesting that he hadn't fired him, but said nothing. "Billy's a good kid, just wants things too fast."

We shook hands and left. Kelly was at the car when we got outside. "I tried to call you today," she said. "A man called, asking for Matt. I did like you said and told him he wasn't around. When I asked who was calling he hung up. I don't want anything to happen to Matt. I need him. But something's wrong. Something he won't share with me."

Her butterscotch hair lifted in the breeze. She was forty-three, but looked younger. Her eyes had character. "Why don't you get him to take off for a few days? Fly down to Dallas, or New Orleans. See some old friends."

"He won't go. Can't. Things are too tight here right now. Maybe in a couple of weeks."

I hoped a couple of weeks wouldn't be too late.

"Anything unusual," I said, "anything at all. Strange phone calls, strange people. Anything. You tell me, immediately."

"Okay," she said. "Is it going to be all right, Wyatt?"

"Sure. With Chick and me on the job you got four hundred pounds of prime, grade A, American assurance."

She smiled. "Be careful."

I told her we would. Driving back to Largo, Chick said, "So now we're detectives, huh? Like Travis McGee and Lew Archer."

"More like Abbott and Costello," I said.

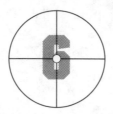

I was getting ready to leave to talk with Billy McCall. I had called him earlier. He'd sounded groggy, slurring his words. Said he didn't have time to talk to me, but I was determined to have my way.

I was thinking about what I was going to ask Billy boy when Sandy called. We were invited to a party. At least she was, and wanted me to accompany her.

"I think I'm busy that night."

"I haven't told you what night yet."

"Will this mean rubbing up against wax figures with American Express gold cards who're concerned about greed and the plight of inner-city youth?"

"Yes, there will be several pretentious assholes in attendance. You can come and be an unpretentious one."

"Now you've done it. I don't have to take this. I ever tell you that I'm an American folk legend? The only man in NFL history to date all the Dallas Cowboys cheerleaders in the same week?"

"A week which pales in comparison to one night with me."

She had a point. "How about renting a couple of Jimmy Stewart movies while you feel my muscles and adore me?"

"I've felt your muscles."

"And?"

"It's a yawn."

"Where is that cheerleader hotline number? I had it here a minute ago."

"Why do you pretend you're not going when you know you are?" she said.

"There'd better be major smooches afterward or I'll pout all night."

"If you're a good boy and don't make fun of anyone, we'll see."

"I'd think you'd let me win a couple of points. Feed my ego a little."

"Your ego is self-sustaining and requires no between-meal snacks."

"Nobody likes smart, self-assured women, you know."

"Except you," she said. "And I'm glad."

After we hung up I got out the Mustang to drive to Billy McCall's. I had decided it might not be a good idea to use the Bronco for a while.

When I got to McCall's he was nursing a hangover. He had swollen eyes and kept working his mouth as if he'd swallowed foam rubber. Billy was five-nine, twenty, dark hair, boyish good looks, slender waist. One of the good-time guys. Every girl's heartthrob in his Tony Lamas and Levi's. There was a BMW in the drive. He had a skier's tan corroborated by the upright skis against the wall. There was a black Stetson hanging on a peg, a bank of stereo components against one wall, and a half-empty bottle of Jack Daniel's bourbon on the coffee table.

Billy was an interesting guy. He ran a big coke bill, drove a fifty-thousand-dollar import, and lived in an exclusive neighborhood. Not bad for a ranch hand. Must have invested wisely.

He didn't want to let me in. "Look, man," he'd said, opening the door a crack. "I'm wasted. Had a rough night. Come back later, huh?"

He tried to shut the door, but I had my boot against it. I was too big to argue with and he was too sick to care, so he let me in.

Score another point for the enduring and irresistible charm of America's favorite ex–wide receiver. Welcome everywhere.

He offered me coffee. I accepted a cup. It was weak. He pulled a seven-ounce bottle of Budweiser from his refrigerator, wrenched the cap off and tilted the bottle back, draining it. Made noises like a distance runner with a pulled muscle and one mile to go. Tapped a cigarette from a pack of Marlboros. On the coffee table were a couple of rolled Zig-Zag papers, fat in the middle, like bloated snakes. Next to that was a salt shaker half full of a white substance that probably wasn't salt. Billy lighted a cigarette with a throwaway lighter. Slouched back against the couch.

"What does Jenkins want?" he asked.

"Nothing."

"I thought he sent you."

"I came on my own. Sometimes it happens that way. I need to ask you some questions."

"About what?"

"What do you know about Jackie Burlingame and a huge cocaine bill you couldn't pay?"

"Aw shit," he said. He looked away, disdainfully, as if I were a foolish old man. I just hate being treated with disdain. "So, that's it. Jenkins wants his money back after doing me his big favor. Screw it. I'll pay it back. It's cake. I just—"

"Shut up. He doesn't want your money. He doesn't want anything from you. When Matt Jenkins does favors, that's what it is. He doesn't ask for payment. Besides, he didn't do it for you. He did it for his niece."

"Cynthia? If he's so into doing good deeds, why'd he dock my pay?"

"You know the answer to that. Should've fired you but he and his wife both like Cynthia."

"His wife?" said Billy, smiling. "Ain't she a sweet piece of—"

"Her name's Kelly," I said, interrupting. "But you can call her Mrs. Jenkins."

"What are you? The morality monitor? She knows what she's got. She knows when to swing it, too."

I decided not to like Billy McCall.

"You know, Billy? I'm getting real tired of hearing you talk. I've heard it a thousand times before from a thousand other jerks. Since I outweigh you fifty pounds I believe I'm going to insist you stop talking that way about her."

"I might be tougher than you think."

"You'd have to be. But it's irrelevant. Either way, one more remark about Kelly Jenkins and I'm going to airmail you to the emergency room."

"Okay, okay," he said, a little chuckle in his voice. "Take it easy. Shouldn't have said it. I know. She turned me down once and I don't get over that stuff."

"What's that mean?"

"Aw. I was drunk. Last summer. She was sunbathing out by the pool. Had on one of those bikinis that look like dental floss for your ass. She has nice . . . a . . . she's a very fine-looking older lady. Anyway, Matt wasn't around and I thought she was trying to tease me. I started talking to her. She was nice. I made a play and she told me to get lost. I pushed it a little and she slapped me. Pissed me off. I said something I shouldn't have, probably."

"What did Cynthia, your true love, have to say about that?"

"You kidding? I didn't tell her. Mrs. Jenkins didn't say anything, either. It made her real nervous though. Like she'd done something wrong. Hey, let's get something straight. I care about Cynthia. I wouldn't do nothing to hurt her. Me and Cyn, we're forever."

A door opened and our conversation was interrupted by the

entrance of a slender redhead in a man's shirt, or at least, in Billy's shirt. She looked all of sixteen. Billy looked uncomfortable at her sudden appearance.

"Billy . . . ," she began. She looked at me, then quickly away.

I bounced my eyebrows like Groucho Marx. "The lovely Cynthia, I presume?"

Billy did a double take. "Just get back in there, will ya, Julie? I'll be with you in a minute."

"I gotta get home, Billy. Daddy's gonna kill me."

She walked back into the bedroom, shutting the door quietly behind her, as if I would forget she was there.

"Ah, the sweet fragrance of forever love," I said. "I'm touched. Billy McCall, Sweetheart of the Rodeo. You're a prize, Billy. I've got shoes older than her."

"Aw, shit, man. That don't mean nothing. You know how it is."

"No," I said, looking straight at him. "I don't know how it is."

"Aw, man. Didn't you ever get a little on the side, when your woman didn't know about it?"

I let that pass. "You said Kelly acted weird about your pass at her. What does that mean?"

"Don't get hot at me, but she about jumped out of her skin when I . . . uh . . ." He looked at me, then said, "Well, you know. It was like you'd put a snake on her, or something. Made me feel creepy, like I was a leper or something. Then she cried and said she was sorry. Said it was her fault. Then she was nice again and told me I was never to think of her in that way. She said she cared about me, but it would never be in that way. It was weird. After that, she treated me just like before."

"And how does she treat you?"

"Nice."

"How much were you involved with Jackie Burlingame?"

"Just buy the powder from him, that's all."

"Peddle it somewhere else. You're driving a BMW and the

rent on this place must run seven hundred a month. Tell me again how you just bought the blow from him."

Billy wiped his palms on his jeans. Lit another cigarette. "That's all there is to it, man. Straight."

"You don't know anything I want to know, do you?" He shrugged. His cigarette hung from the corner of his mouth like he was James Dean. Does anybody have a personality they didn't borrow from a movie marquee anymore? Preened paramours with sour expressions and manicured nails. "You've got a lot of things to explain and you're going to explain them to me."

He looked at me. Tossed his hand at me, dismissing me as if I didn't exist. First the disdain and now this. Sometimes you just have to get their attention. Stepping around the table between us, I cuffed him alongside the face with an open hand. Didn't want to do it, but it was about time somebody woke him up.

"Hey!" he cried. The cigarette flew from his mouth, pinwheeling through the air. It took the smirk off his face. People look at you different once you've popped them. I tried not to feel too much satisfaction. "Shit. You didn't have to do that."

"I'll do it again. Maybe hit the other side for balance. What else do you know?"

"I oughta call the cops."

"Go ahead, Billy. We'll talk to them together." I picked up the salt shaker. Billy sat up when I did. "Wonder what they'll think of this?" I unscrewed the lid. "Hope you don't salt your food before you taste it. Bad for the blood pressure." I spilled a little on the floor. "Oops."

"Hey, don't man."

"Better toss some over my shoulder for good luck." I poured a little into an open hand.

"No, wait," he said. He chewed on his lower lip. "Okay, okay. So I deal a little dope for Jackie. Mostly grass. A little coke, now and then. Doesn't hurt anybody."

I thought about Jackie and Turk. Both dead. Thought about

Matt and Kelly Jenkins. I thought about nasty little guns spitting out twenty rounds per second. He wasn't hurting anybody, though. Something else wasn't right. Maybe it was the BMW in the drive or Billy's smug attitude. I remembered how the gun drop felt like a setup, wondered why they overpaid for the guns. I took a stab at it.

"You didn't owe Jackie any money, did you, Billy?"

He looked at me, wide-eyed. I stood over him. He was thinking about his answer. Wanted to tell the lie, but was considering the consequences.

"Jackie's dead, Billy boy. You had anything to do with this, you'd better spill it, because I'd say you're next in line. If you don't know anything you'll be safe."

"Burlingame's dead?" he asked, eyes wide. He ran a tongue across dry lips. He grabbed the whiskey bottle by the neck and took a good swallow, gave an involuntary shudder, then said, "How? When?"

"You set Matt up."

"It's not that way. Matt's good to me. Shit, I deserved to be docked. Don't understand why he doesn't fire me. Why'd they kill Jackie B.? Shit, this is crazy."

"Who are 'they'?"

"I don't know. Jackie knows . . . knew, anyway."

"What was your part in the deal?"

He ran a hand through his thick hair. Took another knock from the bourbon. He looked tired. And scared. And smaller than when I'd entered. "I know a guy," he said. "Buys a little grass from me, now and then. He was flying on snow one night. Hey, you ever hear that old Steppenwolf song, 'SnowBlind Friend'? Yeah, you're about the right age, sure you have. Like that, flying blind and drinking a little."

Billy seemed to just do a "little" of everything. A little booze. Sold a little dope. Cheated on his fiancée a little. Lied just a little. His excesses were just other people's perception. Just a game to him.

He said, "Anyway, this guy says he knows a guy knew how to get guns. Uzis. Macs. FALs. So, I mention it to Jackie once and he set up a meeting. The guy wasn't kidding. He did know how to make connections on the guns. Jackie'd heard about some big gun collector wanted to get his hands on some autos. Matt knew the guy, but I said Matt would never go along with it. So we cooked up the story and Matt bit."

"You're a class act, Billy."

"I didn't mean any harm. Matt's clear. Ain't no big deal."

"Nothing's a big deal to you. You used Matt. Tried to hit on his wife. Deal drugs, guns, and friends. Just laughs. As long as you drive a BMW and have your toys then everything's cool. Right?" He made me sick. "You stay away from Matt and Kelly, got it?"

"I didn't know anyone'd get killed."

"Cynthia too."

"What?"

"Stay away from Cynthia, too." I was getting the same disgust for Billy I had for Jackie. It was like a virus passed on from one carrier to another.

"Hey, you don't run my life, man."

I pulled him off the couch by his hair. Shook him like a first-grader. "Listen, McCall. You have too many cards on the table, and no trumps. I tell Matt about this, or maybe about you trying to move on Kelly, and he'll be over here. Promise."

"I ain't afraid of Matt. You either." His face was twisted with hate and defiance, like a spoiled child's.

I let him go. "There're some people out there somewhere, hard people, with guns, who are upset about not getting their merchandise. They killed Jackie and Turk—"

"They killed Turk?"

"Like snapping your fingers."

"Damn." He dragged on the Marlboro and searched the floor with his eyes. His face was chalky. His fingers shook as he took the cigarette from his lips.

"So who was the guy wanted to buy guns?"

"Doesn't matter."

"Don't talk in riddles. Why doesn't it matter?"

"The guy didn't want 'em. Jackie asked him but he said he had no interest in illegal guns. Acted pissed off. Made us leave."

"So how did Jackie deal the guns."

"Some guy contacted him."

"Who?"

"Called himself Captain something—"

"Captain Marvel?"

"Yeah, that's it. I never saw anybody though and Jackie didn't tell me nothing else. I didn't know anything about when they were gonna make the drop, or nothing. How do you know about all this?"

"One-way street, Billy. You get nothing. Just do what I say and I won't give your name out to people who'll drop by and punch your ticket."

"Shit, man. You come in here. I don't know you from nothing. You scare shit outta me and don't give me a handle."

"Tough in the fast lane, partner."

He chewed the corner of his lip. "Okay, so what do you want me to do?"

"Keep your mouth shut. Give me the name of the gun contact. And, if you're real smart, you'll go gently into that good night."

"Can't we deal? Isn't anything on the table?"

"Nothing. Your tail, maybe."

"Who are you, anyway?"

"Rocky Roads," I said. "Town Tamer."

Billy gave me the name of the gun contact and I walked out of his apartment and crossed the street to my car. Drove one block west, turned the corner, stopped, got out of my car, and walked over to where Chick was parked in a nondescript tan Ford.

He was reading the newspaper when I knocked on his window. He had the paper open to an article about nutrition. He rolled down the window and said, "You know certain leafy green vegetables contain beta-carotene, a proven anticarcinogen?"

"I just left Billy McCall in a highly depressed state of mind."

"Probably not enough fiber in his diet."

"He struck me as a trifle constipated. If he starts to go rabbit you know what to do."

"I'll stick to him like a cocklebur on a wool sock."

"Good."

"Like Velcro to a cotton ball."

"You been drinking?"

"Of course not," he said. "I'm much more lucid when I'm drinking."

"Just keep an eye on him."

"You find out anything?"

"Only that Billy McCall is distasteful and seduces teenyboppers. That, and I got the name of his gun contact. Guy named Frake Meredith. Used to be a tennis player. Now he owns a couple of upscale restaurants. Fronts for the mob."

"You going to check on him?"

"Eventually. First, I think I'll find out a little more about Crispin Purvis. Like why Jackie B. thought Purvis wanted to buy guns, then it turns out he didn't." I told Chick the rest of what I'd learned from McCall.

"It's more than a coincidence somebody contacted Burlingame after Purvis turned him down."

"Almost like Purvis passed it on."

"Keeps him clear."

"What I figured, too. But, we need to know what they were planning to do with the guns and why so much money was floating around."

"Somebody messing somebody else around."

"I'll catch up to you later."

"As the world's greatest skip-tracer and bodyguard, I'd advise you to ingest massive amounts of beta-carotene at regular intervals."

"Just watch Billy, Chick," I said. "Why can't you read *Playboy* like the other degenerates?"

After Chick left to shadow McCall, I bought a *Boulder Daily Camera*. Nothing in it about Jackie or Turk's deaths. Nothing on the radio. Captain Marvel and the shadow soldiers must have cleaned up the scene. I doubted they would run to the police. We weren't going to the police, either.

I hoped they hadn't got the plate numbers from the Bronco. Things had been hot when they saw it, but it was still a worry. Then there was Sandy. I didn't want to give her any more to worry about.

Sandy had had enough excitement growing up. Her mother died of cancer when Sandy was in her teens, and her father, a nonfiction author, became a self-destructive alcoholic upon his wife's death. Duncan Collingsworth III had been a professor at Colorado State University—during the time I played football there—teaching history and American literature.

His teaching career ended when he abruptly resigned. Gave no reason, just did it. There was talk of a scandal. Happened over twenty years ago now. Fortunately, there was a great deal of money in the Collingsworth estate. Duncan III was heir to a large fortune amassed by his great-grandfather, a rancher and silver miner of the late 1800s, and supplemented by his grandfather, the first Duncan Collingsworth.

As the scion of one of Colorado's leading families as well as a nationally renowned author of a trilogy about the old West, Duncan's reputation could absorb the whispered asides, the stiff-lipped smiles, the gossip. Sandy, however, had to deal with her father's bouts with depression, his absenteeism, his three A.M. dry heaves, his emotional abandonment of her.

But Sandy was from the same tough French-Canadian stock as her mother, Genevieve Castillon Collingsworth, whose great-grandfather had trapped the Missouri river, whose grandfather had been a railroad man, and whose father and mother had turned a small weekly newspaper into the largest chain of newspapers in Colorado. You could look at Sandy and see Genevieve—warm yet fiercely independent. Survivors. Honest sojourners in a world dominated by men, taking them on straight up, playing fair. No feminist slogans, no harping about discrimination, no special favors wangled, no phony checks written on the promise of sexual favors. Just Sandra Veronica Collingsworth. It was enough.

And, she loved me.

An unlikely pair. A princess and the jack of hearts. Or maybe the knave of hearts. Pretender to the throne. She was cool silk and sparkling wine from a fluted goblet. I was denim and black coffee from a speckled tin cup.

Love conquers all.

I drove to Denver in a 1969 Mustang Mach I—a throwback to the halcyon days of my youth. It was a crisp, leafy Colorado September, the sun bursting through the trees with the energy of renewal. The air lean and clear. A wonderful day to be in the mountains, listening for the low haunting bugle of rutting elk. As I slowed to enter the city limits of Denver, I felt a slight miss in the firing sequence of the Mustang's 351 engine. The concrete and steel of Denver enveloped me. Further in, the late afternoon traffic swallowed me and my ancient muscle car—two dinosaurs from another era, trapped in a time for which neither was suited.

On the radio Leonard Bernstein conducted the Vienna Philharmonic through the *Leonore* Overture—the preface to Beethoven's *Fidelio*—the story of a Spanish nobleman, Florestan, imprisoned by his enemy. At the sound of a trumpet, Florestan is to be killed. However, Florestan's wife, Leonore, gains entrance to the prison and puts a pistol to the villain's head, saving Florestan.

Let Guns 'n' Roses top that.

A block from the studio I stopped at a storefront doughnut shop with a green and white striped awning. I bought a cup of black coffee. It came in a thick paper cup, not Styrofoam, with an old-fashioned paper cover with a tab. Life's little pleasures. I peeled back the lid and a small cloud of steam arose. It only smelled marvelous.

I pulled into the studio parking lot. The only parking slot left was reserved for the assistant producer, Richard Caster, who knew me and yet managed not to adore me. No accounting for taste, I guess. I pulled into his slot. Another blow against the empire.

At the door I was given a pass with my name scrawled across it in Sandy Collingsworth's expressive hand. A uniformed guard ushered me through doors and down a hallway into the airy studio. I stepped over cables and wires and stood over to the side, near cameraman Jerry Johnson. Sandy was seated behind her desk getting last-minute touches on her already perfect face. Looking up, she saw me and smiled.

"My God, Jerry," I said, to the cameraman, "the woman is hideously ugly."

"That you, Storme?" he said, looking into the camera monitor. "Won't work. Still won't take down my Sandy Collingsworth swimsuit poster."

"Twenty minutes," said a voice.

At that moment Richard Caster burst into the studio, walking stiff-leggedly, his forty-dollar tie outside his jacket and trailing like a dog's tongue. Seems he'd left the studio to run an errand and upon his return discovered someone had parked in his executive slot.

"There's a Mustang parked in my space," he was saying to the director. "I had to park two blocks down." Then he announced, "Who owns the Mustang parked in my slot?"

Sandy glared at me, head cocked questioningly, hands on hips. I shrugged with my palms upturned. Who, me?

The taping went well. Halfway through it I handed a studio gofer ten bucks to move my car. He smiled and folded the bill into his shirt pocket.

I liked watching Sandy work. She was a pro, taking her cues, reading her text. At the end of the half hour she favored central Colorado with a sensational smile.

Like a sunset.

After removing her microphone and earphone, Sandy stood and walked around the low table. She accepted a glass of water from a stagehand. As she neared me, she was intercepted by Richard Caster.

"I thought we agreed about the end of the show," he said. At five-seven and in heels she was eye-level with him.

"No," said Sandy. "You told me you wanted me to banter with Frank at the end of the show."

"Well?"

"Well, it comes off artificial if I push it. If I think of something appropriate I'll do it. But not every night."

"I think it adds something to the show."

"Give me a break, Richard."

I stepped closer. "Hi, kids. Love the smile at the end, Sandy. Great closer."

Sandy smiled at Richard. "See. He liked it."

"You," said Richard, meaning me. "You parked that car in my slot."

"These accusations hurt me, Richie."

"It's Richard," he said. "I called a towing service and they should be pulling it away, right about now."

"Curses," I said. "Foiled again."

"You won't think it's funny when you pay the tow. And, if you don't mind, I'm talking to Miss Collingsworth."

"Did you know you get these little bubbles of spittle in the corners of your mouth when you're mad?"

His hand started for his mouth, then he checked himself. He turned on Sandy. "As for you. You need to be a little more cooperative." He pointed a finger at her and started to say something else when I interrupted.

"Don't point at her, Richie."

"What?" he said, his face red.

"Wyatt," said Sandy. "I'll take care of this." She gave me a "back off" look. I started to say something else, but thought better of it.

"I don't mind suggestions, Richard, but you're not pulling my strings. I'm all grown up now and when it's appropriate, I'll banter my tail off."

"Worth seeing," I said.

"Wyatt, please," she said. I stuck my hands in my pockets and backed off. She was doing fine without me.

"So, Miss Celebrity doesn't take—"

He was interrupted by a burly African-American with a thick cigar jammed back in his jaw and a shirt that said "Sam" over the pocket. "You Caster?" he asked. "Guy called about the tow?"

"Yes, I am."

"You owe me fifty bucks."

"It's his car," Richie said, pointing at me. Always pointing. So uncouth.

"Wasn't no car in your slot, man. You owe me fifty bucks. Ain't makin' no dry run."

"That's crazy. There was a red Mustang in my slot. It's his. He never left the studio. It had to be there."

"All I know is I'm headed home for supper, running late, when I get a call says I'm supposed to come out here to tow a car outta your slot. Ain't no car in your slot. Now you're givin' me some sorry bullshit about paying. I'm tired and hungry and if you don't pay the fifty I'm gonna peel it off the backa your ass. Pardon me, ma'am."

"That's all right, Sam," Sandy said, smiling. "Whatever you have to do is all right with me."

"Keep an eye on him, though," I said. "Man's a vicious finger-pointer."

The last we saw of Richie Caster, he was asking if Sam took MasterCard.

"Shee-it," said Sam. About summed it up.

Bullet Bob's, despite the hokey name, was the in-place to dine for Denver's elite. I wasn't crazy about in-places or the social elite, but Sandy liked it and their coffee was outstanding. The maître d' was a polished penguin who asked if we had reservations. I smothered the bad joke and he led us to a table without incident.

We were given menus without prices, which I took to mean the food was free. I ordered prime rib, medium rare, with asparagus tips and baked potato. The lovely Miss Collingsworth had broiled rainbow trout, broccoli, salad, and a white wine with a name I couldn't pronounce. I kept an eye peeled for Bullet Bob.

Over New York–style cheesecake and coffee we discussed wedding plans and why I needn't ride to the rescue in each and every case.

"I can handle Richie," she said. "He's touchy because I dated him a couple of times."

"At least he has some taste. I'm not sure I understand why you'd date a lowlife like Richie."

"Maybe I'm attracted to lowlifes," she said, smiling.

"I detect a slur, but I'll forgive it if you'll give me your cheesecake."

"Not a chance. How do you eat the way you do and not become fat."

"Remarkable metabolic rate which is quickened by your presence."

"You say some of the—" She hesitated, her jaw tightening.

"What's the matter?"

"Nothing. Maybe he won't see me."

"Who?"

"Somebody I used to date."

"To save time, maybe you should give me the names of anyone in Denver you haven't dated. Which guy is it?"

She looked down at her coffee cup and nodded her head in the direction of a man in a tailored suit. "Blond-headed man, tanned, gray double-breasted suit, smoking a cigarette. Table near the window." I followed the nod and her description to the man seated near the window. There was another man seated across the table from him. Heavyset guy with Mediterranean features and a bad haircut. The first man looked up as I was looking at him. He stood up and walked across the room.

"Oh, no," said Sandy. "Here he comes."

"What is he? A vampire?"

"Worse."

"Perhaps I'll be able to reason with him."

"No," she said. "Let me handle it."

"I'm a pretty good reasoner."

"No. Just be nice."

The man was at our table now. He held his cigarette in an odd, three-fingered way, like George Raft used to. He was five-eleven and had a slender, waspish nose. Slender waist. Handsome guy. Lots of hair. His socks probably cost more than my entire outfit, though my jacket was genuine corduroy.

"Hello, Sandra," he said.

"Funny," I said. "He doesn't sound like George Raft."

He gave me a nasty look. I smiled engagingly, but he was unaffected by it. The man was made of iron.

"Who's the stiff?" he asked Sandy.

I looked at Sandy and silently formed the words "Who's the stiff?"

"This is Wyatt Storme. And he's not a stiff, he's my fiancé. I've decided to upgrade my choice of men. Wyatt, this is Frake Meredith, who is not a Rhodes scholar."

Frake Meredith. The tennis pro. Jackie Burlingame's gun contact. Hot stuff on the circuit in the late seventies. From the John McEnroe school of etiquette. Temper tantrums and broken rackets. Why would he be involved in gun trafficking? Had Billy McCall lied?

"Look, I've been trying to call you," he said. "I want to get together again, sometime."

I took another bite of cheesecake. Melts in your mouth. Good after-dinner show. I wondered if I'd have to tip Frake.

Sandy said, "Do you have some biological or psychological defect? I don't want to see you. I don't want to talk to you. Not now. Not ever."

I sipped my coffee. Good to the last drop.

"But I want to talk to you," Frake said.

"I'm ready to go, Wyatt."

"You aren't done with your cheesecake yet."

She gave me a piercing look. Women. No sense of the absurd. I decided to stand up. Humor her. Meredith followed me with his eyes as I did. I was four inches taller than him. And I had a genuine corduroy jacket and a remarkable metabolic rate. He had no chance.

I paid the check, took Sandy by the elbow, and we walked to the door.

"Hey," Frake said to our backs. "I'm not through talking to you."

"Are you still handling this?" I asked Sandy as we continued to walk away.

"Yes."

I shrugged. "Okay. Just let me know when you want me to blast him with my power ring."

I tipped the hatcheck girl and she handed me Sandy's coat, which I held while Sandy slipped into it. Frake followed us into the lobby.

"Don't turn your back on me," said Frake. He reached out to grab her arm, but I slapped his hand away.

"That's enough," I said.

"Nobody touches me," Frake said.

"Must make sex difficult."

Sandy said, "I'll take care of this."

"It's past that," I said, looking at Frake.

"You don't know who you're fucking with, cowboy," Frake said.

"Sure I do. A lounge lizard with a single-syllable vocabulary and no manners."

He smiled. Smirked actually. I hate a smirker above all things. "Tough guy, huh? Real badass. Well badass, don't write checks with your mouth your body can't cash."

"Hey, that's really funny, Frake. You'll wow 'em down at the trauma ward."

"You threatening me?"

"Let's go, Wyatt," urged Sandy.

"Can hardly tear myself away," I said.

"Listen here, hotshot. I'm gonna talk to the girl." He jabbed a finger in her direction.

"Don't point at her, Meredith," I said, meaning it.

"I do what I want, shit-for-brains. You understand that?" He pointed at me. As he did I snatched his finger, grabbing it in my fist, the back of my fist toward me. Fastest hands in the

West. Then I rotated my hand outward and twisted his finger, forcing him to rise up on his toes.

"Shit. Ow," he hissed between clenched teeth.

"Wyatt, don't," Sandy said.

"Talking isn't time-efficient. He understands this."

He glared at me with barracuda eyes. The lapels of the expensive jacket bunched. "You're fuckin' dead, man."

"Someday," I said. "Not by you."

Over Frake's shoulder I saw his dinner companion, the guy with the bad haircut, approaching. He was built like a bull seal.

"Get him off me, Carmine," said Frake. Carmine took a step in my direction. When he did I turned up the pressure on Frake's finger. He did a little jig as I did. He must've heard that different drummer.

"You take another step, Carmine," I said, "and I'll break it off and give it to some downtown jackboy to wear on a necklace. Tell 'im, Frake."

Frake grunted in pain, then said, "Back off, Carmine. Do it."

Carmine stopped.

"Now tell him to take a walk," I said.

"Go on, Carmine," said Frake.

Carmine complied. Why did a former tennis player need a gorilla like Carmine hanging around? Maybe Billy was telling me straight, after all.

After Carmine left I released Frake's finger. He jerked the injured hand back and flexed it several times, considering me with slitted eyes. Wolfish eyes. Wounded and dangerous.

"You shouldn't have done that," he said. "I won't forget it. Better watch your back."

"I will. You don't have the backbone to come straight at me."

He looked away. His eyes moved to Sandy, then back to me. "We'll see," he said, then backed away.

We left.

And I watched my back as I did.

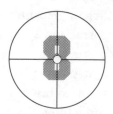

I could have accomplished the same thing without making a scene," said Sandy.

"Maybe. Wouldn't have been as much fun."

"You enjoy that?"

"No." I pointed the Mustang down the six-lane. The street lamps painted circles of light on the asphalt. A hundred years ago this would have been a meadow alive with eagles soaring over columbine and evergreen. Now it was skyscrapers and shopping malls. Progress. "A little, maybe."

I kept driving.

"It bother you that I went out with him?"

"I guess."

"What about Richie?"

"Less so," I said.

"Just Frake Meredith bothers you."

"Particularly Meredith. Especially Meredith."

"I've dated other men."

"I didn't think you were a nun before."

"I didn't just date the Richies and the Frakes."

"No reason they should miss out. Most outstanding woman in Denver."

"Most outstanding person in Denver."

"I'm in town now. Drops you to number two."

"Oh, pooh," she said. "You're jealous and won't admit it." She twirled a finger in my hair. "Maybe I like that. Who was the big guy? Carmine."

"He's a leg-breaker."

"A what? Oh . . . you mean he's a professional thug."

I nodded. "Tell me about Meredith," I said. "I know he used to be a pro tennis player."

"Yes. A good one, in fact. Hotheaded, though. It's where he got the nickname 'Frake.' Short for fracas."

"So what happened to him?"

"Got too old. Partied too much. Got into cocaine. Went broke. But he opened a couple of restaurants and has made a good deal of money."

"What are the names of the restaurants?"

"The Shamrock and the Deuce."

"He's involved in this gun thing," I said.

"I have trouble believing that."

I related my talk with Billy McCall.

"Maybe he was lying."

"I thought about that. But why hang out with the gorilla? And those restaurants you're talking about? They're fronts. I doubt if Meredith owns them, even though his name is probably on the papers."

"Oh." She was quiet. The tires hummed on the pavement. The radio played Eric Clapton. "Sorry. I didn't know."

I turned and looked at her. Smiled. "No need for it. I like coming to your rescue."

"It surprised me. How quick you had hold of his finger."

"Hands like a lizard's tongue."

"Father's in town."

"How is he?"

"He looks great. He's been exercising and is off the booze. He's writing again." She was quiet for a moment, then said, "I love you, Wyatt. Why don't I know you."

"You know me," I said. "Better than anyone."

"No, just better than you let other people know you. It's not the same thing. Where did you learn to do those things? How come you know about people like that? There is a side to you I don't know about. A darker side."

"Which question first?"

"You're being evasive."

"Part of my dark side."

She placed her hand on my right thigh. It burned and soothed. "I think I can penetrate the mist."

"I'm not sure you're adhering to the rules."

"Meaning?" She stroked my thigh down to the inside of my knee. Was the heater on too high? You never knew about these old American muscle cars.

"Meaning you're not playing fair."

"Do you want me to play fair?"

I kept driving.

"Well?" she said.

"I'm thinking about it."

"Don't think too long," she said.

I looked at her.

"Or . . . too hard," she purred, squeezing my knee.

I kept driving. A little faster, maybe.

The next morning we had breakfast with her father at the dough-nut shop with the green-striped awning. By the window. The sun shining through the glass. It painted warm patches on the floor and on my face as it drifted past Sandy's honey-blond hair, giving her outline a cozy glow. I had fresh-ground Colombian coffee and a doughnut. Sandy sipped cinnamon-hazelnut coffee and nibbled on a bran muffin. Her father was using the pay phone to talk with his publisher.

"How can you eat a bran muffin when they've got all this great pastry?"

"Goes with the twenty-four-inch waist."

"Small price to pay."

"What's your waist size?"

"Gauge," I said, correcting her for a change. "You measure steel in gauge."

She smiled a lazy smile and cocked her head. Looked at me. I looked back. Nice view. "Wyatt, I need to ask you some things you may not want to answer."

"So, don't ask."

"Will Frake try to . . ." She was struggling with it. Her eyes showed it. "Will he try to hurt you?" It came out in a rush.

I smiled. "He don't pack the gear, darlin'. Guys like Meredith aren't scary if you drag them into the light. Besides, it's a well-known fact that I'm six-feet-two-and-a-half-inches of high-carbon steel and always keep my edge."

"You're not answering the question. Will he try? What about the . . . you know. What about the mob?"

"He might. But they won't. I doubt the big boys have any interest in me. Meredith is nobody to them. Just a name they can use. Eventually, they'll swallow him."

"What if he keeps after me?" she said. There was nothing else in her face or voice. She wasn't trying to find out where she stood with me. She wanted to know about me. "Will you let me handle it?"

I looked out the window. An attractive middle-aged woman was dragging a little boy by the hand down the sidewalk. He kept trying to pull away. "Ask me something I won't have to lie about."

"Wyatt," Sandy said. "Everything can't be handled that way."

"No argument there."

"I can handle this situation."

"You don't understand the situation."

"And you do?"

"Yes."

Her cheeks colored and her jaw worked. "You're stubborn and annoying. Why do I love you so much?"

"Probably the chiseled jawline. Women have no defense against that."

"What are you going to do with the money and the guns?"

"Split the money with Chick. We buried the guns. Probably squeeze McCall some more. Run the back trails on Burlingame. Check out Burlingame's apartment. Check on Meredith."

"Why was there so much money?"

"Doesn't make sense, does it? Somebody's running a scam. Either that or there was more to the deal than Jackie told me. Or more than he knew."

"What's Chick doing?"

"Tailing McCall. See where he goes. Who he talks to."

"Then what?"

"Then we flush them out into the open."

"To what purpose?"

"It's something to do."

She looked at me, her head turned slightly, considering me. "You like this, don't you?"

I shrugged. Ambiguity my shield.

"You do. I can see it in your eyes when you talk about it. Like they are looking at nothing but seeing everything. That's the part I don't know about. The scary part. The part you keep for yourself. Please be careful. I don't know where I'd be able to find another dipzoid has-been wide-out on short notice."

"I'm always careful."

"Let me handle Frake my own way?"

"How about some more coffee?" I said. "Tell me about Joring Braden."

"Congressman Braden is perhaps the most famous politician

in Colorado, if not the western United States. You mean you don't know anything about him?"

"I'm radically apolitical."

"You don't vote, do you?"

I confessed I didn't. My only political theory was that Congress needed to be dissolved and all new people voted in.

"How can you not vote?"

"I sleep in. You going to tell me about Braden or not?"

She smiled. "Joring Braden was elected to the House in 1964. On the coattails of LBJ and several other hawkish Democrats. Sounds funny now, doesn't it?"

"Not really," I said. "Politicians distill their morality in the opinion polls. They don't allow conviction to stand in the way of progress."

"Boy, are you cynical."

"Pragmatic."

"Braden was a supporter of the war until his son was killed under mysterious circumstances—"

"What mysterious circumstances?"

"The body was never returned to the States. Lost in transit. Helicopter crash. Braden became an opponent of the war. Critics say his conversion was coincident with the national mood Nixon's ascension to the White House created. Now he's primed to run for the Senate. Some say he has his eyes on Pennsylvania Avenue."

"You're kidding."

"There's more. In 1975 Braden's first wife died. His second wife divorced him in 1977."

"Didn't wait long between women."

"He's had a checkered career in that respect. He's known as the Ted Kennedy of the Rockies. Has some DUIs which were covered up. Reputation as a womanizer. There was a big flap in the late seventies when a Miss Colorado candidate filed a palimony suit against him. He denied it and the beauty queen miscarried during an auto accident."

"What were the circumstances of the accident?"

"Hit-and-run. The fetus aborted and that was the end of the palimony suit. There was an investigation but nothing came of it. Braden is almost beyond the law in Colorado."

"So I could run into trouble if I start turning things over in his playpen?"

"Probably," she said.

Her father returned and took a seat. Duncan Collingsworth III was late fifties but looked mid-forties. Handsome in an unobtrusive way. Same expressive mouth he'd passed on to his daughter. His eyes were clear blue and intelligent. They were joyful and contented as he looked at his daughter.

"What did they say, Father?"

"My editor thinks they will be glad to see my new work. He used the word *excited*."

I offered my congratulations.

He smiled, thanked me and took his usual small sip of coffee. The drinking problem had always been in contrast to his restrained personality. "Sandy tells me you are involved in a project of your own."

"Helping out some friends," I said. "Matt and Kelly Jenkins. You know them?"

"I . . . a . . . the name's familiar." He picked up his coffee cup and drained it. He held it a few inches above the table and looked around the room. "Where is that waitress?" he said.

"There's more in the coffee server," said Sandy, indicating the brown thermal pitcher on the table.

"Yes, of course," he said. "Whatever was I thinking about?"

"Kelly was at Colorado State when you were a professor there," I said. "Maybe she took one of your classes. Her maiden name was McArthur. Kelly McArthur?"

"One of Wyatt's myriad former flames," Sandy said, giving me a sidelong look.

Duncan poured coffee into his cup. It overflowed onto the

saucer and then to the tablecloth. "Well, damn!" he said. "Now look what I've done. What a mess I've made."

I reached out to help him by lifting his cup from the saucer, but only succeeded in dribbling more coffee onto the table and Duncan.

"Aw, great," I said. "Sorry."

"It's all right, Wyatt," he said. "I started the whole thing."

Sandy dabbed at the spill with a napkin. "What a couple of clods," she said. "I'll probably be cleaning up after both of you for the rest of my life."

"There are worse things," I said.

"Agreed," said Duncan.

After breakfast I drove Sandy to Channel Seven and then pointed the Mustang toward Boulder and Corning Estates, the home of the more late than great Jackie Burlingame. Before leaving town I called my cabin to see if Chick left any messages. After the seventh ring, the recorded message started. I heard my voice:

"If you waited seven rings you either have something worth saying or you fell asleep waiting. Go ahead."

I punched in the playback code, 83, my number as a wideout for the Cowboys. I heard the whir of winding tape, a click, then Chick's voice:

"Watson, the game is afoot. He's been running all over town. Fortunately, being Captain Midnight I am able to shadow him without his knowledge. I'll meet you at seventeen hundred hours at the Electric Ranch bar. If not met, will leave message with Long Legs at Electric Ranch. Gotta di di, he's got legs."

I waited to see if there were other messages. There were none.

I hung up and got back into the Mach I. I started it and it rumbled beneath me. Apparently, I had got Billy McCall's attention. Either he was covering his tracks or testing the wind. If he bolted it meant the bad guys were after him. Then we'd have to find him first and put him in a safe place, otherwise he might throw me to the wolves. Worse, he might put them on to Matt and Kelly.

Could not allow that.

I arrived at Corning Estates without any idea how to get into Jackie B.'s condo. Worse, I didn't know which unit was his. Then, I got a break. It was about time. Corning Estates had personalized parking slots. The condo number was painted in yellow block characters on each parking slab. There was a mint-green Mercedes 200SE with the license plate, JACKY-B. The yellow paint on the parking slab said 23-B.

I felt underneath the edge of the right front wheel well. Then, I felt along the left front. Found it. A little magnetic rectangle with a sliding lid. Figured a juicer like Jackie would have a back-up set of keys. I slid open the box. Two keys—one with the Mercedes-Benz trademark and one round-headed key with "Safe-T" stamped on it. Either it was the key to his apartment or he had a treasure chest buried in the garden.

Using my powers of intellect and discernment, I ruled out the treasure chest and beat it up to the second floor, my heart filled with expectation. When I got there I put the key in the lock and turned it. At least I tried to turn it. It didn't fit. Maybe I was a little hasty ruling out the treasure chest.

I pondered what to do next. I could shoot the lock off but that might be considered gauche in an upscale neighborhood such as Corning Estates. Could kick the door in like John Wayne, but I was wearing my Adidas. Maybe I could vibrate through the wall like the Flash—I did have my Adidas on, after all. I always wondered what would happen if the Flash sneezed while he was vibrating through walls and stuff. Spenser would just pick the lock. Spenser knew everything. I looked at the door. Nothing happened. I thought about it some more. That didn't work either. Maybe astral projection.

I was stumped.

I heard someone coming up the steps. I ducked around the corner to hide. Actually, I ran around the corner and hid behind a potted tree. Guaranteed to make me look silly if he chose to walk around this corner, which, fortunately, he didn't. Instead he walked halfway down the corridor and stopped in front of Burlingame's door and began to pick the lock with burglar's tools.

Ask and it shall be given you. Seek and ye shall find.

He was successful in getting the door open. He went inside. I reached into my jacket and snapped the Browning from its holster. Walked quietly down the corridor. The door was open a crack so I went inside.

Knock and it shall be opened unto you.

The man was preoccupied with rooting through drawers, and didn't hear me come in. He was tall and slender and dressed like a cowboy—boots and jeans. One of the shadow soldiers? His back was to me.

"Don't turn around," I said, "or the last thing you'll ever see is the handsomest man in the universe." Tall and slender started to look over his shoulder. "Hold it, slim. I know what you're thinking. 'What does the handsomest man in the universe look like?' Well, being this is a nine-millimeter Browning, the gun you load once and shoot forever, you have to ask yourself, 'Do I feel lucky?' "

He stopped trying to look over his shoulder. He said, "You haven't got a gun. You're bluffing."

I shuffled the slide on the gun. It made a nice little heavy-metal *snick*. "Has its own sound, doesn't it? Nothing sounds like that, except that. And it's copiously loaded." He seemed satisfied I was a man of my word. I felt better. "Okay, facedown on the carpet with your hands in your back pockets." He complied. Such a feeling of raw power. I patted him down. Found a .25-caliber auto pistol on him. "What were you going to do with this? Shoot mice? Should've hid it in your purse. I'd never have found it there."

I tied his hands together with cord I cut from the venetian blinds. Blindfolded him and checked his ID. Name was Harold Wallace.

"Okay, once again it's time to play 'Why did Harold break into the condo?' Correct answers are worth ten points. Incorrect answers will be gonged. Now, let's see, what can we use for a gong? I've got it. We'll use the gun. I'm sure you'll be able to hear that."

"Smartass."

"What are you doing here?"

"What's it to you?" I kicked him in the thigh. He grunted.

"Burlingame owes me money," he said.

"So, you thought maybe you'd break into his apartment and find some lying around? Try again."

"Who are you?"

"Ray Stevens. And I'm here to assure you that everything is beautiful. What are you looking for?"

"Just looking," said Harold. "Don't know what for."

"Well, let's see now. I could call the police and tell them I found you tossing the apartment. Then, they could swing by in their uniforms and everything, take you downtown, strip-search your anus, serve you bad coffee, and ask you why you were here."

"Big deal."

"I'm not through Harold. Don't interrupt again. Then, they could ask you where Jackie is, what happened to him and what you had to do with it. Contrary to popular opinion they are persistent and efficient."

"Don't know anything about Jackie."

"Jackie's dead, Harold. But you knew that already, didn't you? You were there when they did it. Isn't that right, Harold?"

"You're the guy in the van," said Harold.

"That is correct, Harold. Now, for twenty-five points and a chance to win an all-expense-paid trip to Terre Haute, tell me what I have to gain by letting you leave here standing up."

"I didn't know they were going to whack him out. They just told me about the drop."

"Who shot him?"

"I don't know."

I stood on the back of his knee. He grunted in pain.

"I didn't see it," he said. "That's the truth. I was looking at the sample gun when the shot went off. Then, there were several shots."

"Why'd they kill him?"

"I don't know."

"Are they looking for me?"

"What do you think?"

"How much money was in the case?"

"I don't know. Maybe thirty Gs."

I decided to throw him a curve. "Sorry, Harold. You're way off. There was only a couple of grand on top with a bunch of bundled Monopoly money underneath that."

He was quiet for a moment. Thinking about it. "That can't be. We were supposed to . . ." He stopped for a moment. "You a cop?"

"Nope. Just a guy wondering where the rest of my money is. I think one of your people ripped me off and that distresses me."

"You still got the guns?"

"Maybe. Who are you working for?"

He was quiet again. I put my foot on the back of his neck and pushed. He made a sputtering noise. "I . . . can't . . . tell."

"I'm getting tired of this, Harold. I could just zap you and look elsewhere for information. Up to you. Choose."

"They'll kill me."

"A moot point. Me or them. Who is it?"

"I don't know."

"You know a guy named Billy McCall?"

"No."

"How about Frake Meredith?"

"Means nothing to me."

"How about Crispin Purvis?"

"No."

I shoved the heel of my Adidas where it would be the most effective. He grunted. I said, "Try again."

"Okay," he said. "I've heard of Purvis. Doesn't mean I know what he has to do with this."

"What about McCall?"

"Can't help you. Don't know him."

"Meredith?"

"Tennis player. Owns the Shamrock. All I know."

"How was this set up?"

"Look, man, we got a call from the Captain. Said the drop was set. I went."

"Who's the Captain?"

"Don't know who he is. We just call him the Captain."

"You active?"

"No. Was. Got eighty-sixed."

"Why?"

"Section eight."

"You crazy?"

"No. Called it battle fatigue. But that ain't the way it was."

I rubbed the side of my jaw. "What'd you do?"

"Nam," he said. "You don't know what it was like."

I did. "Regardless, I have a burning desire to know what you did." I pushed the Browning against the back of his ear.

"Okay. Shit. I'll tell you." Using my thumb, I let the hammer down slowly. "I was an MP. Liaison for military intelligence. Around Saigon. Worked the Golden Triangle, investigating black market stuff. Cigarettes, booze, contraband—"

"Guns?" I said.

"Yeah. Gooks'd steal 'em, pick 'em up after a firefight. Sell 'em to Charlie, use 'em against our guys. Can I sit up?"

"No."

"My back hurts."

"Tough. Think pleasant thoughts."

"You a vet?"

"No," I lied. "I was one of those longhaired hippie types that smoked dope-a-wana, and hung around college campuses with sex-starved coeds while you were buying Asian girls with Lucky Strikes."

"What are you doing here?" he asked.

"We seem to be having a little role-reversal problem here. The guy with the gun almost always gets to ask the questions. It's like a rule or something. What did you do that got you in trouble?"

"Didn't kill nobody."

"Don't talk in riddles."

"They were going to hang it on me if I didn't go along."

"Tell me about it."

"We were onto a cadre of smugglers. They were dealing large amounts of weapons and matériel into Cambodia and into the hands of the VC. We squeezed a street monkey named Tam, found out where the next drop was gonna take place. We went in heavy, got the drop on them. One of the guys was a Caucasian. Kangaroo cowboy. An Aussie."

"What was he doing there?" I asked.

"Some kind of conduit for international sales. He was turning the guns on an open market to the highest bidder. Turns out he was some kind of Australian secret service operative."

"Australia? What was he doing dealing our weapons?"

"Getting rich. He offered to pay us off. 'No use you Yanks going home poor,' he said. He made us a good deal, man. We seized some of the cache, to make it look good, then burned the gooks working for him."

"And took their places," I said.

"Right."

"So where did the military beef come from?"

"A ready-mix lieutenant got fragged in a whorehouse. They needed somebody to take the fall, so I was elected."

"Why you?"

"This lieutenant was a congressman's son. Couldn't have him dying in a Saigon cathouse. So, we cooked up a story where he was accidentally killed when I went crazy killing gooks and got him by accident. Shipped junior home in a rubber bag."

I sat back against the arm of a chair. Gave it some thought. I doubted that Harold was being entirely honest. They always kept something back. I would just have to sift through it. What did the death of Joring Braden's son over twenty years ago have to do with a gunrunning operation in contemporary Colorado? And how did Harold know Crispin Purvis?

"Tell me how you know Crispin Purvis."

"I work for him. On his dude ranch."

"Well, well. First you don't know him and then you've heard of him, and now this. He in on this?"

"No."

"Who set it up?"

"Already told you. Captain Marvel."

I asked him a few more questions, but didn't get anywhere. He wouldn't tell me anything else. He wouldn't tell me who the kid with the Roy Rogers trick draw was. Didn't figure, though. He would have been in kindergarten during the late sixties. Where did they pick him up? Unable to get more out of Harold, I blindfolded him with his handkerchief and gagged him with a pair of balled-up socks I found in Jackie's drawer.

That done, I tossed the place. Found an address book with phone numbers in it. The book was coded. Initials or acronyms beside the numbers. I didn't have time to decipher them, as I'd wasted too much time with Harold.

Jackie's bedroom looked like something out of *Superfly.* Too much satin and velvet. There was a mirror on the ceiling. One of the dresser drawers had a false bottom. Underneath it I found a Walther PPK pistol, some cartridges, and an extra clip. Loaded. I pocketed those items. I checked the bathroom and, at the bottom of the commode tank, I found a brick. As if a guy with a mint-green Mercedes was concerned with saving money on his water bill. I rolled up my sleeve, reached down into the tank and pulled up the brick. It was plastic and hollowed out, yet still had some heft to it. One end was grooved and by twisting clockwise it swung open to reveal a silver plastic bag.

I shook the contents of the pseudobrick into my hand. The silver bag had a Ziploc closure. I opened it and looked inside. White powder. Cocaine. I put the brick back in the commode tank and replaced the lid. Returning to the living room, I found Harold thrashing around on the floor trying to free his hands.

"Give it up, Harold," I said. "I got a merit badge in tying up people. But, just so you'll know I appreciate your help, I brought you a present." I hefted the bag of coke. "Your very own lifetime supply of cocaine." I put it into the pocket of his jacket. He grunted something under the sock gag. "No, don't bother to thank me. Just makes me blush. Now, you be good and maybe the nice policeman will bring you a lollipop."

He let go a volley of muffled expletives. At least they sounded like expletives.

"Here, now. That any way to talk?"

I left the apartment and returned to my car. I drove two blocks and stopped at a pay phone. Dialed 911. When the dispatcher answered, I said, "At Corning Estates, apartment twenty-three-B, you'll find a drug dealer bound and gagged, with a kilo of blow in his jacket. I've had enough of those lowlifes working my neighborhood. You'll have to hurry though. He'll be able to get loose pretty soon."

"Where is this?"

"Corning Estates. Twenty-three-B. The guy can also tell you about Jackie Burlingame."

"Who?"

"Jackie Burlingame. Ask this guy about him."

"Who is this?"

"The Midnight Cowboy. Champion of good."

"Everybody's a wise guy anymore."

"Gotta run. Evil is everywhere and never rests."

The Electric Ranch Bar and Grill was a pleasant enough place to spend a late afternoon. Perched on the outskirts of Boulder, it boasted a saloon-style western façade, and a warm contemporary pseudocountry motif inside, with the usual profusion of Coors and Busch neon. It was more bucolic than cowboy, more 1990s than 1890s. Modest. More a place to have a couple of beers after work than a place to raise a fuss.

Didn't see Chick.

I sat down and waited for my eyes to adjust to the darkness. Kept an eye out for "Long Legs." Then I saw her. Actually, she walked up to take my order. As I sat, the belt of her one-piece shift was at my eye level. And it was a long way to the floor from there. She had large dark eyes and a strong face. More handsome than beautiful, but beautiful nonetheless.

"What'll you have, cowboy?" she asked.

"Coffee, if you've got it. Black."

"You must be Storme," she said. "I've got a message for you from your friend."

"How'd you know my name?"

"Your friend said you'd be the only guy to come in and ask for coffee." She laughed. "It'll only take a minute. I've had it ready to make most of the afternoon, waiting for you to come in."

"What's the message?"

"He said to stick around here and he'd be back. Said, 'The rabbit ran into the briar patch and wouldn't be out for a while.' That make sense to you?"

"No."

"Me either. He's different. Cute though. Oh, something else. He said to check out the hors d'oeuvres. That they were, hope I get this right, 'replete with beta-carotene.' "

"What is on the hors d'oeuvre table?"

"Vegetables and dip."

"Broccoli and carrots?"

She nodded. "Said it was the reason he liked it here. The beta-carotene."

I looked at her. Considered her magnificent freeway-long legs. Smiled. "One of the reasons, anyway."

She smiled. "My name's Cinnamon if you need anything."

She left to make the coffee. Still early. The evening crowd would come in later. Two older gentlemen sat at the bar, sipping draft beer and talking low. Two college kids in CU sweatshirts at a booth with a pitcher of beer on the table. And me, America's sweetheart.

I opened the address book I'd found at Burlingame's apartment. Buried among phone numbers and appointments were the following acronyms and numbers:

```
CP—5/18/67
MB—1-191-1768
JB—100 Grand St., Denver
CP—Mercedes-Benz, 10K, like new, $35,000
J/CS—BAR #5554326
```

I looked at it, turning it over in my mind. A date, an address, and an ad for a Mercedes with ten thousand miles on it. Initials by them. And what was J/CS? Was BAR Browning Automatic Rifle? There were more phone numbers and addresses with names by them. I recognized two of them. One belonged to a backup quarterback with the Denver Broncos, and one was Janet Sterling, a film actress with an Aspen address. She had been in several modestly successful productions. Regular customers or blackmail victims? Or both? Be interesting to check these people out. I'm sure Jackie knew several interesting people.

It was a start.

The college kids played pool and slugged quarters into the jukebox. A mixture of Garth Brooks and Mariah Carey songs filled the room. I was not a big fan of either. Give me Jimmy Buffett and Eric Clapton every time. Cinnamon warmed my cup. The front door opened and three men resembling humans came into the saloon. Bikers. Leathers and tattoos. Long hair and metal dangling from their jackets. Colors on the back of the jackets—a blazing skull with the word HEADHUNTERS in scarlet. One of them had a ZZ Top beard and a ring through one cheek, and he was the best groomed of the trio. Whatever happened to smooth-faced JDs with Elvis sneers. Ah, the good old days.

They swaggered into the room, a dark knot of leather and beast aroma. One of them stopped near my table and said, "Hey, this guy's drinking coffee." His friends walked on as if I didn't exist. I wished the same for this guy. "Why you drinking coffee, man?"

Being socially inhibited, I am often at a disadvantage in these situations. I wanted to say it was liquefied bone marrow from a biker's skull. I didn't. I wanted to tell him to return to the herd. I didn't. Instead, I smiled enigmatically and said: "It's the source of my power."

He rolled his head to one side like a large dog considering

something unfamiliar. He snorted his disgust. "What power, man? You can get coffee at a restaurant."

"Atmosphere. Ambience. Cerebral conversation. Only get those here." I was getting tired of talking to him. Sandy was always after me to become more tolerant. Less confrontational. I was practicing. I was tolerating the crap out of this guy.

"You dissing me, man?" he asked. Geez, this guy was the antidote for tolerance.

"Go play somewhere else, huh?" I said.

At that moment the front door opened again and Chick Easton walked in. The biker glared at me with simian eyes.

"Hey, Wyatt," said Chick, nearing the table. "Who's your friend?"

"Ain't his friend," said the biker.

"Well," said Chick, smiling. "Look's like you've done it again." The biker's friends had stopped walking and were taking an interest now. Never a dull moment. "Let me apologize for my friend," Chick said. "Whatever he did that offended you I'm sure he's sorry. Isn't that right, Wyatt?"

I sipped my coffee.

"See?" Chick said. "He's sorry."

"He didn't say nothin'."

"He always becomes reticent when he feels apologetic. He's a very reticent apologizer."

The biker swiveled his head to look at Chick. "Now you're doing it. Fuckin' with me."

"What'd I do?" Chick said, his arms spread, palms up. "Wouldn't think of it." But, the Cheshire-cat smile was on his face. "Hey, Cinnamon. How about three shots of JD with beer chasers for these guys. Put it on my tab, okay?"

She nodded. The college boys cast nervous looks at each other. The old men swiveled around on their stools. Chick looked at the guy. "There, how's that? Everything's cool. Right?"

The biker glared at me some more, then said, "Maybe I see you guys some other time."

I started to say "What a treat," but remained in tolerance mode. Sandy would have been proud.

"Come on, Bull," said ZZ Top beard. "Free booze, man. You can crack on the straights anytime." The older biker said nothing. He'd already turned away and taken a seat. Bull nodded his head, hitched up his belt, and spat on the floor at my feet.

He was a delight.

Bull joined his friends and they sopped up gratis booze. Chick sat down and smiled. "Once again I have rescued your narrow rump. Chick Easton, soother of mutant bikers."

"What does 'The rabbit has run into the briar patch' mean?"

"Billy McCall is in the drunk tank. They're holding him overnight. Against his will, even."

Cinnamon walked up then. "Get you anything?"

"Sure," Chick said. "I built up a powerful thirst reasoning with those wayward boys. Missionary work is thankless yet not without satisfaction. Bring me a Heineken and a shot of Maker's Mark."

"Okay," she said. She asked if I needed more coffee. I declined. "Thanks for not making a scene. This round is on the house. If they make trouble I'll call the cops."

"Those guys come in here often?"

"Once in a while. They were here this morning when we opened up." Chick smiled at me.

"What about Billy McCall?" he asked. "Slender guy. About twenty. Dark hair. He was in here this morning with them. He a regular?"

"No. Never saw him before today. Heavy drinker, though. I'll be back." She walked away. Chick admired her gait.

He said, "I leave you alone for a few minutes and you almost mess up my investigation."

I unwrapped a cigar. "How's that?"

"Those bikers. They work for McCall and Burlingame." I clipped the cigar, put it between my teeth and lighted it with a Dallas Cowboys lighter. Chick continued. "They mule the dope, make the collections. They are world-class collectors. Master-Card should put them on the payroll. Nothing like a bicycle chain upside the head to shake loose the rent money. The older guy with the long hair? He's a Nam vet."

"How do you know all this?"

He tapped his head with a forefinger. "First, because I'm a genius. Second, because the guy has 'Bravo Company' tattooed on his forearm. Also, because I've been following Billy around and he handed these guys some dope right after I saw you last. Also some money. In fact, Billy's been all over town. You lit a fire under the boy. I think he's making a move to inherit Jackie's clientele."

"A risky idea."

"Yeah, but I don't think Jackie had much contact with the bikers. The bikers make good muscle. They make an immediate psychological impact. If Billy greases them enough and gets them into line, he's got some juice."

"If not?"

He sipped the whiskey. "If not," he said, "then the beast eats him up."

"Could happen anyway," I said. "Sooner or later the guys in the camo will figure out Billy had something to do with Jackie and the guns."

"There's another possibility."

"Which is?"

"Billy's been busier than Monty Hall. Buying drinks. Passing flake. Handing out money. Maybe he was having a going-out-of-business sale. He was tossing down the booze. Saw him toking on a number in his car, too. He's scared."

"How'd the cops get on him?"

"A public-minded citizen, concerned about the dangers of drunk driving, turned him in. I know a guy works traffic. Owes me a favor. Told him I needed McCall out of action for a while. He hauled him off to the drunk tank.''

"They could find narcotics in the car. He could take a big fall.''

"Nah. I swept his car while he was making his last visit. Then I called my cop buddy.''

"You dump the product?''

"Let's see,'' he said, smiling. "What did I do with it? Put the coke and pills down a drain, and what did I do with the grass? I'll be switched if I remember. I'm sure I got rid of it.'' He bounced his eyebrows. Actually, he has an eyebrow and a half. One of them looks more like an apostrophe lying on its side, a little souvenir of his tour of Vietnam.

"That stuff's bad for you.''

"I have just a touch of glaucoma. Fixes me right up. So what did you find out?''

I told him about finding Harold going through Jackie's apartment. Showed him the keys and the black book I'd found. He looked at the book carefully.

"These entries with the initials are weird. Can't make any sense out of them. I know Janet Sterling.''

"You got a swimsuit poster of her or something?''

"Better than that. I've done some bodyguard work for her. Some of it close up. A little kinky, though. She's a biter.''

laughed. "That's pretty fantastic," I said to Chick. "Even for you. You and Janet Sterling?"

"Got the teeth marks to prove it."

"What were you supposed to be protecting her from? You?"

"A rabid fan. Stalker. Turned out to be nothing. Just a fan. He didn't realize how she took it. But anymore, celebrities get skittish when somebody starts dogging them. She gave him an autographed picture. I took it to him. He was all right. Just didn't have much of a life. Besides, I flexed. Works every time."

"And?"

"And," he said, pleased with himself. "She was appreciative. Gave me a case of Glenfiddich Scotch and a five-C bonus. Modesty prevents me from divulging the rest."

"Uh-huh."

"She's in town, right now. On location for a scene from a movie."

"She a user?"

"Part of the lifestyle."

"Could she be one of Jackie's customers?"

"Possible. But it doesn't make sense. She could get the product from a higher-class jobber than Burlingame. What about the quarterback? You know him?"

I did. Randle Lightfoot. A Heisman runner-up and academic all-American out of South Dakota State University, waiting for John Elway to get old or develop arthritis. He had a big arm, but was erratic. He either threw fifty-yard strikes or hit a cameraman on the sidelines. The interesting thing about Lightfoot was not the fact he was a pro football player, or his Indian heritage. It was his off-the-field lifestyle that gained him the most notoriety. He dated starlets and partied with celebrities. Drove a Porsche. Top down and full out. A poor man's Joe Namath.

"Met him once. Funny kid. He's caught between what he wants to be, what they say he is, and what he really is. Wants to be Jim Morrison and Joe Montana. On alternating days. Wants to write his name across the sky in Day-Glo."

"Can he?"

"They all think that when they're twenty-five."

"Even you?" he asked.

Neil Young's "Harvest Moon" played on the jukebox. "Even me," I said.

"Seems you did more than think it."

"I used disappearing ink."

"Ever wish you could do it all over?"

I sipped my coffee and watched the college kids play pool. They laughed when they missed their shots. "No. Mostly I wish I could have it all back."

Chick lifted his glass. "Well, here's to having it all back. To young quarterbacks and high school dances. To things lost or left behind." He put the whiskey to his lips and threw his head back. He put the empty glass back on the table.

Sometimes Chick Easton allowed the clown mask to slip and the dark bruise in his soul would show in his eyes. It was a deep

purple like storm clouds, roiling in the sky. He'd survived the
war but not his part in it. Tried to wash it away with whiskey
and conversation. But it would always tug on him. And he would
always be one of us.

They sent us there, then brought us back when it was no
longer convenient. Blamed us for their malaise. Then two decades later asked forgiveness when it was stylish to do so. In
return we got a black marble wall, bad dreams, and eyes that
could no longer cry. Now they were busy condemning patterns
of speech and thoughts they didn't agree with. Political correctness is the new tyranny. The new intolerance. They want to
make the rules and hope we're not watching them do it.

We hadn't asked to go and some had never fully come back.
Not much to do about it, though. Hang on tight and don't give
them the satisfaction.

"So," I said, "when's McCall get out?"

"Tomorrow, unless he makes bail. My cop buddy will tell me
who springs him. That'll give us another lead."

"Still, all this seems to be taking us away from the gun connection and the money. Who was the money supposed to go to?
And what does Janet Sterling have to do with this?"

The college kids had stopped playing pool and returned to
their booth. "If you don't mind me waxing your butt at billy-
ards I'll play you a game."

He stood up and walked to the table. I followed him. Above
the table Clydesdales endlessly pulled a beer wagon around a
Budweiser logo. Kitsch in perpetuity. I put quarters in the slot
and pushed it in. The multicolored balls spilled onto the lip as
if I'd rolled up three cherries in a Vegas slot machine. We selected cue sticks. Chick chalked his cue, measured the white ball
and sent it into the triangle of colors with a resounding crack.
Two striped balls and one solid ball dropped into pockets.

"Janet is a user," said Chick. "She runs at high speed at all
times. She isn't much of a drinker though she will pop a cork.
Booze saps the youth out of your body." He put a striped ball

in the side pocket and left himself lined up on the thirteen. "I'm the exception, of course. So Janet uses the pills to keep her up, put her to sleep. The usual stuff. Some pretty sad shit, actually." He punched the cue ball and it kissed the thirteen ball into the side pocket.

"So you think Billy was telling the truth about his part in Jackie B.'s business?"

"I'll believe it if you will."

"Hey, old man," said one of the bikers, interrupting us, "we're ready for another round here."

"Your friends are thirsty," I said, smiling.

Chick exhaled. "Westmoreland was right, after all," he said. "Appeasement never works." He started to shoot, hesitated, looked at me and said, " 'Old man'?"

I made a little brushing motion at the side of my head. "Got a little gray over the ears," I said. "I think it makes you look dignified, myself."

"Hey, old man, you hear me?" bellowed the biker. "You deff or something? Get us another round."

Chick waved at them across the room. Smiling, he said, "Fuck yourselves with a can opener, boys." He took another shot and missed. "Damn. Now they got me off my game."

"Excuses, excuses," I said. I drilled the two ball into the side pocket.

Though they couldn't have heard what Chick said, the three bikers walked our way. They spread themselves around the table. "Maybe you didn't hear me?" Bull said.

"You're in my light," I said, lining up a shot on the threeball. Bull reached over and picked up the cue ball.

"We want another round." He stood there flipping the cue ball up and down. "Get us one."

"They want another round," I said to Chick. "This is your fault."

"They're costing me a fortune."

"Tough shit," said the biker.

"Mom told me to stay out of bars," I said.

"Shoulda listened to her," Chick said.

"You guys gonna buy us a round, or not?"

"It's customary," said Chick, standing with his cue stick at parade rest, "for the recipient of the first round to buy the second round. Bar etiquette. Where have you guys been?"

"Fuck you, wiseass," said the biker nearest Chick.

"Be easier to give them what they want," said the biker Chick identified as a veteran.

"Maybe you could wean them," I said. "Buy them smaller drinks each time."

"Who asked you, asshole?" said Bull.

"Conversation doesn't seem to be working," said Chick. "You promised Sandy you'd be good?"

"She knows I'm a backslider. Besides, I'm not reformed enough to listen to any more of this."

Bull was still flipping the cue ball. The guy nearest Chick, the one with the ZZ Top beard, reached into his pocket and pulled a butterfly knife. As he was flipping it into readiness, Chick struck the surprised biker on the wrist, then quickly put the same hand against the side of the man's throat. The knife clattered to the floor. I snaked out a hand and intercepted the cue ball as it left Bull's hand, and smacked it up against his forehead. His eyes rolled back in his head and he fell over a nearby table. Chick spun the cue stick back under his armpit, Chuck Norris–style, then lashed out the heavy end, striking the bearded bandit in the neck. The man put his hands to his throat and Chick drove the cue into his solar plexus. The man sat down hard, wheezing. Chick kicked the knife away, then placed the end of his cue against the biker's throat.

"Will you yield?" ZZ Top started to get up, but Chick front-kicked him, snapping the man's head back to crack against the floor. He looked at the mature biker, who had stepped back, his hands up. He was smiling, almost to himself

Chick asked him, "What about you?"

"Nothing for me today, thanks." He backed up, smiling as if in appreciation, and attended to his companions.

"I didn't know you could do that," I said.

"Do what?" Chick asked.

"That Chinese stick-fighting crap."

"Oh," he said, and sipped at his beer. "I can't. I was just playing around."

I put the cue ball on the table. Lined up the three ball and slammed it into the corner pocket. "Not bad for an old man," I said.

Who're you?" Chick asked the biker with the gray in his beard. Bull was out for the count, but was breathing okay. ZZ Top beard was groaning.

"You the heat?" he asked.

"We were, we'd have arrested you instead of beating the shit out of your buddies."

"They call me Jubal."

"Sounds like a movie title. You work for McCall?"

"Some. With him is more like it. Why you want to know?"

"Little old for a biker, aren't you?"

"What's age got to do with it? Youth didn't help these guys. Special Forces, right?" The way he said it wasn't really a question.

"And you're an ex-Marine."

"*Semper fi,* brother. First on the beach, last to go home."

"Why hang out with these losers?"

"Everybody gotta be somewhere, man."

"What kind of work do you do with Billy?"

Jubal, the ex-Marine biker, smiled and shook his head. "See you around." He turned his attention to his friends. We weren't going to get anything else out of him. We walked out of the bar after generously tipping Cinnamon.

Outside, Chick opened the Ford's trunk and lifted out a log chain. It tinkled and spat as he walked to where our friends' motorcycles were parked. He ran the chain through the spokes of the rear wheels, linking the three choppers together. Then, he padlocked the chain.

"Wouldn't want anybody to steal their bikes," he said.

We adjourned to the parking lot of an upscale specialty mall, one of those vanity emporiums springing up in Colorado and elsewhere—with gourmet coffee shops, vegetarian restaurants, wine and cheese merchants. Something for everyone. Chick used a pay phone to check on Billy McCall while I sat in the Mustang and listened to a classical station. Mozart's Piano Concerto 21 in C swelled in the confines of the Mustang. A timeless tune in a classic automobile. Wonderfully atavistic.

Chick returned and sat in the passenger seat. "He's out. Made bail an hour ago."

"Who paid it?"

"You're not going to like it," Chick said. He scratched the bridge of his nose. "Matt did."

Thirty minutes later I nosed the Mustang into Matt's driveway. A burgundy Cadillac limo sat in the drive.

"Matt's got company," Chick said.

I grunted acknowledgment.

"Important company," he said.

I shut down the Mustang and got out. As I did, the world's strongest chauffeur unfolded from the limousine. His suitcoat fit well, accenting the ax-handle–wide shoulders and fifty-inch chest. His suit was pearl gray and looked expensive. He was in his forties with a square jaw and rust-brown hair. He wore oxblood-colored leather boots which looked about size thirteen. He had an odd strip of mutated white hair running front-to-back.

"Holy-gee-gosh," Chick said. "It's Conan the Chauffeurian."

I nodded at the man. He looked at me and folded his arms.

Chick said, "We must attempt to communicate." He smiled and said to the man, "Unusually typical weather don't you think?"

No response.

He followed us with his eyes as we walked to the front door. "Friendly sort, isn't he?" said Chick. "Nice haircut." He waved to the man while I rang the doorbell. Kelly Jenkins answered the door. She wore a mint-colored gauze shift, open at the throat. Her face glowed with health. The small creases at the corners of her eyes—the only evidence she was in her fifth decade—added depth to the childlike face. She kissed me on the cheek and her perfume made me think of other times, other promises.

"I want to talk to Matt," I said. "It's important."

"He's in his office with three men. One of them you'll recognize. Congressman Braden." I didn't tell her I wouldn't recognize him, or any politician for that matter. "I don't know the other two," she said. Her warm nut-brown eyes searched my face.

She led us to the rear of the large house. It smelled of cinnamon and coffee. There were late-blooming wildflowers, freshly picked, in a vase on a low coffee table. Our footsteps were hushed by the thick carpet. I was aware of her muscles flexing and rolling under the dress. As we neared the den, she stopped and placed a hand on my arm.

"Maybe I should go in ahead of you," she said, standing close to me.

"Busy or not, we need to see him."

"Something's wrong, isn't it, Wyatt?"

"Who else is in there?"

"I don't know," she said. "I've never seen them before."

"How long have they been in there?"

"An hour."

"Kelly," said Matt, from behind the door. "Is someone here?" The door opened and Matt stood in the doorway. Past his shoulder I saw three men, all seated.

He opened the door. He hesitated when he saw us. "Well, Wyatt. Chick. How are you doing?"

"We need to talk, Matt," I said.

"We're finished. Come in."

We followed him into the room. Seated in one of the wing chairs was a man in a safari bush jacket, expensive, his hair slicked back close to the skull, a thin Boston Blackie mustache on his upper lip. His skin was tight on the bones of his face, and he had a long, slender cigar in one hand. Blue-gray smoke wafted up in a fine line toward the ceiling. He had capped teeth and a cleft chin. His eyes were dark and penetrating. Wolfish eyebrows. He seemed amused by our presence.

The second man was slender, five-eight, with quick eyes and a smug expression. Black jeans, alligator boots, and a houndstooth wool coat, western-cut. Around his neck was a rawhide-weave bolo tie with a turquoise slide. On one hand he wore a tan kidskin glove. The other hand was bare. A tan cowboy hat rested on his knee.

The third man was in his sixties. White wavy hair, dark suit, rep tie. Distinguished. Congressman Braden.

"This is Crispin Purvis," said Matt, indicating the man in the bush jacket. "A business acquaintance of mine."

"Business acquaintance, Matthew?" said Purvis. "I would hope more than that. And," he said to me, "you are?"

"Just fine," I said, brushing aside his query. His dark eyes were like an oil slick on a dirty pond. His lips formed a thin smile. He had an odd way of talking as if concentrating on the correct enunciation of each syllable. I couldn't place the faint accent.

"You must not be much of a football fan, Mr. Purvis," said the cowboy. "This here's Wyatt Storme. Used to be a flanker-back for the Dallas Cowboys."

"I will admit I am not much on games," said Purvis. He tasted his needlelike cigar and smiled at me.

"That's okay," I said, looking back. "I wasn't much of a football player."

The cowboy stood up and said, "I wouldn't say that." He removed the glove and offered me the hand to shake. As he did I saw the butt of a gun in a shoulder holster. He wasn't trying to hide it. Wanted me to see it. He squeezed my hand. Hard. Very strong for a small man. Unusually so. He tried to make it hurt. It would have, too, if I hadn't maintained a firm grip. The width of my hand helped, too. I didn't squeeze, just kept him from grinding my knuckles. I looked him in the eyes. He smiled at the corners of his mouth. He said, "Heard you was the best. Fastest hands in the NFL."

"Long time ago," I said.

"Yeah, was, wasn't it?" He grinned, showing his teeth. "Times change. Name's Montana. Coy Montana."

"Named after the state or the quarterback?" Chick asked.

Coy Montana lifted his jaw in Chick's direction. "Who're you?"

"Wild Bill Jesse the Kid," said Chick, smiling. "Who might you be, stranger?" Montana's jaw tightened.

"Coy works on my resort," said Purvis. "A dude ranch, actually. Teaches our clients to ride and fast-draw. Like in the old west."

"That's interesting," I said. It was, but not in the way they thought. "Maybe I'll take some lessons."

"Give 'em to you free," said Montana, his jaw muscles working as he clamped the cheroot between his teeth. The guy was a walking B movie.

"Appreciate it," I said. "Maybe I'll help you find the other glove."

He reached up and slowly removed the cigar from between his teeth and smiled. Not a warm smile. I imagined warmth was a stretch for him. "You got a sense of humor," he said.' "I like that. More fun that way."

"And this," said Purvis, indicating the third man with a sweep of his arm, "is the Honorable Joring Braden."

I turned to the third man. He appeared agitated and uncomfortable. Braden stood up and shook my hand. "Nice to meet you." He nodded at Chick. "We must be going, Crispin. I've a plane to catch."

"Well," said Purvis, "it is time for us to leave, Matthew. It was nice meeting you gentlemen."

Montana put on his cowboy hat, taking care to make sure it was properly seated. He touched the front of it. Nodded at me. "Adios."

I nodded back at him.

"Happy trails," said Chick.

They left. Chick lit a cigarette. Offered the pack to Matt, who shook his head.

"Why were they here, Matt?" I asked. Matt sat down at his desk. The sky was darkening behind him.

"Business."

"What kind of business? The cowboy was there when Burlingame was killed. Maybe the guy pulled the trigger. And Purvis was the gun contact Burlingame wanted to meet."

Matt was quiet. He looked at me. His shoulders sagged. "I thought you didn't recognize any of them. That they were camouflaged."

"You can't camouflage attitude. Coy Montana is the guy flashing the six-shooter that day. Can't be that many guys floating around Boulder carrying a Colt like a pocket comb. And why'd you cut McCall loose? Chick had him on ice so he could check out some bikers."

"He called, so I put up the bail money."

"Why do you keep running interference for him? He's a drug dealer and a parasite. He's soaking everybody around him. He had a sixteen-year-old girl in his apartment. He set you up. I don't understand you."

Matt reached into a drawer, pulled out a square bottle of Jack Daniel's and poured a healthy slug into a square glass. Held the bottle out to Chick, who shook his head. I said, "The answer's not in there, either."

"Maybe I'm not as pure as you, Wyatt," he said. He saluted me with the glass, then drank. He set the glass down and said, "Maybe nobody is."

I looked at him. Let out a breath. I didn't like the vibrations in the room. Didn't understand them. I'd known Matt for years. We'd been through a lot together, but something had come between us. "What's eating you?"

He took a drink, swirled the whiskey around in the glass. "Nothing, Wyatt. Sorry. Things aren't . . . things aren't going too well right now. More than just this."

"What have those guys got to do with you?" Chick said. "They smell bad. Purvis throbs of bad money. He's got a bodyguard thinks he's Billy the Kid and a chauffeur looks like he was born during an electrical storm." Not to mention they had a U.S. congressman as a travel companion.

Matt pursed his lips and dropped his eyes. Started to lift the glass then hesitated. Looked at us. "There *is* something going on. I can't share all of it with you now. You'll have to trust my reasons."

"I trust you, Matt. It's the situation I've got problems with. I can't work in the dark. Billy McCall was our only lead, then when we put him on hold to follow another one, you cut him loose."

"So, what is Billy involved in?"

I told him about the bikers, the link between Billy and Jackie Burlingame, the visits to his various jobbers, and the booze and dope binge that landed him in jail.

Matt had poured another drink by the time I finished. Shook his head. "Knew Billy was up to something. In over his head, isn't he?"

I nodded.

"Can you get him clear of it?"

I looked at him. "Even if I wanted to, it'd be tough. If he's inside and messing around, sooner or later they're going to find out."

He thought about it for a moment. Took another hit from his glass. "Sure you don't want some of this, Easton?"

"Sorry, Matt," Chick answered. "I'm running on straight beta-carotene today. What do they want?"

He looked into his glass. "They want to know if I've heard from Jackie Burlingame."

"What did you tell them?"

"That I didn't want to hear from him."

"What's Braden's interest?"

"He didn't say much. Just that he was concerned about gun traffic in Colorado."

"Why come here?"

"I put Burlingame on to Purvis." He looked at me briefly. Shrugged.

"They mention the money?"

He shook his head. "Avoided the subject. In fact, the entire conversation was vague. They were checking me out. Seeing if I knew anything I shouldn't."

"Do you?"

He nodded.

"Such as?"

"Can't say. Things I wish I didn't know."

I said, "Why don't you and Kelly take a vacation? Go down to the Gulf Coast for a couple of weeks. We'll let you know when it's over."

"Why don't we just drop it?" he said.

I stood up to leave. "Too late for that."

"What if I asked you to back off?"

"Not even then."

Tuesday morning I drove to Denver with a jumble of information; a jigsaw puzzle dumped out upside-down on a table, and no idea what the picture looked like or where anything fit. Somehow Matt was connected to Crispin Purvis, who, in turn, had brought in Congressman Braden. Why? Coy Montana and Harold Wallace had both been present when Burlingame got popped. Both worked for Purvis. One of them may have pulled the trigger, but I couldn't go to the police with the information. "And what were you doing at the time you witnessed the murder, Mr. Storme?" "I was guarding a cache of illegal weapons and shooting indiscriminately into the midst of those blackguards, sir." Hmmm.

Burlingame had said Purvis wasn't interested in his gun proposal. So who had put up the money? Why bring it if you had no intention of handing it over? What was the significance of the strange code in Burlingame's black book? Was that what Harold Wallace was looking for?

Finally, what was it Matt wouldn't share with me? I trusted him enough to know that it wasn't anything that would put me in jeopardy. He wouldn't do that, regardless of the consequences for himself. But what was it?

I was on my way to see Randle Lightfoot, and later I was to escort Sandy to a party for Denver's beautiful people, of which she was one, though I'd rather run a slant pattern into the teeth of a nickel defense on third and twenty.

"It won't hurt you," Sandy had said. "Besides, do you want me unescorted in a room full of party sharks?"

The things I do for love. The only positive about the party was that Janet Sterling was attending, which might provide me an opportunity to ask questions or at least get an autograph.

I dropped Chick at his Ford so he could pick up Billy McCall's trail again. That done, I put in a call to Channel Seven and asked for Sandy. I needed information and she was the only reporter I trusted.

"Newsroom," she said. "This is Sandy Collingsworth."

"So what," I said. "This is your favorite has-been. I need information."

"What do I get out of the deal?"

"My undying gratitude and membership in the Wyatt Storme fan club."

"I'd rather have a romantic candlelight dinner and an evening of heavy breathing."

"I need some background on Crispin Purvis."

"I'll see what I can do."

"Thanks."

"I love you, you politically naïve jock hermit."

The Mach I was still missing a little, so I opened up all four jets on the carburetor. The 351 bellowed a throaty roar and I was pressed into my seat. There was no traffic and I allowed the needle to push past one hundred for about a quarter of a mile before backing off. The needle was still plummeting when I heard the siren. I looked in my mirror and saw the lights dancing on a patrol unit. I pulled over and reached into my hip pocket for my wallet. Looking into the sideview mirror I saw the big trooper unfold from his unit. Couldn't be, I thought.

But it was.

I rolled down my window and handed my license out, keeping my face averted.

"In a hurry, aren't you?" said the familiar voice, taking my license. "I clocked you at eighty-three miles—" There was a pause, then, "Aw, no. What are you doing breaking the law in my jurisdiction, Storme?"

"Just kinda wanted to stay in practice. How are you doing, Cliff?"

He pushed back his hat with a thumb. "Pretty good, until now. What in the hell is your hurry, and don't give me the usual song and dance."

"Engine's missing. My mechanic says I don't drive it enough. So, after carefully assessing the density of traffic and noting its sparsity I pushed it up a little . . . you sure I was going eighty-three?"

"At least that. But, then I was expecting a regular citizen. Like a crack dealer or a teenager. Why can't you drive a regular car like other people your age?"

"You going to cite me?"

"The state can use the money."

"Trade you for it."

"What have you got?"

"You know who Joring Braden is?"

"Of course I know who Braden is."

"You vote for him?"

"Come on, Storme. Get to it."

"I think Braden is involved in illegal activities."

"A politician doing something underhanded? Come on, Storme, that's part of the job description."

A big Chevy rolled by. One of those new ones that looks like an egg on wheels.

"How about gunrunning?"

"Sure. A guy who sponsors gun-control bills is running guns."

"Your job has made you a pessimist."

"Eighty-three in a fifty-five. That's points and a major fine. Maybe I'm supposed to impound your license or arrest you until you bond out." He started to write something in his ticket book.

"Slow down, Cliff," I said. "I'm serious. I just saw Braden with a big-time gunrunner."

He stopped writing. "And who is that?"

"You going to let me off?"

"I don't know. Eighty-three miles per hour. Pretty big favor."

"I ever lie to you?"

He thought about it for a moment. "No. You withhold information and you think that excuses it."

"Eat the ticket and we'll talk."

"I don't know. I was kind of looking forward to taking you into the office and beating you on the kidneys with a nightstick. Could use the exercise."

"Some other time, okay?"

"Give it to me."

I did. He got into my car on the passenger's side and we talked. I'd known Trooper Cliff Younger for several years. He was laced-up straight and nobody to mess with. A good man to have on your side. He kept his word and nobody held anything over his head. A straight-ahead cop's cop. I told him my feelings about Crispin Purvis and the meeting at Matt's house. I left out the part about witnessing Jackie Burlingame's murder. But I did tell him Jackie had approached me about doing some muscle work for him.

"So you think something has happened to Jackie Burlingame?" he said.

"Haven't seen him in a while. Have you?"

"Not looking for him."

I told him about finding Harold searching Burlingame's apartment.

"And what were you doing there?" he asked.

"He had my *Woodstock* album."

"Uh-huh."

"Original soundtrack. A classic."

"Guess we're at the end of the straight answers, right? How is it you get involved in these things?"

I shrugged. "Natural-born busybody, I guess."

"More like a lightning rod."

"I've got a black book with some names in it," I said, meaning the book I'd found in Jackie's apartment. "Anything happens to me you'll be able to find it at my cabin." I told him where it would be.

"I'll pick it up after I get through celebrating. What names?"

"Names associated with Jackie Burlingame."

"Give me a sample."

"Randle Lightfoot."

"The quarterback?"

"We have a winner."

"What does he have to do with Burlingame?"

"I don't know yet," I said. "But maybe I will after I talk to him today."

Younger looked out through the windshield, then back at me. "Why are you conducting an unauthorized investigation?"

"Everybody needs a hobby. Besides, you know any crimes committed by Lightfoot?"

"Rumor is he mules cocaine between NFL cities. The feds tried to sting him, but the Denver cops tipped him off."

"Loyal Bronco fans. Football players are a public treasure."

"And retired ones are a pain in the ass. Okay," he said. "I'll see if I can stir anything at this end. As for the ticket, it'll cost you a cigar. One of those good ones. What do you call them?"

"Roi-Tan?"

He gave me a pained look. "Not smart to play games with a guy who carries a .357."

"In the glove box," I said.

He opened it and pulled out a pair of Macanudos. Baron Rothschilds.

"You said one cigar."

"The price of being a wiseguy," he said.

"Another cop on the take," I said. "Depressing."

"Has its rewards," he said, unwrapping a cigar.

I pulled into Denver, the jewel of capital cities. Where the Rockies rise up from the floor of the Great Plains like a great blue wall. Imposing. Grand. Magnificent. As an artist, God could not be touched. The Rockies were his most impressive work, sculpted from rock and blood. Salted with snow and peppered with evergreen and poplar.

Yet Denver pushed outward; a fungus of concrete and steel and road signs growing in a widening ring.

Fingerprints at the edge of a masterpiece.

My thoughts drifted back to Kelly Jenkins. The way she looked in the gauze dress. Her vitality. The smell of her. A beautiful lady who once had been mine, years ago. And yet not mine. There had been another. A man without a name who had come between us. Invisible, yet as distinct as the boiling black smoke from an oil fire. She had pulled away from me, not physically, but from somewhere deep inside of her, on a level I could not reach or explain. So I looked elsewhere.

She hadn't stopped me, so I guess I got away.

Matt knew of our past relationship, but not of its intensity. Its heat. I had been unable to get enough of her. The flavor of her. I had just returned from Vietnam and my head was filled with pictures of smoke and sweat. And death. She had pushed it all away and filled it with her scent. It was the thing I remembered most. And today I had caught a tinge of it drifting into

my head again. After all these years. It made me uneasy. We
had been friends all these years and I had never felt its pull in
between. But I'd felt it today.

Why now?

Once again, my past was raising its head from the dark pool
in my heart. When it did, it brought the dreams with it. The
dreams that invaded my sleep. My peace. Dreams of gaping
black holes where a friendly face had been. Dark dragons lunging
at me from cold tunnels. Strange men trying to kill me because
my eyes were round.

Memories with serrated teeth crawling around my brain.

I stopped at a Dunkin' Donuts and bought a cup of coffee at
the drive-through window. As I reached to pay I saw the egg-
shaped Chevrolet, again. The same one? There had to be thousands of them that color, a pale tan. Still, I would be careful to
watch for it, now.

I pulled back into the traffic flow, accelerating to make up the
distance between myself and the Chevy. Saw the license plate.
Filed away the numbers so I could get Younger to run them
through the computer. He'd be glad to do it. Right after he got
through throwing a fit.

I watched the rearview. Didn't see anything, so I continued
to Lightfoot's apartment. Lightfoot had a Driftwood address,
out near Deer Creek Lake. I was southbound on Wadsworth
Boulevard when I picked them up again. Same tan-colored
Chevy. Two men in front.

I don't believe in coincidences.

I turned left into the parking lot of a Sack-and-Go. When I
did, the Chevy turned into a Hardee's across the street. Circling
the lot, I pulled into traffic, backtracked two blocks, repeated
the circle maneuver at a Chevron station and resumed travel
in the original direction. Within a block, I met the Chevy again.
In the passenger seat was a man with a square jaw. I waved as
we passed. The square-jawed man smiled and shook his head.

I proceeded to Randle Lightfoot's address.

• • •

Lightfoot's place was a large modified A-frame structure set back off the road with a circle drive. There were two cars parked in front. I parked behind a Mercedes with the license plate BK-UP QB, and a black Beretta. The house was set on three lots and could not be seen from the road or the neighbors', as if it were located in a remote area rather than a nouveau-riche development. I walked toward the house using the native stone pathway.

I rang the bell and waited. No answer. Strange, as he was expecting me. I rang the bell again. A playboy like Lightfoot might have been entertaining late last night and still be in the sack. Alone, I hoped. I remembered the Randle Lightfoots from my playing days—party hard, race the night, see it all, don't miss anything. Sedate your head with booze and ludes at night, taste the flesh, then jack yourself up the next day with Percs and white cross. A cherrybomb flameout superstar. Everybody's hero.

Still no answer. I stepped back from the porch and looked up at the upstairs window. Rattled the door. Locked. I walked around the house. In the rear of the house was a huge wooden deck—swimming pool, hot tub, portable bar. Dry leaves skittered across the floor of the dry pool, and steam rose from the hot tub like volcanic vapor. My boots cobbled against the wood planks.

Through the steam of the hot tub I saw Randle Lightfoot floating jellyfish-style in the percolating waters.

I kneeled down and grabbed the body, which was past caring, by the dark hair and pulled it toward shore. I heard a board creak. I turned around to see who it was.

Too late.

I felt a leathery thud against the base of my neck. My eyes rolled, my head was shot through with one flashing roll of dark thunder.

And I tumbled into the hot, turbulent waters.

Falling.

And sinking.

And slipping into the darkness.

Little flashes of bright white light burst into an ozone of nothingness. No dawn coming. Then rough hands pulling at me, as I drifted up from the void. Couldn't breathe. Coughing, hacking, spitting. Coldness behind my nose, irritating. Real.

Then I felt the scraping, catching hardness of the pool's edge as if a great monster were pulling me from the water. I felt pressure below my ribs then an urgent gushing volcano within me.

Coughing. Swimming in my head. My body spasmed and jerked. Light flickered like a silent movie. Then, a raw bite at the back of my throat as I continued to hack and expel water.

"Pull him inside."

"Sonuvabitch weighs a ton."

"Clothes are wet. Quit crying and pull him in the house. There any blood?"

A hand felt along the back of my neck. Then a sharp tang of pain.

"No. He's got a goose egg. I think I got him out in time."

"You're a hero, Tompkins. We'll have a parade for you. Get him inside before anybody shows up."

I tried to talk, but could only manage guttural sounds as if I had no tongue.

"Garbo talks," said the voice of the man farthest away from me. "Can't understand a word you're saying, son. Nice day for a Jacuzzi. Try it with your clothes off, next time. World of difference." My head was clearing now, and the coughing had become intermittent. My throat and nose were raw and my head was throbbing.

Large hands pulled at the front of my jacket. I heard the splatter of water against concrete as I sat upright. I let my head loll, playing opossum, buying time, sliding a hand inside my jacket, readying myself to pull the Browning from its holster. There was a sharp shooting pain as the blood shifted from the back to the front of my skull. A wave of nausea shipped inside me. I was afraid I would black out, again.

"You all right, Storme?" came the voice of the standing man. There were two of them. The younger man who'd pulled me from the water and an older man, the one with the deep, soothing voice. I lifted my right knee to cover the movement of my hand. Shifted my weight to my left hip, eased a hand into my jacket, then . . . nothing.

I heard a chuckle, then, "You looking for this?" I looked up and the older guy was holding my Browning, nonchalantly. Big guy. Overweight but square-bodied, like Dick Butkus gone to seed. Square jaw, Irish eyes, straight teeth. It was the passenger from the tan Chevrolet, the one who'd smiled and shaken his head when I'd waved at them. It was the two guys I thought I'd given the slip. Couldn't understand it. Always worked for Jim Rockford.

I let my eyes slide over to where the younger guy was standing near the edge of the hot tub. I pretended to cough, assessed my chances of dumping him in the water and then kicking out at the older guy. From where they were standing I might be able to pull it off.

"Don't even think it," said the man with my gun. "Tompkins, you better take a step back. That crap in the file about retiring because his knees went bad is bullshit." They both moved back a step and looked at me. Professionals. The big man pulled up a deck chair and sat down, pointing my gun at me. He crossed his legs and smiled a lazy, killer-shark smile. I shivered, involuntarily.

"So what's it gonna be, Storme?" he said. "You want to go inside and get dry or you want to freeze to death out here?"

"Why are you following me?" I asked, buying time.

"Wanted your autograph."

"Give me your address," I said. My teeth were beginning to chatter. "I'll mail it to you."

"Hate to put you out like that."

"No trouble. A special service I have for guys that knock me in the head."

"Didn't do that," he said, leaning back in the chair. "Might've prevented it if somebody hadn't pulled that little double-back maneuver in town. Or if Tompkins wouldn't have crowded you."

"I didn't crowd him," said the younger man. "I just didn't take into account the highway patrol stopping him."

"Young guys," he said, indicating Tompkins with a nod. "Come out of training with their heads packed with scenarios and percentages. The Company sends 'em out to me with simulated field experiences. They're high speed on the shooting range, but they never shot anybody. Never had anyone shoot at them and don't know the difference." The voice was upper Midwest, maybe Michigan or Wisconsin. North of the Missouri River, anyway. "Tompkins here runs into somebody like your buddy Easton, same thing happens."

"Who's Easton?" I said, playing dumb, something for which I have a real flair.

He smiled, and said, "Play it any way you want, Storme. I know Easton. Worked with him in Nam for a while. There's a pro. Like a shadow with legs. Worth twenty of these dental assistants the Company turns out now. They read *The Wall Street Journal,* drink Perrier, and wear colored underwear." He looked at Tompkins. "Follow the tail too close."

"I went by the book on it," protested Tompkins. "We have him, don't we?"

"Yeah, fished him out of a Jacuzzi along with a corpse. Top-drawer work."

"You CIA?" I asked.

He laughed, looked away, then back at me. "Heavens, no," he said. Big smile, letting me see the teeth. Inside joke. "There are no Langley agents operating within the domestic sector. Why, that would be a jurisdictional trespass. Wouldn't do to have that, now, would it?" He rubbed his jaw, then asked, "Why are you here with the dead quarterback, Storme?"

"Who are you?"

"Name's Donovan." He put out a hand, but hadn't relinquished the gun. I shook the hand. "Dirk Donovan. You want to go inside now, Storme?"

I did.

I undressed in the kitchen with Donovan attending. He sat in a chair turned backward, resting bear forearms on the back of the chair, my gun dangling from one of his paws. He had an easy confidence about him, yet his laughing eyes took in everything. I had no intention of running. No reason yet. Probably a good thing. To Donovan I would probably just be another shooting-range exercise.

Tompkins found one of Lightfoot's jogging suits and I put it on. A dead man's clothes. Donovan appropriated a bottle of Wild Turkey from the bar and poured from it into two heavy rocks glasses. Offered one to me. I shook my head, which made it hurt. "Give it to Tompkins," I said.

Donovan smiled and poured the contents into his glass.

"Okay, Storme. Why are you here and why is Lightfoot doing the big float?"

"Friendly visit," I said. Lightfoot's jacket fit, but the pants were a little long.

"Why'd you duck us back in town?"

"Thought you were undercover seatbelt cops. Besides, I don't like being followed."

"You always that suspicious?"

"Why are you following me?"

"What are you doing at the house of a dope mule?"

"He's a football player. I used to be."

"Now you're an ex–football player and he used to be. He's dead and you're the first guy on the scene. Your reunions are a little rough. Maybe I'll call the cops and let them sort it out."

"Go ahead," I said. "I've got nothing to do today. He was dead when I arrived. The body was stiff when I tried to pull him from the water. Thought about calling the cops myself. How'll you explain following a law-abiding citizen in the continental U.S.? Wonder how the FBI and the locals will like that? Everybody mad at everybody else."

Donovan rubbed his jaw. Sipped his whiskey. "Good stuff," he said. "I prefer Bushmill's." He went with the change-up, figuring me for a fastball hitter. "Why'd you quit playing football, Storme? Better yet, why'd you quit without telling anybody? Every other one of you narrow-hipped marvels calls in the press for one last round of adulation and mumbled clichés. Why not you?"

"Knew there was something I forgot."

He tipped the chair forward, balancing on two legs, and said, "I'm guessing you just decided you didn't owe an explanation. Maybe you don't figure you owe one now."

Tompkins returned to the room. "Found this," he said, holding up two baggies of cocaine.

"Good work, Tompkins," said Donovan. "Go out and arrest Lightfoot before he makes a break for it. Be sure you read him his rights."

"Maybe there's a connection," Tompkins said, his face red. "What do you know about it, Storme?"

"Let's see. I'll guess Lightfoot is dead and you have a baggie of cocaine in your hand."

"Being a smartass won't help this situation."

"Passes the time."

"You know a guy named Jack Burlingame?"

"I know Jackie."

"He's disappeared."

"You mean like Mandrake the Magician?"

Tompkins frowned. "Recently, Jack Burlingame has been in contact with Matthew Jenkins, a businessman who is a friend of yours. Yesterday, Purvis and Senator Joring Braden visited Jenkins. An hour after they arrived, you and Chick Easton, a former Special Forces rogue, show up. How do you explain that?"

"Special Forces rogue?" I said. "Does that mean he has abbreviated affairs with the ladies only to discard them, or does it mean he crashes through the jungle with tusks flashing?"

"Why can't we do this the easy way, Storme?"

"You're not enjoying this?"

"We have reason to believe that Jack Burlingame is dead. Do you know why we think that?"

"He's starting to stink?" I said.

Tompkins pursed his lips in a thin line. He looked at Donovan, who smiled and stood up. "C'mon Storme, play nice. We just want to know what's going on."

"What is going on? I came here to visit Lightfoot and I find him dead in his hot tub. I get knocked on the head, then fished out by a couple of spooks. My head hurts, I'm wearing pants that are too long, my Tony Lamas are probably ruined, and you guys want to know what's going on. You tell me."

"We think Crispin Purvis is dirty," said Donovan. Tompkins started to interrupt, but Donovan held up a hand. "The powers that be are very interested in keeping Congressman Braden free of controversial figures."

"I thought this administration was against covert operatives. Against door-smashing secret agent work."

Donovan shook his head. "You've got a lot to learn. Doesn't matter which side is in office. Job's the same."

"So you guys swing back and forth. How do you handle not knowing who the good guys are?"

"We're professionals."

"That easy, huh?"

He shrugged, then sipped whiskey. National politics has become so clownish and cynical that it is like looking into a kaleidoscope. We've become so indolent and numb to the lies and the subterfuge that we just change channels.

"What I want to know right now, though, is why I've got a reclusive football player at a meeting involving Purvis and a congressman and the next thing I know he shows up at the home of a murder victim. A football player known for sticking his nose in where it's not wanted. A football player who denies knowing Chick Easton, a guy who I know is his best friend. Why is that, Storme?"

"We walked in on the meeting with the congressman and Purvis by accident."

"Uh-huh," grunted Donovan.

"Believe what you want." I needed to give them a little information if I hoped to walk away from here. These were the big boys. The kind of nasty world-hopping feds who live in a savage world and take no prisoners. There would be no Miranda warnings or probable cause. I didn't need them breathing down my neck. Or worse. Also, I needed to feed them a little to get a little from them. "A few days ago, Jackie Burlingame offered to pay me to accompany him on a business deal."

"What kind of business deal?"

"I don't know," I said, lying. "I figured it was illegal. Probably drugs."

"Why come to you?"

I still wondered myself. Jackie's answer hadn't satisfied me, but I gave it to them. "Said he needed somebody with a knowledge of the outdoors."

Donovan was silent, turning his head sideways to consider it.

"Can't help it if you don't like it," I said. "That's the reason he gave."

"How do you know him?"

"He was a student at Colorado State University when I played football there. He was the campus dealer."

"Everybody was doing it, right?"

"I'm not defending it," I said. Wish I hadn't done it, in fact. I wished a lot of things. Mostly things better left undone. But I didn't owe Donovan anything, least of all an explanation for my poor choices. "But the statute of limitations has run out on most of my mistakes."

"How much did he offer to pay you?"

"A thousand dollars."

"That's a lot of money."

"Don't need it."

He nodded. "What is it you do to make a living?"

"I collect baseball cards."

"How is it you live so well?"

"In the immortal words of Bob Dylan, 'I can't help it if I'm lucky.' Besides, I live downhill from money."

He chuckled, closing one eye as he did. He swept one hand in Tompkins's direction. "See," he said. "Why can't you be this interesting?" He looked back at me. "You live off the interest of a six-figure trust you set up. High six figures. You saved your money, invested wisely, and now you live off the interest, high up in the mountains, like you were Jeremiah Johnson. You're a maverick and a wild card and you better back away from the table. The stakes are higher than you think. Besides, you're mucking up the waters and I'm getting too old for this shit." The smiling eyes turned hard. "You need to understand that I don't want to bump into you again. None of this better end up on Congressman Braden. I don't like him much better than you do, but I got a job to do and you better not bet the rent money against me doing it. Now get your stuff together and get out."

"We're not letting him go, are we?" said Tompkins.

"Naw. I planted a homing device on him. You know, like the man from U.N.C.L.E. used to." He made a sour face. "What do you think? He's not going to give us anything he doesn't want to give and probably doesn't know much we don't already suspect." He looked at me. I gave him my helpful patriot smile.

"I'm going to call the police," I said.

"We'll take care of it. They'll never know you were here."

I shook my head.

"What's the problem. Don't you trust the U.S. government?"

"No. I don't."

He laughed. "Don't blame you. Well, Tompkins, looks like we need to clear out. Wouldn't do to be here when the locals show. Might not look good. They are awful thin-skinned, sometimes." He looked at me and said, "You have any idea who did Lightfoot?"

I thought about Coy Montana, but it didn't seem like his style. Besides, if I gave them a string they might trace it to Matt Jenkins, and I didn't know what Matt's involvement was. Somebody had Matt over a barrel, and I didn't know who or how. Until I found out, I couldn't afford official intervention. I thought about it some more to give the impression I wanted to help them, then shook my head. "Can't think of anybody."

"I'll bet," he said. He handed me my gun.

I gathered my wet clothes and followed them outside. I had some camo pants and a pair of tennis shoes in the car. Lightfoot's clothes were too big, and I didn't like wearing a dead man's clothes. At the front door I wiped my fingerprints from the doorbell, causing it to ring. Nobody answered.

As I approached the Mustang I saw the two spooks walking to the tan Chevrolet, which was sitting back from the drive, out

of view of both the road and the house. The Mercedes sat own-
erless now. My head hurt. I opened the Mustang door and put
my clothes in the back. Then, I remembered.

The black Beretta GT was gone.

"Where's the Beretta?" I asked Donovan as he opened his
car door.

He smiled his big smile. "What Beretta?" he said and shut
the door.

I squished back into the house in wet boots. The tennis shoes had not been in the car like I thought. Once inside I found Lightfoot's dryer, tossed the wet clothes in, and padded back into the living room, where I used the phone to leave a call for Cliff Younger. I was told he'd call back.

Donovan and Tompkins knew about the Beretta. It had been there when they drove up. Which meant they knew who it belonged to and were covering up, or, at least, they weren't sharing the information with me. Who were they protecting, and why were they following me? I hadn't thought to take the plate numbers off the Beretta. I'd assumed it belonged to Lightfoot or to an overnight guest. There was little doubt in my mind that I'd been sapped by the driver of the Beretta. Not to mention what he'd done to Elway's understudy.

At least Lightfoot wouldn't have to worry about contracting a social disease anymore.

Or about anything else. Ever.

I turned on Lightfoot's stereo. I didn't think he'd mind. A classic rock station was playing Neil Young's *Harvest* album without commercial breaks. Not everything about the media explosion was bad. Just almost everything.

"You had so much and now so much is gone," sang Mr. Soul.

So much. So much done. Too much gone and nothing to be done about it. Lightfoot didn't even get to flame out like a comet sinking into the green sea. What had he left behind besides broken hearts, fancy cars, and the unfulfilled promise of his potential? He was no longer a bankable commodity.

Throw a million miles of passes, kid. Lift a railroad yard of weights. Take more hits than a heavyweight boxer. Sign right here at the bottom, kid. We're selling dreams. And broken bones. And torn cartilage. Got a pain? Here, take this, kid. We'll make a household name of you. A celebrity of you. Hawking underarm deodorant, and after-shave, and any other damn thing we can think of. We'll even make you believe you're making a significant contribution to civilization.

But basically, it came down to playing a kid's game, wearing a jock strap, and community showers with physical mutants. Wearing an assigned number.

A moratorium on growing up.

It had no significance.

And now Randle Lightfoot, wannabe and fantasy date for thousands of lovelies, was just dead.

The phone rang. It was Younger.

"What's up, Wyatt?"

I told him.

"You stay right there," he said. "Call the sheriff. I'll be there as fast as possible. You can get in more crap faster than anybody I know."

I hung up and dialed 911.

Then, I waited.

•   •   •

I heard car doors slamming as the last note of "Natural Beauty" died. I retrieved my clothes from the dryer and put them on. The weather report came on the radio. The temperature was in the low fifties and the weatherman predicted snow by early next week.

I heard the clomp of hard-soled shoes on the wood deck. I looked out and saw three policemen—a plainclothes detective and two uniformed deputies—looking at the body. I opened the sliding glass door and heard the detective say: "Don't touch anything. The forensics boys will be here in a minute."

I said, "Hello. I'm the guy who found the body."

The detective raised a palm, and said, "In a minute, I'll be right with you."

Typical cop, I thought. Rude. Happens every time there's a corpse floating in the hot tub.

They examined the lump of waterlogged flesh that used to be Randle Lightfoot. Took photographs of him. He was used to that. That done, the detective walked to the glass doors and entered. He flashed a badge and with an authoritative voice said, "Detective Elliot. Sheriff's office. Who are you?"

"Wyatt Storme."

Detective Elliot was in his early fifties, slight paunch from too many Coors after his shift was over. A wiry block of reddish-brown hair was receding on both sides, like sea water swelling around a jutting rock. A rusty shadow of whiskers dotted sagging jowls. His dark green eyes were the sharp, no-nonsense orbs of the career interrogator.

"What's your connection to the deceased?"

"I just know him."

"You find him like that?" he asked, digging a cigarette from his coat. "Or did you put him there?"

"Had to. Couldn't lift the piano high enough to drop it on him."

He gave me a look that wasn't friendly.

"I didn't kill him," I said. "He knew I was coming by but no one answered the door so I walked around back and found him floating in the hot tub. As I was reaching in to pull him out somebody hit me and I fell in with him." I told him about Donovan and Tompkins fishing me out. Also about the black Beretta.

"How come you're not wet?"

"I dried my clothes in the dryer."

He lighted the cigarette, waved the match in the air to extinguish it, and dragged deeply. "Let me get this straight," he said. "You come here to visit Lightfoot and find him floating in the Jacuzzi. Then somebody, you don't know who, whacks you on the back of the head, and two feds, probably CIA, who won't admit they're CIA, fish you out and then play coy about a black Beretta you say was parked outside when they got here. So you call us, then while you're waiting you dry your clothes?"

"Didn't have time to do a full load."

"I don't like your story, Storme."

I shrugged.

"How well you know Lightfoot?"

"Just know him. We're not close."

"You know he was muling dope?"

"I'd heard it."

"How do I know you didn't do him and then call us and play innocent?"

"Didn't have any reason to."

"How do I know that?"

"Because I told you so."

"We can do this downtown, you know. With the cuffs on and the siren wailing."

"How many times you use that line?" I said. "My alibi is on the way and the forensics guy will corroborate him. Why don't you give up on the *Dragnet* routine and try something pertinent?"

"Like what?"

"Like checking the grounds for footprints, checking with

Langley to see if they have agents named Donovan and Tompkins.
Like seeing if a guy named Coy Montana has a black Beretta.''

"Who's Montana?"

"A cheap imitation Clint Eastwood who carries a gun and
works for a guy named Crispin Purvis."

"Who's Purvis?"

I told him.

"Maybe I like you for it."

"Look, Lieutenant. When you're looking for a size ten you
don't try on every pair of shoes in the store, you just look inside
the shoe. I'm not a size ten."

"You're carrying a gun," he said.

"Yes."

"Give it to me."

I did so.

He hefted the Browning. "You a private cop?"

"No."

"Why you need this, then?"

"Insecure, I guess."

I heard a car door slam. The boots against boards.

"Tell me why I should believe anything you say, Storme."

The door opened and Trooper Cliff Younger said, "Because
he's telling the truth." He put his hand out to Elliot and they
shook and introduced themselves to each other.

"Why should I believe his story?" Elliot asked Younger.

"A little over an hour ago I stopped him for speeding on
Highway Thirty-six."

"You two friends?" he asked Younger.

"We do some hunting and fishing."

"Did you cite him for speeding?"

"No."

"How fast was he going?"

"Too fast," Cliff said, in the tight-jawed way he had when
you were stepping over the line.

"Look, Younger," said Elliot. "Don't get your nose out of joint. I'm trying to conduct an investigation."

"I'm not part of the investigation. Storme's no murderer. He's not a liar either, but if he's got a personal stake in this somewhere he'll stonewall you."

Elliot flipped open a little notebook, looked out to the rear deck where the uniforms were taking measurements. "Been easier if he'd have done it. Now it'll mean a bunch of extra shit."

"Know how you feel," Cliff said.

After an hour of questions I was released into Cliff's custody. He escorted me to my car.

"Boy, you were magnificent. 'How fast was he going?' 'Too fast,' " I said, imitating his clipped tones. "Love the way your jaw sets when you're mad."

"What's going on here?"

"You heard the questioning."

"I did. And I know you never give something for nothing."

"I'm not sure. But it has something to do with what I told you before. They warned me off Braden."

"I hate when you get me involved in your crap," he said. "It always turns out to be something that might affect my pension. Keep me posted or I'll drop you down a hole."

"Sweet talker."

Leaving Lightfoot's, I headed north. Twenty miles later I pulled down a blacktop road, turned onto a gravel lane that led to a defunct railroad spur, the iron-and-wood widow of a nation which had expanded past needing it. Some things change forever, not for better.

Sitting on the rusted rails was an old Pullman car. There was a wooden deck built onto the front of it, and a Continental flag flying over the top of it. Thirteen stars in a circle. A blood-red 1970 Barracuda, a decade-old four-by-four Ranger pickup, and the nondescript Ford sat in a chipped rock drive. A pair of peacocks and a raccoon named General Sherman roamed the grounds. Wildflowers grew in the yard and waved in a breeze that carried the silvery scent of mountain air. Behind the Pullman, the Rockies erupted from the plains, pushing upward into the distant blue-white haze.

I got out of the Mustang. The rumble of the 351 was replaced by the metal vibrations of Iron Butterfly pulsating from the

Pullman car. General Sherman waddled up and stood on hind legs. I patted his head and stepped onto the wooden deck. There was an empty Wild Turkey bottle on a picnic table.

I opened the door and was hit by a wave of sound. Chick lay in a pile of Turkish pillows, a can of Coors in one hand and a bottle of Jack Daniel's in the other. The heavy thud of tom-toms banged off the walls of the old Pullman. And my head. The drum solo of "In-A-Gadda-Da-Vida." In that long thumping climb, which led full circle to the strange, dadaist lyrics. Seventeen minutes of sixties anesthesia. More anthem than song.

A thick cloud of brown smoke fouled the air with the acrid smell of burnt rope. The lights of the CD player cut through the dimness of the old car.

I left the door open, to let either the smoke out or the air in.

Chick raised the whiskey bottle and said, "Going for the world's record. Most hours of continual listening to 'In-A-Gadda-Da-Vida.' I once went five hours in Vietnam."

I stepped across the room and turned off the stereo. The silence was immediate and wonderful. "War's over."

He grinned a crooked grin and took a swallow of the beer. "So they tell me."

"Where's McCall?" I asked.

"Under sedation in the guest room." He lifted up a blanket and a Turkish pillow and uncovered Billy McCall, mouth open, passed out.

"Why?"

"I'm protecting him. I ever tell you I was a piledriver bodyguard?"

"What are you protecting him from?"

"Says somebody's trying to ace him. Anyway, he's scared and it's easier than following him around, so I offered my services."

"What's he paying you with, Cambodian Red?"

"He tried to tempt me, but I was strong, though the secondary smoke thing ain't bad. Can't blame me for breathing. He pasted his brain shut with ludes and the roach. Not to mention about half a bottle of Wild Turkey." He looked down at the snoring McCall. "I think the kid has potential, coach."

"Why does he think somebody's trying to kill him?"

"Said he knew too much."

"That's a contradiction in terms," I said. "Randle Lightfoot is dead. Somebody croaked him."

He chewed a corner of his lip. "So he wasn't wrong. Said it was going to happen. Said he was next. So I'm hiding him out under these pillows. They'll never look there."

"What about Janet Sterling?"

"I didn't have a chance to talk to her. She was out. But she'll be at the party tonight. The one you're going to. You can talk to her."

"Who does he think is after him?"

"Doesn't know for sure. Just knows. How did Lightfoot get it?"

"Drowned in his hot tub."

"Doesn't sound very relaxing." I gave him the details of my meeting with Donovan and Tompkins. And the black Beretta.

"Dirk Donovan. That old mick. There's a guy can bust a cap on you with a smile on his face."

"You think he's protecting whoever was driving the Beretta?"

"Sure."

"Why?"

"Because somebody told him to. You were smart not to take a powder when he offered. They might've framed you for Lightfoot's killing. That is, if they didn't cover it up entirely."

"There's too many players. We've got drug dealers, bikers, congressmen, and now the CIA taking an interest. They're almost tripping over each other. You know what I think?"

"Yeah, I do," Chick said. He took a swallow from the whiskey bottle. "Isn't just about a few handguns and machine pistols."

"Couldn't be. Too much money and too many power-trippers hovering around. Wake up Sleeping Beauty. I want to talk to him."

Chick shook McCall. "Come on, kid. Reveille." McCall's head lolled and his mouth worked, but he didn't wake up.

I knelt beside McCall, grabbed him by the lapels and pulled him into a sitting position. "Hey, Billy. Wake up." I grabbed his face in one hand and shook his head. He groaned and opened one eye.

"Wha . . . oh shit, not you," he said.

"Nice to see you, too, McCall. I want to know what's going on."

"Head . . . hurts."

"Can't imagine why." I glared at Chick, who shrugged. "Lightfoot's dead, Billy."

Both eyes opened wide, then he squinted as if I'd flashed a camera in his face. "What?" His head nodded. His eyes looked like the flesh of a beached catfish, bloated and rheumy.

"Doggone it, Chick," I said. "Why'd you let him get like this?"

"Always glad to help out. Bodyguarding requires a creative mind, a willingness to stretch the normal boundaries of—"

"Shut up and get me a glass of water."

Chick brought the water, which I splashed in Billy's face. McCall sputtered and shook his head.

"Dammit, Storme," said Chick. "I got those pillows in Istanbul."

"Why do they say 'Made in Taiwan' on the tag? Okay, Billy, who's after you?"

"Don't know."

"Why are you running around town politicking?"

"What?"

"Moving product. Making contacts. What do you know that you didn't tell me the other day?"

"Nothing. My head hurts."

"Tough. I want to know what's involved in this affair besides a few weapons."

"I don't know what you're talking about. I need a beer and some aspirin."

"Why is there so much involved? You better start talking or I'm gonna let Chick start working on you."

"What? Him? Hey, what are you doing here, anyway? You

guys know each other? He's working for me. Ain't that right, Easton?"

Chick made a face. "Well, Billy, not exactly. You see, there was never a formal contract drawn up. Then, there's the question of my retainer which you drank. Besides, Storme has a prior claim. Just tell him what he wants to know and everything will be copacetic."

"And if I don't?" asked McCall, shifting his eyes from Chick to me. He put a hand alongside his head.

"Chick is world-class at getting people to tell him things, Billy. He used to do it for a living. In Vietnam, where the sun never sets on a good time. Tell him what he'll win if he doesn't talk, Chick."

"Well, Bill, I'll tell you. I'm not going to enjoy it, but I've got a little trick with a fillet knife and lighter fluid. Hurts like a bitch, but it's one hundred percent effective in laboratory tests."

McCall's mouth worked. "You're bluffing."

"Real men don't bluff," I said.

"And I'm a real man," said Chick.

"Fuck you guys."

"See how he is?" I said to Chick. "I told you."

"You were right," Chick said. Reaching into his pocket he pulled out a Schrade lockback folding knife. With a flick of his wrist, he snapped the blade open.

"Okay, okay. I'll tell you what's going on. But you've gotta give me something for this hangover first."

"It's your lucky day, son," said Chick. "I've got the cure. Uncle Chick's miracle midday hangover tonic." He walked over to the kitchen cabinet and began mixing ingredients into a big tumbler while singing Dylan's "Subterranean Homesick Blues": "Johnny's in the basement mixing up the medicine, I'm out on the pavement thinkin 'bout the government . . ."

When he was finished, he brought the concoction over to Billy. "Here you go. Fix you right up."

"What's in it?" Billy asked, eyeing the tumbler with a side-long gaze.

"Tomato juice, Tabasco sauce, red pepper, raw egg, instant coffee, two ounces of Budweiser, a splash of whiskey, and a secret ingredient. Generations of Easton men have been greeting the day and sobering up with this unique brew. Drink it all at once."

"Thiz'll work?"

"Satisfaction guaranteed. Bottoms up, sailor."

McCall drank the muddy red liquid, his Adam's apple bobbing as he drained the glass. Twin rivers of crimson ran down the corners of his mouth and dripped bloodlike onto his shirt. My stomach churned in sympathy for what was going on inside him. He handed Chick the glass.

"We better get him outside," said Chick.

"I want to ask him a couple of questions first."

Chick grabbed McCall under one arm. "Outside first. The secret ingredient is kind of fast-acting."

Billy McCall was showing the first signs of photosynthesis as we hustled him to the door. "Not on the deck," Chick said. "Out in the yard." We bumped him down the steps and out to the lawn. We stood him up and Chick said, "Now, give him some room."

Billy wavered like a straw man in a high wind and said, "What's this stuff s'posed . . . ohh." He gagged, hacked, then a gusher of red spewed from his mouth.

"Aw, geez, Chick," I said.

"Kinda like watching Linda Blair in *The Exorcist,* ain't it?"

"What's the secret ingredient, anyway?"

"Ipecac syrup."

I made a face and looked away. "You have no values."

"Never had 'em," he said. "Never will."

Billy McCall, on his hands and knees, groaned and vomited for the larger part of ten minutes. He sounded like a seal. Chick sat on the deck and smoked a cigarette while I averted my head. I finally lighted a cigar, mostly to cover the fetid smell of peristaltic acid drifting our way.

"If projectile yawning ever becomes a spectator sport," said Chick, "we've got ourselves a gold medalist."

"This isn't helping anything," I said.

"The healing arts aren't always pretty."

Finally, the bark-and-color show ended. Billy Mac sat on the lawn, spent with the efforts of his cure. General Sherman waddled over to the puddle, sniffed at it, turned his head, then trotted away. Chick went into the Pullman and returned with a glass of water and two aspirin, which he set on the deck table. Then we helped Billy up off the grass and onto the deck. His breath was sour on my face.

We sat him down on the deck. His face was drained of color

and the skin under his eyes sagged like crumpled sacks of flour. His lips were pale and dry.

"I think you killed him," I said.

"Just smells like it. He'll live. Here," he said to Billy, holding out the glass and aspirin. "Take this."

Billy accepted, hands shaking as he swallowed the tablets and drank the water. He wiped his mouth on a sleeve. His teeth began to chatter and his body shook. I took off my jacket and draped it over his shoulders.

"I feel like shit," he said.

"If it's any comfort, you look like shit," said Chick. "Give it a couple hours and you'll be up to feeling only miserable."

I said, "I want to know what's going on, Billy."

"I'm not sure I know all of it."

"Give me what you have then. Chick, can you make some coffee? Black. And lots of it. And leave out the secret ingredients."

"You're unappreciative," he said, going inside. "Bet nobody asks Dr. Kildare to make coffee."

"Sonuvabitch tried to poison me," said Billy.

"What's the deal on the guns, Billy? What was Burlingame up to?"

"If I talk, who's gonna protect me? There's some rough people involved."

"We will. Look, no matter how Chick acts, he's tough. The best bodyguard in Colorado. We'll take care of you. Now talk."

"Okay." He coughed, dryly. "You already figured out we set Matt up. Jackie said he had a sweet deal working, one that'd make us rich, but there'd be risk involved."

"Guns and drugs."

"Yeah, and more than that."

"Like what?"

"Heavy stuff. C-4, M-60 machine guns, AT-4 antitank weapons."

"Where'd he get his hands on that stuff?"

"Not sure. But I think somebody's taking a cut at both ends.
Making the connection and then buying them back and distrib-
uting them."

"That doesn't make sense."

"Didn't to me, either. But that was the feeling Burlingame got."

"Why did Burlingame want me along?" I asked.

"I don't know," he said. "Don't know why they killed him
either."

Chick returned with the coffee. He gave a cup to Billy and
one to me. Billy sipped at the black liquid. "What do you get
out of this?" I asked.

"Burlingame gave me a bigger cut of the drug business. I
served the customers while he did the weapons deal."

"Where are the rest of the weapons?"

"I don't know. He didn't trust me on much of that stuff."

"Do you know who is buying the guns?"

He shook his head, winced, and put both hands on either side
of his head.

"How did you know Randle Lightfoot was going to get
whacked?"

"Because he knew things."

"Such as?"

"Him and Burlingame were pals. Hung out together. Jackie
gave him free stuff and Lightfoot would mule it to other NFL
cities. Stuck the packets under the padding of his helmet. Equip-
ment guy was in on it. They fired the guy last month. Jackie
liked hanging out with a football player, like a groupie or something, and Lightfoot liked pretending he was a tough guy.
They'd get drunk together and brag about shit. How they were
badasses and all."

"They mention any names?"

"Just one."

"Frake Meredith."

"Yeah."

"How's he involved?"

McCall chewed his lower lip, hesitating.

"Meredith is small fry," I said. "Forget him. The big boys won't come after you because of him."

Billy McCall began to talk. It was a strange, involved tale. Somebody—I figured Purvis or Burlingame—was trying to monopolize the Colorado gun market. Somehow Burlingame had gotten his hands on some of the guns and wanted in on the action.

"How was Jackie going to make himself rich?" I asked.

"He had a source and a buyer with a steady cash flow. Least that's what he said. Said he was going to sell a sample, then make the big score."

"What made him think he could pull this off? Why not just stick to the dope or play the gun deal straight?"

"You know Jackie. His head's warped. Liked to think he was putting something over on people. He was scared, but it appealed to him too much to walk away from it. Had to try it. I think it made him feel hard-core. A tough guy. He used to chuckle about it, talk about what a beautiful scam it was."

"Scam? Was that the word he used? Called it a scam, not a deal?"

"Yeah. It was weird. Jackie's a juicer and a doper, but mostly he was a greedhead. Wants his and yours, too." He snuffled, and squeezed his eyes shut, then opened them.

"Guns are tough to deal," I said. "They're big and bulky and hard to conceal. Drugs are easier. To move guns you need a network. A good one. Or the feds are all over you."

"Said he had that doped out. Had protection at a high level."

"Burlingame? Who would he know?"

McCall shrugged. He took a big swallow of the coffee and made a face. Burned his tongue. "Damn," he cursed. "I gotta lay down."

"In a minute. Where did Jackie keep the guns?"

"I don't know."

"But he had them stashed somewhere. Right?"

"He sure bragged a lot if he didn't have them somewhere."
He told us more, but nothing we didn't already know, though
he confirmed things we suspected.

"Go take a nap, Billy," I said. "I'll get back to you." I jingled
the keys in my pocket. Keys to my Mustang and keys to my
cabin. Keys to a Mercedes of a dead drug dealer and wannabe
gunrunner.

And a key that didn't fit an apartment door.

So what do you think?" I asked Chick. We let Billy sleep after having him drink some Gatorade to keep his fluid levels up. He would not feel great when he woke up, but you can't fix everything.

"He knows a few things. Doesn't know all of it. Probably hasn't told us all he does know. Too sick to bullshit too much. Don't know how much it helps."

I agreed. What did Congressman Braden have to do with it?

"Lot of money floating around," said Chick.

"Fortunately, much of it floated our way."

"We must remember to do something good with it. Like liberating a case of Scotch from some back room."

"Or maybe use it as bait. We've got a key that fits something. I'll bet when we figure out what it fits we'll also find some illegal weapons. Let's check out Purvis's dude ranch. Get some riding lessons."

. . .

The Sun King Dude Ranch was a five-star, six-gun, wood-and-steel complex of buildings sprawling across twenty acres of prime mountain real estate. Part ode to the West, part resort, it had it all—tack house, corral, heated swimming pool, Jacuzzi, par-three golf course, tennis courts, walking trail, gift shop, A-frame lodges and cowboys—both dude and the hired type in full cowboy regalia. In the middle of the compound Old Glory and the Colorado state flag flapped on a flagpole. The dust and mountain rock felt good under my boots. The air was cool and carried the rich smell of horse and leather mixed with hickory smoke and pine.

Pale-skinned Easterners in cowboy boots and virgin Stetsons unloaded Jeep Cherokees. Their political correctness didn't prevent them from purchasing vehicles named for Indians. The hired hands wore chaps and tied-down Colt .45s in case the clients rioted.

"You think John Wesley Hardin would take a soak in a Jacuzzi?" Chick asked, as we got out of his Barracuda.

"Maybe after a quick round on the golf course."

"Let's mosey over to the saloon and have some red-eye."

"Later, maybe," I said. "I want to look around a little." I had a theory that some of the shadow soldiers worked on this ranch. Coy Montana did, anyway, and I wanted to poke a stick in his hidey-hole.

"You realize we have discovered ground zero of the American wet dream?" said Chick. "Stud horses and cowgirls. Heated swimming pools. Tennis rackets and six-guns. I mean to tell you, we are there. I am obligated to conduct tests, then drink till I can't stop smiling."

A cowboy on a tall horse stopped. It was Harold Wallace, the guy I'd caught tossing Jackie B.'s apartment. The drug collar must've slipped off him—which meant somebody with clout had sprung him, which probably meant Crispin Purvis. Wallace didn't recognize me. I didn't expect him to as he had only heard my voice. He looked long, tall, and authentic. "Howdy," he said, touching the brim of his hat. "Can I help you gentlemen?"

"Yeah," Chick said. "We're lookin' for a hoot owl name of Coy Montana. Know where we might find that varmint?"

"Yes sir," said cowboy Harold. "He should be just about done with his fast-draw class." He pointed us in the direction of the shooting range.

"Much obliged, partner," said Chick. "Happy trails."

Cowboy Harold tipped his hat again and sauntered away.

I said, "That was the guy that broke into Burlingame's apartment."

"Well, I'll be switched," said Chick.

"Give Gene Autry the day off, huh?"

"Pretty authentic, huh?"

"Tedious."

"Them's fightin' words, hombre."

We found the shooting range. Five "dudes" were practicing their quick-draw technique with .22 revolvers. Three men and two women waiting to grow up, leather holsters tied down with rawhide tethers. Nike tennis shoes and hand-tooled belts. The short, staccato yelp of .22s crackled like popcorn and the sharp smell of cordite swirled in the air. The gunslingers were drawing, firing, then spinning guns back into holsters.

"Don't bow your leg out," Montana told one shooter. "It puts the gun in a bind when you pull it. You want your gun leg straight, but relaxed, that way the gun comes out clean. Cock the hammer as the gun clears. See the target. Concentrate, don't stare. Stay loose." An accountant drew his gun, cocked it, and fired. The bullet kicked up dirt at the foot of the silhouette target. "You're rushing it and shooting too soon. Here, watch."

Montana took up position on the firing line and removed the glove from his gun hand. His body was loose, hand dangling by the holster. "Okay," he said. "Call it when you're ready."

The dude said, "Draw!" and the gun jumped from the holster as if spring-loaded. The heavy bark of the .45 was a marked contrast to the popping .22s. Very loud. Louder than the gun that killed Jackie Burlingame? Or had the van muffled the noise?

Five shots ripped into the target as he fanned the cut-down trigger. He reholstered, then spun around, twirled the gun up and pointed it directly between my eyes. The black hole in the end of the Colt looked like a drain pipe.

I didn't move. For half a heartbeat he locked onto me, then smiled and whirled the gun in a silver pinwheeling flash back into its holster. Scary quick. He laughed.

It was too sudden for me to react. At least I didn't wet my pants. His students, the cowboys in the fresh Levi's, stood wide-eyed and slack-jawed.

"Don't do that," I said, lowly, meaning it.

He pounded my shoulder with an open hand, letting me know everything was okay and we were old buckaroos. He gave me the capped-teeth smile, enjoying himself. Chick removed his hand from inside his jacket.

"Good to see you guys," said Montana. He turned to his class and introduced me. "This here's Wyatt Storme. The football player." He turned back to me, smiled and said, "The ex–football player." He emphasized the "ex." Wonderful guy. He dismissed the class and they ambled off in their new boots and Nikes. Back to their cellular phones and Wild West fantasies.

"What can I do for you boys?" he asked us. He tugged on the kidskin glove.

"Looking around," I said.

"Lookin' don't hurt nothing. Help yourself."

"Thought maybe we'd take some fast-draw lessons while we were here."

He cocked his head and squinted in thought. "Sure. Let me get you a couple of guns."

"Got my own." I reached under my coat and pulled out the Browning. I pointed the automatic and sighted on the neck of the target. Squeezed. Fired. Then I did it again. And again. Fourteen times. I got in a rhythm. On the tenth shot, the splintered neck caused the head to lay over. The last three severed the head from the body. The slide clacked open on the empty clip. My ears were ringing and the air smelled like the Fourth of July.

"Pretty good shooting," Montana said. "Not very fast though."

"Shooting straight's the important thing," I said.

"Different with someone shooting back at you."

"No doubt about it."

"You needin' something?"

"Not a thing. Already got everything."

He smiled. "Well, you boys enjoy yourselves. I've got chores to take care of." He walked off. Swaggered, actually.

"Well," Chick said, "that was productive. Love watching you and Montana show off for each other. Why didn't you draw a line in the dirt and dare each other to cross it?"

"You think that would've worked?"

The trip to the Sun King Ranch was less informative than I'd hoped. The only thing certain was that Coy Montana was hairline crazy and faster than a Bufferin. I was convinced he was the man who'd killed Jackie Burlingame, though I didn't know why or if any of the ranch hands besides Harold Wallace had been there.

We left the resort and I dropped Chick back at his place and drove up my mountain. When I got back to my cabin there was a note pinned on the door.

Wyatt,

I was here and you were not. See you tonight. Wear a suit and a tie and try not to act smug and impossible. You know I love you.

Sandra

P.S. I'm serious about the tie.

Since quitting football I only wore a tie on Sunday mornings. Used to have to wear one on team flights. Ties were okay, but they symbolized something I'd left behind, not something I was searching for. However, it was ill-advised, though interesting, to anger the lovely Sandra. Sometimes I pushed the envelope just to watch the fire start in her blue eyes. Watch the lovely jaw grow taut. I smiled to think about it, and cut myself with my razor. Never happens on the shaving commercials.

I put on a brown tweed jacket, a tan oxford shirt, a pair of jeans, and a pair of Tony Lamas. Wasn't a suit, but it was close. I looked at a rack of ties. I selected one that was creased from hanging on the wire. I held it for a moment and hung it back up.

Can't always have it her way, I thought.

Forty-five minutes later I was at the door of her apartment. In my hand was a red rose, wrapped in green tissue. I held it over my heart and knocked.

"If that's you, Wyatt," she said, "just come in. I'm not ready yet."

"It's bad manners to yell through a closed door."

"You have a key."

"We must retain certain formalities or risk losing the magic in our relationship. Besides, I was taught not to enter houses without knocking."

"God, you are so provincial. This is the nineties."

"Don't remind me. I have knocked and await your answer."

I heard a muffled curse, then the syncopated sound of shoeless feet scuffing across carpet. She opened the door and leaned against the doorframe with a smile on her heart-stopping face. "You are a pain in the butt, Wyatt Storme."

I held out the rose. "But a romantic pain in the butt." I held out the rose. "For you, my love. It pales beside your beauty." She looked at it momentarily. "Aren't you going to squeal with delight?" I asked.

She took it and grabbed me by the lapel of my jacket and

pulled me inside. She pulled me close and kissed me. Long. Deep. She released my jacket and pushed me back.

"There," she said. "Isn't that better than squealing with delight?"

"Ask me later," I said. She hadn't mentioned the tie. Suspicious. "When I've had something to compare it with."

"You're wearing the tweed jacket," she said. "I knew it. Wait right there." Not "Where's the tie?" She was postponing the execution. Highly suspicious. She left the room and returned with a wrapped gift, a narrow box with a gold ribbon tied around it. I opened it. Inside was a handpainted tie, dark brown with cream and tan patterns. It went well with my shirt and jacket.

"How do you do that?" I asked.

"Simple," she said. "You're stubborn. I knew if I told you to wear a suit and tie you wouldn't. However, I also knew you wouldn't risk wearing that damn corduroy thing. Which leaves the tweed. Knew you'd wear a solid shirt, since you have some psychological aversion to calling attention to yourself. So I figured either white, tan, or goldenrod." She smiled in triumph.

"How is it that you know me so well, when I am a stranger to myself?"

"Because I love you, stupid. Every little idiosyncrasy. In a world of thought-balloon cardboard cutouts you are a flesh-and-blood declarative sentence. You are my anchor. And, you are predictable."

"You don't know everything."

"Yeah?" She touched my chin lightly. Smiled. "Were you thinking of me when you cut yourself shaving?"

Our destination was a large house on the east slope looking down on Boulder—a huge, sprawling home with a glassfront wing. The lights of Boulder twinkled and danced and played off the huge windows. I bypassed blue-coated parking valets and parked the ancient Mustang among the BMWs, Mercedeses, Cadillacs, Lincolns, and stretch limos. There wasn't a car in the heliport–parking lot worth less than thirty thousand dollars. The Mustang snarled to a halt, as if objecting to being tethered next to its glitzy, gelded cousins.

I stepped out of the car, into the chill mountain air. It was clear and bracing. I pulled some into my lungs and looked up into the mountains, wishing I could take the backpack and sleeping bag from the trunk and walk steadily up into them, to where I could drink coffee from a tin cup, look down on the city and dream of bugling elk and eagles riding currents of rising heat.

As ever it were so. Grounded once more by my love for Genevieve Castillon Collingsworth's daughter.

I walked around the car and opened the door for her. She accepted my hand and unfolded herself, long and willowy, from the car. She wore a dark evening dress with a matching cape. Her hair was up—winding golden curls spilling onto her shoulders. The smell of perfume drifted into my face, familiar and comforting. I took her by the elbow and escorted her to the house, my boots and her heels in concert.

A man in a tuxedo met us in the foyer.

"Good evening," he said. "And who may I say is attending?"

"Popeye and Olive Oyl," I said.

He attempted a smile, but with difficulty.

"Pardon my escort," said Sandy, giving me the taut-jaw look. Excellent. Like lightning in the mountains. "He often confuses lack of maturity with wit. Sandra Collingsworth and Wyatt Storme."

He looked at his list. "Yes. Here it is. Enjoy your evening."

"I just hate it when you call me down in front of the help," I said as we entered the house.

"You love it," she said. "In fact, you do everything possible to elicit it since you have some sort of twisted male hypothesis about anger and beauty."

"Country girl," I said, "I think you're pretty."

"You're no Neil Young."

"And Neil couldn't run a post pattern with track stars chasing him, either. Whose place is this?"

"Friend of Janet Sterling's. Some kind of globe-trotting industrialist. Has a weird name. Crispin something." She smiled and raised an eyebrow.

"Crispin Purvis."

"Said you wanted some background information on him. Here it is close up."

The tie felt tight at my throat.

I sipped club soda and endured.

Sandy was mingling, leaving me to contend with the elite and the other social cripples who circled each other in their strange ritual dance, expounding and pontificating on politics and issues on which they had been expertly misinformed. Like buffalo, they grazed, sniffing at one another.

Boulder is the politically correct center of the new civil religion. Fads and causes the new faith. Its practitioners don't smoke, smile or question articles of faith. And they are not amused by those who do.

Grieg's Piano Concerto in A Minor spilled from speakers embedded in the walls and ceiling. Glasses tinkled and voices chattered and chased each other. There was a John Gross steel sculpture which looked like a pregnant Thanksgiving turkey. It was *Venus,* I was informed. The goddess or the planet? I asked. I was given a tight-lipped persimmon smile and dismissed as a peasant. The bandleader of a late-night talk show flitted about the room, soaking up admiration and recognition as if it were sunlight. Three wet bars and three banquet tables were laden with multicolored beverages, foods, and appetizers—exotic and traditional. Waiters in red waistcoats circulated through the throng with trays of hors d'oeuvres and champagne. I searched the crowd for evidence of life and cigarette smoke. There was neither, so my cigars lay dormant, nestled in the liner pocket of my jacket.

I had already removed my tie. That'll teach her to leave me stranded with mutants, I thought. There was not another tweed jacket in the place. Probably no one wearing a Timex watch, either.

I survived a monologue about the greenhouse effect from a thin-haired, cocaine-impaired, mustachioed middle-aged flower child whose parents had left him a trust fund, freeing him to discuss such things. I'd heard the argument before. Only a few years ago the same people were predicting a new ice age. My prediction? The same as my friend from Woody Creek—Bad Craziness.

"... fluorocarbons and factory smoke floating into the stratosphere causing a buildup of chemicals which are superheating the atmosphere. Not to mention the rent in the ozone which is causing the increase in skin cancer." He finally paused to ask, "What do you think?"

"I think they should remove the asterisk from Roger Maris's sixty-one home runs because Ruth made more plate appearances in 'twenty-seven. I think Archie should dump Veronica and date Betty Cooper. I think contemporary art is suffering from an elitist malaise." I looked at him, trying to will him to disappear.

His eyes widened as he backed away from me, probably to retreat to the men's room for another snort. At least it wouldn't add to the rent in the ozone.

Grieg had given way to the Rolling Stones, and several people danced to "Gimme Shelter." Of course, there was, and still is, none—though I've searched hard. Across the room I spotted

Crispin Purvis, in white tuxedo, working the crowd, with a stunning brunette on his arm I recognized from a half dozen movies. Janet Sterling smiled like diamonds at her subjects.

A tall blonde sidled up next to me. She was wearing a dress cut to separate and support ample breasts. I studied her. Needed to be ready in case Sandy asked if I talked to anyone. Didn't want to come off as a wallflower. She was a gorgeous creature. Straight teeth. Lovely hands and long legs. I kept an eye on her and watched for furtive movement—or any other kind. Detective work requires vigilance.

She said, "I'm Lauren. What's your sign?"

I looked at her blankly. Turned my head and bit my lower lip. Tried to think serious thoughts. Didn't work. The laughter bubbled up to my mouth and escaped. " 'What's your sign?' "

She looked at me, her head tilting like a fawn's when considering something new. "What's the matter?" she asked.

"Nothing."

"You're cute." She had bedroom eyes and no design flaws. "What's your name?"

I told her.

"You don't look like you're in the business."

"What's the business?"

"You know. Acting. Dancing. I'm an actress."

"How do you know I'm not an actor."

"You've got a little scar along your jaw. Your nose has been broken and you didn't get it fixed. You don't seem very aware of yourself like actors do. You aren't mingling. You look more like a stunt man. You a friend of Crispin's?"

"No."

"You want to go somewhere?"

"I'd better not."

"Why not?"

"I'm with someone. Exclusively."

"You afraid of AIDS?"

"No. I'm afraid of her left hook."

"Hey Lauren," said a voice I'd heard before. It was Coy Montana. He was hatless and gloveless. "Why don't you go powder your nose? I want to talk to this man. Heard they've got some blow in the sunroom."

Her eyes widened and her nostrils flared. "I'll see you later, Wyatt," she said. She bustled through the forest of night creatures, nose to the wind.

"What are you doing here?" he asked me.

"Didn't recognize you with both hands exposed. Where's the hat?"

"You didn't answer my question."

"I asked you second."

"You're here with the news lady, right?"

"Pretty inquisitive for a hired guy."

His lips tightened. "Just trying to make conversation."

"Maybe you should take a remedial course."

"This is the third time you've shown up."

"Didn't know you were keeping track. What's your interest?"

His shoulders relaxed. "Just want to make sure all the guests are having a good time."

"There's an honest job," I said. "Me, I always wanted to be an elevator operator."

"What do you mean by that?"

"Why are you crowding Matt Jenkins?"

"Who says we are? He and Crispin are friends. Hell, we're all friends, tonight."

"I don't like it," I said. I was tired of his friendly cowpoke routine. Time to cut-block him at the knees, get him mad. "And I want you to back off."

"Is that supposed to frighten me?"

"Naw. Takes brains to be scared."

He leaned toward me. His eyes had become dull blanks. "Look, Storme. I don't know why you're trying to rile me. But not tonight, okay? Why don't you get drunk? Get high on something. Plenty of everything. Enjoy yourself. Don't nose around.

You got a nice girl and your life is pretty much in order." I said nothing, just looked at him, which seemed to irritate him. He said, "Don't mess with the bull or you get the horn. Savvy?"

"That's genuine sagebrush rhetoric if I ever heard it. You forgot, 'Next time I see you, you better be packin' iron.' "

He nodded his head, as if considering the solution to a puzzle. "See you around, Storme. Have a nice time."

"One more thing," I said, leaning into his face. "Next time you pull a gun on me it'd better be smoking or made of chocolate. You savvy that, Kimosabe?"

He glared at me, then smiled. Nodded, then backed away, his eyes on me for a last look before pointing a finger at me and dropping his cocked thumb like the hammer on a gun.

No doubt about it. We were making progress in our relationship.

I looked across the room and saw Janet Sterling momentarily separated from the throng. I made my way toward her. She accepted a glass of champagne from a waiter. A woman approached her to express admiration. Ms. Sterling sipped her champagne and looked over the rim of the glass at me. Magnetic eyes—dark and inviting.

I waited until the fan left and moved closer.

"Miss Sterling," I said. "I need to talk to you if I could."

"Ms.," she said, correcting me. "Ms. Sterling." She smiled. "You can call me Janet." Looked me up and down. "My," she said. "Certainly a lot of you, isn't there? Is everything in proportion?" She bit her lower lip with a white tooth and raised an eyebrow.

"I'm a friend of Chick Easton's."

"Wyatt Storme," she said. "Yes, I know. I'm a big football fan. Where have you been hiding all these years and can we hide there together?"

"Do you know Jackie Burlingame?"

"Rather know you," she said. "You certainly look like the real item."

"Very flattering. How do you know Burlingame?"

"This is disconcerting," she said. "Every man in the room wants to bed me and when I find one I like he's interested in talking about some little snake who sells pills and powder." She flashed the marquee smile. "Wouldn't you like to get to know me better? You have a nice face. Would you like a part in my next movie?"

"No thanks. Afraid it would cost too much."

She laughed. "Well, well. One with a brain."

"Is there someplace we could talk?"

"That's much better," she said. She took my hand and led me from the room. I looked for Sandy, who had noticed and was following me with her eyes and shaking her head. In trouble again. I looked back and gave her a "Don't look at me" shrug.

Janet Sterling led me into a sitting room off the ballroom. There was a large-screen television, a bar and trendy furniture decorating the room. She sat down on a love seat, pulling my arm as she did. I maneuvered myself to sit on the edge of a heavy birchwood coffee table.

"Don't be shy," she said, cocking her head.

"Tell me about Jackie Burlingame."

"Why are you so uneasy? Don't you like the 'new woman'?"

"Hadn't adjusted to the old one. Would you feel better if I shrieked and ran around the room with my hands clapped to my mouth?"

"My. Certainly clever for a football player. How did that happen?"

"I used to be an actor before I passed a literacy test."

She threw back her head and laughed. "You are delicious," she said. She ran her hand through her mane of black hair and shook her head. I could smell her rich perfume. "Do you have a cigarette?"

"Sorry. Want a cigar?"

She smiled wickedly and said, "That'll do."

I gave her a tubed Portofino. She made an elaborate show of

slowly unscrewing the cap, then placing the long, slender cigar between her perfect teeth. I lighted it for her, then did the same for my own. She inhaled the smoke, then languidly released a blue-gray cloud, all the while looking at me with ebony eyes, as a cheetah eyes its prey. She suggestively worked the cigar in and out of her mouth, then touched the tip of her hummingbird tongue to the underside of the cigar. I was in over my head on this one. This was her territory.

"So let's forget about Jackie and resolve the problems at hand," she said. She placed a hand on my knee and caressed the inside of my thigh. A fog formed and thickened in my throat. I am, after all, flesh and blood. I moved my knee and readjusted so I would be out of reach.

"Men who play hard-to-get turn me on."

"What about men who give in?"

"They turn me on also." She tilted her chin to expose her lovely neck. I thought chaste thoughts. Wasn't helping much.

"Why would Burlingame have your name in his little black book?" I asked.

"What difference does it make?"

"Jackie's dead."

"Doesn't surprise me."

"Why do you say that?"

"He was a drug dealer."

"Did you buy from him?"

"Are you from *People* magazine? Or just a nosy bore?"

"A friend of mine is in trouble with some lowlifes. Jackie was one of them and now he's off the board."

"Sounds like your problem is solved."

"Your name was in his book," I said. "Crispin Purvis, too. Then you are the guest of honor at his house. That a coincidence?"

"Crispin is rich and influential. He's investing in a production in which I am interested in getting the lead. He invited me to stay here while I am in the area."

"Doesn't sound very progressive and 'new woman'-ish."

Her lower teeth showed in a hard line against her uppers. "You are kind of a shit, you know."

"I didn't start this."

She leaned back and placed her hand against her temple. Smoke trailed away from her and dissipated. She was more beautiful in repose than in attack mode. A highly chauvinistic attitude I'm sure. "The project will be shot here in Colorado, so when my agent got the invitation I came. I'm getting close to forty. After forty, female stars get secondary parts—psychotic menopausal matrons and bizarre comedies with *Saturday Night Live* refugees, if they get anything. It's a fast-dance life so I do what I have to. I use a little cocaine to keep me going, some grass to relax. Jackie gets it for me. I didn't know he was taking notes."

"Did you know Jackie's dead?"

"What difference does that make?" She clicked her fingernails agitatedly. I looked at her, waited. "Okay," she said. "No, I didn't know."

"What do you know about Crispin Purvis besides he's rich and wants to invest in a movie?"

"He imagines himself a kingmaker."

"Meaning?"

"Congressman Braden. He's promoting him as a senatorial candidate. You know, photo ops, big fund-raisers. Let him be seen at the right places with the right people. Crispin thinks big thoughts. He's pumping a lot of money into a push to get Braden the nomination. Gives him advice. Crispin is full of advice, love."

"The price of taking his money."

She laughed at the back of her throat. "I've been around Hollywood for almost twenty years and have seen all the little boys with the big muscles and *GQ* haircuts. The pretenders with the notches in their zippers. Most men are little boys. Just give them what they want . . . hell, you don't even have to give them what they want, just make them think it. There are few who are all grown up. Crispin, for instance. But it's in a dark, unsettling way. Cold-blooded. His brain is moving so fast you can hear it hum. Then there's you. Who'd have thought it? The football player who became an adult." There was heat in her eyes now. "Who are you really, Mr. Storme? What do you want?"

"Just a guy who needs help with a problem."

"I think," she said, crushing out her cigar, "you're just a bit more than that."

I left Janet Sterling to smolder along with her half-smoked cigar, and moved down the corridor checking rooms, getting the layout of the huge house. The thrum of the party vibrated like a distant heartbeat in the stillness of the main wing. I walked with the gingerly tread of a man conscious of his trespass. I checked some of the rooms and found nothing unusual until I came upon a locked door. There was no light under it, so it was locked for safekeeping, not privacy. Why lock a room in your own house? I tried a credit card along the door seam, but only got a bent credit card for my trouble. How do they do that, anyway? I'd starve to death as a burglar. Maybe subcontract the breaking-in part.

To satisfy my curiosity I tried the Safe-T key on the Mercedes key ring. Didn't fit.

I tried to imagine the house from the outside, considering how to gain access from a window. I walked into an adjoining room. It was a large wood-and-leather room decorated in taxidermist motif—heads of jungle cats, Cape buffalo, elk, moose, and mule deer peered at me from the wall. There were display cases of various firearms. Some antique, yet many new. This is in the home of a guy who was backing a gun-control congressman? Curiouser and curiouser. More interesting were two framed pictures of Purvis—one with Richard Nixon, another with Bill Clinton.

I walked over to a window and looked out on the darkened back lawn. There was a tarp-covered pool and a large patio. The grounds tailed off into the foothills. Having had my look, I walked back into the corridor, where the overmuscled chauffeur hollered at me.

"Hey! What are you doing back here?"

"Hello," I said, adopting a bumbling guest demeanor. "Boy, this is a big house. I was looking for a bathroom and got lost. Guess I've had a little too much to drink. Could you show me how to get to a bathroom?"

"You're not supposed to be back here," he said. His bulk filled the hall. His thick arms and chest made his forearms point at twenty-five degree angles from his body, and his hands dangle from his wrists. I wondered where he bought shirts with collars big enough—Michelin?

"Come with me," he said.

I followed him and he showed me to a bathroom. I thanked him, went into the bathroom, flushed the toilet, and ran water into the basin. I wet my hands and flicked some water on my shirt and jeans for effect. When I opened the door he was waiting for me. Mistrustful. It made me more interested in the locked room.

"Sure is a fancy bathroom," I said cheerfully.

He grunted and ushered me back to the ballroom. If there's anything I despise, it's a blabby chauffeur. I thanked him for his help. I took a dollar bill out of my pocket, grabbed him by a thick wrist, pulled his arm up to parallel and put the dollar in his palm. He looked at me from cold depths. He turned his hand upside down and the dollar fluttered to the floor. He walked off.

Couldn't even buy a friend. I blame it on the declining value of the dollar.

I made my way to the banquet table. I got a cup of coffee and some kind of exotic pastry filled with boysenberry jam. I thought about the room. Why was it locked? What was so important that Purvis couldn't risk someone stumbling in? Purvis had plans for Joring Braden. Kingmaker. A Senate seat was nothing to sneeze at. A gun collector backing a gun-control senatorial candidate? When an alligator lies basking in the sun next to a fawn, you're at the Weirdville Zoo. When the dove rides on the predator's back, you're at the circus. This is Colorado, where the NRA and the Fund for Animals are right on top of each other, and only the most fragile peace exists.

Something was not right.

While thinking these things I looked across the room and saw Purvis shaking hands with a familiar-looking guy. Frake Meredith. My buddy from Bullet Bob's.

Meredith and Purvis together? Why? What did a cache of illegal weapons and two hundred thousand dollars have to do with any of this? And who had tried to trip off the principals involved? Better, who whacked Randle Lightfoot? I was no less confused than I had been at the start. In fact, I was more so, if that was possible.

I saw the thick-necked chauffeur talking with Coy Montana across the room. They looked my direction then made their way toward me. I was convinced the chauffeur was the big shadow soldier I'd seen prior to somebody putting a bullet in Jackie. Counting Harold Wallace, that made three I knew of. But who had been their leader that day? Who was Captain Marvel? It wasn't Purvis, as Captain Marvel had been taller, but I thought Purvis was the money man.

"Skunk here tells me you were snooping around the house," Montana said, referring to the chauffeur as the two men approached.

"Well, you big tattletale," I said to Skunk.

His fists clenched and unclenched. I could almost hear stones grinding in his head. I recalled the way he'd dispatched Turk. "You need to learn a little respect," he said, hissing between clenched teeth.

"Take it easy, Skunk," said Montana, enjoying the exchange. "He's just pushing your buttons. Isn't that right, Storme?"

"Something like that."

Purvis joined our circle. I felt him before I saw him. It was like hearing something slide through damp grass. "Well, Mr. Storme," he said. "Are you enjoying yourself?"

I looked at Skunk. "Sure. Wouldn't have missed this for the world."

"Good," he said. "Met your lady friend. She's a beauty. Quite intelligent, too."

"Evidenced by her choice of escort," I said.

"He's been snooping around," said Dumont.

Purvis cocked his head to one side. "What are you looking for, Storme?"

"See if I could find Skunky here a personality."

Skunk stared at me.

"There are wiser things than badgering Mr. Dumont," said Purvis.

"But few things more fun."

"Maybe you should let sleeping dogs lie."

"Not when they're lying on my porch, stinking it up."

"You're quite sloppy at this, aren't you? A more subtle approach might be in order."

"You know, when I played football I really liked to block. I liked hitting the guys who were taking shots at me. I especially liked blocking on counterplays and reverses when the guy I was blocking had to change direction suddenly. That's when I could really lay 'em out."

"What's your problem, Storme?"

"You show up at Matt's with a politician who looks uncomfortable and a bodyguard. Why does an honest community leader, patron of the washed masses, need that?"

"I'm a successful businessman. A ruthless one, in fact. There are people who might wish me dead."

"Certainly understand that."

Purvis's brows pursed, narrowing his hooded eyes by another tenth of an inch. "You're a guest in my home," he said. "Let's try to be civil for the duration of your visit."

"Matt was a little on edge after you left the other day. Why?"

"Do you fight all your friends' battles?"

"When the mood strikes me," I said.

"Want me to throw him out?" Dumont asked Purvis.

"Better go on a diet first," I said. "Lay off the pork rinds."

"You're begging for it."

"Coy," said Purvis. "Why don't you buy Skunk a drink?"

"Sure," Montana said. He chuckled and led Skunk away.

"We have a saying where I'm from," Purvis said.

"Can't wait to hear it."

He forced himself to smile. "Sometimes you must leave a sheep so the wolves don't take them all."

"But I'm such a selfish sheepdog."

"There are more wolves than you think."

"What's Meredith doing here?"

"You know Frake?"

"We've met. Thinks he's connected but they just use him."

"You seem well informed."

"Got a subscription to *People* magazine. Read it every morning in the bathroom."

A voice hailed Purvis from behind me. He waved and said he'd be right with them. To me, he said, "Nice to chat with you. Tonight you're my guest. Tomorrow, stay clear of my affairs." He walked past me.

I wanted a look at that room. But first I wanted out of here. I went to get Sandy but she was already looking for me.

"You ready to go?" she asked.

"Boy, I don't know," I said. "I can't remember when I had a better time unless it was the first time I tore the cartilage in my knee."

"I know something you don't know."

"Several things, probably. What have you got?"

"Wait until we're in the car."

Crispin Purvis is a naturalized U.S. citizen," Sandy said as we were walking to the car. "He was born in New Zealand."

I recalled his odd habit of enunciating each syllable—the sheep-wolf thing, then, the faint accent I couldn't identify. Could it be Aussie? Harold Wallace said he had worked for a rogue Australian operative in Nam. Purvis? Purvis had become a U.S. citizen and had built an empire. With black market money?

"New Zealand, huh? You may have something for me." I told her about the black market gun operation in Vietnam that Harold Wallace had told me of.

"You think Purvis is the Australian agent?" she asked.

"Possible," I said. "Quite a coincidence if he's not. Wallace isn't exactly a genius. He could have the accent confused. Or Purvis took the Australian identity as a cover." We were at the car. I pulled out the car keys, which were tangled with Jackie Burlingame's keys. What did the other key fit? What was in the locked room in Purvis's house?

"Meredith was there," I said.

"Why?"

"That's what I want to know."

"He called today."

"What did he say?"

"Asked me out."

"Popular lady."

"I told him not to call again."

"To which he said?"

She looked uncomfortable. "He got angry. Started swearing. Said something about 'breaking your little boyfriend's elbows.' "

"That'd hurt, wouldn't it?"

"Stay away from him, Wyatt."

"After he apologizes to you."

She pursed her lips and inhaled. She had magnificent lung capacity from cycling the back roads of Colorado. Also, she had a little natural head start on the lung thing. Something to do with genetics, I think. She let out her breath and said, "We've talked about this before. You don't listen."

"I listened."

"But you want to handle it in your usual macho-bull-in-rut manner. Right?"

I said nothing.

"Don't close me out, Wyatt."

"Nobody swears at you."

"You can't go around beating up everybody that talks dirty to me."

"How about if I confine it to a withering glare?"

She smiled whitely in the dark car, then laughed. "You big dope."

"Kind of a lovable big dope, don't you think?"

I thought about the situation. I now knew who three of the soldiers were. I'd bet Dumont had military experience. Coy Montana was the wild card in the deck. Had he aced Randle Lightfoot? Or had someone else? I voted for Montana. He smelled of predator, walking territory where his kind had long been extinct.

What hold did Purvis have over Congressman Braden? They were at opposite ends of the political spectrum; strange, unnatural bookends holding up several volumes of power and bad history. And what did they have on Matt Jenkins? I could no longer offer Matt the luxury of withholding information.

I said, "Let's wait a while. I want to see when Meredith leaves."

"I think this is an elaborate device to get me alone in your car so you can make out with me," Sandy said.

"Am I that transparent?"

"Well, you can just forget it, because I promised my parents I'd be home by midnight." Gary Puckett and the Union Gap played on the radio. Incredible voice. Bringing it all back—young love and dancing in the velvet night, dawning awareness, and the expectant hope that it would continue to get better.

"I miss Mother," Sandy said. Her hands were in her lap and her head was tilted down and slightly forward, her eyes distant. I said nothing. Gary Puckett continued to sing in his unique, clear-toned tenor. "It's good to see Daddy writing again." Since I'd known her she had never called Duncan "Daddy," it was always "Father." "For a while it felt as if I'd lost them both. It's taken me a long time to get over . . . to get over Father's behavior while Mother was dying." Puckett's voice died in a blaze, trailing off to a fade-out. I fidgeted in my seat, suddenly uncomfortable. I looked out my window toward the house.

"He had an affair with a college student," Sandy said, in a rush to get it out, as if thought would rob her of the courage to do so. "That's why he left Colorado State. I found out after Mother's death."

"We don't have to talk about this."

"He began drinking heavily," she said, ignoring me. "It was as if he couldn't bear to watch Mother wither away. The writing stopped. The tenderness stopped. It was like the whole family was dying instead of just Mother. When I found out . . ." She paused, as if to gather a second wind. I wanted to stop her. I didn't want to hear this—it was a selfishness that couldn't abide hearing her misery. Her pain was mine and I was not made to handle it. It created an anger deep inside, raging against things I could neither explain nor control.

Nor assail.

"I was young," she said, continuing. "In many ways. I was confused, and bitter, and hurt, and finally, angry. I never knew who the other woman was, but I hate her. How could he do that? How could he do that to Mother? To himself? To me?"

I had no answer.

"It made me feel selfish and small. Abandoned. My mother was gone and I had estranged myself from my father. Then, over time I forgave him. You helped. I saw in you the strength Father lacked. Not that he wasn't strong in his way, but you have a strength I hadn't encountered before. Except in Mother. You and she are alike in some ways.

"I love my father, Wyatt. Like I love no one else, except you. He needs me and I need him . . . and I cannot forgive myself for wasting so many years. Years apart from him when I could have been with him. I won't make that mistake again."

I spotted Meredith. Walking to his car, accompanied by a tall red-haired man. He hadn't been at the party long, which affirmed that it had been a business visit. I started the Mustang.

We drove into Denver. I pulled the Mustang into the parking garage beneath her apartment building. She looked at me, a golden curl dangling near her eye like Christmas ribbon. I traced it with my finger. Looked into her eyes. A man could get lost in those eyes. I knew one that had.

"It's difficult for you, isn't it?" she said. "To hear me talk about these things."

"I don't like you to hurt."

"But no matter what you do, sometimes I will. You can't keep it all away from me."

"I can try."

"You will, won't you?"

I said, "I've waited all my life for you. Once I confused what life and love really were and in the process became someone I didn't like or want to be. You changed that for me. I won't give you up for even a moment."

She smiled. A solitary, perfect, sparkling tear formed and trailed slowly down her cheek, gaining momentum, and in a rush fell to her lap.

"Stay with me, Wyatt Storme. I need you. Nothing else. The rest will wait."

"And I need you," I said. "Nothing else. And the whole world can wait."

The next morning, accompanied by Chick, I drove to a midtown restaurant, where, according to Billy McCall, Frake Meredith conducted affairs that included drug traffic, bootlegging, and prostitution—all under the auspices, protection, and permission of the local mob family. Meredith was allowed to operate as long as he paid tribute, a certain percentage of his take, to his sponsors. He could never be a made man but still operated a small underground empire, supplemented by his legitimate businesses—a chain of funeral homes, a memorial headstone company and a couple of upscale restaurants.

The sign on the door said CLOSED, but the door was unlocked. The cafe, the Shamrock, was a restaurant-lounge of some repute that had received notice in Denver tourist propaganda. It was dark, leathery, and finished with dark walnut. A four-leaf clover adorned a huge mirror behind the antique bar.

A hostess met us as we walked into the restaurant. "We're not open yet," she said.

"We're looking for Frake Meredith," I said.

"I'm afraid I don't know whether . . . and you are?"

"Frake Meredith," I repeated. "I want to see him."

"Just a moment," she said. She walked to the bar and used the phone. She turned slightly away from us and spoke into it. She nodded her head twice, then put the phone down and walked back to us, a nervous smile on her face.

"Someone will be right with you," she said. "Would you like a table?"

"We'll wait here," I said.

Soon a man shaped like a bull sea lion, with jet black hair and large pallid lips, entered the room. It was Carmine, the gorilla who had been with Meredith at Bullet Bob's. His suit was tailored. "What do you want?"

"Meredith," I said. "We need to see him."

"Who are you?"

I told him.

He left us, then returned momentarily. "Mr. Meredith isn't here today. Come back some other time."

"You got the feeling he's lying to us?" I said.

"Surely not," Chick said.

"Is he in the back?" I asked.

"You got something in your ears? Get the fuck out."

"He's in the back," I said to Chick.

"Yep," said Chick. We started to walk around the heavy man. He put a hand out to stop Chick. Before the hand reached Chick's chest, Chick grabbed the man's wrist with his right hand and placed his left hand behind the small of the man's elbow. With his thumb on the back of the man's hand, Chick twisted and forced the arm downward. The man gave a small grunt as his body tilted. He tried to recover, but Chick increased the pressure on the back of the hand and marched Carmine backward through the lounge to a rear door. He shoved him through a swinging door into a room where Frake Meredith was drinking coffee and eating pastry. Also on the table was an electronic calculator with curly strips of paper lying about.

There was another man with Meredith. A red-haired man with

a florid face and muttonchop sideburns. It was the same guy who'd been with Meredith last night at Purvis's party. Chick released Carmine with a shove.

"Well, lookee here," Chick said. "Meredith is here after all."

"What the fuck is this?" said Meredith, arms extended.

"Profanity," I said, "is the vocabulary of the ignorant." Carmine had recovered and stepped forward.

"Relax," Chick said. Carmine took another step forward and Chick swept the dark man's arm away and followed with the heel of his hand against the dark man's forehead. He stumbled backward over a chair.

"Get the hell out of here, Storme," said Meredith. "Before I call the cops."

"Yeah," I said. "Bet there'd be a race over to see who gets to rescue you. Heard you're a favorite. We just want to talk, Meredith." I looked at the third man who was glaring at me. "That okay with you, sweetheart?"

He stood up and I stiff-armed him back into his chair. "Stay seated."

" 'Tisn't healthy to be messing with someone you aren't acquainted with, laddy-buck." The accent was Irish.

"Hey," said Meredith. "You come into my place and Bogart my help. You interrupt my breakfast. What do you want from me?" He turned his palms upward.

"Stay away from Sandy."

"You crazy? All this over some gash?"

"Don't call her that, Meredith. Call her that again and you'll need a proctologist to do your dental work."

"You don't run my life."

"You come near Sandy again and I'm going to become an important part of it. Are we together on this point?"

"What am I supposed to do? It's a small city. What if I accidentally bump into her?"

"No bumping. No accidents. You even call her you'd better

be doing it from Jupiter. Any more profanity and you'll be taking your meals through a straw. Another thing. You were at Purvis's last night. What were you doing there?"

"None of your business."

"It is when it involves friends of mine."

"You've got friends?"

"Matt Jenkins. Somebody is squeezing him and I don't like it."

"I don't know anything about that."

"What's your connection with Purvis?"

"You got a hearing problem?"

"Chick," I said. "I need some help here." Chick walked around the table. Carmine started to intercept him, but Chick side-kicked the man in the solar plexus. Carmine, the slow learner, crumpled to the floor, gasping for air, his mouth working like a fish's. Meredith started to get up from his chair, but Chick pinched him alongside the neck and forced him back into the chair. Once Meredith was seated, Chick dug his thumb into the soft flesh under Meredith's chin.

"Now," Chick said, leaning down by Meredith's ear. "You're going to talk straight or I'm going to start hurting you very badly. In ways you never knew existed. Raise your hand if you understand."

Meredith raised his hand.

"That a boy." He patted his shoulder. "I think you have his attention now, Wyatt."

"Why were you at Purvis's?"

"He wants me to invest in a movie."

"What else?"

"That's all."

"Don't blow smoke at me. What else?"

"That's it. That's all—" Chick dug the thumb in, again. "Okay. Okay." Chick relieved the pressure. "We've got a couple of business deals going."

"What kind of business deals?"

"I'm a dead man if I talk."

"Maybe even if you don't," Chick said.

"Then do it. I got nothing else to say about it."

"Where's Jackie Burlingame?" I asked.

"Haven't seen him."

"But you know him."

"Yeah. I know him."

"Do business with him?"

He laughed. "Not anymore."

"You know Billy McCall?"

"That the guy hangs out with Jackie B.?"

I nodded.

"Yeah. I know him. Wants to be a swinging dick, but he's just a little punk. Girls like him."

I asked more questions but gained no information I didn't already have. I laid off questions about guns, as I didn't want to tip my hand on that yet. I was satisfied he was in on the gun deal with Purvis and that he knew what had happened to Burlingame.

"Okay, Frake," I said. "We're going now. You're out of Sandy's life. Permanently. We're clear on that. You don't mention my visit to anyone. Not to Purvis. Not to Sandy."

"Not to Sandy?"

"I don't want her to know. She doesn't like the way I handle things."

His eyebrows knitted into little concentric furrows. "You come in here and beat up two guys and you're afraid your girlfriend will find out about it?" It confused him. "You're a fucking mental case," he said.

"You're not the first to notice," said Chick.

Two hours after sharing sunshine and wisdom with Frake Meredith, I was back at Matt Jenkins's house. Chick left me to check with a lawyer about a skip-tracing job.

Kelly answered the door barefooted, wearing terry-cloth shorts and a T-shirt. There was a sheen of perspiration on her forehead and her body glowed with the incandescence of health. Her naked legs were smooth-muscled and tanned. As always, Kelly's engines idled at a high rate. There was an innocent sensuality about her. No hard edges. All round and smooth and full of the vitality of female.

"Matt's not here right now," she said. "But come on in. I just made coffee." She didn't wait for an answer, just bounced into the kitchen. I didn't have time for a visit, but followed her anyway.

"I'm a mess," she said, pouring the coffee. "I've been working out. Getting a little flabby." She had the body and muscle tone of a college cheerleader. She sat down and crossed tan legs, causing a small ridge of muscle to form in the calf and thigh. "So, what have you found out? If you don't mind my asking."

I didn't. I told her most of what I knew so far. About Purvis. About Congressman Braden. I left out anything that might worry her concerning Matt. Call it chauvinism. Call it condescending. Call it macho conceit. I just do not derive any pleasure from watching people—and particularly women—worry. Too late to be anything other than what I am. She sat, sipping her coffee and nodding, as I talked. She uncrossed and recrossed her legs. The room was warm.

"So, you think Purvis is involved in something criminal?" she asked. I nodded. "And you think Congressman Braden is involved with him. Where does that leave Billy?"

There's a funny question, I thought. Billy McCall? Since I'd known Kelly I'd been impressed by her intellect as well as her compassion and capacity for forgiveness. But Billy McCall? An irresponsible, selfish, substance-abusing drug dealer?

"It leaves Billy as a small-time hood operating at the edge of a razor-toothed beast which will swallow him whole." I said it with more heat than I wanted to.

"What's the matter, Wyatt?" she asked.

"Your attitude toward Billy is weird. You realize he was cheating on your niece with a teenybopper?"

"Girls grow up faster than they used to."

"There's an interesting spin on the situation."

"Don't you think you're being a little judgmental?"

"Don't you feel you're being a little naïve? This kid is dealing drugs and may be hooked up to a deal which will put dangerous weapons into the hands of criminals."

"I'm not trying to make you mad," she said, standing up. She walked over to me, leaned over, placed her hands on either side of my face and kissed my forehead. Her aroma in my head again. The kiss lingered between too long for a friendly peck and too short for an invitation—ambiguous, yet pleasant. As always the contradictions of Kelly McArthur Jenkins were part of her intrigue.

She lifted my head by the chin. "We've known each other too long for this, Wyatt Storme," she said. "Too long to play games. Too long to lie to each other. You remember what we used to mean to each other, don't you?"

Sometimes I remember more than I'm comfortable with, I thought. "Time changes things."

She leaned over and kissed my lips. I put my hands on her upper arms and gently pushed her away. "Can't do that," I said. "We've known each other too long for this. Also, too well. The end of this is disaster. For both of us. There is too much history. Some good, some bad. The good is I'm all grown up now and I have Sandy. The bad is some of the choices I've made, but I'm dealing with that. This will only confuse things. A selfish attitude maybe, but I'm stuck with it."

"You probably think I'm terrible," she said.

"No. Flattered. You are one of the most intelligent and beautiful women I've ever known. But things are swirling around for you and it has you off balance. Besides, you couldn't help yourself. I do have magnetic gray eyes." She smiled, then I said, "What is Matt keeping from me?"

She took a step back and held her elbow with her opposite hand. "You think Matt's keeping something from you?"

"Says he is. What is it?"

"I can't tell you if he doesn't want it told."

"What happened to 'people who've known each other too long to play games'? If you don't tell me, I'm going to have Matt tell me anyway. That's what I came for. It's become too complicated for secrets."

"It doesn't have anything to do with what's happening."

"Then why not tell me?"

"Because it's personal and it has to do with things that happened a long time ago. Old mistakes."

"Do these old mistakes involve Matt?"

"What do you mean by 'involve'?"

"Kelly, this conversation is wearing on me."

"I'm not trying to be evasive," she said. "No, that's not true. I am being evasive. The mistakes are personal ones. Mistakes both of us made."

"They have leverage over you two?"

"Not directly."

"What does that mean? I have to know. There's too much danger for too many people for me to be nice about it. You're worried about old mistakes. Old dragons. But what if they turn into new mistakes and bigger dragons? What if other people are hurt?"

She looked down at the floor. She sat down in her chair, her shoulders sagging in defeat. She placed her forehead in a hand, then raised her head. Ran a hand through her hair. She made a little circle with her mouth and let her breath out and looked at me.

"Dammit, Wyatt," she said. Her eyes glistened like smooth pebbles in water. "Always has to be your way. You never let go. Always so sure of yourself. So confident that your little house is clean. I'll tell you our dirty little secret."

"We don't have to pursue this," I said. "I don't want to—"

"No, it's too late for that now." It came in a rush, as if she were in a hurry to say it before she forgot it. Too late to stop her. Too late to erase the past.

"Billy McCall is my son."

Kelly Jenkins's eyes glistened yet remained unyielding in their defiance. Quite a thing to find out after all these years. Billy McCall was her illegitimate son. It explained why the Jenkinses put up with so much from him.

"That's the secret?" I asked.

"Part of it," she said.

"What's the rest?"

"Same old Wyatt Storme," she said. It had an edge of bitterness in it, like the taste of old vinegar. "Never change, never let go." She laughed. "That is, you never let go unless you have to invest emotionally. Never take a chance with your feelings."

"This is counterproductive."

"You walked out on me."

"Your memory is flawed," I said. "You found someone else."

"Why didn't you take me back?"

"Come on Kel. That's ancient history."

"Don't even want to know if he's your son?" Her face flushed with color, the pale crimson mounting beneath the fading tan, one hand clenched, the other clutching the hem of her shorts. I felt a dull pang at the pit of my stomach as if an air bubble were being forced through it with a bicycle pump. Billy was about the right age. It would explain Matt's strange behavior the last time I talked to him. I searched for the words. The words that would make twenty years of bad decisions and old wounds better. I could think of nothing.

"Is he?"

Her eyes dropped. I watched the fall of her breasts as she exhaled.

"No," she said. "That was cruel of me. Forgive me, please. It would have been better if it were true."

"Who is the father?"

She placed her hands together in her lap, then sat back in her chair. "It's not important."

"Does it have any bearing on this situation?"

"No. Not as it relates to Matt's problems. There's more, but that part is up to Matt. It only matters that Billy is protected. He doesn't know I'm his mother. Is he okay?"

"Chick's watching him. And it's obvious he doesn't know you're his mother," I said. "He told me about his indiscretion."

"What indiscretion?" she said—then recognition. "Oh. When I was sunning myself he . . . that is . . ." Her eyes closed momentarily. She put a hand alongside her face. "I've messed things up for everybody. For Matt, for Billy, for myself, and for . . . you." She closed her eyes tight.

I didn't know what to say. There was too much to say. To think about. Too much to wish hadn't happened. Old people live in the past, and wishing is what you do when hope runs out. Sufficient for the day is the evil therein.

I watched her struggle with it. In a way I probably represented her past for her, but had never been part of her future. Nor had she been part of mine. We had known each other very well a long time ago when I needed someone to bring me back into the world. But we'd collided with circumstance and the pressures of what we were becoming.

She was older then, and I was older now.

But I couldn't go back.

"Don't take so much on," I said.

"What?" she said, looking up.

"You can't undo it. But you can live with it. You can start by telling Billy the whole story."

"I can't. He'll hate me."

"Be his choice. I'm not excusing what you did or how you handled it. I learned a long time ago that I can't excuse my faults, but I can be forgiven for them. There's a difference. Forgive yourself. He'll be mad at first. Who wouldn't be? You're hard to dislike. He'll come around."

"There's too much I've done to be forgiven."

"Then bury your head in the sand and feel sorry for yourself. Self-pity is a great refuge. You can stay in there forever. Won't even have to come out and—"

"Oh, shut up," she said. "Sometimes you can be a complete bastard. You know that?"

"Years of practice."

She smiled. "We were in love once. Weren't we?"

"We're still in love. Aren't I sipping coffee in your kitchen? Didn't I ride to your rescue?"

She gave me a suspicious look. "Sometimes you go somewhere inside yourself and hide," she said. "You move up on your mountain and try to escape. But life keeps drawing you back down, doesn't it? You can't hide forever, Wyatt."

"Heard that before." I took a deep breath. "I don't know if we were in love or not. Sorry, but that's the truth. I needed you. You were everything I dreamed about and hoped for while I sat in my bunker and listened to the war. I liked being around you. The rhythm of you and me together was nice. But you were looking for more than I could give and deserved more. You helped me when I needed someone and I'll never forget you for that."

She stood and walked to me. I held her and she held me and we hung on for the moment, shielded from the storm.

The phone rang, interrupting the moment. She answered.

"It's for you," she said, holding the phone out. "It's Chick."

I took the phone. "What's up?" I asked.

"You need to get back here," he said. "Been talking to Billy. Some interesting stuff comes out of this kid when he sobers up. He's not always very forthcoming. The truth kind of comes in bits and pieces."

"What have you got?"

"So Billy thinks Jackie B. was blackmailing somebody?" I asked. "What makes him think that?"

"He knows about the little black book," Chick said, sipping at a silver flask. We were down below my cabin taking target practice with our bows. Billy McCall was up the slope in the cabin taking a nap. "Probably not a great idea to let people know you have it. It's also why he was spooked when you told him Burlingame had been killed. Billy has been a bigger part of this whole thing than he has been letting on."

"You mean," I said, "somebody would actually mislead us?"

"Hard to imagine, isn't it? He says there are more weapons than what we've seen."

A cold wind blew down the canyon, rustling the multicolored leaves of the aspen trees, and across the Little Silver River. I could feel and smell snow brewing in the north. Soon this valley and the slope of my mountain would be snow-covered. A few more weeks and I'd winterize the cabin and move to Missouri.

I pulled the string of my Browning X-cellerator compound to anchor and released the string. The arrow buried itself in the heart of the elk silhouette target with a hearty *thwok*.

"We still don't know where the other weapons are stashed." I removed a glove and dug in my pocket and fished out the Mercedes key and the key that didn't fit Jackie's apartment door. I held them up so Chick could see. "I still don't know what this fits."

Burlingame had said he had a regular customer in these guys. That they wanted more and wanted it in volume. So why kill him? Why not just pop him somewhere else? Why kill Turk? And if they were going to whack him out anyway, why bring the money? And why did Jackie want me to go with him, then change his mind?

"For the sake of argument," I said, "let's say Jackie had something on Purvis. What would happen?"

"Montana whacks him. But I don't like it."

"I don't either. Why don't we like it?"

"Because Purvis is too aloof. Too damned nasty. There is nothing Jackie could have on Purvis that would do more than piss him off. Illicit love affair? Strange sexual appetite? The usual stuff people get blackmailed for Purvis does for recreation."

"That, and Jackie would have to be crazy to try it with Purvis. He would be afraid to mess with him." I placed another arrow on the string. "But what if Jackie had something on the congressman? Something that would blow up Purvis's plans to put Braden in the Senate? Would he ace Jackie if that were the case?" I released the arrow and it dug into the target next to my previous effort.

"Sure. But why so much money?"

"What if somebody, say Montana or Skunk Dumont, was in on the blackmail scheme? What if one of them gave Jackie the handle on Braden? Told Jackie what to blackmail Braden with? If they were in it together maybe the bag contained both payoffs."

"One for the guns and one for the blackmail?"

I smiled.

"Aw, that's crazy," Chick said. "But what the hell. The whole thing's crazy."

"Harold Wallace thought there was only thirty thousand."

"Which eliminates him as Jackie's partner."

"Maybe," I said. "But he was tossing Burlingame's apartment. For the money or for information to help him find the other weapons? Or maybe for the little black book I found."

"Which pretty much leaves Montana, Skunk Dumont, and the leader."

"Captain Marvel."

"Who we wouldn't know if he fell over us unless his name was tattooed on his forehead."

Something fell into place in my head. "But whoever Captain Marvel is, he knew Randle Lightfoot and he's important enough for political protection from your friend Donovan."

"Why do you think he knew Lightfoot so well?"

"Lightfoot was a big, strong kid. There was no blood and no sign of struggle. Whoever held him under knew him, knew his habits. Some booze, some pills, then hold the sedated friend under the water. Any struggle would be minimal and sluggish."

Chick took another shot at the target. He set the tip of the bow's limb on the ground and leaned on it. He looked across the river for a moment, then said, "Let's say Jackie was blackmailing the congressman. Braden sends money to pay off Jackie. Purvis sends money to pay for the guns. Purvis tells Montana to whack Jackie . . . Wait, I don't like it. They do Burlingame, they don't know where the rest of the guns are."

"Unless, they know somebody who knows."

"Who?"

I looked up the slope toward the cabin. "I think we may be sitting right on top of the answer."

"I request the privilege of beating the information out of him."

"Sorry. He's Kelly's kid. Makes it a different ball game." I fitted another arrow to the string. I drew the string to anchor and released. The arrow flew off the string. There was a clicking sound as the arrow broke one of Chick's arrows. "Broken arrow," I said. "Sign of peace."

Suddenly, there was a staccato, burbling sound, as if a metallic giant was gargling. Once you've heard it every day for two years you never forget it. It was the rattle of automatic weapons. It echoed down the canyon accompanied by the crashing sound of shattering glass and the splatter-crack of lead smacking wood.

"The cabin," I said. "Billy."

We ran up the slope, bows in hand. I had Burlingame's Walther PPK in a hip holster. It wouldn't be much help against automatic weapons, but more than the bow. I kept the bow in case I could get behind one of the gunmen.

As we neared the cabin, the noise increased, covering our approach. We circled behind the shooters. Meredith's henchmen. Carmine and the redheaded man. They were laying down a fusillade that was tearing up the cabin. They were so intent on the job at hand that they didn't notice Chick and me closing in behind them, nor did they notice when I nocked an arrow and sent it flying to bury itself up to the fletching in the redheaded man's back—right under the scapula on the right side. His back arched and he dropped his Kalashnikov. He was luckier than the Sicilian, who turned around in time to see Chick Easton put a bullet in his mouth. The back of the man's head exploded, his arms flew out, and his body was blown backward.

The noise stopped.

The Irishman was on his knees, groaning and reaching for his weapon, his right arm pulled into his body as if he were a wounded praying mantis. The clear mountain air stank of hot metal and cordite, and the mountains, sparkling with sunlight and multicolored leaves, were silent of animal noise—hushed by the undesirable presence of the man-wolves and the smell of aftershave, sweat, and carnivore breath, and the rolling stench of death.

Red moaned as he crabbed closer to his weapon. I pulled the Walther. "Leave it," I said. "Or you'll never see the Emerald Isle again."

He sat back on his haunches, his face contorted in pain and shock. "Get . . . it out," he said. "Please."

I picked up the Kalashnikov and tossed it down the slope. I looked at my cabin. It was pocked with bright slivers of peeled wood. The windows were gap-toothed with shiny splinters of broken glass, refracting the sunlight at odd angles. "I oughta put one in your throat," I said. "Keep your gun on him, Chick, and I'll get the arrow out."

"Fuck 'im," said Chick. He rolled the hammer back on the big revolver. It made its ratchety triple-clicking noise as it snapped into readiness. He moved closer so the hood could look down the dark hole. "Say hi to Saint Pat when you get there, asshole."

"Pull the trigger, then, ya black-hearted bastard."

"Wait a minute, Chick," I said. "Let's call the sheriff. Let him handle it."

"Wait," said the Irishman. "Aw, mother, my shoulder's on fire. I can't go back inside. Can't stand to be locked up. I'll trade you something."

"What's the trade?"

"Pull the arrow, fix me up, and don't call the constable." He winced. "And I'll tell ya things ya might wish to be knowing."

"We'll see," I said. "I pull the arrow, then you tell me something and I'll decide if it's enough."

Chick said, "Can't I sorta shoot 'im . . . you know, just a little bit?"

I handed Chick the Walther, pulled a lockback knife from my pocket and cut away the man's topcoat, his sports jacket, shirt, and undershirt, so the arrow wouldn't catch when I pulled it through. I couldn't back it out as the friction of the arrow channel dictated continuing forward. I cut material from the shirt to use as bandages. The wound had bled little, and, judging from the entry and exit points of the arrow, I saw no danger in removing it other than infection. I stepped behind the wounded man and sheared the fletching from the end of the arrow so it wouldn't drag, then shaved the hot-glue residue down until I was satisfied I had most of it.

"I need some whiskey," I said to Chick.

"Good idea," he said. He pulled the silver hip flask from his jacket and took a swallow. "Yessir," he said. "Now what?"

I looked at him and waited. He shrugged and handed me the flask. I poured some on the wound—at the entry and the exit— then handed the flask to the Irish hood.

"You're a fine lad," he said. He tilted his head and took a good jolt. "Aye, that's good whiskey. Go ahead, now."

I wound a handkerchief around my right hand and placed my left hand gently on his chest, with the shaft of the arrow between thumb and forefinger. "It'll have to be all at once. If there's a bone splintered, it'll hang up. This isn't going to be any fun. It's going to hurt, so you take another swallow before I pull it through."

"One more tug then into the fire," he said. *"Erin go bragh."* He was swallowing whiskey when I jerked the arrow free from his flesh. He screamed and spat whiskey. I held the bloody shaft in hand as he thrashed and cursed, his teeth clenched.

I poured whiskey on the wound, then padded that with shirt bandages. Removing my belt, I lashed the bandages tightly to him to prevent further bleeding.

Wyatt Storme, backwoods medicine man.

"Waste of good bourbon," Chick said.

I looked at the still form of the Sicilian. A cold breeze blew across his body, fluttering his dark hair. His mouth and eyes were open in mute testament to the surprise that death is. I wondered if his mother knew where he was. Would there be a marker for his grave, and would she come? Could she forgive me my part in his death?

I stood on the hill, autumn's winds washing over me.

Then I walked to the cabin to check on Kelly McArthur's son, Billy.

Billy was all right.

Like the cockroaches that survived the blast at Nagasaki, Billy was all right. I found him hunkered down in the bathtub, his pants down around his ankles.

"I was hanging a rat when I heard the shooting start. I jumped into the tub and waited for it to end. Man, it was like World War Three. Who was doing the shooting?"

"You weren't hit?"

"No. Banged my knee jumping into the tub."

"Good."

"Good that I'm okay or good I bumped my knee."

"You figure it out."

Twenty minutes later, with the redheaded man's wound cleaned and freshly bandaged, I surveyed the damage. Wasn't as bad as I had thought. The thick logs had absorbed the bullets. The east windows were shot out and wind was whistling through them. The television set was a gaping black hole and no loss.

The pockholes from nine-millimeter bullets and broken glass were the biggest problem. Miraculously, the stereo was untouched with the exception of one speaker, which had a corner of its walnut cabinet ripped loose.

The redheaded man's name was Kevin. He told us Meredith had sent him and his dead partner up to "throw a scare into that asshole," meaning me. However, Carmine, still smarting from Chick's handling of him, had wanted more than just a scare. He also told us that Billy had called Purvis for a peace parley. In exchange for protection he had promised Purvis information he wanted.

I glared at Billy McCall. "You're incredible," I said.

He shrugged his shoulders, palms up, in explanation. "Hey, I was just watching out for myself."

"What you're best at," I said. "You called Purvis and gave us up. Oughta break your neck."

"I saw him first," said Chick.

"So what is it you have?" I said to Kevin.

"How am I knowing you'll let me free?"

"You don't. Your other options are worse. If what you tell us is good enough and you dispose of your partner, then I think something can be worked out."

He didn't like it, but he gave the information anyway.

It went like this:

Crispin Purvis was smuggling guns nationwide. Trying to gain a monopoly on the illicit trade west of the Rockies to the coast. He'd already locked up the Denver area. Meredith was in it with him. Kevin didn't know Burlingame.

"They hollow out headstones," said the hood, "and fill them with handguns or cocaine. The bigger guns are transported in false bottoms in coffins—sometimes even with the poor departed soul inside."

"It ain't bad," Chick said. "Who'd check a tombstone or a coffin with a body inside?"

"What's Braden's connection?"

"I don't know him."

"So who pays for the damage to my house?"

"Carmine carries a large amount of cash. 'Flash money,' he calls it. He won't be aneeding it, now."

"How'd you ever hook up with a lowlife like Purvis?"

He smiled a knowing dimpled smile. "How would you think an Irishman ends up in Colorado?"

"IRA?"

He said nothing. Didn't deny it. Didn't confirm it.

There was over two thousand dollars in the dead man's wallet. Not enough to cover the damage, but I could patch the bullet holes myself. I warned Kevin if we saw him again or he went back to Purvis we'd call the cops.

"I've no use for Purvis, anymore," he said. "Time to head across the sea." He left and took Carmine with him. Carmine didn't object.

I made Billy retrieve spent shell casings while Chick and I built fires where blood had splattered the leaves. That done, we pulled Billy inside and sat him down.

"I need a drink," Billy said.

"No booze," I said, "until you answer some questions. You've been holding back all along and that's over now. You talk or I'll toss you to the sharks. They'll be glad to see you. You've had more to do with the gun business than you've been telling."

"Just a beer," he said. "All I need."

"Start talking."

"All right. All right. What do you want to know?"

"Where are the other weapons?"

"Locked up in a storage place. One of those places with all the garages where you store your boat and stuff. Place called Safe-T U-Store."

Matched the key in my pocket. Bingo.

"Who was Burlingame blackmailing?"

"Not sure."

"Was it Joring Braden?"

"Could be. I don't know." I looked at him. "I don't. That's straight. He just said he had some shit on a 'big dog.' That's all he said."

I handed Burlingame's black book to him, open to the page with the strange code on it. "This make any sense to you?" He looked at it for several moments and handed it back. I examined the cryptic numbers and letters again:

```
CP—5/18/67
MB—1-191-1768
JB—100 Grand St., Denver
CP—Mercedes-Benz, 10K, like new, $35,000
J/CS—BAR #5554326
```

"No," Billy said.
"What about Randle Lightfoot?"
"I told you. He hung out with Jackie some."
"That all?"
"All I know."
"What about Janet Sterling?"
"He sold her some flake, now and then."
"This code doesn't mean anything to you." He looked at it some more.
"No."
"Been thinking about it," Chick said, the smoke trail from his cigarette framing his face. "CP is Crispin Purvis and JB must be Joring Braden. But the date 5/18/67 means nothing to me and there is no 100 Grand Street in Denver. Maybe it means one hundred thousand dollars. If so, it could mean Braden paid him one hundred Gs in extortion money. Or it could be the price of drugs or guns. There is no 191-1768 phone number in the area. Why the ad for the Mercedes? Another payoff? I'm lost on the last one."

Something tugged at the back of my mind. Something Harold Wallace had said.

I picked up the phone and dialed Sandy's office number.

She picked up the phone and I asked her what Senator Braden's son's name was.

"He has two," she said. "Which one do you want?"

"The one killed in Vietnam."

"Wait a minute. I can find out."

"Hold on," I said. "Can you give me the date of his death?"

She said she could. I waited. Chick pulled two beers from the refrigerator. He looked at me before handing one to Billy. I shrugged in resignation. Chick resumed looking at the black book. Three minutes passed before Sandy came back on the line.

"Got it. Senator Braden's son's name was Michael and he was killed in action on January 7, 1968."

"You sure it wasn't May 18, 1967?"

"Positive."

"Small wonder you're the top reporter in Colorado."

"Bet you say that to every beautiful journalist."

"Only if they come across."

"Don't get your hopes up," she said. "I need a favor. Could you go by Father's and pick up a book I left there? It's Mary Higgins Clark's newest."

I said I could and hung up the phone. "MB stands for Michael Braden," I said. "He was listed KIA on January 7, 1968."

"Matches the numbers," Chick said.

"What do you mean?"

"K is the eleventh letter in the alphabet. I is the ninth and A is first. KIA. Eleven-nine-one. That leaves 1768, which can be read 1/7/68. January 7, 1968."

"That's pretty good," I said. "And all this time I thought you were just another bounty hunter with a drinking problem."

"What problem? I drink all the time. It's not a problem."

"Doesn't give us much. So what if he died on that date?"

"Why bury it in code?" Chick asked. "Why kill Jackie then send a guy to toss his apartment? They wanted this book. But why kill Lightfoot? They don't know where the other guns are."

"What if something strange happened January 7, 1968? Harold Wallace said he'd been discharged from the military because of his implication in the death of a congressman's son. Had to be Michael Braden. Said he was discharged on a section eight rather than take a murder rap. Now, he's working for Purvis, who had to be the rogue Aussie operative. Wallace lied to me. His connection to Purvis goes back twenty-five years. Purvis pretends not to be interested in Burlingame's guns, but sends three guys who work for him to make the pickup."

"And to whack Jackie Burlingame."

"Jackie had something on Joring Braden. Something to do with Michael Braden's death in Vietnam. Something big enough to knock him out in the political arena. But what? Purvis found out and had Montana or someone kill Jackie, which made Braden even more his puppet. Not only had he killed the blackmailer, Purvis now knew the secret."

"If Jackie knew what happened, then Purvis probably knows," I said. "Who else?"

"Congressman Braden."

"Anybody else?"

"I'm hungry," Billy said.

"Eat the beer can," I said. "And shut up."

"Don't get hostile."

I was getting tired of being around Billy McCall. Didn't care if he was Kelly's son. "You know, Billy. I'm through listening to your voice. Why don't you contribute something besides noise?"

He shrugged. "Why not? Couldn't do any worse than you geniuses. You guys weren't so busy playing Sherlock Holmes you could answer your own questions."

"Meaning what?"

"Meaning, shit-for-brains, that the other person who knows what happened to Mike Braden might be your old buddy Matt Jenkins."

Years ago the Giants had a cornerback named Ivory Conners. He'd been around the league for a long time and caused me much grief. For some reason I couldn't shake him when we played them. He had the unnerving habit of hitting me at the precise moment the ball arrived. Worse, he had an irritating laugh he shared with me each time he hit me or deflected another pass. He always had an extra shove or comment when the play ended. That, and constantly throwing it in my face that he had my number.

So when the Cowboys traded for him late in his career I wasn't overjoyed—partly because I didn't like him and partly because I wanted to burn him big time, just once before he quit. But old Ivory was smart. Smarter than a young wide receiver.

"Boy, you can't take it personal," he said. "I just take advantage of you. Mess with you and get you mad. Throws you off your game. You're a hothead. Besides, you've got a habit. You always give a look opposite the way you're gonna cut, just as you come off the line. Think you fooling people and you fool most. But old Ivory's been around. Don't get into routines and don't let your feelings affect the job. Emotion is not part of it, whitebread. Just get the job done." Then he smiled the smile that had been in a dozen commercials.

I learned from that. And now, driving back into the flats, I learned it again. I had a blind spot where Matt was concerned and didn't want to think he was more involved than he'd said, and especially didn't like hearing it from Billy McCall, but it needed to be checked out. I called Matt's office and found out he was at his gun club. I knew its location. First, I'd stop by Duncan Collingsworth's hotel and pick up Sandy's book. I called his room and the line was busy, so he was there.

Chick was in the passenger seat, drinking beer and bobbing his head to the Rolling Stones' "Street Fighting Man." Billy was sitting in the backseat, sulking.

"Where we going?" Billy asked.

"Don't worry about it," I said.

"Don't you guys listen to any music from this century?"

"You mean that drone-syndrome crap they spit out of computers and play on MTV?" Chick said.

"I need to see Cynthia sometime."

"Who's Cynthia?" Chick asked me.

"His forever love that he cheats on. Matt's niece."

"You mean Matt's going to be related to the little bacteria?"

I said nothing. There was no exit in that direction.

Duncan was staying at the Denver Sheraton out on the interstate. Sandy wanted him to stay with her, but he didn't want to be a burden. We parked in the lot and went inside. Chick and Billy went into the lounge while I took the elevator up to the fifth floor of the main building. I stood in front of room 512 and lifted my hand to knock.

I heard voices inside. Duncan's and a female's. Was he entertaining? Should I leave? If I didn't get the book Sandy would think I forgot. Just because there was a woman in his room didn't mean something was going on. Besides, he was postpubescent.

I knocked.

Footsteps muffled by thick carpet. As they neared the door I heard the familiar female voice say, "The room service is quick here."

I wanted to be gone from there. No mistaking the voice and too late to leave. Everything fell into place. Why hadn't I seen it coming? I had the pieces. I'd been blind just as I'd been blind with Matt.

Duncan opened the door, and his eyes widened in recognition of his future son-in-law. Past his shoulder I saw the woman I was afraid I'd see. A woman who had complicated my life before and would now complicate it again. Perhaps beyond repair.

Kelly Jenkins.

I watched her eyes close in pain, her cheeks flush. Duncan stood, hand on the doorknob, eyes expressionless. Nobody said anything for too long. Finally, Duncan said, "Wyatt. Come in. Please."

"I . . . just stopped by to pick up Sandy's book."

He nodded. "Certainly." He walked woodenly to a nightstand, picked up the book, and walked back, the book hanging from his hand. He handed it to me and I thanked him.

"Wyatt, I—"

"No," I said, shaking my head. "It's okay."

We looked at each other momentarily, knowing what the other knew, then he nodded. I turned and walked away. I was at the elevator when Kelly caught up to me.

"Wait a minute, Wyatt," she said.

I turned and looked at her.

"There's nothing going on here," she said.

"A little late for that, isn't it?"

She slapped me. I took it. Probably deserved it.

"I'm sorry, Wyatt," she said. She placed a cool hand on the spot she'd struck.

"Forgive me," she said.

"I do."

We stood and looked at the carpet.

"What are you going to do with this?"

I stepped inside the elevator and pushed a button.

"Live with it," I said.

The elevator doors closed and I went down.

A thousand things went through my head. I felt like a bit player, working for scale in a bad soap opera. Billy McCall was Sandy's half-brother. Worse, though time had dulled some of the impact, my future father-in-law and I shared something better left unshared. Duncan was the invisible force, the unknown man who had drawn Kelly away from me twenty years ago. This was the unspoken shame that had driven Duncan away from the world of academe and put his head in a bottle—the source of Sandy's teenage trauma. Which is why the sexual revolution was a big fat bust. We'd run a big tab—unwanted pregnancy, venereal disease, divorce, fractured homes, angry children, and the nuclear bomb of the whole thing: AIDS. We'd laughed and played, couching responsibility in semantic terms, giving short shrift to the truth. We are very selfish, spoiled children. Now it was time to pay up, and rather than make hard choices, we declared bankruptcy and erected new semantic buzzwords, skewing reality to fit desires.

Duncan and Kelly had left Colorado State around the same time. I didn't see Kelly again until Matt and I became friends. At the time I thought it interesting to come across an old girlfriend. Glad she'd married well and vice versa. If she'd married an Alaskan pipeline worker or some Silicon Valley executive I would never have known. I'd prefer not to have known. I'd spent the last ten years trying not to know.

Life is not an even bet. You erect these little fences around your life, then you start putting up the framework and insulate. Then, just as you start to put in the gate and decorate a little, you notice the torn places in the fences, the leaks in the roof, the trampled places in the back where the thief has sneaked in and taken things you'd forgotten were there.

And the part that hurt—ached where there was no way to reach—was that it had taken so long to build.

What would I tell Sandy? Nothing. I would keep it to myself. Which created another dilemma. One of the cornerstones of our relationship was honesty. Nothing held back. But I sometimes hedged, neglecting to tell her of the danger I often encountered, even courted, tempering the telling of it. A year ago I had killed two mafia hit men. They had been hired to kill me. She knew the first part, but not the last.

And I was not being honest with myself. I had pretended to accompany Jackie Burlingame on Matt's behalf, which was only partly true.

What was true?

I'd wanted to do it. Wanted to taste the bitter edge of danger, smell the aroma of my own fear. I was a mainline danger and adrenaline freak. There was no cure.

But I could not tell Sandy about her father. No. That was up to Duncan, if he chose to do so. And if he didn't, well, then I would respect that also. I couldn't live his life for him. Had enough trouble with my own.

When I hit the lounge, Chick and Sandy's half-brother were drinking Scotch and playing liar's poker. Chick was winning all the money.

"You're cheating," Billy said, handing Chick his dollar.

"The essence of the game," Chick said. "It's why they call it 'liar's poker.' I'm a better liar than you are. I do it convincingly and with panache. You? You're just a liar."

"Least I'm not some schmuck-ass bounty hunter."

"You're right. Better to be some bottom-feeder druggie with the morals of a weasel. Three sevens." He saw me. "Hey, Wyatt. You ready? I've been fleecing the sheep here and it's been . . . Hey, you don't look so good."

I sat down next to Billy. "Give me a little room, huh?" I said.

"How much do you need, man?"

I ran my hand over my face and said, "Billy, why is it every time I talk to you I feel the urge to flush."

"Hey, man. Don't be—"

I leaned into his face. "You aren't getting it, are you? I hear your voice again this month I'm going to drop you off a building. Shut up." He put his hands up and made a ceremony of running two fingers across his mouth in a zipper motion. Then he made a little twisting motion and mimed putting the key in his pocket. I gritted my teeth.

"Much as I'd love to see you bounce Billy boy around the place, I'd say we're having a little problem with transferral," Chick said. "What's eating on you?"

I looked down at my hands.

Chick said, "Billy, take a walk."

"Who wants to stay here?" he said, getting up.

"Don't wander off, though," Chick said. Billy gave him the finger. "Charming youngster. Next time he does that I'm gonna put my thumb on his carotid. What's the matter, man?"

"Nothing."

"You're going to bullshit me, right? It's me. Chick. Your ace sidekick and mental superior. You sneeze, I say gesundheit. You cut, I bleed. But, it's okay. You wanta play deaf mute, you got your reasons."

I told him. Everything. About Billy. About Kelly. About Duncan. About Duncan and Kelly. About Kelly and Billy. He didn't interrupt. When I finished he ordered another drink and I ordered one, too. He raised the apostrophe eyebrow at that and lit a cigarette, took a deep drag, burning a half inch off the white wrapper, then blew a large cloud of smoke at the ceiling.

"Son," he said. "Somebody just tossed you in the shit silo, gave you a spoon and told you to dig."

The waiter returned with the drinks and set them on the table in front of us. I looked at mine. Looked at the golden-brown liquid. It had been a long time. I reached a hand for it but Chick reached out and pulled the glass away from me.

"No," he said. "Don't do that. One of the things I like best about you is you're always you and not somebody else. Don't start doing things make you somebody else."

I shook my head and said, "Ain't life swell?"

"Life is just one damn thing after another," he said. "We come expecting one thing and go away disappointed."

"Poor Sandy. What is she going to think if she finds out?"

"There you go. Bullshitting again. Bad enough when you do it to me. Worse when you do it to yourself."

"I'm not in the mood for your whiskey-colored insights."

"Because you know I'm right," he said.

"Yeah. You're a regular sage."

He chuckled low in his throat and took a swallow of my drink. "Agh," he said, grimacing. "Bar whiskey. See? They had you spotted for a novice. Good thing I'm here to save you from it. So, what's it gonna be? We gonna sit here and watch you pout all day?"

"I'm not pouting."

"Bullshit, bullshit, bullshit. You can change the words but the song remains the same."

"Why don't you get off me?"

"May I speak honestly?"

"No."

"Thank you. As one of two living people who can kick your butt around the block and make you like it I'm going to tell you something you don't want to hear. First, you don't feel bad for Sandy. Or her dad. It's the white-picket-fence dreamland you've erected in your mind you're lamenting. Your perfect life with Sandy. The perfect life you think will redeem all the past failures and trespasses. But somebody just drove a shit train through your flowerbed and you don't like it. You can pretend it's something else, but that's what it is. And it's crap to lay it on your selfless concern for Sandy. Not to mention it's patronizing. She's a grown-up. Probably the most woman and finest lady I've ever met. And she's yours. Quit beating yourself up over her as if you didn't deserve her. You don't, of course." He leaned back and sipped his Scotch. "So, there it is. The kind of outstanding off-the-cuff advice you would have to pay a psychiatrist three hundred dollars an hour for."

He was close. Which was the worst part. I hated that he had seen it before I did. I looked at him and smiled.

"You think you know everything," I said.

"And you're a cluck ex–football player with no job who orders bar whiskey then doesn't drink it. Crybaby jock mama's boy."

" 'Crybaby jock mama's boy'?" I said. "What kind of talk is that for an ace sidekick? And just who else do you think can kick my butt around the block and make me like it?"

He gave me a superior smile and said: "Sandra Collingsworth."

I rubbed my chin and squinted one eye at him. Couldn't think of anything to say.

He sipped his Scotch, leaned back, sighed deeply and said, "Sometimes I get tired of being outstanding."

When we got up to leave we were unable to find Billy McCall.

"That little ferret," Chick said. "Whenever you don't want him around, he's around. Whenever you want him around, which isn't often, he's gone."

"We ought to try to find him," I said.

"He's on his own."

"What if they find him and whack him out?"

"Stop trying to cheer me up."

The Outfitter Club was a large complex set in the rising plains east of Denver, complete with swimming pool, skeet range, clubhouse, lounge with smoking room, and an indoor shooting range. The clubhouse foyer was wood and leather, decorated with outdoor prints by Remington and glass-fronted gun cases filled with Parker shotguns and Weatherby rifles. Big game heads from around the globe jutted from walls. A huge reddish-gold grizzly, at full height on hind legs, teeth bared, stood guard in the lobby. Next to it was a trophy bull elk, its rack magnificent and spreading like the boughs of an oak tree. A plaque at the foot of the elk read:

SIX-POINT BULL ELK
taken by
Matthew Jenkins
Nov. 15, 1985

"Nice elk," Chick said. "You think they got Teddy Roosevelt stuffed around here, somewhere?"

"No," I said. "That'd be tacky. They do have Cleveland Amory in the lounge with an apple in his mouth."

A man in a maroon blazer with a gold-plated badge that said he was the club director asked if he could help us.

"Yes, you can," said Chick. "I'm Marlin Perkins and this is my faithful gun-bearer, Jim. Doesn't speak a word of English you know. I'd like to donate a Cape buffalo I stopped in full flight with a slingshot. If he hadn't been carrying the slingshot I don't know how I'd ever have bagged him."

The supervisor looked confused. "I'm afraid I don't understand."

"Ignore him," I said. "We're friends of Matt Jenkins. He asked us to meet him here."

"Oh," he said, relieved to find out we weren't lunatics or representatives from Fund for Animals. "Yes. Mr. Storme and Mr. Easton. He's on the range. If you'll follow me."

He led us downstairs to a door he opened with a key. "All the members have a key," he said. "Follow the corridor. There are windows outside the range. Mr. Jenkins should be on number seven. Enjoy your visit."

We walked down the corridor. Through windows various members of both sexes fired into silhouette targets of elk, moose, deer, and bear. When we reached number seven we saw Matt Jenkins, ear protectors on, firing a .40-caliber Glock into a target used by law enforcement agencies—the silhouette of a man. The only target like it on the range.

I pressed a button outside the door and a red light flashed on the bench in front of Matt. He turned, waved to us, pressed a button next to the light, and then there was a sharp clicking noise in the door, followed by a buzzing. We opened the unlocked door and walked in.

"Sharpening my eye," he said, pulling the protectors off his head, draping them across his shoulders. On the firing bench was a snub-nosed .38 and a Colt government .45. Strapped at his waist was a Colt Peacemaker holstered in a tooled leather belt. First Chick, then Coy Montana, now Matt. Every man a gunslinger.

"You expecting a Marine assault?" I asked.

"Let me show you something. I've been practicing." He handed us each a pair of ear protectors. That done, he laid the Glock down on the table and took a bent-legged stance with his right hand dangling near the holstered Peacemaker like Audie Murphy. I looked at Chick, who raised the apostrophe eyebrow he'd brought back from Indochina. Matt rolled his shoulders, then drew the Colt and fanned five shots at the silhouette. He put the six-shooter back in the holster, shrugged out of his ear protectors. "Take a look," he said.

We removed our ear protectors. Using the tripod-mounted spotting scope I saw four bullet holes in the target. One in the thigh, one nicked the left elbow, and one that hit the border outside the outlined figure. The best shot had struck the target in what would be just below the lower right rib of a real man.

"Look," he said. "Put two in the silhouette with the fast draw." I didn't make any comment about three shots that missed or caused little damage. "Won't be long before I'm a regular Wild Bill Hickok." I also didn't comment that Hickok was shot in the back while dying of venereal disease.

"Did you know Burlingame was blackmailing Congressman Braden?" I asked.

"Not surprised," he said, ejecting spent cartridges from the Colt. "That's the way Jackie did things."

"What would Burlingame have on Braden?"

He leaned back from the waist and looked sideways at me. "Why ask me?"

"You're the only person I haven't considered."

He holstered the gun. "Kelly called just a little while ago. Just before you got here."

I looked at Chick and then back at Matt.

"It's okay," Matt said. "I don't mind that Chick hears this. She told me everything. I've known everything for a long time now. About Billy. And about Kelly and Duncan Collingsworth. I even know about Kelly trying to seduce you in my kitchen. Said you turned her down flat."

"She's got it backward," I said. "I tried to put the move on her and she ran me off."

Matt laughed. "She said you'd say that." He shook his head, smiling. "Boy, there's only one like you, Wyatt. Something I need to tell you. Both of you." He looked down at the floor, then out toward the target silhouette. "I'm not trying to do a number on you, but I'm dying. Cancer."

The heavy smell of cordite took on a funereal aroma in the vaultlike cubicle. The walls closed in. Chick was tight-lipped for a change, considering Matt with weary eyes, eyes that spoke of distant wars and other comrades fading with time.

"Shit," Chick said.

"Sorry, Matt," I said. "I didn't know."

"We've known each other too long for sympathy. I don't even like telling you. I've had a good run. No complaints. They found it a year ago," he said. "Thought they'd got it all. Took some pretty extreme measures, in fact. Funny thing to do to a cattleman. Made a steer out of me. Oh, get those asshole looks off your faces. It gave me another year of life. Kelly's been without a real man since then."

"Aw shit, Matt," said Chick. "Save it for somebody else."

"I'm with Chick. You're no less a man for that."

"Yeah," said Chick. "I often go longer than that, which I can't understand, breathtaking handsome as I am."

"Little easier to understand than you might think," I said.

Matt laughed. I wanted to laugh with him but was afraid it would echo in the room with the emptiness of a child humming in the dark.

Matt said, "Kelly stood with me through all this. She's a beautiful woman. A vital woman. She has the needs of a vital woman. I told her she needed to find someone. Someone to fulfill those needs. She refused. But I could see the signs. We both became irritable. Her because of the repression. Me because I couldn't do anything about it. Finally, she mentioned you, Wyatt. Don't be uncomfortable. It's done.

"When you found Kelly and Duncan together they were discussing what to do about Billy. There is nothing between them now except the son they created years ago. They've both paid enough, since. He was before me. So were you. Doesn't mean anything. Time they quit hating themselves. They discussed whether to tell Billy they were his parents or not. I think they'll tell him and accept the consequences."

I nodded. I was embarrassed. Unusual for me.

"What if I'd taken Kelly up on her offer?"

"Might as well be somebody I like and respect as some drunken cowboy on a one-night stand."

"I've still got to ask you about a few things," I said. "Can't help it if it appears cold-blooded. What did Burlingame have on Braden, and what hold does Purvis have?"

"If I tell you will you let it go?"

I looked at him.

"What I thought," he said. "How about you give some thought to backing off for my sake if I tell you?"

I nodded. "Okay."

"Tell me, first, what you've found out so far."

It took twenty minutes to tell him everything—about the

weapons Burlingame had held back, about Purvis's shady past and gun dealing. What we'd found out about the funeral parlor and memorial headstones and smuggling of guns. About Randle Lightfoot and the Langley agency's interest. About the mysterious black Beretta and the strange code in Burlingame's little black book.

"You care if I see the book?"

"Don't have it with me," I said.

"I can tell you what it says," Chick said.

"You memorized it?" I said.

He shrugged. "Haven't burnt all my brain cells yet. Just most of them." Using the range phone, Matt asked for a pen and paper. A young man in a white shirt and bow tie brought a beige pad with the club's logo across the top. Chick wrote down the code and told him what we'd surmised so far. Matt looked at it for several moments before reaching into his wallet and producing a slender case with phone numbers and addresses on it.

"That first number," he said. "The one that looks like a date—5/18/67? Purvis's phone number is 555-1867. It's unlisted. You guys are right about Mike Braden's KIA date."

"How do you know we're right?" I asked.

"Because Michael Braden is not dead. That's what Burlingame had on Braden. And," he said, "because I was there."

Michael Braden's death in Vietnam was faked," Matt Jenkins told us. "An elaborate hoax. Congressman Braden, like any father, was afraid his son would be killed in the Tet offensive."

"Thought Tet was a surprise attack."

"To the public and to the soldiers in Vietnam, maybe, but the CIA reported that the NVA was gearing up for a major offensive for the Tet holiday."

"Who knew about it?"

"A few generals and a few select congressmen and senators."

"Why didn't they get ready?"

"Didn't believe it," said Matt, loading the clip for the Glock. "Couldn't believe it. It would have made them look bad if the attack came even if they made it privy to intelligence and operations."

"And," Chick said, "they would have looked bad if they reported it and it didn't occur."

"That's right."

"Doesn't make sense," I said.

"You were there," Chick said to me. "What did make sense? It was the turkey shoot of the century. See the hill. Take the hill. Count the bodies. Abandon the hill. Tune in tomorrow for the same fucking charade, the same tune, sponsored by the people who brought you the war."

"If they'd reported it and asked for reinforcements and no attack occurred it would have looked like the Pentagon was just jacking Congress for more bucks," said Matt. "It was an election year."

"So they just let Tet happen?"

"Pretty much. And by that time, the brass had blown so much smoke that nobody believed them when they reported they had dealt the NVA a serious defeat, which *was* the truth."

"So where is Michael Braden now?"

"I don't know," said Matt.

"How do you know he's alive, then?"

Matt palmed the loaded clip into the Glock and said, "Because I helped them cover up his fake death." He told us the story. He had been part of the contingent which, along with Harold Wallace, smoked the Vietnamese black marketeers. One of the black market hoods was a Frenchman, the same height and coloring as Michael Braden. They dressed him up in Braden's uniform, hung Braden's tags around his neck, shotgunned him in the face, and Michael took a powder. There was little time for the niceties of verification in Nam, and as Congressman Braden was in on the subterfuge no official fuss was raised. Michael Braden was free from the horrors of Vietnam, but was also cut adrift of his identity and his country.

"We were given a healthy cut of the booty and promised more when we got home."

I got a sick feeling at the pit of my stomach. "Matt, tell me you didn't sell guns that were used to kill American GIs."

"No. I did take the money to cover Braden's desertion, though." His eyes dropped. "I'm not very proud of that moment. I've had to live with it a lot of years."

"If the government knew about Purvis, why didn't they take him out? Or arrest him?"

"We were operating under the authority of the CIA at the time. Purvis was helping them smoke out the double agents and giving them inside info about who was dealing guns and contraband among the ARVN and South Vietnamese citizenry. He got so good at it that he continued in the gun business after the war ended. But Purvis didn't know about the phony KIA."

I chewed on it for a bit. Congressman Braden, who wanted to be Senator Braden, had faked his son's death while sending other sons to die in his place. Thus, the switch from hawk to dove. How had Burlingame found out? Burlingame had probably told his drinking buddy Randle Lightfoot, who had been killed for knowing. Or maybe just because somebody *thought* he might know. Burlingame had used his knowledge to extort money from Braden and finally to weasel his way into the gun operation. Purvis had found out and ended the nuisance of Burlingame's interference. Now, Purvis was pulling Braden's strings. The White House needed Braden because of his important position on several committees integral to the administration's success. To that end they had sent the CIA to protect Braden.

Something clicked into place in my head. It was a long shot but when I inserted it into the drama it made the thing make more sense. I had an idea who Michael Braden was. I said nothing at the moment, but kept the thought as a hole card. I needed a picture of Michael Braden. Sandy would be able to get me one. However, I still didn't have the complete answer. I still didn't know who Captain Marvel was, nor did I know why so much money was involved when only part of the munitions had been delivered the day I accompanied Jackie Burlingame.

"So now you know what I know. And some things I didn't want to tell. Will you back off and let me handle it myself? I need to do this for myself. You've seen me fast-draw."

"Fast doesn't matter," I said to Matt. "You've got to take your time and make sure."

"I don't have any more time," Matt said.

The room was too small for conversation.

I called Sandy and asked her to find a picture of Michael Braden. She said she'd try. I told her what had occurred. Told her about Matt's cancer, which upset her. I left out the part about her father. One blow at a time.

We drove out to the Safe-T U-Store, a complex of low Butler-style buildings arranged in long rows separated by gravel aisles. We tried the Safe-T key on several doors until we found it. Fourth row, fifth door.

Inside the garagelike building was a Honda motorcycle, some steel patio furniture, a sixteen-foot Bass Tracker boat, and at the rear of the garage, a pile of boxes and crates with a tarp draped over them. Underneath the tarp were rectangular crates painted in desert camouflage with the words U.S. ARMY stenciled on them. We opened one. Inside was an M-60 machine gun. Checking several other crates we found grenades, Browning and Beretta handguns, M-16 rifles, AK-47 rifles, grenade launchers, grenade fuses, a half-case of C-4 plastique and the grand prize, a half dozen AT-4 Viper antitank weapons. I pirated one of the Browning pistols. It was identical to my own.

"Let's call up a couple guys and take over Colorado," Chick said. "You can be emperor and I'll be in charge of the treasury and the Coors brewery."

"There ought to be something we can do with this," I said. My voice sounded strange in the hollowness of the tin building.

"We could put up a sign, go into business. 'Ever wanted to blow up your county? Mount a counterinsurgency against that troublesome family down the street? Are you tired of that kid who drives his car past your house late at night with his radio blasting? If so, come to Revolution City, where you'll be able to get that hard-to-find antitank weapon. Wrap your fingers around our fragment grenades and you'll never shop anywhere else.' "

While Chick rambled on, I spotted another tarp near the west wall. It covered something long and low. I walked over and pulled back the heavy tarp. Underneath was something out of a science-fiction movie. They looked like guns, but not like any guns I'd seen before.

"What the hell's that?" Chick said.

"I don't know. Looks like some kind of machine gun."

"Let's get a closer look." He kneeled by the long weapons, felt along the barrel, examined the breech. He whistled lowly and chuckled.

"You know what it is?" I said.

"Think so. These are aircraft machine guns. Probably off a jet or something like it. Doesn't look American. Maybe off a Mig. These guys are nuts."

We covered them with the tarp. Did the same for the crates.

"What now?" Chick said. He started to light a cigarette, looked around, changed his mind. He removed the cigarette from his mouth and stuck it in his pocket.

"I need to get hold of Younger and tell him what's going on."

"You do that and he'll be over here confiscating crap and asking cop questions. You know how he is."

"It's time to let the cops handle things. What you pay taxes for. Cliff will take care of this. He'll call in the ATF and they'll clean this up."

"Great plan," Chick said. "What connects Purvis to these guns? How come you have a key? How did you find this? What do you mean you know who killed Jackie Burlingame?"

"Always a pessimist."

"Dumb idea. One of your dumbest. Cops'll get the guns, bug you with questions. Purvis and Montana and Braden will all walk away from this another day older and infinitely more cautious from now on."

"So what's your idea?"

"Sit on it for a while. We got the guns. And the money. Purvis wants both. Makes him look bad to get stiffed. Pretty soon he'll get suspicious of his people, get irritable. Maybe he'll make a mistake."

"Something else bothers me," I said. "Let's say Jackie Burlingame was aced because he was blackmailing Braden, and Purvis didn't like it. Why was Randle Lightfoot killed?"

"Simple. Jackie told him he was blackmailing Braden."

"Maybe. If Jackie's off the board, Braden no longer gets blackmailed, Purvis removes unwanted baggage and gains exclusive rights to Braden. We know three of the soldiers from the day Jackie was killed—Montana, Dumont and Wallace. But who was Captain Marvel? And . . . here's the real kicker. If Michael Braden is alive, where is he? And if he's alive, did Jackie tell Lightfoot who he was?"

Chick smiled. "That's pretty good, Storme. Michael Braden has an interest in keeping his existence a mystery."

"Everybody involved has an interest in keeping Michael Braden's existence a secret—his father, Purvis—even the White House. We find Michael Braden and we can put this all together."

"We better find him before they find out we're looking for him."

I nodded. "When we find him maybe he'll tell us who Captain Marvel is."

The sun had disappeared, transforming the sun-dappled mountain into an inky, cold hill as I hammered the last sheet of plywood into place over the broken windows. I had called a glass company, but they wouldn't be able to come up until Monday, five days from now. I had been insistent, but the guy had a good point when he said, "It's too late to get up there today. You don't exactly live down the block, y'know."

So, until Monday, I would have to put up with plywood or freeze to death. I chose plywood and 3M plastic. It cost me a fifth of Glenlivet Scotch, as Chick was in a single-malt phase, but between us we were able to winterize the last window. That done, I built a huge fire in the natural stone fireplace and made a pot of coffee. My fingers were stiff from the cold and from swinging the hammer. While I was building the fire, Chick cut up onions and browned deerburger for chili. He added tomato sauce and beans to the meat and seasoned the whole thing. I kept a watchful eye on the proceedings, as I remembered his hangover remedy. On the radio, the weatherman was predicting a cold front including snow by the first of the week.

We ate chili and drank coffee, and the warmth from them spread through my body. A satisfying sensation of spent energy and fatigue settled in my shoulders. I put an Otis Redding tape on the stereo and his rich voice filled the room, singing "Cigarettes and Coffee." Opened my cigar humidor and selected a Hemingway Masterpiece, clipped it and lit it slowly with a wood kitchen match. The heady aroma began to fill the room.

I offered the box to Chick and he chose an H. Upmann Monarch. He lighted his with a kitchen match, struck off his thumbnail. We settled back, secure in a masculine cocoon of tobacco smoke and Otis Redding soul. After a few puffs, I retrieved my Browning compound bow and began waxing the strings with a beeswax stick in anticipation of the early morning hunt we had been putting off while we ran around playing crimebusters.

"So," Chick said, holding his glass of Scotch up to the firelight. "Kelly Jenkins tried to hit on you?"

"Halfhearted attempt," I said.

"Hmm," he said.

"What's that mean?"

"Just hmm," he said, smiling and rolling his cigar between his fingers.

I waxed the bowstring. It made a low-decibel hum as I stroked the wax across it. The fire popped and sizzled in the fireplace.

"Kelly Jenkins, huh?" he said.

"You trying to say something?"

"You are the man of steel if you resisted her. She's looking for fulfillment, shoulda called me. I've been stoking up on beta-carotene."

"She probably wanted someone of her species."

"My Indian name is Ever Ready."

"I'm worried about Matt."

"You're afraid he'll cowboy Purvis and Montana."

I nodded.

"Me too," Chick said.

"We can't hover over him."

"He's a big boy now."

We awoke at three A.M., drank coffee, pulled on coveralls and boots. Grabbed our bows and walked into the darkness of the Rockies. Using pocket flashlights, we made our way to our stands and waited for daylight, our breath forming steamy clouds in the rarefied air.

The sunlight pushed back the night and slipped and painted its way across meadow and slope, revealing a skin of frost on the forest floor. Multicolored aspens and emerald spruce trees stretched across the mountains as the sky shifted from early morning golden orange into azure. A magpie croaked from somewhere up the ridge and was answered by the regal screech of an eagle drifting on thermal waves. No honking cars and sirens. No politics. No reserved parking lots. No temptations.

I thought about Kelly Jenkins. Thought about my self-imposed abstinence, a kind of penance for past excesses. There was a peace in it, a fibrous inner strength that fed energies and built comfort zones. I have long been suspicious of people who defined themselves by sexual prowess and preference. We are more than that. More than beasts that must be fed and sated. We think. We reason. We live. We love. Love and reason separate us from animals. And as we reason and love, we are able to hope. And hope enables us to resist those things that would enslave us. Resistance, not capitulation, is liberty. As Hemingway puts it, "Gluttony takes the pain out of having to be a man."

And yet the essence of Kelly lay on my mind, the scent of her lingered, a bittersweet residue of love's memory, from which there is no escape, only periods of respite.

I was shaken from introspection by the haunting, low bugle of a bull elk. A ghostly, ancient sound that sent a cool electric shiver down my neck, as thrilling as a Beethoven flourish.

I circled upwind of the sound, careful of my footsteps. With a bow you get one shot and then only after considerable time and effort. Weeks could pass without another opportunity. Every step, every movement was important. The moaning of the elk sounded again, seeping through the aspens like a love song. Closer.

Gingerly, I picked my way through the trees. I could hear him moving about. Soon, if I did everything right, I would have him. I was doing everything right.

He stepped into view. His rack was magnificent, spreading like the boughs of an oak tree, more like beams than antlers, the tines sparkling with frost. His dark mane contrasted with the buff color of his large body. Steam rose from his nostrils and his mouth was wet with the juice of his desire. He raised his head and bellowed into the mountains.

At such times the shot didn't matter. The experience was manifest. The mind was a camera, preserving the moment forever to be called up to warm a chill night or sweeten a cup of coffee by some campfire. The part of the hunt nonhunters will never understand. You don't have to kill to enjoy the hunt. But the kill is an inevitable part of the hunt.

I raised the bow.

The fickle mountain wind shifted slightly as I pulled the string to anchor. The elk snorted and searched the slope with his keen eyes. As he did so he moved to a spot that gave me a tougher shooting angle. A killing shot would be difficult. Not impossible, but difficult. I do not shoot unless assured of a killing shot. I didn't come to stick him so he could run off. He was more than a mere target, he was the monarch of this mountain.

I waited, holding the bow at full draw. A cool northern breeze chilled my neck. The bull scented me, turned, and bounded away. The opportunity had been missed. Foiled by forces be-

yond my control. There would be another day, another encounter, where the wind would be in my favor. Yet, the moment
was four stars. Transcendent. More than could be hoped for
or planned.

They didn't always get away.

I walked down the mountain, the birds serenading me. It was
a beautiful morning. And I could feel it all the way down.

I linked up with Chick at eleven-thirty. He asked if I had seen
anything and I casually mentioned my encounter with the bull
elk. In fact, I casually mentioned it for the next twenty-five minutes. He demonstrated his interest by asking me to shut up. I
told him his life would be miserable as I would continue to give
him things to be envious of. And so on. We kept it up down
the mountain to the truck, forgetting for a moment the troubles
around us, the sun warming our backs.

We arrived back at the cabin a little before two in the afternoon. By that time thunderheads were forming in the western
sky, billowing and pluming into white mushrooms that would
turn slate gray, swell with precipitation and dump snow like
shaking down from a feather pillow.

We dumped our bows and tackle and warmed the chili. Chick
unlaced his boots, poured himself a Glenlivet, neat, and leaned
back on the couch.

"I been thinking," he said. "We could have a big mess on
our hands if we expose Braden. With Deadeye Dirk of the CIA
floating around to clean up and Purvis and Montana willing
to whack out anyone who threatens Braden, we might become
moving targets."

"I thought Donovan was your buddy."

"He is. But he'll do what he has to. If they sent him to cover
Braden's backside, he'll do that. If they sent him here to kill all
the Coors drinkers in the state he'll do that. He is nobody to
mess with." He unlaced his boots as he spoke. "Once when we

were barhopping Saigon a group of jarheads started messing with us. For a while we made fun of them and laughed. Had a good time. One thing led to another and one of 'em got ballsy and took a swing at Dirk. Now, Dirk looks big and slow. He'll fool you. He slipped the punch and got the Marine down and shaved the guy's eyebrows with a pocketknife. Made him look like a mutant. No, we'll have to make it in his best interests to go the other way, otherwise he'll be a great big turd in our punchbowl. You can reason with Dirk. He's smart. He doesn't like having his strings pulled by Harvard lawyers and sons of politicians. We might be able to use that."

"Matt's in deep on this one. Need a way to pull him clear of this."

"Keep your eye on Montana when you do," Chick said. "That boy's got ideas. Think he wants to go independent."

I heard the sound of a car engine. As the windows were boarded up, I had to get up and open the door to see who it was. Looking out I saw the tan Chevrolet that had followed me the day I found Randle Lightfoot floating in his hot tub.

"Speak of the devil," I said.

"Who is it?" Chick asked.

"Dirk Donovan."

irk Donovan unfolded his bulk from the driver's seat. He waved hello. "Hell of a trip up here. Thought I'd drug the transmission off the bottom of the Chev a couple times. Don't you like people? What happened to your cabin?"

"Decided to redecorate. What brings you up here?"

"Care if I come in?"

From the back deck I heard Chick say, "Sure, but first put your gun on top of the car." I looked over and saw the silhouette of Chick with a gun in his hand, pointed at Dirk. He must have slipped out the back door.

"Aw, you don't need that," the big man said. "This's a friendly visit."

"Well, hell, Dirk," Chick said. "I feel bad about it, but I shot a guy here yesterday, one shot and it was over, and you know how it is, once you're in the groove and all . . ."

Smiling, Donovan reached into his jacket and pulled out a Glock auto and placed it on the hood of the Chevy. Then he showed empty hands to us in a "What the hell?" gesture.

"There," Chick said. "Much better. Sure good to see you, Dirk."

Inside, Chick poured Scotch for Donovan and himself. "I'm here for a parley," Dirk said. He took a sip of the whiskey. "Wonderful stuff. The Scots are good for something."

"Instead of good for nothing like the Irish," Chick said.

"I come to lay my cards on the table and you insult my heritage. Old friends shouldn't do that."

Chick shrugged. "You want to cut to it, old buddy? I'm getting all misty-eyed."

"I want to know what your involvement is."

"Storme loves a media babe and I'm a free agent. That's it as far as involvement goes around here. Come on, Dirk, you know better than to go fishing with vague open-ended questions hoping we'll fill in the blanks. Kinda insulting. You want to know something you ask straight."

"What is your interest in Congressman Braden?"

"Just good Americans with an interest in the political process," I said.

"You don't even vote, Storme," he said.

"Thought it was a secret ballot."

"Not anymore."

"Why I live up here."

"The people I work for have an interest in seeing that Congressman Braden becomes Senator Braden. Like most of them, Braden has fucked up once or twice in the past. Means nothing to me one way or the other. But if you have information which could harm him and you back off, it could work to your benefit."

"You haven't got anything I need," I said. "I've already been on one of the government's expenses-paid field trips and I didn't like it much. While Charlie was trying to kill me for the sin of youth, guys like Braden exempted their sons and sent in the second team. I got nothing for him or the government, so peddle that somewhere else."

"We don't have to be at cross purposes here."

"Who're you protecting?"

"My country."

Chick groaned. "Come on, Dirk. Don't soap us with that sorry shit. Wyatt says there was a black Beretta there the day Lightfoot was killed. Who was driving it?"

Dirk sat back. "You know better."

"Thought I'd give it a try anyway."

"No harm in that." He turned his attention back to me. "I'm also looking for a little book. Do you have it?"

"Don't ever come here uninvited again," I said.

Donovan had a wry smile on his square Irish face. He looked at Chick, and Chick said, "Coulda told you." Donovan looked back at me, said, "You know, then?"

I nodded. "I can forgive a father trying to save his son's life. The rest of it? . . . No." The phone rang. I answered it. Donovan followed me with his eyes.

It was Sandy. Her voice was neutral. Had her father told her? No, it wasn't that. Worse than that.

Matt Jenkins was dead. Murdered.

Matt had been found sprawled out in the corral of his horse stable, a western holster strapped on, an unfired Colt lying on the ground beside him. Dead. The news lay against the base of my medulla like a lead weight.

"When?" I asked Sandy.

"An hour ago."

"Thanks."

"Are you all right?" she asked.

"I'll be okay." I hung up the phone, turned to Donovan and said: "Get out."

"Not very hospitable."

"Get out before I throw you out."

Chick said, "What's up?"

I told him.

"You're not blaming me for that, are you?" said Donovan.

"Indirectly."

"You're wrong."

"If it's the same person who killed Randle Lightfoot, I blame you for protecting him. If it turns out to be the same person there won't be anyplace for you to hide."

"I'm not protecting anyone."

"Who does the black Beretta belong to?"

"Don't know what you're talking about."

"Was it Michael Braden?"

"I don't know what you're talking about."

"Chick," I said. "I want him to tell me if it's Braden's. I don't care how you do it."

"Won't go any good. He's tough. I set him on fire, skin him with a paring knife, he won't say anything. Anyway, he is telling you," Chick said. "In his own way."

I looked at Donovan and said, "That right?"

He shrugged.

He said, "I'm sorry about your friend."

"You like working for people who'd protect Purvis and Braden?"

He smiled. "There are larger forces at work here."

"Yeah? You government people give me a pain. I've heard it before. Politicians pull that crap like a gun. Justifies everything, whether it's body counts or more taxes. Everything's okay as long as you have good intentions."

"Pretty cynical attitude."

"Brought it back with me," I said. "Thank 'em for me next time you're in D.C."

We were at Matt's within the hour. Police of different affiliation and uniform were on the scene. Members of the press stood outside the police barricade like hyenas awaiting their chance.

"This is a fucking three-ring circus," Chick said as we got out of the Bronco. I no longer worried that they would recognize the Bronco—I hoped for it. I told a uniformed deputy I was a friend of the Jenkinses and wanted to see Kelly. He used a walkie-talkie to communicate with the house.

I heard a voice come back over the radio saying Mrs. Jenkins wanted to see me. As I stepped over the barricade a guy stuck a microphone in my face, and said: "Did you know the—"

I jerked the mike from his hand and threw it toward the woods.

"Hey! You can't do that."

I kept walking.

Inside the house, Kelly Jenkins was being attended by a doctor. He was encouraging her to take a sedative and she was resisting.

"Wyatt," she said, with a small cry, when she saw me. She ran to me, burying her head in the hollow of my shoulder, her body trembling as if she'd come in from the cold. I held her tightly as if we stood on a precipice and were afraid to look over the edge. After a few moments she composed herself, holding my upper arms between her hands and taking a deep breath. Then she used her fingers to wipe the damp away from her eyes and cheekbones.

"I'm okay," she said. "Tell him I don't want a sedative."

I looked at the doctor. He said, "I think it best."

I shook my head. The doctor shrugged and said, "I'll leave a sample here if you need it later."

She thanked him and he left. I sat her down at a kitchen table while Chick made coffee.

"I know it's tough, Kel," I said. "But I need to know what happened before the police make me leave. Can you handle that?" She nodded her head. She was outstanding. "Do you have any idea who did this?"

"No."

"Why was Matt wearing the gunbelt?"

"I don't know."

"Were there any targets out there? Like cans or bottles or anything like it?"

"No."

"Where did they shoot him?"

"In the chest . . . and . . . in the—" She couldn't get it out, so she pointed at her abdomen.

"How many shots?"

"Th . . . three."

I looked at Chick. He said, "It's who you think."

"Yeah."

There was a commotion at the front door. Someone was angrily addressing the deputy posted there.

"Dammit, no one is to be allowed in here without clearance from me." Heavy footsteps pounded the carpet. Detective Elliot stomped into the room. He seemed unhappy to see me.

"What the hell are you doing here?" he said.

"I'm a friend."

"Being a friend of yours isn't too healthy."

"Being his enemy ain't so hot, either," said Chick.

"Who the fuck are you?"

"Watch your language," I said.

His face colored with heat. He started to say something, changed his mind. "Sorry Mrs. Jenkins." He looked at Chick and asked his name. Chick told him. Then he asked me, "Where were you at approximately eleven o'clock this morning?"

"Up on a ridge above the Little Silver. Elk hunting."

"Anybody corroborate that?"

"I can," said Chick.

"How'd you find out?"

"My fiancée called. She's a reporter."

"Her name?"

"Sandra Collingsworth."

"The girl on Channel Seven?" He looked at me. "That's hard to believe."

"I'll send you a wedding invitation."

"This is too much of a coincidence. You know things you haven't told me and I'm going to find out what they are. Either of you own a .45?"

"I do," I said. Chick said nothing, though he owned one.

"I may impound it."

"Suit yourself."

"Cooperative, aren't you?"

"It's your slick interrogation style. Afraid you'll just trip me up."

"What was your relationship to the deceased."

"His name was Matt."

"Quit instructing me, Storme. I don't care much for it."

Chick chuckled.

"You got something to say?" Elliot said to Chick.

Chick smiled. "He's hard to get along with, Inspector. Was me, I'd get one of those deputies beat his ass with a nightstick. That'd fix him. Teach him to get uppity with the law."

"You look familiar. Where've I seen you before?"

"Used to be a famous female tennis star. Then, one day, I knew there was a man inside trying to get out. So I started taking estrogen shots, watching John Wayne movies, and before you knew it, my voice dropped and hair began growing on my chest. Then, there was the transplant from an Angus bull and before you know—"

"I remember now. Bounty hunter. Two years ago. You brought in the Gillis twins. Big as bears. They skipped on an assault charge. Beat up a couple cops. You brought them in, we had to check them in at Emergency."

"They didn't want to come back," Chick said. "Had a funny attitude about it. I asked nice and everything."

"Yeah," Elliot said, settling it in his mind. "You thought you were a comic then, too. But this is a homicide beef and both of you are going to cooperate. Now," he said, turning his attention to me. "What was your relationship to Mr. Jenkins?"

"Close friend."

"Do you know anyone who had reason to kill Mr. Jenkins?"

"I know who did it."

He glared at me. "Who?"

"Coy Montana. Works up at the Sun King Dude Ranch."

"Montana? That's who you said killed Lightfoot. I checked. He doesn't own a black Beretta. Why do you keep trying to hang it on him?"

"I was wrong before. This time I'm sure he did it."

"How's that?"

I looked at Kelly, then back at Elliot. "It was a shoot-out."

"What?"

"You know. Like the old West." I told him about Matt dying of cancer and practicing his fast draw at the shooting range. About Montana's unusual predilection for gunplay. When I finished, Elliot was shaking his head.

"Sheriff's going to love hearing this," he said. "Okay, guess it won't hurt to ask this Montana guy where he was this morning. Why kill Jenkins?"

"I think he likes it."

"Why do you say that?"

"Can't help you there," I said, hedging, not wanting to tell him I was there when Montana, or someone, smoked Jackie Burlingame. "Just a feeling I get."

"Will you be willing to testify if I can put Montana at the scene?"

"Detective Elliot," I said, "if you don't arrest him and throw him in a hole, I'm going find him, no matter where he is, and pull him inside out."

The Bronco boomed down the highway toward Denver.

"The police will take care of Montana," Chick said. It was the first thing either of us had said since we'd left Kelly Jenkins, her lips tight, her life in disarray.

"Sure."

The speedometer registered eighty-five.

Kelly had said Matt seemed happy that morning when she went to town. Animated and talkative. She asked if he wanted to go with her but he said he had something to take care of at the house and for her to go on without him. Told her she was as beautiful as the day he'd met her. That he loved her. At the time she checked it off as the maudlin mood of a man dying of an incurable disease. Now she knew there was another reason.

She also told me Duncan was going to tell his daughter everything. I told her there was no necessity in it.

"There is if you've been living a lie for twenty years," she said.

Then what?

Would the strange triangle of father and fiancé put a kink in our relationship that could not be removed, assuaged, or forgotten? When Sandy looked at me, would she see Kelly and her father? Would it hover over our married life like a dark cloud of rotted memory? When will it let go? When are we free of past mistakes? How long must we pay? I hadn't even known Sandra Collingsworth then. Duncan Collingsworth had been just another college professor, one of several. But I'd known Kelly McArthur too well. I'd used her to heal myself of the anger burning inside me like a poisoned toad, to take the edge off the hurt, my mind off the myriad trespasses and compromises I'd made in Vietnam. To forget. The brutality. The killing. And my part in all of it. To forget I'd been a willing participant.

Purgatory, sometimes, is where memories live.

When I returned from Vietnam, a long-haired guy in sandals and beads spat on me and a crippled vet who had lost a leg when he tripped a wire. The hippie called us baby-killers. Murderers. How could he know? How could he judge? I'd lived the nightmare while he was drinking Boone's Farm and listening to Jimi Hendrix. I found out who he was and where he lived. I knocked on his door. He didn't remember me. Didn't know me. Somehow that made his trespass worse in my mind. I threw him down the stairs leading to his crash pad. I spat on him as he lay moaning. Then I stepped over him and walked out the door into the sunlight. Wasn't proud of it. Took one more hill and retreated to count casualties.

The speedometer reached ninety-five, the tires and engine whining.

"Well, what the hell," said Chick. "Good a day to die as any, I guess."

I backed off the accelerator.

"Sorry."

" 'S okay. Feel the same way."

I headed downtown to see Sandy.

She was at Channel Seven, getting ready for the six-o'clock report. I parked in Richie Caster's parking place, again.

"Signs says Richard Caster," said Chick.

"Inside joke. We're old buddies."

Chick waited in a bar across the street. I walked into her dressing room. She looked up from her prelim copy with tired eyes. Eyes which revealed that her father had told her. She knew.

She said, "Why didn't you tell me? Better, why couldn't you tell me?"

"I didn't know what to do," I said, my hands in my pockets.

"You could have trusted me to handle it."

"Sure. Come in and say, 'How you doing, Sandy? Nice weather, huh? How about those Broncos? You know your dad and I were having an affair with the same woman years ago?' "

Her eyes looked hurt and I knew I'd gone too far. "Sorry," I said. "I decided to leave it up to him. I didn't know whether he would want you to know or not."

She put her hand to her forehead and massaged her eyes. "It's a load, isn't it?" she said.

"Yeah."

"He was drunk when he told me. That, of itself, was bad enough. He hadn't had a drink in three years. Been attending AA meetings. Doing fine. Then he hit me with the rest of it . . . and, well . . ." Her lip quivered as she struggled with it. "Dammit, Wyatt. I don't need this. It's . . . too much." She recovered, then said, "This Billy McCall, what is he like?"

I swallowed. "He's a good kid."

She turned hot blue eyes on me. "You're doing it again. What's the matter with you? I'm not a paper doll. Quit treating me like a child."

"Okay," I said. "He's a lowlife. He should be sterilized and not allowed to reproduce. He's distasteful. I wouldn't spit on him if he was on fire. If he was dead, buzzards wouldn't eat him, because—"

"Stop it!"

We glared at each other. The heat of the air between us was eating the oxygen in the room.

"I'll shut up," I said. "Won't say another word. Just don't make me feel like crap because I love you and don't want to hurt you. We're not going to get anywhere beating each other up."

Her eyes softened. "I need some time," she said. "This is tough."

"I know. You're tough enough."

"Is she . . . is Kelly all right?"

I nodded, said, "Yeah. It'll get rougher when she has time to think about it."

"What happens now?"

"I'll wait and see if the police pick up Montana, but I don't look for it to happen. He'll have an alibi. Somebody, Dumont or Purvis, will say he was with them. I've gone about as far in that direction as I can for the moment. I haven't pursued Purvis much but he hasn't given me much of a handle. He's slick. I'll probably check on him next."

"Why not just let it go? Let the police handle it."

"They just put an old friend in a bag. Shot him three times after goading him into a gunfight. A thrill killing. And you think I'm going to let that go?"

"You don't have to bite my head off."

"I was trying for the new honesty."

"Don't be a smartass."

"Hard to suppress natural talent."

She shook her head as if telling herself something she already knew. "Why do I love you? You're impossible. It's like having a pet gorilla. I want to hug you but I never know when you'll drag me off into the jungle where you live."

"Worth the gamble. All the girl gorillas say so."

She smiled. "I need some room. Some time apart. Can you give me that?"

A response rushed from gut to mouth, one that would have reignited the fire. But I beat it back. We'd been through this before. A year ago. It took three months then. Three months like a dry dusty cave at the back of my throat. She saw it in my face. "Not like last time," she said. "Not like that. A few days. That's all."

"Okay." I started to leave.

"This isn't the way I want you to leave," she said. "You know I'll always love you."

"Knowledge is power."

She managed a smile. "Don't be cynical."

"Everybody says that, but I don't believe in it."

I collected Chick at the Mile High Lounge and we left. He had just ordered a drink.

"Leave it," I said. "You can afford to. You just inherited a hundred grand, remember?"

We walked across the street to the Channel Seven parking lot. I was about to unlock the Bronco when a cream-colored Lexus sedan pulled into the lot. It was Richie.

He got out of his car. "You son of a bitch," he said. "You parked in my spot again." The cords on his neck stood out above his carefully knotted tie.

"This your spot?" I said, feigning confusion.

"You know it is. Says it right on the sign."

"You're right. I see it now. 'Assistant Toady.' Should've known it was yours."

"Get the hell out of here before I call the police."

"This is your buddy?" Chick said, smiling.

"Yeah. We kid like this all the time. Isn't he cute?" I waved at Richie. He shivered with anger. "No," I said, putting both hands up. "Don't ask us to stay. Gotta run."

I backed the Bronco slowly out of the slot. Majestically, I thought. Richie glared us out of the lot.

Chick was smiling serenely in the passenger seat.

"Sometimes," he said, "you are crazier than me."

Matt's funeral was Saturday afternoon. The blue Colorado sky turned smoke gray and the wind lay down as if gathering to exhale. I wore a suit and tie I bought for the occasion. Sandy accompanied Chick and me. But accompany was about all. There was an invisible veil between us. Our attempts at conversation were stiff and formal.

We stood under the moldy sky with fifty other people and listened to the minister compare Matt's body with an old shroud that was now cast aside for a new one. All my trials, Lord, soon be over.

Kelly's parents were dead and she had no brothers or sisters, so I escorted her back to the limousine. She stumbled once as we neared the limo, but I held her up. I opened the door for her and she got in, thanking me.

"Will you come out later, Wyatt?" she asked.

"Sure," I said. "I'll come by."

She nodded, thanked me, and I shut the door.

I watched as the limousine left the cemetery, all waxed black and sparkling chrome. Red taillights disappearing over the hill.

One more gone. One less to laugh with. To remember with. One of the good ones. It never got easier. One after another they squeezed themselves into the photo album in my head where I kept such things. To be opened at some later date when the laughter would be more remembered than this moment. For at this moment I was afraid of the long ride home alone. Afraid I'd known what Matt was thinking the last time I saw him. Afraid to speak with any moral certainty about warning him off his intentions. Better to die of cancer, inevitable, yet without any moral gray area? Or better to die with boots on, knowing you were committing an unusual suicide? And what was Matt saying to me from beyond the grave? Was he telling me to avenge him—setting up Montana—or was his death a gesture of warning, showing me the futility of vengeance?

I looked across the graveyard into the blue mountains and said his name.

I felt Sandy's hand on my arm. I turned and she held me. It was motherly, feminine. Needed.

"You can let go, Wyatt," she said into my ear. "You can cry if you want." She said it as if it were an intellectual choice.

But I couldn't. Even though I wanted to. Years ago in the Far East I'd cried because I was away from home. Cried because the smell of gunpowder irritated my eyes. Cried because another comrade had fallen. No tears left. I'd used them up. There was no release anymore, only a pain that I couldn't salve. It didn't make me feel heroically tragic, just lonely and sad.

We drove Sandy to Denver. Conversation was stale and measured as between strangers forced to share air space. I tried to understand but it made me resentful of her and of her father. Chick sat in the back, smiling into my rearview mirror and saying "Hmmm" like a clinical psychologist responding to the stilted, overly polite dialogue between Sandy and myself. I wanted to choke him.

When I let Sandy out at Channel Seven, I asked if she wanted to have dinner later. She declined. I made a comment about her being "unrelenting" and Chick said "Hmm." She walked to the building, her heels clicking on the cold concrete. I watched her go through the front door and disappear.

Chick got into the front seat, cleared his throat.

I said, "You make that noise again I'm going to break your neck."

"Sure are touchy. Hormones'll do that. You'll feel better when your testicles drop."

I muttered something and drove on. Chick chuckled softly and unscrewed the cap on a half pint of Jack Daniel's.

Of my three best friends in the world, one was dead, one had abandoned me, and one was a half-crazy bounty hunter who drank too much and amused himself with my life.

At least someone was getting something out of it.

When we pulled into the gravel driveway of the Pullman car we saw Billy McCall's BMW. Chick reached down, rolled up a pant leg and produced a derringer, larger than any derringer I'd ever seen.

"What's that?"

"Davis .38," he said. "Don't leave home without it."

"Just Billy," I said.

"Maybe. What if they smoked him then drove his car up here to wait for us?"

But it was just Billy. He walked out on the custom deck with a bottle of chardonnay in his fist, arms spread wide as if we'd just returned from a long trip.

"What's happening, dudes?" he said.

"We've been to a funeral," I said. "You should have been there."

He dropped his arms to his side. "I know. I don't like funerals. Can't take them. Matt was okay."

Here was a change. He seemed sincere. Was Billy McCall turning into a human being?

"Hope you don't mind I helped myself to your wine."

"Don't mind," Chick said. "What I bought it for. Besides, my inheritance money came."

"Listen, I got some inside shit for you guys. Yeah, that's right, me. Don't look so surprised. I'm not always a lowlife. I've been pounding the streets, asking around. Found out that Jackie B. knew Coy Montana from ten years ago. Montana was playing a small part in a western they made down around Canon City. Jackie was supplying dope to some of the actors. Montana was one of them."

"Step in the right direction," I said. Helped affirm a link between them. One that Purvis might know of and might not. "Why'd you run off the other day?"

"Needed my car. Besides, I told you I wanted to see Cynthia, so I did. Figured a couple badasses like you'd be safe without me around to protect you."

I looked at Chick. He was chuckling. He nodded at Billy. "What the hell ya know? Junior's growin' up."

There were about thirty people at Kelly's when I arrived. Friends, business associates, relatives. I didn't know anyone there. The kitchen was covered with food—a meat and cheese platter sent from the cattlemen's association, a similar one from the Outfitter Club, various salads, pies, cakes and one chilling dish—a smoked turkey sent from Purvis Enterprises, Inc.

Kelly hugged me, clinging to me momentarily in a sisterly way. I kissed the top of her head and held her. Her hair smelled of strawberries, her skin of perfume and soap. She introduced me and I obligingly went through the ceremony. She was called away as another guest arrived. I popped open a Coke and considered escape, but thought better of it. One guy recognized me from my playing days and cornered me, droning on about the Cowboys, the Broncos, the Colorado Golden Buffalos.

"You played for the Buffalos, didn't you?" he asked.

"No. Colorado State."

"Fort Collins? You were a quarterback in college, weren't you?"

"Yeah." I looked for Kelly.

"Why'd you switch to wide receiver in the pros?"

"Injured my shoulder. Couldn't throw long anymore."

He clinked the ice in his bourbon. "Funny. Matt never mentioned knowing you. Can't wait to tell the guys at the office I ran into you here. Why'd you quit playing when you did?"

Thought he'd never ask.

I caught Kelly's eye and she rescued me. Told her I needed to run but she looked at me, asking me with her eyes to stay. "Where do you have to go?"

I thought about it. "Nowhere," I said.

She smiled.

The crowd thinned and left, expressing sorrow, offering to help clean up. Kelly thanked them. No, she'd clean it up herself, give her something to do. Yes, lunch would be wonderful. The flowers were lovely. Good to see you.

I realized I was seeing Kelly as I hadn't before. As a woman. I'd known her as a lover, then as the wife of a friend, and then as my friend. But now she was a woman. A beauty of a woman, taller than she looked. Takes me longer than most.

Finally, there were only the two of us. I picked up stray dishes and glasses, rinsed the glasses, threw away the paper plates and loaded the dishwasher. Kelly excused herself to change clothes. She returned wearing a Colorado State sweatshirt, jeans and a pair of Topsiders.

"Don't think I've ever seen you wearing a suit," she said. "At State you always wore jeans and tennis shoes. You haven't varied much since."

"I'm making a minimalist fashion statement."

She smiled. "Thanks for staying. I know you don't like crowds. I thought maybe you'd be uncomfortable after the other day."

"I'm not. You set me up to be the good guy."

"Sorry about that," she said. "Matt had moments . . . times when he'd get melancholy about the operation. Like he wasn't a real man. That's when he'd start drinking. Like the day you came by and he was short with you. I thought about lying to him. Telling him I was having an affair with some imaginary man, but I knew he'd see through it, and deep down I also knew he didn't really want me to have another man. He was relieved you turned me down. He didn't say it, but his eyes gave him away. I knew you would turn me down."

"What if I hadn't?"

She smiled. "I don't know, Wyatt. I really don't."

We finished the cleaning and went down to the family room to watch television. I asked what was on. She said *Casablanca* and she'd seen it a million times, but loved it anyway. "It's like a painting or a favorite song. It has a rhythm and poetry about it."

"You sure you want to see it?" I said, thinking of the ending where Bogart tells Bergman to leave him and go with her husband.

Her eyes were round and soft and glistened in the dim light when she said, "I can stand it if you can."

So we turned it on and sat at opposite ends of the love seat, where she'd watched hundreds of movies, snug against Matt's shoulder. I watched with half my mind, the other half thinking of Sandy and where we stood. I was okay until the movie reached that part where Bogie stands in the train station, Dear John letter in hand, the rain causing the writing to run and disappear, and I felt his anger, his despair.

I'd seen the movie over and over, and this time it was like the first time. It had been in Vietnam and the old sixteen-millimeter film flickered on the makeshift screen. The sound of the guns in the Paris scenes eerie, as if they echoed the guns outside the bunker. I was nineteen and the pain of separation was acute. It made me think of summer nights filled with top-down convertibles and longhaired girls, hair billowing in the wind like flags, and the distance between them and me. A door opened on an empty room in my heart. There was no hand on the knob.

Kelly moved toward me and I raised my arm, allowing her to snuggle against me. It happened without preamble or hesitation, as natural as the sun bursting gloriously over walnut trees in the backyard of my childhood home, then filtering through the fingers of venetian blinds to paint my bed with stripes of sunlight and shade, beckoning, waking me to another day of high experience.

She was warm against me, the aroma of her wonderful and heady, the rise and fall of her breathing a comfort. We were grieving and it was good to share the warmth against the night.

When the movie reached the part where Bogie was giving his climactic speech to Ingrid Bergman, I felt a convulsive catch spasm through Kelly's body—just once, then her breathing returned to its normal rhythm. The movie ended and the titles rolled and before I knew it I was kissing Kelly McArthur again, as if uninterrupted by two decades. She held the kiss and turned her body toward me. I felt the dampness of her tears against my face. Reaching up I caught one with a finger and traced it from her face. She wore no makeup to run and ruin her perfect face, a face beautiful enough in its natural state to get away with it.

I was afraid to speak, as if speaking would break the spell. She stood up, holding my hand in hers, tugging on me. "Stay with me, Wyatt. I need you." Her eyes were like those of a child afraid of a sudden noise in the night.

I stood. A thousand things rushed through my head. A thousand protests and arguments, but I wasn't listening this time.

Because I also needed her.

I woke up with the three A.M. guilts. Alone. I had a moment of disorientation, waking up in a strange place. Where was she?

I got up and put my clothes on. Rubbed my eyes in an attempt to get them to focus. There was a light on in the kitchen. I padded down the hall, shoes in hand. A million excuses floated through my head, all of them rationalizations in fancy clothes.

It had been tender, not grasping or desperate, yet still a mistake. I could tell myself I had been a good boy for a long time, that she'd done me wrong, that it was healing for Kelly, but in the end I knew it had been selfish and punitive. An attempt to recapture the past. An attempt to punish Sandra Collingsworth. It had it all—sated desires long at bay, rewarded my goodness, restored my manhood, recaptured my youth, satisfied my sense of adventure and experience, unleashed the beast thought dead these past ten years, and basically made me feel selfish and sinful and small and brutish.

When I walked into the kitchen Kelly was sitting at the breakfast bar with a rocks glass filled with cracked ice and clear liquid. A bottle of Beefeater's gin on the counter.

Sunday morning coming down.

She looked up as I walked in and her face fell. She said, "I was afraid you'd have that look on your face."

"Kelly. I—"

She held up a hand. "It's okay, Wyatt. You don't have to say it. I took you down with me. There's no excuse for it. It was selfish of me."

"No." I shook my head. "You can't take the blame for this. I'm a free agent. We didn't do anything that I didn't participate in willingly."

She smiled wanly. "Want a martini?"

I shook my head. "No. Better hold a few sins in reserve."

"Don't blame yourself," she said.

I said nothing.

She said, "Years ago I made mistakes, one which I regret more than the others. I was in love and never said it. I wish I would have said it. So I'm saying it now. I loved you, Wyatt. Maybe I always have. Tonight was a fantasy. I didn't want to hurt you or cause problems for you. I don't feel badly about this, except for how I've made you feel. Matt wouldn't mind, he didn't have any ridiculous illusions about the sanctity of the dead. I held off for a year, a hard thing to do, and I did it for him because . . ." She caught her breath, wiped at the corner of an eye. "Because I loved him and still do. Tonight was for me and I don't regret it, won't regret it, and would damn well appreciate it if you wouldn't look like that."

"What do I look like?"

"Like you just witnessed a three-car accident."

I put on my shoes. Thought of things to say, but everything I thought of sounded corny, apologetic or self-pitying.

"You know what one of your problems is?" she asked.

Great. Character analysis. I looked at her with a "Give me a break" look. "What?"

"You don't scare me, Wyatt Storme," she said. "Your problem is you're not as tough as people think. Not that you ask people to think anything. And not that you aren't tough. I remember when you played the second half against Wyoming with a broken nose, and you kept taking your helmet off to wipe the blood out of your eyes. One of the linemen left the game and threw up from looking at you, but you finished the game. It's the other kind of tough you don't have. You hurt for things. Inside, you hurt. When I first met you I'd never met anyone who hurt so bad or was so good at concealing it. Things get to you and you won't admit it, won't let anyone inside to share it. You wear a mask. A mask that looks like your everyday face but I see it in your eyes and hear it in your voice and it makes me remember the scared little boy, home from Vietnam, who took risks and played tough guy so nobody would know how bad they'd hurt him and crippled him up over there.

"The other little boys can't see those things, because they're too busy flexing their muscles and talking tough, but a woman can. Particularly one who cares for you. If I see it, then so does Sandy. Playing hurt is what you're good at. Don't be afraid of it. You're still trying to purge yourself of some thing or several things that happened over there and you've got to let go. Even cry."

I looked at her, felt the rhythm of my breathing. I felt something come to the crest of the dam, lapping at the walkway, then recede. I wanted to stay with her, avail myself of the comfort she afforded. The solace and shelter from the high winds of life. This time they were bending something inside me, something that might break.

"Another thing," she said. "It's okay to be mad at Sandy. She expects it. Get her off the pedestal and quit treating her like a porcelain ballerina. She's a woman now, and you don't have to protect her from everything."

"I've gotta go," I said.

"I know," she said. "That's okay, too. Probably best."

I kissed her forehead. She placed a hand alongside my cheek, letting it fall from my face as I stood.

"You're going to tell her, aren't you?" she said.

"Probably."

"Will she be angry?"

"Probably."

"But you'll tell her anyway?"

I nodded.

She pursed her lips, shook her head and tried to smile.

"Nobody else like you, Storme."

"Thank God, huh?"

I sat in the wooden pew and listened to the young preacher. I was an intruder, squirming on the hard bench like a junior-high kid in the principal's office, out-of-synch with the spiritual atmosphere. I had done that which I should not have done, and there was no way to candy-coat it. I had come for the peace, the assurance.

When they passed the collection plate I dropped in a large amount of money. Not for penance. God didn't play the buy-off game. All the revisionist, situational ethics garbage didn't change that. Like Paul, I had done the thing I didn't want to do rather than the thing I wanted to.

So I sat looking at the rough-hewn cross cut from native timber, behind the preacher, and listened and soaked up the healing words. I came to ask forgiveness, to seek shelter from Storme. But the preacher's words kept ringing over and over in my ears like the clanging of a warning claxon at sea.

At two o'clock, I was at the door of Sandy's apartment, feeling like a Jewish immigrant about to take a citizenship test in Iraq. When Sandy opened the door, her face was radiant, glad to see me. I'd soon fix that.

She ushered me in, poured me a cup of coffee and told me about a human-interest piece she was working on involving an East German woman whose husband was the last person killed trying to escape into West Germany before the wall came down. She had harbored anger and hatred for the Communist soldiers. It had grown in her like a poison weed. Then the wall came down and she and her daughter had walked freely into West Germany, and the feeling of freedom, bought with her husband's, and others, blood, lifted her above hatred and anger. And she knew her husband, a Christian man, was at peace and rejoiced in her forgiveness of those who had killed him.

"It's a wonderful story," she said. "She lives here in Denver with her daughter and son-in-law, a serviceman. She goes around to churches and schools giving talks about freedom and forgiveness. She is a wonderful woman. You've got to meet her. Her name is Leonore, like the woman in Beethoven's opera." She was smiling, animated, energized by her work and interest in this story. So interested she'd forgotten her own problems and that she'd wanted time to herself.

"Sandy. I have something to tell you."

It was like turning off a record. The music of her personality stopped. Instinctively, she knew she would not like what I was about to say.

I told her about Kelly. Without embellishment or reserve. All of it.

Her mouth worked. She stood up and walked about the apartment, hand to her mouth, back to me. I saw her hug herself with her arms. Finally, she turned around abruptly.

"Why?"

"I don't have an explanation that doesn't sound like an excuse."

"What is it about her? Is it her face? Does she have magic powers? Maybe it's her perfume. What kind is it? I need to get some for myself. Whatever it is turns intelligent men into jackasses in rut." Her voice was rising in pitch and intensity now.

"Maybe she puts off some kind of heat only men feel, like the high-pitched whistle only dogs can hear. Is that it?" I started to shrug, but stopped myself. "You son of a bitch. How could you?"

There was no shelter from her fury. I had no argument. I could only endure whatever came.

"God, I hate it when you sit there so smug in the virtue of your honesty, as if it excuses everything. Explains everything. You're no different than the rest of them. No different than . . ." She let it trail off before she said the thing she didn't want to say. Tears filled her eyes. "I guess you have nothing to say?"

"What could I say that would change what I've done?"

"You're shutting me out again," she said. "Safe in the armor of the autonomous Wyatt Storme. Safe in your personal code of honor. Liberated from having to explain yourself. That's why you live on that damned mountain. Safe from having to feel. You just turn it inward and endure. But it's still running away, Wyatt, any way you slice it."

She paused, her shoulders rising and falling with her breathing, like a distance runner coming down from a workout.

"I think you'd better leave now," she said, wiping at one eye with a quick swipe of her hand.

I stood up. I felt as if my heart were being squeezed between the talons of a beast. My head swirled with emotion, but I couldn't bring words to my defense. I loved her. I love you, Sandy. I wanted to say it, but it stuck in my mouth like the dry knot of tears in my heart. My game face, which had served me so well in combat and on the field, betrayed me now, making me appear unfeeling—a defense mechanism once useful, now automatic.

"I want my apartment key back," she said. I reached in my pocket, numbly, pulled out the key and handed it to her. As I did she wrenched the engagement ring from her finger and put it in my palm. I looked at it. Such a tiny thing. It lay in my palm like a stone plucked from a fire.

"I love you, Sandy," I said.

Her mouth pursed into a oval. "I know. It just makes it harder."

"We need to talk about this."

"No. Not now. Just go."

I stepped into the silent hallway.

She closed the door behind me and I heard her muffled sobbing behind the door.

I walked down the hall. It was longer than I remembered.

3·6

I'd killed a girl in Vietnam. An accident. Not because I hadn't meant to kill her. I thought she was a man. And she was trying to kill me. No other option. I still regret it. A regret I refuse to apologize for, as if chauvinism carried greater weight than death.

I shot her in the face, the bullet from my sixteen ripping through the side of her face, exposing bone, tooth, and muscle, knocking the hat loose from her head. Her pinned-up hair fluttering loose.

Sometimes she visited me in my dreams. She did so now. The first time in more than a year. She came back, charging me, her Kalashnikov chattering, bullets ripping into the dirt around me, half her face split into a skeletal leer, throbbing with damaged nerves, growing closer, screaming now . . .

There was snow on the ground when I awoke from a fitful sleep. I made coffee and drank it in the bay window that hadn't been touched in the fire fight. Watched the snow drift to earth, dancing in the intermittent breezes peculiar to the mountains. The steam from the coffee wafted up as I lifted it to my mouth, warming my nose and eyebrows.

I looked down on the river, which cut through the mountains like a silver ribbon. Thought about Sandy. Felt the ache in my gut. How had it come to this?

I looked down on the river.

I'd bought this mountain from a guy who'd lost big in Las Vegas. We were on a layover on a flight to play the Seattle Seahawks in a preseason game. He'd recognized me and figured I had money. Told me he owned a mountain. It was in a prime hunting area, he said, and worth several times what it would cost me to stake him. If he lost I got the mountain. I called a realtor in Boulder and it checked out. I staked him, he lost, and I won the mountain for the cost of a good used car. He shrugged, said, "Sometimes it goes like that." Then he shook my hand and said, "It's all yours."

It had taken me two years to build the cabin, living out of a trailer. No hurry. I'd hurried everything else up to then, so I had plenty of time. I'd learned three things in the NFL: You can't eat prestige, you can't buy back time, and the difference between slave and freeman was the price of the ticket. I'd been a rich slave and opted for a more modest freedom.

It was counterproductive to sit here and dwell on things I couldn't control. It would just tie me up in knots. Get up and move around.

It was early, so I grabbed a Ruger .22 pistol and went out to bag a breakfast rabbit. Two hours and two shots later I returned with a rabbit and a squirrel, which can be done if you are patient, quiet, and take your time picking your shot. I dressed them, sliced them into the desired cuts, soaked them in milk to wick away the wild taste, basted them in a mixture of whipped eggs and milk, floured them, and placed the pieces in a cast-iron frying pan. The aroma filled the cabin as the skillet

popped and sizzled merrily. I made more coffee, and broke
a couple of eggs.

After breakfast I showered, shaved, fired up the Bronco, and
headed down the mountain and over the river, heading for the
flats. I couldn't get her off my mind. She was wedged in there
and wouldn't come loose. I thought this stuff would have all
stopped twenty years ago when my voice changed.

I had to see her. Talk to her.

I stopped at Channel Seven. It was twelve-thirty. She had
gone to lunch, I was told. Where? At the mall. I drove there.
Got out of the truck and walked inside. I checked the restaurants, looked through fast-food places but couldn't find her. I
was in the parking lot when I saw her walking my way accompanied by a man wearing a topcoat and scarf, Nunn Bush shoes.
He had manicured nails, moussed hair, and was carrying a pair
of black leather gloves in his hand. I walked up to them. Her
face fell when she saw me.

"Sandy," I said. "We need to talk."

"Wyatt," she said. "This is Barry Maunder. Barry, this is
Wyatt Storme."

"Good to meet you, Wyatt," he said.

I nodded, seeing him only peripherally.

"You got a second?" I said to her.

"I need to get back," she said. "Besides, there's nothing else
to say."

"There's a lot to say."

Barry decided to intervene. "Come on, old man. She says she
has to get back."

"Stay out Barry," I said, not looking at him.

"Some other time, Wyatt," she said. "Please."

"When?"

"Look, fella," said Barry, stepping closer to me. "The lady
doesn't want to talk to you."

"Go stand in a store window, Barry."

Now he moved between me and Sandy. In my face. I detest

a crowder. "Now look, Storme," he said. "I'm going to have to ask you to leave."

"Sandy. Have Rob Lowe step aside or the dry cleaner will never get the wrinkles out."

"That sounds like a threat, old man."

"Barry, don't," Sandy said. "I can take care of this."

I stepped back and to the side to avoid having to smell his cologne, which smelled like the price of a new car. I said, "Sandy, I'm not trying to cause a scene. I want to talk with you. I know I messed up and I can't do anything about that—"

Barry had stepped closer again and put his hand on my shoulder. "Last chance, old man," he said. "Move along."

"Don't touch him, Barry," Sandy said.

I looked at his hand on my shoulder. Closed my eyes momentarily and gritted my teeth. Tried to count to ten. I opened them and he was still too close, his hand still on my shoulder, nudging me away. "You want to keep that hand, get it off me."

He increased the pressure. I heard Sandy say, "Don't touch him, Barry," again, as I removed his hand with a wrenching motion, causing him to grunt and his body to dip to one side. I held on to the hand and straightened his arm, holding it out like a broomstick. His topcoat bunched at the shoulders and his teeth clamped together.

"Now, Barry," I said evenly. "I don't want any trouble, but you touch me again and I'm not promising anything."

"Stop it, Wyatt."

"He dealt it."

"You're not mad at him. You're mad at me."

I released Barry and he came at me. I sidestepped and stiff-armed him in the chest. His feet came out from under him and he sat down hard on the asphalt.

"Quit it, Wyatt," Sandy said, stepping up to me. "Stop it right now."

"He gets up again, I'll put him right back down."

She slapped me. I saw it coming in time to duck or stop it,

but chose to take it head on. It smacked resoundingly. Twice in one week. I just have a way with women.

I looked at her momentarily. It hurt on a lot of levels. She looked surprised by the force of it. I turned around and walked to my truck.

"Damn you, Wyatt Storme," she said to my back.

I kept walking.

"Damn you," she said, softer this time, her voice breaking.

I neared the Bronco. The cold air made my face sting. I started the truck and left the parking lot.

Since I was already mad, it might be a good time to go visit my good buddy Coy Montana.

Nothing to lose by it.

They had taken Coy Montana into custody for questioning, but didn't hold him. As predicted, Skunk Dumont had given him an alibi, saying he'd been with him at the projected time of Matt's death. State trooper Cliff Younger told me this over lunch. He'd passed on the information about the "alleged" gun activity, his word, to the ATF and they were investigating. He wouldn't tell me anything else.

"Privileged information," he said. "For us in the law-enforcement business. Which leaves you out and you stay out. And stay away from Montana."

I said nothing.

"I mean it, Storme. I know how you think. They'll get him eventually."

"And if they don't?"

"Just stay away from him."

"Whatever you say, Officer."

"Don't be a wise guy, either."

"Boy, nothing makes you happy."

I gave him another cigar and headed out. Coy Montana was free. Michael Braden was alive. Sandy was gone. And the fact that I was breathing was no indication I was still living.

I drove up to the Sun King Dude Ranch. The snow was beautiful in the clear Colorado sunlight, painting the mountains in an angelic coat of brilliant white. The aspens and blue spruce and poplars rose from the blanket, their shadows a signature on the landscape.

, I got out of the Bronco and went to find Coy Montana. I saw Harold Wallace again, and asked where I could find Montana. He looked at me funny.

"I know you from somewhere?" he asked me. "You were here the other day, weren't you?"

"Where's Montana?"

"You're the guy . . ." He didn't finish.

"I came to see Montana." I saw him then, walking across the grounds carrying a saddle. I cut across the complex to intercept him.

When I got close to him he raised a hand and gave me his smirking grin. "Good to see you, *compadre*," he said.

"Save the cowboy crap for somebody impressed by it."

"What're you all worked up about?" he said, sticking a wood match between his teeth with a gloved hand. "Oh, yeah. I'll bet you think I popped your buddy, whatsisname." He cocked his head and smiled. "That's all been cleared up. I'm as innocent as a baby chick—"

I ripped a left jab into his mouth. He dropped the saddle as I hooked him beneath the ribs with a right uppercut. Air whooshed out of him and he bent double. I slapped him on the ear, which turned him, exposing his kidneys, and I pounded a fist into them. He groaned and I kicked the side of his knee and he dropped to the ground. I plucked his six-shooter from its holster and tossed it. He looked up at me in surprise, blood trailing from his mouth. His hat fell off and I grabbed a handful of hair and jerked his face up.

"That's for Matt, you low-rent punk," I said. "Cops don't turn the key on you I'm going to do this every time I see you."

"I'll . . . kill you," he said between swollen lips.

"Anytime you want to take a cut in the big league just let me know. I'll saw your head off." I pushed him down in the snow-patched dirt.

By this time several ranch hands were rushing to his aid. As they neared I opened my jacket, let them see the Browning. "Back off, guys, or you're headed for the last roundup." They froze, staring at me like a circle of cattle eyeing a snake. "Tell Purvis he's next," I said to Montana. I kicked him in the thigh.

" 'The last roundup,' " I said to myself as I left. "Incredible."

I was five miles from Purvis's when the highway patrol car pulled me over. Cliff Younger. He got out of his unit and strode stiffly to my Bronco.

"Nice work, Storme," he said after I'd rolled down my window. "Soon as the call came through I knew it was you. Told you to stay away. Pulling a gun was dumb. Why'd you do it?"

"He said you weren't the greatest cop in Colorado. I couldn't let him get away with that."

"Yeah. That's funny. You're a regular David Letterman. Come on, we're going for a ride." I got out and locked the doors. Cars zipped by, whipping the cold air. "Oh yeah. You gonna give me the gun or do I take it?" I reached inside my jacket and handed it to him. He shucked the clip into his hand and shuffled the action, but there were no bullets in either. "Are you the king of stupid or what? You threatened those guys with an empty gun?"

"Seemed like the thing to do. I just showed it to them, anyway. I didn't threaten anybody."

We rode to the county jail where they took my wallet and belt, and frisked me. I called Chick.

"See if you can guess where I am?" I said.

"Let's see. No phones in the woods. Cindy Crawford's not in town. No rodeos or rattlesnake roundups going on. I give up."

"I'm in jail."

"Man, leave you alone for a minute. What'd you do?"

"I thumped around on Coy Montana a little bit."

"Selfish of you."

"And I flashed my gun some. Seems to have struck a nerve with the police. Can you come bail me out?"

"I don't know. I'm right in the middle of an *Andy Griffith* marathon. But if you promise to be my friend and personal slave I can swing by."

I gave him the location and hung up the phone. They placed me in a cell, which reeked of urine and old sweat, with a couple of practicing genetic mutants complete with tattoos, three-day beards, and tropical armpits. They were smoking generic cigarettes and practicing their tough-guy acts. I looked around the cell and sat down on a bed that was little more than a mattress stuffed with the feathers of a half dozen sickly chickens and smelling of must and tobacco.

"Hey, fresh meat," said a heavy guy with receding hair and a denim shirt with the sleeves cut out. "That's my bed." There were four beds hanging from chains on the wall and they were sitting on two of them.

"Whose bed you sitting on, then?" I said, still in a bad mood.

"He's sitting on my bed," said the other, a slender-faced guy with teeth like a fox squirrel. "I give him permission."

I didn't move. I nodded my head at the empty bed. "Whose is that?"

"That's ours too," said bad hairline.

I chuckled. "Got this all figured, don't you?"

"You laughing at us?"

"Think you'd be used to it by now."

Squirrel teeth stood and said, "You gotta pay us for your bunk. Cost you a pack of butts."

I patted my shirt and jeans. "Well, how you like that?" I said. "Fresh out."

"He ain't takin' us serious, Willy," said squirrel teeth. "You oughta take us serious, meat."

I pulled a cigar from my shirt pocket and stuck it between my teeth. "You know, guys. I'm not having a great day. We're stuck here awhile so let's make the best of it. Now, you just go back to naming the parasites currently inhabiting your bodies and I'll sit here and smoke my cigar." I lighted the cigar with a book of matches. The jailer had taken my lighter.

"Hey, asshole. Who you think you are?"

This was pleasant. "Just a guy," I said, "wants to be left alone." I wondered if they had another cell. Maybe one with cable TV and a vibrator chair.

"What're you in for?"

"Assault and battery," I said. They looked at each other.

"Yeah?" said Willy. "Who'd you assault? A coupla girls?"

"Hired killer, actually," I said.

"I don't believe you."

"Don't care what you believe." I wouldn't have to have the vibrator chair, I guess. They were both standing now.

"You oughta not fuck with us," said squirrel teeth. "Me 'n' Willy're in for armed robbery." He said it as if it would impress me. It didn't.

"Congratulations. Just shows what I know. I had you pegged for a couple of perverts run in for molesting farm animals."

"That's some mouth you got on you, asshole."

"Kind of a pretty mouth, though," said Willy.

"Yeah," agreed his friend. "Really pretty mouth. Nice to have a guy with a pretty mouth around." They took a step in my direction.

Maybe a black and white TV with local stations. I wasn't picky. I stood up and puffed my cigar. They closed the distance between us. I took another puff.

"You ain't got no sticks, maybe you can do something else for us," said squirrel teeth.

"Yeah," said Willy. "That'd be nice."

"You mean like be your girlfriend, right?" I said, taking another puff.

"Yeah, like that."

I took my cigar from my mouth and looked at it. "Naw. Thanks anyway, but you guys stink."

Squirrel teeth took a step in my direction and I put my cigar out. Unfortunately for him, I put it out on his face. He screamed and jumped back. I swiveled and kicked the fat guy in the nuts. His eyes rolled back and he doubled over. I whacked him on both temples with my fists and he sat back on the floor. I returned my attention to squirrel teeth. He ran at me. I head-faked left, shuffled right and stuck a left uppercut into his solar plexus. He fell, skidding on the floor and groaning.

Maybe just a radio tuned to a classical music station.

By this time a deputy had heard the commotion and came running. He saw the pair on the floor and me standing. My damaged cigar lay smoldering on the floor of the cell.

"What's going on?" demanded the deputy.

"Don't know," I said. "They don't jail very well. Maybe it's their first time."

I was moved to a private room, but there was no television in there, either. Took my matches, too. That did it. This place gets no more of my business. Willy and squirrel teeth kept yelling out all the unpleasantries they were going to subject me to if they caught me out alone. Thirty minutes later the deputy returned with Chick.

"About time," I said.

"Don't thank me. It just embarrasses me."

"You're free to go, Storme," said the deputy. "He paid your bail."

"I hope that doesn't make you think you can take liberties now," I said. We walked by the cell where Willy and squirrel teeth were. They muttered some obscenities and threats and generally terrorized us.

"What's this?" Chick said. "Some kind of lab experiment?"

"These are my sorority sisters, Buffy and Hillary."

I picked up my belongings. The deputy said that the Sun King ranch had called and dropped the charges. All a misunderstanding.

"Decent of them," Chick said.

"Innate charm. Works every time."

We got in Chick's Barracuda and drove to the impound area to pick up the Bronco. "Sandy called," Chick said. "Right after you did."

I looked out the window. "What'd she want?"

"Wanted to meet Billy. He knows she's his half-sister, now."

"How'd he take it?"

"Weirded him out. Kelly being his mother, especially. Knocked him for a loop. Maybe it'll shock him into having some sense. He could use some. Another thing she told me. Looks like you're making a day out of smacking people around."

"He had it coming."

"Three times in one day? Sounds lunatic to me."

"I've been having cramps and hot flashes all day."

He drove on. We passed billboards and convenience stores. "It ain't no good, Wyatt. I know about anger burning in your gut like fire. It'll twist you up inside. You can't go around beating the shit out of everybody."

"I skipped a couple of old ladies that took a parking spot from me."

"You're mad at Sandy, not the whole world."

And Montana. And myself. I told him about Kelly.

He whistled. "Man, you're on a hot streak. What was Montana doing while you were using him for a cymbal?"

"Bleeding," I said. "And moaning and looking surprised."

"Feel better?"

"Worse. I'm going to go see Purvis."

"Why?"

"I'll know when I get there and feel it out."

"You're not thinking real clear. Too much emotion. You're going to have to drop back and punt. You're usually more deliberate than this. Chill out some. You can get hurt real bad with these guys if you don't stop and study things."

I don't care, I thought. "I'm going to see Purvis. I'll watch what I do. You get Billy to a safe place. I'm pretty sure Harold Wallace was looking for something that would tell him where the weapons were the day I braced him." I didn't tell him Harold might have connected me to that incident. "Or the money. We've got both."

We were quiet for a minute.

Finally, Chick broke the silence. "Go slow, huh?"

"I have been," I said. "Didn't kill him, did I?"

The Mustang climbed the foothills below Crispin Purvis's estate. The floor of the rising plateau that was Colorado spread behind and below me—a mile high and rising. I parked on the heliport tarmac and walked to the house. A man I hadn't seen before answered the bell—mid-thirties, sandy hair, scar below his left ear. One of the shadow soldiers? I asked to see Purvis. He chuckled, shrugged and walked back into the house, saying nothing.

I walked in.

Rachmaninoff's Piano Concerto no. 2 in C Minor spilled into the room as if the walls were breathing it. Had to give Purvis credit for his taste in music if nothing else. He sat in a large den, smoking a pipe and examining a short, elaborately decorated sword, with a small flintlock pistol attached to it. A drink on the antique table at his side.

Lounging on a trundle bed near a small sunroom at the rear of the den was Janet Sterling, wearing a bikini bottom and earrings. I walked into the room, the sound of my shoes muffled on a huge Turkish rug, the real item. As I entered she swiveled, revealing heavy breasts. Saved me the trouble of having to frisk her. There was a clear martini pitcher on a glass cart nearby. Half empty. A lazy smile on her face.

"Well, look," she said, stretching like a tawny cat. I didn't gasp or gape. My mouth didn't fall open. What willpower. "It's the football player with the brains."

"Mr. Storme," Purvis said, placing the weapon on the table. His hair was slicked tight against his skull. "What a pleasant surprise. Please, have a seat." He indicated the pistol-sword. "Unusual weapon isn't it? I collect them. The more exotic, the better. Can I get you something? A drink?"

I shook my head. The television was tuned to a station where stock-market prices were trailing along the bottom of the screen. There was a lion's head on one wall.

"Nice lion," I said. "Yours?"

"Yes. Took him in Zambia. He was a rogue. A man-killer. I was commissioned by the government to kill him. Traveled around Africa and Asia for several years exterminating animals that were dangerous. Out of control." He leveled his eyes at me, and the corners of his mouth twitched into a malevolent smile. Behind him, Janet Sterling shrugged into a short robe, allowing one breast to stare at me for an extra moment before she covered it. She smiled at me with her head cocked.

"Dangerous work," I said.

"Yes, it is. However, it has its own rewards. There is little excitement left. We've civilized the thrill out of society. I've hunted wild boar in Germany, Kodiak and grizzly bear in Canada, Cape buffalo in Africa. However, nothing quite compares with combat. Someone shooting back. You were in combat. Didn't you find it exciting, even exhilarating?"

I looked at him. Janet Sterling looked at me.

"No? Come now, Storme. I've examined the record. Decorated. Silver Star. Two tours of duty. Confess. You found the field of battle fascinating, even intoxicating. The iron whore, as it were." Janet Sterling raised one eyebrow at me. "Come now, how was Vietnam?"

"Like Disneyland except scarier and people were dying. I blame quality control. I don't think they checked the rides. You know how it was, anyway. Why are you looking into my war record?"

"I might ask the same thing? Why are you looking into my background?"

"Matt Jenkins is dead. Jackie Burlingame is missing. You were at Matt's with Representative Braden and your pet snake, Montana. I don't like coincidences."

"Surely you don't think I or an employee of mine had anything to do with Mr. Jenkins's unfortunate death, do you?"

"What do you think?"

"Is that why you went up to the Sun King?"

I shrugged.

"Harold Wallace, one of the ranch hands, told me about it. Other things as well. Coy is very worked up about the whole thing."

"Yes," said Janet Sterling. "You hurt his pride. He'll be all pouty now."

"Maybe you can console him," said Purvis, without looking at her. "Lick his wounds, as it were. Perhaps favor him with new ones."

"Screw the little bastard," she said. "You, too."

"We're forgetting ourselves, aren't we?" he said.

"I do so love it when you speak in the corporate third person," she said. "It's so sexy. Almost makes me forget you're a eunuch."

He turned his head to look at her. "Pull your claws in, darling. We have company."

She ignored him. "Will you be staying for dinner, Wyatt?" she asked me. "We're having raw meat."

"You are, of course, welcome to stay for dinner, Storme," said Purvis.

"No thanks."

"Janet, I need to talk with Mr. Storme. Why don't you dress for dinner?"

"Maybe I'd like to hear it," she said. "Would you like me to stay, Wyatt? Or maybe just watch me dress?"

"I need to talk to him privately," I said.

"Man talk?"

"Just talk."

She left the room and I willed myself not to watch.

"She is a beautiful woman," said Purvis. "But like most beautiful women, she can be troublesome and disruptive."

"You two playing house?"

"No. I don't sleep with whores. Not even high-priced ones. Not knowingly, anyway." He said it without venom. As if we were discussing stock prices. Very controlled.

"So why have her here?"

"The entertainment industry is an unusual business requiring unusual arrangements. What do you hope to gain by coming here?"

"I know a secret," I said.

He folded the paper into a small square. "There are many secrets. Which do you think you know?"

"I know about Michael Braden."

His ears gave a little twitch, betraying the otherwise impassive face. "Joring's son died tragically, in Vietnam."

"He's alive and I think Burlingame was blackmailing Braden with the information and you knew about it."

"How do you know that?"

"No denials?"

"Fairy tales do not require debunking."

"Got another one for you," I said. "Once upon a time there was an Australian gunrunner who wanted to grow up to be a real guy. Along the way he used blood money to establish legitimate businesses. You with me so far?"

He placed his fingertips together forming a triangle in front of him. "I'm enthralled. Please continue."

"But that wasn't enough for him. He was into danger and intrigue. Wealth insulated him from the thrill of peril and adventure. So he began to slip into old habits. There is something powerful about destructive weapons, and power was alluring to him. Especially political power. But he knew his background wouldn't stand scrutiny, that he was a naturalized citizen with phony papers. Am I boring you?"

His expression had evolved from relaxed bemusement to sharp annoyance. "Hardly," he said between his teeth.

"Love a good audience. Anyway, he opened an old door and found himself a nasty skeleton. This skeleton belonged to a politician. So he bought the legislator. Which isn't that tough anymore. Everybody's got one." Then to let him know I was aware of his real nationality, I said, "And they have even less dignity and integrity than some low-born pirate from New Zealand."

His hand dug into the arm of his chair. Composing himself, he puffed on his pipe. He stood and walked over to the lion's head. "I have several heads like this one," he said. "But you know that, don't you? Yes, of course, you do. You were prowling around my house the other evening like some cat burglar instead of a guest. But, no matter." A satisfied smile appeared on his face and then, like the blink of an eye, was gone. "This particular lion is special. A worthy adversary. Cunning and powerful. He had been wounded by a local who had killed his mate. He began to take livestock. Goats, cattle, pigs, the occasional villagers. It was as if the wound had driven him insane with a lust for vengeance." He paused to smile at me again. "He eluded me time and again, outwitting snares, baits, and native beaters. The locals thought him magic. A demon.

"Then he began to make mistakes. Became bolder. I shot him as he lay just outside the village with his latest kill, a yearling calf. As I raised my gun he roared at me. A terrible bellowing. It had scared others off before me. I shot him and he charged. I shot him twice as he came on. He wouldn't stop. Kept coming. He dropped dead within a few yards of me, his heart and lungs shattered. A magnificent warrior." He looked up at the lion, then back at me. "Dead, nonetheless."

"When I was a kid," I said, leaning back, "my uncle Fred had a stray dog he'd taken in. A mongrel. What we called a Heinz fifty-seven. One day my uncle found some of his chickens killed. There were feathers around the dog's favorite sleeping place. Fred shot the dog. 'Once they've tasted blood they're good for nothing,' he told me. 'You gotta get rid of 'em.' "

Purvis took the pipe from his lips and exhaled a plume of smoke. He looked along the pipe at me. "Is there an analogy here?"

"I'm not happy about Matt's death. Extremely agitated as a matter of fact. To the point I might not be much fun to have around. It might become uncomfortable for those I blame. I'm hurt by his death. You might say wounded. And I won't lie outside the village waiting for the great white hunter to come after me."

"Is that a threat?"

"You know Montana did it."

"That is up to the police to determine."

"Did you see Montana the day it happened?"

"No. But Dumont did."

"Fortuitous."

"There seems to be an edge of sarcasm in your voice. Do you doubt the veracity of Mr. Dumont's account?"

"He's a liar."

"Did it occur to you that he might be telling the truth?"

"The truth never occurs to guys like Dumont and Montana. You either, now that I think about it."

"I don't think I care for your conversation."

"I expect that from someone who surrounds himself with puppets and sycophants."

"Miss Sterling tells me you have a book with my name in it."

"Maybe."

"I would like to have it."

"Unrequited desires are the worst."

"I'm willing to pay. How much?"

"Two hundred thirty million dollars and an autographed picture of Julius Caesar."

"Perhaps I'll just take it."

"Perhaps you should try."

His eyes narrowed, like the flinching of a cat whose tail has been stepped on. He pushed a button on the house intercom, which interrupted the music. "Taylor," he said. "Come in here at once."

"I have things to do, Storme," said Purvis. "Things much more important than listening to the delusions of some half-literate jock."

The man who answered the door came into the room and said, "What can I do for you, Mr. Purvis?"

"Mr. Storme is leaving, Taylor. Show him the door."

I laughed. "You'll have to do better than him, Crispy."

"Come with me," said Taylor.

"When I'm ready. Wait at the door for me," I said.

He took a step toward me. I looked at Purvis and said, "He touches me, I'll put him on the wall next to the lion."

"Tough guy, huh?" said Taylor.

"Two hundred pounds of molten lava. Touch and you get burned."

Taylor pulled a snub-nosed .38 from his jacket. Pointed it at my chest.

I looked at my watch. "Will you look at the time," I said. "Just gets away from me. Late for another appointment. Love to hang around, chat with you guys, eat dinner, stick the gun up Taylor's ass, stuff like that, but I have to go."

Taylor waved me toward the door with the gun. "Let's go, smartass," he said.

"I'll be back," I said. And I left with as much dignity as the situation would allow.

I spent the rest of the day and the next morning thinking about what to do with Purvis. No matter which way I turned it, I couldn't fit him into a scenario where he would be caught with the guns and a red face. Finally, I left the cabin and went for a drive in the Mach I before I shaved my wrists.

I like isolation. Those moments of peace when you are not assailed by crowds, living bras, underarm deodorant, political action groupies, this year's next thing or life's doomed dramas and unrequested soap operas.

I'd sought solitude, removing myself from the crowd. My choice. But solitude is often a hard bargain, and there were times when I couldn't turn off my head. Too much history crowded into the quiet places.

Sandy gave me order and purpose. Somebody to shower and shave for. My tendencies were to live for myself, selfishly seeking only my way, my definitions. Social lethargy creates the cultural hobo. But that avenue was a dead end. When I played football

I had found people who would forgive any transgression on my part, any indignity, as long as I caught passes in the end zone on Sunday. Celebrity became cathedral. Worship the light of the famous.

Once we'd been forced to endure the presence of a famous action-movie hero who was the friend of team owner T. J. Crawford. Guy was a complete ass who offered criticism and advice to anyone who'd listen. He'd stand on the sidelines, wearing a Cowboys jacket, rare cologne, and a two-hundred-dollar haircut, secure in the knowledge that no one would deny him anything.

He tried to tell me how to run my patterns. Being me, I politely invited him to shut up and get lost. "This isn't a movie and I get no stand-in. They're hitting me for real and the harder they hit me, the more they like it. So go stand somewhere else."

For my insight I got a trip to the principal's office.

"T.J.'s very upset," said team VP Richmond Butler. "You insulted his close personal friend."

"He likes him so much, have him sit with him in his personal box."

"Do the other players feel that way?"

"I don't speak for everybody. Just me."

"Your problem, Storme, is you don't appreciate the benefits of celebrity. Not even your own."

"And your problem," I said, "is you don't see that celebrity hasn't anything to do with it."

"T.J. wants you to apologize."

I laughed. "You want me to block three-hundred-pound monsters. I do that. You want me to catch the ball across the middle. I do that. But that's all you get."

"Maybe we'll trade your ass to Green Bay. Gets cold up there."

"Hot or cold, the field is a hundred yards long and I can catch the ball either place. No movie stars up there."

But they didn't trade me.

I was up against the same thing now. The Honorable Joring Braden was a phony—a womanizing carpetbagger who hung out

with thugs and had federal protection to do so—tolerated because he had the right political viewpoint for the moment. And
because he was a celebrity in the political arena. Neither meant
anything to me. To me, he was just another self-serving creep
standing on the sidelines telling the players how to get the job
done. No dirt on his uniform. No sweat on his face.

A sideline pass is not a ticket to the game. Me? I was a gate-
crasher armed with a crowbar and a monkey wrench. They were
going to have to catch me before they threw me out.

I pushed the Mustang up the highway. Rolled the window
down and cold air rushed in, blowing my hair and taking my
breath. After about five miles of balls-out driving in dogsled cold
I rolled up the window and slowed down. Turned the car around
and headed back to the cabin.

Chick was there when I got back. He was nibbling the throat
of a long-necked Coors and smoking one of my cigars, one leg
lounging across the arm of a chair, a Cool Hand Luke smile on
his ageless face.

"It was too easy," he said. "Our luck's changing, partner."

"Your luck's changing, anyway," I said. "I take it you stroked
your old hide-and-seek buddy Dirk."

"Played him like a violin. Told him we wanted to make a
deal. Let Braden off the hook. At first, he was suspicious, but
that comes with the job description. Told him we weren't interested in Braden, that you had a major hard-on for Purvis and
Montana. He dumbed up, like he didn't know what I was talking
about, then said he'd like to get together, have a couple drinks,
talk over old times. Then he wanted to know where we could
get together. That's when I shook the line. Told him, I didn't
know. Might not be safe to be seen with him. That the Company
still followed me around trying to screw me over. That's when
he said he could shake loose, but only if I really wanted to shoot
the shit, nothing heavy. He bit and I popped the jig, hung it in
his jaw and reeled him in." He smiled, happy with himself.

"If you only had a little more confidence . . ."

He held up the bottle, said, "Here's to all the little people I had to climb over to be stupendous." Then he took a healthy knock.

"What's that do for us?"

"Gives us some breathing room. Dirk's a heavyweight. I don't wanna be watching for him."

"I want to visit Congressman Braden's office in Denver."

"Thought you were about as political as an Eskimo."

"Time to come out of retirement. I'm concerned about the issues confronting our nation."

"Land of the free, home of the brave. We could lobby him on gun control. Tell 'im to always use two hands."

We drove to Denver in Chick's blood-red Barracuda, me driving, him drinking. Joring Braden's Colorado office was downtown near the state capitol, in a two-story dark-steel and smoked-glass building. I parked a block away and we walked across the raw concrete sidewalks, as alone, with the exception of the downtown traffic, as if we were on another planet.

Braden's office was on the second floor. The carpet was thick and mauve. The executive assistant and the receptionist were both young and beautiful. No chauvinist, he. He respected all women, as long as they were leggy and beautiful. Chick has a theory that guys only talk the feminist rap so they can get laid.

The office was well appointed and furnished, hushed by the carpet and the gravity of the position. Two men waited in the office—one a young exec type in a tailored suit. He held a long tube probably containing plans for something Colorado couldn't do without unless the voters saw the price tag, which mustn't happen, as they—naïve children that they were—couldn't possibly understand what was best for them. The other man was past middle age, heavy-jowled, and unused to waiting. He looked at his watch intermittently and patted his foot like a drumming grouse.

"Good afternoon, gentlemen," said the receptionist. "May I help you?" Not "Can I help you?" but "May I help you?" Semantic posture was the first lesson of modern politics.

"Yes you can," I said. "We're here to see Joring. We have an appointment. And I'm sorry we're running a little late. Should we go on in? Old Joring," I said to Chick. "Be good to see him again, won't it?"

"Like old times," Chick said.

"Pardon me," said the middle-aged guy with the watch and the nervous foot. "But *I* have an appointment which is thirty minutes overdue."

"What do you think, Morris?" I said to Chick. "Can we wait?"

Chick turned his head sideways, as if in thought. Made a lips-parted grimace, his teeth together. "Don't see how, Chester. Joring said he wanted to see us as soon as possible. Said he'd cancel all other appointments if we'd come by."

"This is intolerable," said the man. The man with the rolled plans looked like he'd swallowed an icicle. The receptionist was nonplussed, but the executive assistant—Barbara Faring-Cross, by the triangular nameplate on her desk—was less so. She looked like a seasoned campaigner, despite the soft brown eyes, tapered waist, and aerobicized legs. Couldn't trust good-looking women to be demure anymore. More's the pity.

"What are your names, gentlemen?" she asked. I flashed my brush-three-times-daily Dentyne smile, but she shrugged it off. Definitely a contender. Her hands were on her hips. She'd obviously witnessed similar performances.

But never by any so adept. She was melted cheese before us.

"I'm Chester Flankerout and this is my friend Morris Oldman. We're good friends of Joring Braden. Haven't seen him in years. Faring-Cross? That English?"

"No, it's not. Do you have him in your appointment book, Sara?" Ms. Faring-Cross asked the receptionist.

"No ma'am, I don't." She looked at us. "Sorry."

I scratched my head in bewilderment. "Don't understand it. Old Joring said to come by today. You think he could've forgot to tell you?"

"Not a chance," said Faring-Cross, hands on hips. "If you'd care to wait, maybe I can work you in. About an hour?" She cocked her head sideways.

I looked at Chick. "What do you think, Oldman?"

Chick shook his head. "Think we need to see him immediately."

"Afraid of that," I said. I gave Ms. Faring-Cross a palms-up shrug. "We need to see him right away."

"That will be impossible."

"All things are possible," I said. "If your heart's right with God."

"Gentlemen," she said evenly. "Congressman Braden is a busy man—"

"No doubt about that," I said.

Her eyes flashed, then she remembered that diplomacy was the second lesson of modern politics. We might be voters. "Congressman Braden will be glad to receive you. But you'll have to wait your turn. So please have a seat and I'll get you in as soon as possible."

"She's convincing," Chick said.

I looked at her. "Tell him Wyatt Storme is here to see him. Not later, not tomorrow, right now. If that's unacceptable, tell him my next stop is the *Denver Post* and I'll accept the consequences of that but he can't. Tell him the magic word is January 7, 1968. Do it now or we're going in anyway."

"See here," said the foot tapper. "I've important business and I have an appointment."

"Ain't it a bitch?" Chick said. He turned to the receptionist. "You single?"

Faring-Cross's jaw tightened. She walked stiff-legged to her desk and asked for security.

"Bad choice," I said.

"Rather force my way in anyway," Chick said.

We opened the door to Braden's office and walked in. Ms. Faring-Cross yelled for us to stop. We ignored her. Braden was seated behind an aircraft-carrier walnut desk. Behind him a glass wall framed him with the Denver skyline. Nice effect. A subliminal atmosphere of imputed power. I would have been impressed if I were the type. Across from him sat two men in business suits who swiveled in concert to see who was interrupting their congressional audience.

"Excuse me?" said Braden, in a tone suggesting we were the ones who needed excusing.

"Good afternoon, gentlemen," said Chick. "We represent the Clean Oxygen Foundation of Colorado and we're hear to clear the air. If you'll pardon us, this will only take a minute."

"What is this, Joring?" asked one of the men.

"I . . . a . . . don't know."

I said, "Yes you do."

Ms. Faring-Cross bustled through the door behind us. "You men will have to leave immediately. I'm sorry, Congressman. I've called security."

"You hear that, Braden?" I said. "She's called security. That what you want? Think about it. Think about January 7, 1968, while you're at it."

Braden was turning a pen over in his hand. He addressed his invited guests. "A . . . gentlemen, I'm afraid our business will have to wait. I apologize for the inconvenience." He looked to Ms. Faring-Cross. "Security won't be necessary."

"But these—"

Braden held up a hand. "It's all right, Barbara."

Faring-Cross glared. She was good at it. Chick smiled at her. She looked like she wanted to bite us.

The two men stood, looking disgruntled. Braden shook their hands, his polished smile in place again. The show must go on. They left the room without looking at us, escorted by Faring-Cross, congressional pit bull.

"What is it you want?" Braden asked, sitting down.

"Not supposed to call them by their first name anymore," I said. "It diminishes her. Makes her feel subordinate. I'm surprised a politically correct guy like yourself doesn't know better. Gonna get picketed by severe-looking women in slacks if you don't watch it."

"I would appreciate it if you would get to it," he said. "I've much to do today. I don't have time for some fantasizing busybody with too much time on his hands."

Chick looked at me. "See," he said. "Not everybody likes you."

"Hardly anybody, in fact," I said.

"It's because you're always fantasizing."

"Probably," I said. I turned to Braden, who was leaning back in his swivel chair and considering me with hooded eyes, not yet defeated, but contemplating that eventuality. "Congressman, we know about your son. Eventually, we'll find him. When we do, we're going to expose you."

"I don't know what you're talking about," he said. "I think it is reckless and insensitive to come in—"

"Knock it off. I've got nothing for you. I saw too many guys die while you played political football. Guys you sent over there. I've got no use for politicians, but you exceed the slime limits of even that group."

"I don't have to take this kind of talk."

"Yes, you do. Not only did you spirit your son out of Vietnam, you helped cover up the black market weapons scam he was involved in. Worse, I think two men died because of your son."

Braden jumped up from his chair and slammed a hand down on his desk. "That's enough. You are chasing shadows. There is not one shred of evidence that anything you've said is true."

"Sit down," I said. "It's too late for theatrics. It's the truth and I can prove it. Just a matter of finding someone who knew Jackie Burlingame and Randle Lightfoot and drives a black Beretta." His shoulders slumped as if he'd been punched. He sat down slowly. "That's right, Congressman. You saved your son from Vietnam but the lesson he learned was corruption, deception, and outcomes justifying the means. Make a tremendous congressman. Got all the moves."

Braden looked at his desk, then, without looking up, said, "What is it you want from me?"

"Nothing," I said. "You make me sick. Withdraw from the Senate race and we'll never reveal what we know."

"But . . . but, I've got important legislation pending. I've done a lot of good for this country. For my constituents. I chair important committees. Influential committees. Colorado and its people benefit from that."

"You 'Greater Good' guys give me a fucking pain," Chick said. "Same old argument. What's a little graft? A little corruption? You guys are taking care of the public interest. You're too good to us, boss."

"Announce your withdrawal," I said.

"But—"

"You got forty-eight hours."

"Maybe you won't be around that long," said Braden.

"That's much better, Congressman." I leaned across his desk. "No more pretense. No more filibuster. Just you and me. Straight up. You try to take me out before I burn you down. If you're thinking about the way Jackie Burlingame was handled, I'm not that stupid. Anything happens to me, the story goes right to the press and the police. All of it."

"Gentlemen," he said, a smile spreading across his face. Joring Braden shifted gears in his demeanor. "We've gotten off on the wrong foot. Please accept my apology." Trying to work us now. When things get tough we revert to practiced habits. In Braden's case that meant the soft soap. "What do you have to gain by this? Why not use this to your advantage? I could be very helpful to you."

I looked at Chick. "What do you think?"

He smiled. "Can't hear a word he's saying."

"Me neither. Forty-eight hours or your political career goes in the toilet, Braden."

"You can't do this," said Braden.

"Oh sure," Chick said. "We can. We will. In fact, we'll consider it a public service. Have a nice day, asshole."

We adjourned.

We left the office building and walked back out into the cold autumn afternoon.

"Faring-Cross forgot to wish us Godspeed," Chick said.

"Your fault," I said. "You have an overbearing manner."

"We still don't know where Michael Braden is. Without him, threatening to expose Daddy dearest is a bluff."

He was right. We needed Michael or we needed documented proof that Michael was alive. "I'd bet my Gloria Steinem blowup doll we find Michael Braden, we've found Captain Marvel."

"Yeah, but where is he? We could go hang around the Electric Ranch and ask around."

There were other questions. Somebody was double-crossing Purvis. Somebody in his orbit. But who? "Which one of them do you think is trying to rip off Purvis and how do we smoke him out into the open?"

We were outside the double doors of the building. Chick paused to light a cigarette. "Don't know," he said. "But the money could be used as bait."

I nodded my head. "We've just got to figure out how to dangle it without Purvis knowing we've got it."

"Donovan will be sniffing around when he finds out we neutered the congressman. You call Purvis and offer the guns. That'll pin him down for now. Then . . ." He stopped walking. He snapped his fingers and said, "Got it."

"What?"

"I'm an intellectual Godzilla. The little black book. The last code. J/CS—BAR #5554326. A phone number?"

"Worth a try."

We walked to a phone booth. Chick dug a quarter out of his jeans and punched in the numbers from memory. I looked at the sky. The late afternoon sun peeked through the clouds.

Chick put the phone to his ear. He smiled and said, "Sorry, wrong number," and hung up.

"Who answered?" I asked.

"Chicken Sam."

"Chicken Sam?"

"Chicken Sam's is a biker bar."

I thought about our confrontation in the Electric Ranch with the three bikers and the information Billy gave us. "Jubal?"

"J for Jubal. CS for Chicken Sam's. Could be."

It fit my conjecture about who I thought Jubal really was. "One way to find out."

"First, we set up Purvis," Chick said.

I called Purvis with the other phone number from the black book. A lackey answered the phone, but Purvis came on when I told the guy who I was.

"What do you want, Storme?" said Purvis.

"Your phone etiquette could use a little work," I said. "I've got something you might be interested in."

"Which would be?"

"A product."

"Not on the phone," he said.

"The line isn't being monitored."

"How is it you have this number?"

"ESP?"

"Talk to Montana."

"No. Not Montana. You. You were ripped off once and the salesman was killed. Montana may have been part of that. I deal with you or nobody."

There was a pause on the other end. A long pause. I thought he might have hung up. Then abruptly he said, "How do you want to do it?"

"Not now. Soon. I'll need time to—"

He interrupted me with curses. "I'll not play silly games."

"No games," I said. "You want this or not?"

"Congressman Braden called. You are squeezing him."

"Just as hard as I can."

"He is important to me. Perhaps—"

"Give up on him. Regardless of which way you jump, no matter what happens, he goes down."

"You're a hard one, now, aren't you?"

"In or out?"

"I want the black book."

"No. The guns are all you get."

"Call me back when you decide how you want to do it."

He hung up.

"Well?" Chick said.

"He was glad to hear from me. You blame him? Come on, let's get out of here. I'll buy you a beer."

"Any place special."

"Little out-of-the-way place I heard about."

"Okay." He smiled. "Just as long as there aren't any low-lifes there."

Chicken Sam's was a low cinderblock building painted a faded maroon. The parking lot looked like a Harley-Davidson outlet. There was a double-wide trailer behind it. There was only one car parked outside in the dirty gravel. But it wasn't a black Beretta. Maybe Billy was wrong.

A dark-headed guy with a Rambo headband was lying across the seat of his bike, long-necked Coors in hand, talking to a biker babe. Another biker was passed out on the ground nearby. It looked like the setting for a Roger Corman movie.

I parked the fireball-red Barracuda away from the knot of chrome-and-iron hogs and we got out.

"We *would* be driving my car," Chick said.

"Wouldn't be so bad if you'd buy something a little more sedate."

"Any of these sleazoids key my baby I'm gonna thread 'em through the spokes of his Harley."

"Talk, talk, talk."

We opened the ratchety screen door. It was brown with rust and no longer screened much. Then we wrenched open a hollow-core door pocked with splintered depressions. The hardwood floor was several years overdue for a waxing, the finish nibbled away by leather boots. A low cloud of smoke hung between the lights and the cue-scarred pool tables. The bittersweet smell of marijuana was heavy. Bad electronic music belched from the jukebox.

There were thirteen people in the bar, not counting the bartender, all wearing denim and leather and do-it-yourself haircuts; all fitting the description. Nine males, four females. The bartender was a fat guy with a black beard, an earring dangling from the ear that wasn't missing. As we walked across the floor, heads swiveled and followed us. I felt like a vegetarian at a cattlemen's barbecue. At least the music didn't stop when we came in. A mixed blessing.

Chick had his "Isn't life funnier than a sandpaper condom?" smile on his face. If you knew Chick you got used to it, since it didn't matter to him whether you did or not. If you didn't know him you got the impression you were the object of his amusement, which, believe it or not, ticks some people off. Chick looked around the room, pivoting 360 degrees as he did, taking it all in, as if this were a scientific expedition. Stanley and Livingstone go to a biker bar.

"My God, Storme," he said, completing his panoramic spin. "We have stumbled upon an experiment in broken chromosomes and arrested development. Call the Smithsonian immediately. Bartender! A boilermaker here. Bud and Blackjack. And fresh horses. We're Pony Express riders. The mail must go through."

The bartender set a long-necked bottle and a shot glass on the counter. Filled the glass with whiskey. He looked at me. "Whadda you want?"

"A Coke," I said.

"Want a nipple on it?"

I heard Chick chuckle down in his throat. Tolerance, must remember tolerance. "No thanks. But if it's not too much trouble, could you serve it with a plate of Oreos and a nice paper napkin?"

"We don't get many straights in here," said the bartender, plunking down my can.

"Can't understand it," Chick said. "Family atmosphere. Friendly service. Maybe it's the location."

"Seven bucks," said the bartender, ignoring Chick.

I handed him a twenty. "You can keep the change," I said. "If you'll tell me how to get hold of a biker named Jubal."

"Don't know anybody by that name."

"Six-foot. Looks like a Marshall Tucker fan. A little gray in the beard. Rangy. Intelligent eyes. Older guy. Said if I ever needed to get hold of him this was the place."

"You look like the heat." He handed me the change. "Besides, I don't know nobody looks like that."

"We're not cops and I need to get hold of him. Keep the change and I'll add another Alex Hamilton."

He walked to the other end of the bar and ignored us.

"Well," Chick said. "Handled that like a pro."

"You could've done better?"

"Couldna done worse. This is a closed society, man. They don't talk. Won't rat out a brother."

"Didn't know you were a sociologist."

"One of my myriad talents."

"So what do you suggest?"

"We're in Indian country. They're watching us. Know we're looking for Jubal. We hang around long enough somebody'll come to us. The word'll get to him and he'll either show up to eyeball us or he'll saddle up and boogie."

"Doesn't help us much."

"There's a third possibility," Chick said, sipping whiskey.

"Which is?"

"They could beat the shit out of us with chains."

"Prefer they didn't."

"That's the trouble with you. Never open to new experience."

"That music is dissolving the enamel on my molars. Do something about it."

So, we waited. Chick fed quarters into the jukebox and punched in some numbers while I drank my Coke and reveled in the ambience of Chicken Sam's. Steppenwolf's "Ride with Me" rumbled from the jukebox. Chick returned.

"Is that great?" Chick said. "There's a whole string of sixties stuff on the box, mostly Steppenwolf."

"I'll take it," I said.

John Kay's voice faded and Jim Morrison began singing "Riders on the Storm." Chick ordered another boilermaker and I decided against another two-dollar lukewarm Coke. The bartender had just given Chick his change when three arguments against allowing the species to continue walked up behind us.

"The fuck you guys doin' here?" asked a guy with a pock-marked face and a tangerine-colored topknot on his otherwise bald head. He looked like an Algonquin Indian with a bad rinse, or a big troll doll. The guy on his right hand was shorter, with mean weasel eyes set in a pinched face. Looked like the product of child abuse. The third guy was wearing a black leather vest over bare flesh adorned with a galaxy of tattoos, like Rod Steiger in *The Illustrated Man*. He looked like he could bench-press his Harley.

The bartender walked to the back room.

"Didn't I see you guys in that Clint Eastwood movie with the orangutan?" Chick said, smiling as always.

"You see something funny, motherfucker?" said topknot.

"Lots of things."

"Wonder how funny you'd think it was we stomp the shit outta you?"

"Guy's a poet," Chick said.

"Some people just have a way with words," I said, my hand inside my coat. All three of the guys had blades. From the bulge inside weasel-eye's jacket I'd say he was carrying.

It was then that Jubal, who I'd concluded was a.k.a. Michael Braden, came into the bar from a back room. The bartender was with him.

"Let's get down," said topknot.

"Wouldn't do that, Banjo," said Jubal, approaching.

"Why I gotta listen to you, Jubal?" Banjo said. "I'll buzz the straights any fucking time I want."

"Not these," Jubal said, stroking his beard. "Saw them kick hell out of Bull and Little Frank." He smiled at us as he walked between us and our new playmates. "Put them on the ground like it was nothing. Didn't even break a sweat." He turned to face us. Smiled. "You guys gonna fight every brother in the bar?"

"Fight some," Chick said. "Shoot some."

"You'd have to," Jubal said.

"Be a lot of motorcycles for sale."

"You have someplace we can talk?" I said.

"In the back."

"I ain't taking his shit," said Banjo.

"That's up to you," Jubal said. "We've drunk a lot of beer together, Banjo. Smoked a lotta dope. I'm telling you this guy'll

put you in traction. It's what he does, man. He's good at it."
He put his hand on the back of Banjo's neck. "Let it go, babe."

"He's gotta 'pologize," said Banjo. "He can't dis me in front
of the guys when I'm wearing colors."

Jubal looked at Chick. "What's it cost you, huh?"

Chick said, "Sorry for the misunderstanding." He reached
into his pocket, pulled out a ten-dollar bill, placed it on the bar
and said to the bartender, "A round for these guys."

"We talk now?" I said.

"Sure, man," said Jubal. "This way."

We started to follow him out. But, as we turned, Banjo pulled
a knife and came at Chick. Chick whirled, swept the knife hand
away with his right hand and drove the fingers of his left hand
under the armpit of the biker. Banjo groaned, as if giving birth,
and the knife clattered to the floor. Chick followed that with a
knee to the solar plexus. Banjo fell to the floor. I reached inside
my jacket and lifted the Browning from its holster but kept it
inside my jacket, watching the other two, particularly weasel-
eyes. As Banjo hit the floor, Chick stomped the man's right
hand. There was the sound of walnuts cracking. Chick backed
up a step and stayed in a crouch, hands ready. It happened so
fast Manbeast and weasel-eyes had no time to react. They had
been waiting for free beer when it started. Now they stared wide-
eyed at the hapless Banjo, laid out on the weathered floor, his
orange topknot splayed out like a tassel, his hand shivering in
pain.

Chick relaxed.

Jubal sighed, walked over to the groaning man, squatted on
his haunches, and said, "Tried to tell you, man."

I own the place," said Jubal. We were in the back office, which contained an old desk, a few kitchen chairs, and a cot. The walls were decorated with biker-babe calendar art, posters of Jimi Hendrix and the Grateful Dead, and the Beatles' *Abbey Road* album cover. The bartender brought a pitcher of beer and set it on the desk.

"Bought it three years ago. Doesn't bring in much money but it gives the guys a place to hang out. Snow's coming. Not much riding now. They're outcasts like me. Believe it or not we're not welcome many places."

"Look, Jubal," I said. "We've got to ask you things you may not like."

"Like what's my real name?" he said. He was calm about it. Poured Chick a glass of beer. Then himself. "That's why you came looking for me, wasn't it? Knew somebody'd figure it out sooner or later. How'd you catch on to it?"

I told him about the coded phone number in Jackie Burlingame's little book. "Then we just played the hunch."

"Poor Jackie," he said. "I didn't know that was gonna happen. That's straight. Montana and Dumont are predators, man. Greedheads. One of you guys was in the van that day, right? Has to be."

"And you're Captain Marvel."

He smiled. "You got this all doped out, don't you? What the hell? Tired of it, anyway. How long can you be a ghost? You guys gonna turn me over to the pigs, man?" He said it as if he'd been informed he had an overdue traffic ticket.

"Don't know," I said. "I understand wanting to get out of Nam."

He smiled a weary smile. "I really hated it over there. Still have these wiggy dreams about it. Ever have those? What's really weird, man, is I was pretty good at the soldier thing, dig? Made corporal. Was about to make another stripe. Bizarre to be good at something like that, y'know?"

"I don't blame your father for getting you out," I said.

He laughed. Threw back his head and laughed heartily. He settled down and said, "You think Mr. Capital Gains got me out of Nam because he was concerned for my safety? No way, man. I went over the hill. AWOL. I got busted in a whorehouse raid. Had a bag of Cambodian Red and two Oriental chicks with me when they came in. Wouldn't do for the congressman's son to be eating dope and consorting with whores. So my loving father made a deal with the M.P.s—who were dirty, by the way—to get me out. The M.P.s dusted some black-market gooks. I helped in exchange for my freedom. Nice story, huh? No, the honorable Joring Braden spirited me out of there because it was an election year. Look bad if his son was a deserter, a doper, and a whore-monger. They faked my death and made a fucking hero out of me. That way he got the sympathy vote and the hawk vote. My old man's got all the bases covered all the time."

"You don't sound like an appreciative son."

"I hardly know the bastard," he said, with a dark glint in his eyes I hadn't seen before. "He was never around when I was a kid. Messed around on Mom until she couldn't stand it any-more. I know his bullshit's what caused her heart to burst." His thoughtful brown eyes darkened. "He married one of his sticks, but that didn't last very long either."

"How long has it been since you've seen your father?"

"Recent. But he didn't see me. Before that we hadn't talked since 1972. And then he said it wouldn't be good for him politi-cally for us to be seen together, so I hit him up for some bread and split to California. He sent money for a few years, then just stopped."

"Did you know Jackie Burlingame was blackmailing him?"

He rubbed a hand across his face. "That why they snuffed him?"

"I think so."

"Shit." He leaned back in his chair, pursing his lips together. Then he leaned forward with his head down and rubbed his face with both hands. " 'S afraid of that," he said to the floor. He lifted his head. "Jackie wasn't blackmailing him entirely for himself."

"What do you mean?" I asked.

"Helping you blackmail him, wasn't he?" Chick said.

"He owed it to me." He shook his head. "No, that's not entirely right. I wanted to stick it to him. Like he stuck it to me. All these years living without an identity. Without a name. I don't exist, man. You know how that feels?" I chanced a glance at Chick. He looked over at me and arched the apostrophe eye-brow at me. Michael Braden kept talking. "I watched him get powerful. Rich. He didn't even tell me Mom died. I had to read it in the paper. He just shuffled Mom and me out of his life. I still remember when he sent me off to Nam. 'Chance for you to prove your manhood. Do your patriotic duty,' he said."

" 'Prove your manhood'?" I said.

"Yeah. Like that. You believe that shit? Like it was getting your driver's license or something. Here's a guy pulls off a scam so his son doesn't become a political liability, then reverses his

position on the war, talking about 'patriotic duty.' So it doesn't
bother me too much to soak the son of a bitch."

I thought on it for a moment, then said, "Were you expecting
a payoff the day Jackie B. was killed?"

His brows knitted, making him look his age. "No. What are
you talking about?"

"Jackie went into business for himself." I explained about the
varied estimates as to how much money was in the bag. "It
explains some things," I said. "Why Jackie was killed. Why
Purvis didn't know how much was in the bag. Why Harold Wallace didn't know there was so much. There was money from
two sources in the bag. One from Purvis and one from the congressman. Who were the other soldiers with you that day?"

"Bikers," he said. "I won't give you their names. Nam vets.
We were just trying to turn a buck. Montana and Dumont were
sent by Purvis. We had to agree to it or lose the deal. Didn't
understand it then, but the payoff was too good to turn down.
I knew Harold from Nam. I think he must've said something
where he shouldn't have. He works for Purvis."

"You own a black Chevy Beretta?" I asked.

He nodded.

"You kill Randle Lightfoot?"

"No. Lightfoot's my buddy. I was there though. But it'd already happened by then. It was me thumped you on the head."

"Thanks a lot. Why'd you do that if you didn't kill him?"

"I found Lightfoot floating in the tub. Didn't know what to
do. I heard your car pull up and I hid. Got scared. Didn't know
if you were a cop, or what. Couldn't afford to be there with a
dead body and have people find out I had no ID. Find out who
I really was. There's no statute of limitations on desertion."

"So who killed him, then?"

"I think it was Skunk Dumont. You know him?"

I nodded. "Why do you think he did it?"

He explained that after they killed Burlingame, Dumont and
Montana had asked him a lot of questions about who hung out

with Burlingame. He'd mentioned Lightfoot. He'd also mentioned that Lightfoot was a buddy of his.

"Also," he said, "I saw Dumont on the road about a mile from Lightfoot's that day."

How did Dumont get there so quickly? I thought. He would have had to dump Purvis, Braden, and Montana first. Something didn't fit.

"He see you?"

"No."

"Anyone with him?"

"No."

Interesting, I thought, but said nothing.

"Won't stand up in court, anyway."

"Randle was all right, man. Used to get me tickets to Broncos games, which are, like, rare. We partied together. He liked thinking he was a tough guy. Besides, the guys didn't know who he was, so he could relax when he was here. Bought himself a chopper, rode it up here. Hung out."

"Did Lightfoot know you were Braden's son?"

"No."

"Then they killed him for nothing."

"What good would killing Randle do them?"

"Gave them exclusive control over your father. Also, if they were running a scam with Burlingame to soak Purvis they'd be afraid Burlingame told Lightfoot about it. A truly bad thing for Purvis to find out. As bad as they think they are, Purvis is a professional mercenary. An international gundealer and a killer. Lightfoot was an insurance killing. Making sure they'd covered their tracks."

"Just thought of something," Chick said. He looked at Jubal. "You ever go public with any of this—who you are, anything like that—then you're in big time jeopardy."

"How you figure?" said Jubal, stroking his beard.

"You endanger Daddy's shot at the Senate. Also, long as

you're a fugitive Montana and Dumont feel safe. You come out of the closet, then you know too much."

"No chance of that," said Jubal. "I don't want to do no time in a federal lockup." He paused. "Unless . . . what're you guys gonna do with me?"

I looked at Chick. "You want to keep him?"

Chick looked at him a moment, as if appraising a horse. "Naw. He's too hairy. Besides, he hangs around with a bunch of lowlife bikers. Forget him. Make him promise not to run guns anymore or we'll come back and chain their motorcycles together."

"How about it?" I said. "Can you take the oath?"

He looked at both of us. A life on the dodge had made him hypersuspicious. "You guys cutting me loose?"

"No more gunrunning, though."

"And you got to promise to brush and floss daily," Chick said.

He smiled. "You guys are some weird dudes, man."

42

I scooped fresh-ground Colombian into the coffeemaker basket and filled the reservoir with water. Set the built-in timer to start making at four-fifteen A.M. I got my camouflage coveralls, boots and bow ready for the next morning. I tried to call Sandy again, but only got her recorder.

I couldn't think of anything to say and was too proud to ask her to call me.

Funny how things worked. Captain Marvel turned out to be some poor guy they'd shipped off to Nam twenty-five years ago, and as with so many others before and after him, the Lewis Carroll world of war on the half-shelling had ruined the rest of his life. Now he was living like the phantom of the opera in the shadowy underworld of chrome and leather. Besides, I couldn't fix everything, and he'd been in a prison of his own making for twenty-five years. Nice of his dad to ship him off, spirit him out, then forget about him.

I may register so I can vote against him.

I called Kelly Jenkins to see how she was doing.

"This is Wyatt," I said when she answered. "You okay?"

"Yes. Thanks for calling. Are you all right?"

"Sure."

"They let that bastard go." She meant Montana.

"I know."

"It isn't right. He killed Matt and now he's walking around free. That isn't all . . . He . . ." Her voice trailed off.

"What is it, Kel? What are you trying to say?"

"Somebody's been calling. I think it's him."

"How do you know?"

"A feeling I get. No, that's not true. At first they'd call and hang up when I answered. That didn't bother me so much. That happens sometimes anyway. But then . . . then one time he said something about Matt and about you and me."

"What did he say?" I felt heat behind my ears.

"He said—" She hesitated. "Oh crap, this is gross, Wyatt."

"You don't have to tell me if you don't want to."

"No, I'm okay. What he said was, 'You gonna shake that stuff for Storme you might as well let a better man have some of it.'" Her voice quavered at the end. I said nothing, but could feel the tempest forming and swirling deep inside, building and rising again. It boiled and pushed through the thin plate I had constructed over the years to restrain it. It wasn't enough for him to have killed Matt. His was a special sickness. A savage conqueror fascinated by the theatrics of death and notoriety. He couldn't stand it that no one had witnessed his triumph. He wanted applause. Maybe I'd give him his day in the sun.

"Wyatt . . . are you there? Wyatt!"

"Yeah. Yeah, I'm here."

"I thought we got cut off for a minute."

I talked to her for a while. Tried to make her feel better. Tried to make us both feel better.

"Listen," I said. "I think I'm going to call Chick and have

Billy and him come over there. Billy can stay inside and Chick will be outside but you'll never know it. That okay?"

"Maybe Billy doesn't want to come."

"I think you're wrong there."

"It's not necessary. I'm all right. I'll just unhook the phone."

"I'd rather you didn't do that. I may have to get hold of you."

"He calls on the residence number. I'll just unhook that one. You can still call me on the business number."

I told her that would be fine.

"There's one more thing, Wyatt."

"What's that?"

"I want you to get him. Make him pay."

After we hung up, I called information for the number of the Sun King Dude Ranch. They gave me the reservation desk and I asked for Montana's number.

"I can transfer you, sir," said the receptionist.

He answered on the fifth ring. His voice was slurred, sleepy with booze. There was noise in the background. A female voice.

"Whazzit," he said.

"You make one more call to Kelly Jenkins I'm going to disconnect your line."

"Who is this?"

"You know who it is. You leave her alone or I'm coming after you."

"That you Storme? Yeah. Is, ain't it?"

"I mean what I say, Montana. You and me still have to settle over Matt. Don't make it worse."

"You're a tough guy, aren't you, Storme? Yeah. Just like your buddy Jenkins. He was a tough guy, too. Last time I saw him, he didn't look so tough." He started laughing. A silvery flash of cold fire shot through my brain. Easy, Storme, I thought. He's trying to make you mad. It was working, too.

"You and me," I said, "will dance again. But you bother her anymore I won't wait for high noon. It'll come when you're not looking for it. Won't even know it."

"You threatening me?"

"I'm telling you." I hung up.

Give him something to think about.

I was up at four-thirty. I got a cup of coffee and poured the rest into a steel-lined thermos, ate a couple of Pop-Tarts and an apple, pulled on my boots and coveralls, grabbed my bow and headed up the mountain.

The air was cold and bracing, thin and fine as a film of cabernet in a fluted goblet. The moon was a bright snowball in the blue-black sky reflecting off the blanket of white on the mountain and bathing the deep forest in a luminescent glow. There was no need for the small flashlight in my pocket. I arrived at the desired location at six-fifteen. The sun rose over the mountains fifteen minutes later and I picked up tracks. I followed them for an hour, but caught only a glimpse of the mule deer off in the distance.

I took a break at ten, unslinging the coffee thermos and pulling the cellophane-wrapped ham-and-cheese sandwich from inside my coveralls. It was compressed and warm on one side from body heat. I sat down at the base of a huge evergreen, where its boughs had shielded the ground from snow, save the small amount that had swirled underneath like powdered sugar dusted on a chocolate brownie.

I thought about Crispin Purvis and how I could lure him away from his stronghold. How to put him at the U-Store with the armaments at the moment the police showed. While he was there I could break into the locked room at his estate. Chick had given him his burglar tools and showed me how to use them. But it was a long shot. Purvis was careful. He'd been at this game a long time and nobody had tied a can to his tail yet.

Then I thought about Randle Lightfoot. Something still bothered me about his death. Had Dumont known I was coming that day, and tried to set me up for the fall, or was it just a coincidence? If he knew I was coming, why not wait and take both of us out? What had made them think Lightfoot would spill information about Jubal being Michael Braden? Forget it, Storme. Why can't it be easy for once?

I gave up the chase at noon. By the time I neared the cabin the clear mountain sky had become cluttered with clouds and in the distance I saw a bank of blue-gray rolling in like a wave. Clouds swollen with snow. The wind had shifted and was picking up velocity from the north.

Chick was waiting for me at the cabin. He'd let himself in and was helping himself to some Canadian Club whiskey.

"Make yourself at home," I said, taking off my coveralls.

"Glad to." He raised his glass to me. "Sandy called."

I looked out the bay window. "What'd she want?"

"Wanted to meet Billy. I think he kinda likes it. Having a family. He's doing okay."

"She say anything else?"

He shook his head. "No." He looked into his glass. "Sorry, man."

tried Sandy at Channel Seven but she wouldn't take my calls.

"Sure are good with women," Chick said.

"Shut up."

On the television, a voice-over was telling of another shooting in downtown Denver. The commentator mentioned the proliferation of illegal weapons in the inner city. He cited Joring Braden's proposed gun-control bill.

I thought about our next step. What to do about Purvis, Montana, and company. How to burn all of them in the same fire. Or should I start several small fires in different places and hope they converged into one bonfire? I had the weapons and the money. Couldn't let Purvis know I had the money. Somebody on his side had tried to rip him off, and I could use that to my advantage. For now Purvis would not move against me, as he wanted the guns. But he could grow tired of waiting.

"The way I got it figured, these are your options," Chick said. "You call Younger and the ATF, give them the weapons and get out of the way, but you don't like that because you're afraid Montana will slip out of the noose. Or we could pull a scam of our own."

"I didn't know you had given it any thought."

"Shows what you know. How could I become the definitive bounty hunter and bodyguard if the wheels weren't always turning? Course, like I said, ol' Dirk's gonna be a little pissed we squeezed Braden, which complicates things."

"You think the government knows about Jubal?"

"The government knows and sees all."

"With that information they can play Daddy Braden like a yo-yo."

"Big Brother loves games. Got him to run for the senate, didn't they?"

"Anything bother you about Lightfoot's killing?"

"You mean, like, sure was lucky Jubal saw Dumont in the area? Or, how did Dumont get there so fast from Matt's?"

I nodded.

He shrugged. "Don't know what to think about it. Maybe Jubal lied."

"Maybe our luck's changing."

He chuckled. "Maybe."

After Chick left I called Channel Seven again. This time I tried disguising my voice, using an East Coast accent. I was pretty good with it.

"Channel Seven. This is Cheryl speaking. May I help you?"

"This is Francis Falsworth with ABC News. Is a . . . Sandra, ah . . . Collingsworth there?"

"Why yes she is."

"May I speak with her, please?"

"Of course you can, Wyatt. Great accent."

"Like it, huh?"

"Much better than the Southern one earlier. Hold please."

Elevator Muzak played on the line. Why do companies think people want to hear that drivel? Why not bombard the public

with something good for them, such as Chopin, Schumann, Beethoven, Creedence Clearwater Revival . . .

"What is it, Wyatt?" said Sandy's voice sharply.

"We need to get this settled."

"It is settled."

"Sandy, this is infantile. You're acting like a junior high girl
giving back her mood ring."

"I've got an idea," she said. "Why don't you marry Kelly,
then you can be my half-brother's stepfather."

"Come on, Sandy . . ."

"We could see each other at family reunions and picnics.
Then you'd be able to keep an eye on me and beat up every
male who looked at me."

"I didn't beat him up. He kept pressing it . . . What was I
supposed to do? Screen every female I took out twenty years
ago? I didn't know you then."

"You just had to keep pushing, didn't you? Can't leave anything alone."

"I was invited in."

"How nice for you."

I struggled with the anger and frustration that were nibbling
through a thin cord in the back of my neck. "Can't we start over?"

"No." There was a loud click. I looked at the phone momentarily, placed it back on the cradle. At least she was talking to
me again. Yelling at me, actually. Progress. Ever the optimist. I
picked the phone back up and dialed the highway patrol and
asked for Cliff Younger. Miraculously, he was there.

"Younger," he said, answering.

"Younger than what? Springtime?"

"Ah, shit. It's you. Just got a call that some guy'd run into a
gas truck with a Mustang. Got my hopes up. I've been walking
around the station whistling 'Happy Days Are Here Again.' "

"You've still got my gun."

"You want it, you got to come down, fill out a form to get
it back."

"That's okay. I know where there's a whole bunch of guns."

There was a pause at the other end. "All right, Storme. What have you got?"

"Oh, no," I said. "You jump in first and I'll see if the water's deep enough."

"All right. What an asshole. You know how it is with the patrol anymore. We don't get invited in on this stuff. But here's what little they've let me in on. Nobody knows where Jackie Burlingame is. Was a guy picked up at Burlingame's apartment last week, a guy works for Crispin Purvis. Name was Wallace. The locals received an anonymous call and they found Wallace tied up at Burlingame's apart . . ." His voice trailed off. I waited. "It was you. You tied him up and made the call, didn't you?"

"I know not of these things."

"That's where you got the little book you're telling me about. Just run around everywhere screwing things up. Why don't you get an honest job?"

"Think you could get me on the patrol? I could wear a snappy uniform, drive fast, carry a gun, eat for free in restaurants, never get another speeding ticket . . ."

"I want the book, Storme."

"What book?"

"I could get a search warrant."

"On what grounds?"

"There's still the beef on Lightfoot. I could tell the judge there was a book at your cabin that might help us find out who killed Lightfoot."

"I may know who killed Lightfoot," I said.

"Yeah? Who?"

I told him about Dumont and about Lightfoot's connections with Burlingame.

"Who told you this?"

"Can't tell you."

"You know you're crazy? You're going to tell me the backup quarterback of the Denver Broncos was whacked out and an anonymous tip told you who did it? I know I'll regret asking this, but why would Dumont kill him?"

"Because he thought Lightfoot knew Congressman Braden's dark secrets."

"How do you know all this?"

I spent the next five minutes explaining what I knew so far, omitting how I knew some of it. I didn't want to implicate Billy McCall. I owed Matt and Kelly that much. And Duncan and Sandy.

"Well," he said. "You've uncovered something, but I don't know what to do with it. There's nothing to link Purvis and Braden with any of this."

"You could run a sting on them. Catch them with the goods."

"How? I can't entrap a U.S. congressman."

"Sure you could," I said. "Especially if someone calls in an anonymous tip and you show up with guns blazing, catching them red-handed."

"That isn't the way it works, Storme. We're the cops and you are the citizen. You've seen too much television. You call us, then I'll take it to the right people."

"I'll call you when I get it set up."

"Listen, dammit," he said, voice rising. "You stay out of this or I'll cuff you to the next train west."

"Wait for my call, Cliffy. I still love you best."

I hung up.

I sat down on the couch and unwrapped a cigar. Felt a little better. Not great, just better. For the past two days I'd battled a depression that circled me like a buzzard. What had I accomplished so far? One of my oldest and dearest friends was dead, I'd scraped an old sore better left alone, pushed my fiancée's father back into the bottle, ruined my engagement, and my last friend was a bounty hunter with bad health habits.

What a life. Chock full of fun and adventure.

Wyatt Storme—king of the starlight cowboys.

The phone rang.

It was Kelly Jenkins.

I think Billy's going to do something stupid," Kelly said.

"Like what?" I asked.

She told me that Billy said he was going to "square things."

"What's that mean?"

"I don't know. He was talking about how he had messed everything up . . . for me, for you, and for Matt. And that he knew how to square everything with Purvis."

"Do you know where he is now?"

"No. But I think he's going to Purvis's estate."

I added the numbers in my head. They weren't good. So much for my plan to lure Purvis away. I told her I'd take care of things. I said Chick was on his way to watch her place and yes, I know she said she didn't need it, but to tell him what was going on and that I was headed to Purvis's place. She said she would. I hung the phone up, grabbed the little .25 auto I'd taken from Harold Wallace as well as the PPK from Burlingame's apartment and fired up the Bronco. I figured if they frisked me they'd find the Walther and maybe leave me the .25. And maybe it would be sunny and warm this Christmas.

As I made my way through the meandering mountain roads I knew this one was trouble. Joring Braden knew there was a connection between his son and me. And what Braden knew, Purvis knew. If Purvis had had Montana snuff Jackie B. and then had Dumont burn Lightfoot for what they knew, or even if Montana and Dumont had gone independent, then I was probably next on the hit parade.

I was driving into extremely bad weather.

But I couldn't turn away now. The mangled machinery that made up my relationships—past and present—had set things in motion. No way to turn away from a plea to save Kelly's son and Sandy's half-brother. It was almost a relief, in fact. When I tried to think about the web of past mistakes, bad steps, and fractured history, it was too much to crowd into my head. I was basically a simple person, I think, and the whole thing had become too complex for extended philosophical contemplation.

Sometimes it just got bigger than me.

After an hour of driving I stopped at a gas station and used a pay phone to call Chick in case he stopped at his place first. No answer. I tried Kelly. No, he hadn't arrived yet. She told me to be careful and I told her I would. I didn't tell her that being careful might make little difference.

Driving up the mountain to Purvis's estate, I thought about a plan of action. I briefly considered ditching the Bronco and sneaking down the mountain behind the house, but was afraid it would take too long as I didn't know how much time Billy had. Besides, it might not require any more than just making him leave with me. He was in way over his head. I had no idea how he thought he could fix things, but they were at a much more precarious juncture than he could know.

Chick could probably get there from Kelly's by six o'clock. I could go straight in, pretend to pitch a weapons deal and stall until Chick arrived. It was the best I could hope for. The worst?

They could have already killed Billy or beat information out of him that would leave us both hanging.

Approaching the house, I spotted Billy's dusty BMW parked in the circle drive. I parked the Bronco, got out and felt the hood of the BMW. It was warm. Good. He hadn't been here long. Now, if I could get inside and figure out some way to clue Billy in and still string along Purvis.

If there was still time.

If not, then all my other troubles would soon be over if not solved.

I rang the doorbell.

My buddy Taylor, the gun-toting doorman, opened the door.

"You," he said.

"You're a man of few words and most of them one-syllable."

"What do you want?"

"Money, prestige, youth, and power. I already have brains, good looks, and a dazzling smile. Now, run along and tell your master I want to see him. There's a Milk-Bone in it for you if you hurry."

"Don't push it, wiseass."

"Sorry, Taylor. You don't impress me much without your gun," I said, then added, "Don't impress me much with one, either. I've got a business proposition for C.P., and he'll want to hear it."

Taylor clenched and unclenched his fists. His eyebrows were working. He didn't know what to do. He wasn't afraid of me but was afraid the boss did want to see me. While he was turning it over Harold Wallace walked into the foyer and said: "You."

"Neither of you will get far with such limited vocabularies."

Harold pulled a .38 from inside his jacket. Pointed it at me. "Frisk him, Taylor."

"No need for that," I said. "I'm not carrying."

Taylor frisked me, despite my assurances. He found the Walther and the little hideout gun. I'd made a sickening blunder bringing Harold's .25. Taylor handed the .25 to Harold.

Harold hefted the gun, then looked at me, his eyes dark and sunken in his long face.

I shrugged. "So I lied."

"This is my gun. You're the guy in Burlingame's apartment. You sonuvabitch."

"Don't know what you're talking about."

" 'Don't know what you're talking about?'—You stepped on my neck. You sonuvabitch."

"Are you suffering from echolalia?"

"Shut up and get in there." He motioned with the gun in the direction of the trophy room/sunroom.

I entered ahead of Wallace. Billy McCall was seated in a chair facing Purvis. His face looked anxious as I walked into the room. Once again, Janet Sterling was seated in the sunroom, only this time she wasn't bare-chested, which made the whole day a bust. She was wearing a body stocking with a man's shirt tied beneath her ample lungs. Somehow, no matter what Janet Sterling wore, it brought attention to what was underneath it. She was filing her nails with a silver file, stereo headphones wrapped around her head. She looked up as I came in, tilted her head, smiled and winked. Purvis uncrossed his legs and stood as I entered.

"And to what do we owe this unexpected pleasure?" Purvis said.

"I'm ready to deal," I said.

"He's the guy that jumped me in Burlingame's apartment," said Wallace. "Had my gun on him."

"Is that true?" Purvis asked.

"My gun. I don't know what he's talking about." I was going for disinterested. I said, "I'm ready to offer you a proposition."

"I'm afraid you might be too late," Purvis said. "I have a prior offer from Mr. McCall."

I looked at Billy. He was smiling smugly. He was going to square things. The little rodent. It would take two steps and one swing to wipe it off his face but I needed to stay focused on the issue at hand. This was trouble. I was highly expendable if Purvis thought he didn't need me to deliver the guns. But I had an ace.

"Billy doesn't know where the guns are."

"Oh, but he does," said Purvis. "In fact, he has already delivered a sample shipment, which Skunk moved to a safe place on the grounds. In fact, as we speak Meredith is picking up the balance of the shipment." Billy McCall looked ill. "You needn't worry, Billy. I fully intend to pay as promised."

Janet Sterling removed the headphones and moved in our direction.

"And so, Mr. Storme," said Purvis. "Why do I need you any longer?" He pulled a .32 Beretta from beneath his jacket. I thought about the Browning, which Cliff Younger still had. I'd had three guns taken from me in recent days. Maybe I should just give them away. Save some time.

"I've had enough a you," he said, the Aussie accent thick now, his *h*s and some *t*s disappearing and his vowels taking on strange guttural baggage. "You bloody well better know I'm good with this little gun."

I looked at the lion's head.

"Just keep your hands where I can see them." I shrugged and lifted them slightly away from my body. "There's the lad." He spoke to the intercom. "Skunk," he said. "Come to the house." He released the button and a voice said, "Be right there."

He looked at me. "Sit on the floor with your legs crossed, hands in your hip pockets. And don't entertain any fantasies about me being unwilling to use this gun."

"Why doubt a big lion-killer like you? What're you going to do?" I said, as I complied with his wishes. I make it a point, a rule actually, to discount caliber as a meter to determine compliance in the face of a weapon. They come in all sizes and they all hurt. "Kill me?"

"Not just yet. A pleasant thought, though. You have, after all, been a pain. First I have a few questions. What is your connection to Burlingame?"

"State cop, named Younger, mentioned Burlingame was missing. Jenkins said Burlingame visited him about arranging an introduction to you." Might as well give him something. Might as well be something of no consequence. Might as well not get shot immediately. My left knee, the bad one, hurt. I was not used to sitting with my legs crossed.

"And he did. Mr. Burlingame was an unsavory character. He's a wanker, too, like most Yanks. Do you have my money?"

"No."

"Come now. I haven't time for this nonsense. Where is it?"

"If I had it I'd give it to you." I needed to buy some time. Dumont entered the room. Taylor came in behind him.

"Ah, here they are," said Purvis. "Skunk, I wish to ask Mr. Storme some questions. Could you make him a bit more cooperative."

Didn't like the sound of that. If he wanted to shoot me, he could go ahead. But I wasn't going to let them kick me like a dog if I could help it. I scrambled to my feet, but Dumont was on me too quickly. He kicked me in the ribs as I tried to stand and the force of it knocked me down. When I hit the floor, I tried to roll away, but Wallace grabbed me by the back of my jacket and hair, lifting me. As he did I uppercut him in the solar plexus. He *whoof*ed and his hands went slack on my hair.

I pulled away, but not before Taylor, the happy houseman, slugged me.

"Careful," said Purvis. "I don't want him all marked up, just malleable."

Skunk grabbed me and I could smell him, stronger than his aftershave. His stocky arms pinned my elbows behind me and I felt old lesions tear loose in my shoulders. A grunt of pain escaped clenched teeth, then I felt a fist dig in my stomach. My sails folded and my head slipped to half-mast, my knees sagging beneath fish-slack weight.

They tied my hands behind me and lashed me to a wooden chair. My stomach felt like they'd dropped bricks on it.

"Whassa matter, punk?" said Dumont. "Where's the wiseass shit now?"

"I thought . . . we were going for physical humor."

He slapped me with an open hand which felt like a bag of sand. My head jerked and things swam inside it. He hit me again. Maybe he thought he'd missed.

"Lay off him," said Billy McCall. My hero.

"You telling me what to do?" said Dumont. He backhanded me in the chest, knocking the chair and me over. "What do you think of that, Billy boy?" Reaching down he pulled me and the chair erect, grabbed my hair and started to hit me again, when Purvis said, "McCall's right. Take it easy. I want him softened up, not dead."

Skunk smiled at me, patted my cheek with a hammy hand. He released my scalp with a toss, taking a few hairs with him.

"Plenty of time," Dumont said.

There was quicksand slogging around in my head. I shook my head to clear it and was rewarded by a sharp pain shooting from behind my ears to my eyes. Looking up, I saw Janet Sterling watching the proceedings. Her hummingbird tongue touched the corner of her lip, her eyes wide with voyeuristic interest. I noticed a wall clock: five fifty-nine. Chick would be here if I could hold out long enough.

"Now," said Purvis. "What do you know?"

"You . . . can only lose weight by increasing metabolic rate. Diets are passé. Eric Clapton is the greatest living guit—" Dumont slapped me again. This time it took longer for the dust to settle in my head.

"You'll do nothing except cause yourself unnecessary pain with all that," said Purvis. "Harold says you're the man took my money and guns. Come now. Enough of this. Do you have my money?"

"Don't know what you're talking about."

"Skunk," said Purvis.

"Wait a minute." I looked at the clock again. "Tell me what you're talking about and maybe I can help you. There may be something I know which could help us both. I'm not really enjoying this."

"I'm missing a large amount of cash," said Purvis.

"How much?"

"You tell me, mate."

"I'll take a stab and say it's in the thousands."

"Check him for electronics, lads," said Purvis.

Rough hands tore at my shirt and along my body as they looked for a microphone. "I'm not a cop," I said.

"He's clean," said Harold.

"Should be," I said. "I shower daily and use Irish Spring, for that fresh manly scent—"

"Shut up!" said Dumont, shaking me by the hair, causing me to bite my tongue, leaving the slippery metallic taste of blood in my mouth. I spat on the Turkish rug.

"Well, there you've done it," said Purvis. "You can't get that out. If he shows up dead with his blood on my rug how will that look? Fucking amateurs. Taylor, get some newspapers."

"He's tough, isn't he?" said Janet Sterling, her breathing shallow. She moved closer to examine the blood on the carpet. "Don't mark him up, Skunk. I may have a use for him yet."

"I know what I'm doing," said Skunk. "There's no marks on him. He must've bit his tongue."

"Maybe I'll bite his tongue, too," she said. She stepped toward me and straddled me, wrapping her arms around my neck and taking my lower lip between her teeth. At first she nibbled, as she wriggled in my lap, sliding her tongue into my mouth to taste the blood—I felt her hand on me, down low, caressing and running her hand in my pocket where I felt a sharp stabbing pain—then she bit harder, causing me to wince and jump. What a ghoul.

"Leave off that," Purvis said. "Get her up, Skunk."

Dumont lifted her from my lap. She gave me a final squeeze with her thighs as he did. She laughed as he sat her down.

"Only one man in the room and you tie him up."

"Shut up, bitch," said Dumont.

"I don't believe you'd better talk to me like that, you fat bastard. Are you going to let him talk to me like that, Crispin?"

"I believe I will not," Purvis said. "Leave her alone, Skunk," he said, with ice in his tone. "You know how she is."

While Taylor fetched and they argued, I gained some respite. I'd wandered into a nest of crazies and perverts. "You were saying?" I said, trying to stretch time and catch my breath. "About some missing money?"

"I was supposed to receive a shipment of arms brokered by that low-born, Burlingame. But there was a third man, one un-seen by my emissaries, who bitched the deal and got away. A fourth man, also unknown, helped him escape with the guns and one hundred thousand dollars of my money. Sounds very much like you and your Special Forces friend Easton."

Only one hundred thousand dollars? I thought. Everybody had a different figure. It affirmed the blackmail scam. Which meant nothing at the moment. My head hurt.

"Wasn't us."

He went on to say that Matt Jenkins was indirectly implicated, which I already knew. "So why does an arms dealer back a gun-control congressman?" I asked him.

"Simple economics. Supply and demand. Gun-control laws drive up the price of my inventory."

"Kids are killing each other with your inventory." I looked at the clock. Six-fifteen. Soon.

A strange look came over Purvis's face. "That's the third time you've looked at the clock. What's the interest?"

"Don't want to miss *McNeil-Lehrer*."

"Are you expecting someone?"

"A highway patrolman and Dirk Donovan of the CIA," I said, lying.

"I doubt that. Donovan's interests run almost parallel to mine."

"You know Donovan?" I asked.

"Since Nam. Don't expect him to bail you out. He only works for flag and country, and then only for the powers that be. He's quite flexible that way. And the current administration is delightfully duplicitous and very taken with the Honorable Mr. Braden. Skunk, show Storme to the guest room and then take Wallace and Taylor and go outside. I'd say Storme is expecting help and unless I miss my guess it'll come in the form of his friend Easton. Be careful of that one. He's more dangerous than this one, as he harbors no heroic illusions. And just to be on the safe side, put McCall in another room."

"Why?" said Billy. "What have I done?"

"Nothing," said Purvis. "We'll keep it that way."

Dumont untied me from the chair, leaving my hands tied behind me. He pulled me up by the front of my jacket and ushered me from the room by grabbing my bound hands and then lifting them behind me, forcing me to bend over, my face parallel to the floor, head racing to stay ahead of my feet. Most undignified.

He trundled me down the hall. I stumbled and he jerked on the rope, causing me to yelp in pain.

"Enjoying yourself, Storme?"

I said nothing.

He took me to an empty room at the rear of the house. It was in the process of being painted and smelled of latex and turpentine. He used my head to open the door. I was starting to develop an affinity for him. He threw me down on the floor and I skidded on carpet, burning my face. Using an electrical cord, he bound my legs and ran a length of it up around my hands, linking them to my legs.

Dumont took my face in a massive paw and said, "I'll be back. Don't run off."

He kicked me good-bye and left.

I felt the throb of the heating system as I lay on the floor, struggling against my bonds. Dumont knew what he was doing. The more I struggled, the tighter the knots became. I gave that up and looked about the room. Nothing. I had a headache like a waterwheel, and various sore spots contended with each other for attention. However, there was nothing broken and no cuts, save the self-inflicted one inside my mouth, and some swelling where Janet Sterling had bit me. I was never going to watch another of her movies again. Teach her to mess with me.

Several minutes passed before I heard footsteps coming down the hall. Sounds of struggle. The door burst open and a bound Chick Easton was thrust into the room by Skunk Dumont and Taylor. Wallace trailed them, hunched over slightly, rubbing his ribs.

"I think he broke one a my ribs," said Wallace, grimacing.

"Purvis warned you," said Dumont.

"How'd I know he had anything left? C.P. knocked the shit out of 'im with that thing."

"Careful means careful," said Dumont. "You know better." Dumont kicked me in the back once more. Must've been glad to see me. Pain sailed along my spine and up my neck. With his hand on the knob, he said, "You ladies enjoy yourselves. I'll be back directly."

Wincing, I rolled closer to Chick, who was moaning softly.

"Some rescue," I said. "Thanks a lot."

"Hah!" Chick said, his eyes squeezed together. "Is this your . . . idea of detective work? You can't do anything right."

"I had them right where I wanted them. Was about to tell them the path of crime was dark and twisted."

"Boy, I am never going to come to your rescue again."

"Well, you do crummy work, so it's no loss."

He groaned, then said, "So what's your plan to get us out of here?"

"You think I don't have one, do you? What happened?"

"Was doing all right. But Purvis zapped me with one of those Tasers. Like being kicked by a Clydesdale. Then the Marx brothers started using me for a soccer ball. I sulled up a little, got a shot at the skinny guy. Think I busted a rib on the asshole. But Purvis electrocuted me again. Wears you right out."

"You okay?"

"Think so. You?"

"Yeah. Want to wiggle in there and bite their feet?"

"Naw. They're expecting that."

I rolled toward him to see if he was all right. As I did I felt a little stab above my right thigh. "Wait a minute." I remember Janet Sterling reaching into my pocket. She'd put something in there. Something sharp. Something I might be able to use to cut the ropes. "There's something in my right pocket. I think the movie star put it there. Can you get it out?"

"How?"

"See if you can roll with your back to me and use your hand to get it out."

He did so, and after considerable effort was able to get his hand in my pocket.

"Can't feel it," he said. "Got it! Hold still now." I felt something slide from my pocket. "It's out."

"What is it?"

"Feels like a nail file. Small one."

So she slipped me a file. Might forgive her biting my lip. Might even watch her movies again. We rolled back-to-back and Chick began sawing at my ropes. It was a slow process. He'd been at it several minutes when the door opened.

"What's going on?" said Skunk. He had the Taser in hand and Taylor was with him. They checked our ropes, found mine partially cut through and took the file. Dumont looked accusingly at Taylor. "Thought you frisked 'im?"

"I did."

"Where'd you have it?" he asked Chick.

"Trade secret."

"Another smartass."

"We come in pairs. It's the mating season."

"Come on. Boss wants to see you."

Dumont grabbed Chick and Taylor escorted me. "How come your date's so much prettier than mine?" said Chick.

"Shut up," said Dumont. "Unless you want another power spike. This one'll be up the ass."

"Maybe it'll cure my prostate problem."

They led us into another part of the house. It was the room Janet Sterling and I had been in the night of the party. Purvis was sitting on the couch, waiting for us, drink in hand. Janet Sterling gave me a quick look. I smiled at her, in thanks. She looked away. We were made to sit on the floor.

"Well, gentlemen," said Purvis. "What are you doing here?"

"We're an advance party for Colorado's man of the year award," Chick said. Dumont cuffed him along the ear. Chick took it silently.

"You have become a problem," said Purvis. "I think you have my money and I think you are more trouble than you're worth. I want my money back. It'll be to your advantage to accommodate me. You could cause great problems for me and for Congressman Braden. Where have you been getting your information? Most of it is false, of course. By the way, what is your connection with Billy McCall?"

I said, "What connection?"

"Don't play games with me, Storme. Billy is not as intractable as you. Skunk was able to get his attention almost immediately. We know McCall is your girlfriend's half-brother and Mrs. Jenkins's bastard. I thought I detected a softness on his part when we were establishing a rapport with you." I heard Skunk chuckle. "Come now. Where's the money? This is doing neither of us any good. You tell me what I wish to know and we'll dispatch you humanely."

"You'll spoil me if you keep it up."

"Your smart mouth and insolent attitude is starting to wear on me. Your evasiveness could turn out to—" A bell chimed. "Who the hell could that be?"

"Want me to get it?" Chick asked, brightening.

Purvis raised an eyebrow at Chick. "No thank you. Harold will get it. He's in the kitchen drinking some pain reliever. You broke his ribs, you know."

"Damn. I was trying to break his neck."

"You ain't tough as you think," said Dumont.

"Just let me have me spinach and I'll mop the floor with yas," said Chick.

"Just a couple of minutes—"

There was a commotion at the door. We looked up to see Harold Wallace backing into the room. Behind him, with a Colt automatic pistol pointed at Harold's chest, was Denver's most popular television personality.

And she had never looked lovelier.

Stand over there," Sandy Collingsworth said, gesturing with the Colt at Harold. Her eyes were wide and excited. "That's a good boy."

"Who're you, lady?" Dumont said. "The skirt brigade?"

"Just put your hands on your head and shut up," she said. She nodded at Taylor. "You. Untie them." Harold was starting to do so when Dumont interrupted.

"Don't do it. What's she gonna do if you don't?"

"I'll shoot you," she said.

"Bullshit," Skunk said. "Bet she don't even know how it works." He started walking toward her. "Give me the gun, bitch."

He had his hand out when she shot him in the foot. The report was a high-pitched, ringing whine in the confined space. My ears echoed with it. Skunk's leg jumped and crimson issued from a tear in his shoe. He yelled and fell to the floor, grabbing at his foot. The .32-caliber bullet wouldn't make a big hole, but there are more pleasant sensations.

"Is that how it works?" she said. Her shoulders rose and fell with rapid exhalation. She looked at Taylor and said, "Well?"

He hurried to comply with her wishes.

"Very unladylike, Miss Collingsworth," said Purvis. "How will this look on the six-o'clock news?"

"I doubt anyone hears about it," she said. "You're not going to say anything unless you have an excuse for tying and beating two men. That would be helpful to Congressman Braden's campaign, don't you think?"

"A valid point," he agreed, a smug smile on his face.

Harold untied my hands. I stood and walked, limped actually, to her side. She handed me the gun. "Here, take the nasty thing. I'm just a dumb little girl." The last part she directed at Skunk, who was still clutching his foot. His blood had stained the carpet.

I frisked Taylor and Dumont, who no longer had the Taser, while Sandy untied Chick, who walked over to Purvis and patted him down. Took his gun and the Taser from him. He took a step back and shot Purvis with the zapper. Purvis's body spasmed and he slumped on the couch.

"There. How you like it?" Purvis's eyes were large, his teeth gritted. "No," Chick said, "don't bother to thank me." He feinted with the Taser in the direction of Taylor, who jumped back. Chick laughed.

"Quit picking on everybody," I said. "Let's find Billy and get out of here." I didn't know what to do with them and didn't know how long it would be before Purvis and the Three Stooges figured out Janet Sterling had slipped me the nail file. "We need some insurance," I said. "You." I pointed at Sterling. "You're coming with us."

"I should've known," Sandy said. "Why not the skinny guy?"

"Knew you had your eye on him," I said. "Get your coat, Miss Sterling, you're going for a ride."

"You're not going to let him take me, are you, Crispin?" she said. An Oscar performance.

"I don't see that I have a choice, love." He looked at me.

"I want Billy," I said. "Where is he?"

"I'm right here," said Billy, entering the room. He had a closed eye and his lips were split and swollen. A nylon cord dangled from one wrist.

"How'd you get loose?" I asked.

"I know a few things," he said, surly.

Dumont moaned and rolled on the floor.

Purvis said. "Show a little backbone, Dumont."

Dumont looked up at him with the look I'd seen at the party. A dark, simian look of repressed hatred.

"We need to get outta here," Billy said.

"In a minute."

"What now, Storme?" asked Purvis.

"You've got your guns back."

"And my money?"

"Don't have it. Besides, you ever wonder why this whole thing blew up? Maybe your own people have been scamming you."

"I've considered that possibility," he said. "Continue."

"Ask Dumont and Montana where the money is. Bet they know."

"I should very much like to vent my anger on the correct person." He shot a look at Dumont, who was rocking on the floor, teeth clenched in pain.

"Bet that hurts, doesn't it, Skunky old pal," Chick said.

"I ain't . . . got the money," said Dumont, between grunts of agony.

"You had bloody well better not have it," said Purvis.

"This . . . asshole," he said, tossing his head in my direction, "comes in, makes accusations and you believe him over me. Whyn't you ask your buddy Montana if he's got it?"

The skin over Purvis's face stretched tight, making it appear skull-like. "Coy would not do such a thing. We'll talk about this later." The two men glared at each other for a moment before Purvis said to me, "What are you going to do with us now? Shoot us? I think not. Have us arrested?"

"There's not a lot I can do to you. You're too big and I have nothing to tag you with. But the congressman is coming off the board. That's a done deal. I've got the leverage to do it. So forget about him. It's Montana and Dumont I want. Montana for Matt and Dumont because he killed Lightfoot. Both deserved better. After you give it some thought I'm sure you'll take care of that without me."

"You can be sure of that," he said.

"I didn't kill the Indian," said Dumont.

"I think different," I said.

"You don't believe *him*, do you?" Harold asked Purvis. "He's the guy shot us up that day."

"That's right," said Skunk. "He's got the guns."

"And," said Purvis, "if he has the money why is he here now? I find that most strange. And why has he continued to pursue this affair? There are many questions. I do hope, for your sake, you have the correct answers."

"I've had about enough of your shit," said Skunk. "You need to have some respect." He pushed himself from the floor.

"That's precious," said Purvis, his voice crackling with sarcastic venom. "Your vocabulary bears expanding. You fucking genetic freak. I'm—"

With a roar, the bearlike Dumont pushed himself from the floor, the white streak on his head bristling like the hairs on a wild boar's back.

There was nothing I could do to stop what happened next. As Skunk rushed him, Purvis dug at his belt buckle and pulled a shiny object from his waistline. The savagery of Dumont's charge bowled Purvis and his chair over. The guttural snarls and scrabbling limbs of men in combat filled the room as they crashed and rolled on the carpet. Hand-to-hand combat is an ugly thing whether it's two skinny punks in an inner-city alley or soldiers with bayonets holding a hill. It's desperate and savage in its finality.

Purvis's arms reached between his body and Dumont's, then there was a sudden bunching of his shoulder muscles as if he were lifting something. Dumont's face convulsed and the cords of his neck went taut. Purvis smiled tightly. Wickedly. He continued to dig at the front of his opponent. Twisting and pushing.

Dumont shivered with pain yet managed to get Purvis's chin and the back of his head between his hands. With a chilling roar of pain and effort he wrenched his employer's head, as if attempting to unscrew it. There was an obscene crunching sound, like a branch snapping, and Crispin Purvis, with an involuntary shiver, ceased to exist.

Then it was quiet. With the exception of the rattling of Dumont's breathing. He pushed himself off the Australian, spat in the corpse's face, looked at me. He slumped sideways, revealing a bloody torso with a gleaming spike sunk beneath his rib cage.

"Shit," said Harold.

Sandy slumped against me and a small cry escaped her lips. I put my hands around her waist. Looked at the two dead men, fascinated by the macabre death waltz.

"Belt buckle blade," Chick said. "That's comic-book crap. Who knows to frisk a guy for something like that?"

Taylor took a step to his right. Both Chick and I pointed weapons at him. "Take it easy, Cinderella," Chick said. "Nobody leaves the dance till I say."

"What happens to us?" Harold asked, his long arms raised.

"Nothing, if you're smart," Chick said. "You call the cops. You don't mention we were here. You tell 'em these two killed each other and you found illegal weapons on the premises and you know nothing about it."

"And if we don't?" said Taylor, ever the troublesome child.

"Then, sweetheart," Chick said, "the cops take you in on the gun beef and they put you inside. Also, you tell the cops to pick up Meredith at the U-Store. Makes you upstanding crime-busting citizens."

"We rat him out we could get popped."

"Either way," Chick said, snapping back the hammer on the gun. "Decide."

"Don't leave us much choice," said Taylor.

"Almost none," said Chick.

"How did you know we were here?" I asked Sandy, outside.

"Kelly called."

"Thanks for coming."

"Maybe I came to save Chick and Billy," she said.

"Whatever the reason."

"Is this like what happened in Paradise, last year?"

"Some," I said. The corners of her mouth turned down and she paled.

"Some men like drinking beer and watching TV. But you like being the masked marauder? That it?"

I said nothing.

She said, "Well, I can't stand it. It scares me. Those two . . . those two men. They were going to—" She stopped, as if completing the thought would bring its realization. She turned and walked to her car and made a dismissive gesture with a hand. Her shoulders convulsed and I knew she would cry.

"Are you going to give me a ride?" asked Janet Sterling, standing beside me.

"Look Sandy—" Too late. She was in her car. She started the engine and headed down the mountain, leaving me standing in the cold wind.

"I'm sorry," said Janet. "Did I cause that?"

"No," I said. "You probably didn't."

"Well?" said Janet. "Could we go, then? I'm freezing."

"Yeah," Chick said, touching her elbow. "Good idea. You can come with me. Don't mind, do you?"

"No," Janet said. She shoved her hands in her coat pockets. "That'll be . . . a . . . fine."

Billy walked up and stood beside me. Chick helped Janet into his car. I watched Sandy drive down the hill. "Why'd you come?" Billy asked.

"Slow day," I said. "What were you thinking coming here?"

"Wanted to do something. Tired of being a liability. Thought I'd give them some guns then call the cops."

"Well, you tried."

"You came because you thought I was in trouble, didn't you?"

I didn't say anything. Watched Sandy's taillights grow smaller, more distant. The air was cold on my neck.

"Love her, don't you?"

I nodded.

"You risked your life for me."

"You did the same for me."

"Nobody's ever stuck their neck out for me before."

"Don't make a big thing out of it, kid," I said, as I watched Sandy's car disappear around a bend in the road.

Dammit, Storme," said Cliff Younger as I let him into my cabin. "What the hell do you think you're doing?"

"Coffee?" I asked. It was two days after the incident at Purvis's and I was still sore from the beating. No broken bones, but my body was a minefield of purple blotches. Chick was asleep in my guest room.

"I thought I told you to stay out of this thing."

"What thing is that, Cliff?" I said, easing myself into a chair.

"You know what thing." He relented, and eyed my movements as I searched for a comfortable way to prop myself up. If I leaned a little to the right and straightened my left leg slightly the soreness was only unbearable. "What happened to you?"

"My lumbago is acting up again."

He shook his head. "Arapaho County told me they found Crispin Purvis and one of his gorillas dead. Also, the ATF arrested Frake Meredith as he was transporting illegal automatic weapons, some of which were stolen from the military. Anonymous tip, they said. And it looks like somebody beat the shit outta you and I didn't get to watch."

"Your concern touches me."

"They found an unidentified blood spot in Purvis's house. Type A."

"What a coincidence. You know I was type A?"

"I want to know what went down." He pursed his lips as if deciding something, then said, "Off the record."

I told him. When I was finished he ran a hand through his short-cropped hair.

"Well," he said. "Don't get the big head. You didn't do it all. The ATF had been watching Meredith for six months. We law-enforcement types do manage to stumble around and make an arrest now and then."

I gave him my satisfied-taxpayer smile. "I'll make sure you get your due at the next vigilance committee meeting."

"They had nothing on Purvis but suspicion. But they found ordnance on his property. This is gonna cost you big time, Storme. I figure a box of cigars oughta do it. Rothschilds."

"A box?" I said. "That's highway robbery."

"And a cup of coffee."

"Glutton," I said as I struggled to my feet to fetch his coffee. He didn't offer to help me. Never a cop around when you need one. After drinking his coffee, Cliff left.

Purvis and Dumont were dead. Frake Meredith had been placed under arrest and indicted for transporting illegal weapons with intent to traffic. Harold Wallace had disappeared, as had Taylor, the doorman. The guns had been recovered with the exception of those still buried on my property.

Nobody had been indicted for the murders of Matt Jenkins and Randle Lightfoot.

Sandy hadn't called.

Billy McCall was staying at Chick's place so Chick stayed at the cabin.

We took a couple of days to recover from the bruises and injuries we received. Chick used the time to smoke cigarettes, drink large amounts of Scotch, and watch daytime television. He was addicted to *Jeopardy*, and *Wheel of Fortune*, and he whistled and hooted when Vanna would turn the letters. After a couple of days of this I was restraining an impulse to strangle him with the television cord.

"What do you make of Dumont's denial?" Chick said.

"I don't know," I said. "I've turned it around in my head a hundred times. It wasn't his style."

"So who do you like for it?"

"Not sure. But I've got an idea."

I wanted to call Sandy, but didn't. Male pride. Nearly useless. I sank lower into the dark pool inside. Finally, I decided to visit Duncan Collingsworth. I called and he said he'd be glad to see me.

I bought two cups of coffee in the hotel restaurant before ascending in the elevator to Duncan Collingsworth's apartment. A young married couple rode up with me. They wore involuntary smiles and smelled of soap and sexual anticipation. I could've hated them if they hadn't radiated such guileless charm.

Duncan ushered me into his room. He was warm and courteous, as if nothing had transpired. Between Sandy and myself. Between him and Kelly and me. A conundrum of soul and emotion—of hearts and lives, tossed together by circumstance, then spat out into a heap of smaller questions, larger dilemmas. Hopelessly hoping.

He was packing to leave.

"I'm going to teach a spring course at the university," he said, folding clothes neatly into a suitcase. "It will occupy the time." He stopped what he was doing, then looked at me. "That didn't sound quite right. It will more than occupy the time. I'm looking forward to it. These past few days have been a little rocky, yet cathartic. I am free of my past now. You needn't blame yourself, Wyatt. I realize you intended no harm."

"Appreciate your saying that."

"There is no need to appreciate it." He smiled. "Wyatt," he began, then indicated a chair, "please, sit down. I have things I wish to share with you." I sat. He said, "It's easy to see why Sandra cares for you."

"She hides it deep," I said.

"Hides her feelings? Doesn't allow others to see the pain? Hmm." He sat and pursed his lips as if pondering the observation. "Seems to be more than a little of that going around."

"I want you to know the thing with Kelly and . . ." I stumbled for the words. Like an eighth-grader who hadn't completed his history assignment. "Want you to know it's all right and I—"

"It is most certainly not all right," he said, rising to his erect professorial posture—but there was a note of self-mockery in it. "And I'll not have you excuse the most selfish and unjustifiable act of my life. No, sir. Please do not patronize me. It insults the nature of my offense."

"I did the same thing."

"Yes, you did. And it was wrong and you feel badly. You blame yourself for too many things, but on this one I think we can agree." He turned his head and gave me the sidelong look of the lifetime pedagogue. "As her father I harbor a certain degree of resentment for your actions. But, as a fellow sinner, I understand. Do you suppose, Wyatt," he said, patting his fingertips together, "that we could confess our sins, pat each other on the back, and go on about our business? Some of that male-bonding nonsense?"

I sat back in my chair and considered it. Smiled.

"Not your style, of course," he said, standing. "We both made mistakes. Yours did not compound mine. In fact, yours has, in an ironic twist, allowed me to finally forgive myself. However, mine may have complicated yours. Still, you come here to make this gesture—"

"Listen. Duncan. I'm not trying—"

He raised a hand. "You don't have to try. It is part of you. You know nothing else. I remember a young man beaten down and bruised by war. A young man who played football with fury. A young Midwestern boy who had been thrown into a hellish conflict. You channeled your rage into athletics. Then one day the football no longer mattered. You realized you had traded demons. But you were able to walk away. Am I close?"

"This is not what I came for," I said.

"Then come to the point. What *are* you here for?"

"I love your daughter," I said. "And I'm asking you to forgive things I've done which hurt you and her." I stood to leave.

He looked at me. "Sandy was right," he said. "There is no way to predict or anticipate what you will say or do next."

"What are my chances?"

"She has a tenderness for you. Also her mother's temper. Like you, she is sometimes difficult to predict. I'm afraid I can't offer much comfort. However, I've observed she is happiest when she is with you. It's not much, but I offer it."

"Appreciate it." We shook hands and I started to leave.

"Wyatt," he said at the doorway. "I get the feeling you are often involved in things better left alone. You'll do what you want, but I would counsel you not to follow your anger."

Good advice, I thought.

When I arrived back at the cabin, Chick said I had a couple of calls. One was Detective Elliot. I was supposed to call back. I did so and he answered on the first ring.

"I don't know how you did it," he said without preamble. "But I'll bet my pension money you were in this thing up to your neck. You live a charmed life."

"What thing?" I said, for the second time that day.

He chuckled. "That's the way you're going to play it? All right. I don't know whether to thank you or arrest you."

"I've got something for you," I said.

"No more interference."

"No, this will be easy. Routine arrest." I told him what I had in mind. He finally agreed to it after considerable argument and hung up.

"That's what you've come up with?" Chick asked.

I nodded. "Yep."

"It ain't bad," he said.

I looked at him. "Who else called?"

He had a funny look on his face. Not a happy look. It was a face he used when he was about to do something distasteful.

"What is it?" I said.

"Billy called. Said Montana's been calling Kelly again."

"Time we broke him of that," I said.

"No use trying to talk you out of it, I guess."

"None."

"Then I'm with you," he said.

"First, I have to take care of the thing with Elliot."

"Always something."

"I need a favor from you."

"You got it."

"You get over to Jenkins's and watch Kelly while I do this. I'll call when I'm ready for the other thing."

"What other thing?"

"Montana."

There was a pause at his end. "What've you got in mind?"

"I'll let you know."

There was a lull in the snow, as if it were taking a breath before building to the main event. I parked the Bronco next to a Plymouth minivan with Hertz rental plates.

Michael Braden, a.k.a. Jubal, was packing his belongings when I knocked on the door of the trailer behind Chicken Sam's. "Come on in," he said, greeting me. The trailer was a double-wide with walnut cabinets and showroom furniture. The recession hadn't reached here. There was a new luggage set opened up and boxes everywhere.

"Pretty nice place for a biker," I said.

"Want a beer? What brings you by, man?"

I declined the beer. "Where're you headed?" I asked.

"New horizons, man. New places. And I got you to thank for it. You scared the old bastard, bro. I got fifty large, yesterday. And all I gotta do is get outta here. Already got a buyer for the trailer and the boys can have the bar. Bright lights, big city."

"You killed Lightfoot, didn't you?" I said. "Burlingame, too."

He laughed. "Man, what you been smokin'? I didn't kill nobody."

"You didn't need Jackie B. anymore once you figured out your old man would pay you to keep quiet. You just eliminated the middleman and took direct payment."

"Don't know what you're talking about. Besides, who gives a fuck? Jackie was a piece of shit."

"I could let that pass," I said. "But there's been too much. Somebody's got to take a fall for Lightfoot. He wasn't bothering anybody."

Braden stopped and looked at me. "All this over some toot-nose backup quarterback? Not exactly a choirboy, was he? Besides, I thought Dumont did it."

"That was your mistake. Dumont had no reason to do Lightfoot. You overplayed your hand when you told me you saw Dumont close to Randle's house. Dumont would have had to hustle to beat me there that day. He wasn't in on the extortion scam anyway. It was just you and Montana, wasn't it? I don't like Montana so I assumed he killed Lightfoot. He's crazy, but I don't think he's a backshooter. That's more something a lowlife deserter would do. The only thing I can't figure out is why? Why'd you hold Lightfoot under the water?"

"You're fucking stupid. Got no reason to kill Lightfoot. Just a big dumbshit football player. Fucking half-breed couldn't hold his booze or his flake. Tried to be a swinging dick, but he couldn't even collect on the blow. The dipshit was giving it away." As we talked, the Jubal façade slipped away and he sounded more and more like his congressman father.

"You and Montana thought you'd split the take on the guns and the extortion. Turk was a setup. That's why Burlingame brought him along." Also why he originally wanted me along, I thought. Could've been me instead of Turk. "Sacrificial lamb. Montana shows Purvis the dead body and he thinks you tried to stop it. I'll bet Montana didn't know you were going to do Burlingame. More difficult to explain to Purvis. Your dad, the congressman, didn't know who the blackmailer was. The whole thing was so screwy I couldn't get a handle on it."

Michael slowed his packing. "Man, you do too much thinking. You sure you don't want a beer? Maybe some tequila? Got some good José Cuervo." I declined again. He said, "Don't mind if I have one do you?" He reached into the cabinet and pulled out a bottle of tequila and a Bowie knife. I looked at it. Nothing nastier than a big knife. He turned it over in his hand and it flashed in the light.

"Y'know, Storme, it's too bad. I kinda like you."

"Put it away, Michael," I said. "They've got nothing on you for Lightfoot. Burlingame either. I just wanted to know for myself." He didn't know that the CIA had already covered him on the Lightfoot killing. He relaxed the knife hand and took a hit off the tequila.

He smiled and put the knife on the counter. "Lightfoot couldn't hold his booze, man. Typical Indian. A little firewater and he'd tell everything he knew. Told me he knew I was a deserter. Blurted it out in front of people, man. That asshole Burlingame tried to use it to get a bigger cut of the money. Couldn't have that." He shook his head. "You're one crazy motherfucker, for sure. Get yourself killed fucking around."

"I don't think so. I don't walk out this door under my own power Chick comes after you. And he never stops coming. Worse than the IRS. Besides, they can't hang either killing on you unless you do something stupid. Only Montana and Dumont know you're Captain Marvel, and Dumont's dead and Montana can't talk without implicating himself. I've already talked with Detective Elliot. Real frustrating for him. The press is after him to make an arrest on Lightfoot's killer."

There was the sound of a car engine outside the trailer.

"So," I said, opening the drapes to look outside. "He decided he'd just have to be satisfied with, in his words, 'some chicken-shit bust.'" I opened the door to the trailer to reveal Detective Elliot approaching the trailer, the thatch of burnt-copper hair blowing in the wind. There were two marines with him—an officer and an MP. Braden's eyes widened when he saw them.

"Hey, Michael," I said. "Remember telling me there's no statute of limitations on desertion?"

"I thought you was a brother, man," Braden said.

"Not yours." I opened the door to leave and let Elliot and his military escort in.

"You're a shitty dude, Storme."

"Seems to be the reigning consensus," I said, limping down the steps.

By the time Chick and I arrived at the Sun King ranch the blizzard had covered everything in a wash of swirling white, leaving only blurred edges of scenery. The amber shooting glasses I wore painted everything a pale urine color.

The Sun King was abandoned, as dude season had ended. The only light came from Coy Montana's cabin. A four-wheel-drive Nissan Pathfinder was parked outside.

We got out of the Bronco and I checked the Browning holstered under my coat. It was one I'd pirated from the illegal stash. No way to trace it to me. It was the same model as the one Younger confiscated.

"I'm better at this than you," Chick said.

"This is my deal. The last loose end."

"He's fast."

"Faster than me, in fact."

"Then this is stupid."

"Maybe." I put the gun in the holster. "I know what I'm doing. Maybe."

He started to say something then gave up. He got the voice-activated microcassette recorder out of the glove box and checked to make sure it was working. We walked through the driving snow to Montana's cabin. The door was unlocked so we went in, guns drawn. Montana looked up from a table where he was cleaning his Colt. The cylinder was removed so there was no chance for him to react.

"What do you guys want?"

"Your butt buried in the snow. Me standing over you with a smile on my face," I said.

"So that's the way it's going to be, huh?"

"Told you to leave her alone."

"Just gonna whack me out. Kinda chickenshit, ain't it?"

"Not like that," I said. "Considered coming up here and beating the crap out of you but I'd just enjoy it too much. And it wouldn't be enough. Too easy for you and too much energy to waste on a weasel."

"The champion of good, huh?" He smiled and leaned back in his chair, putting his hands behind his head.

"Put 'em back on the table," Chick said, snapping back the hammer on his .380. "Where I can see them. Do it now."

Montana put his hands, palms down, on the table. "Boy, you guys're sure jumpy. Relax. You want a drink?"

I ignored him. "How'd it feel, Coy, shooting a guy dying of cancer? Having a gunfight with some guy that didn't have a chance."

"He wanted it that way."

"You like being Coy Montana, fastest gun in the West, don't you?"

"Yeah. I am the fastest."

"So tell me, how was it with Matt Jenkins?"

He smiled. My jaw tightened as I squeezed my molars together. "It was just fine. He called it. Wanted to shoot it out. We went out to the corral and he was all worked up. He'd been drinking. I told him he could draw first. He said something about him winning either way it went down. That I was doing him a favor. Must've meant the cancer. Said somebody'd come after me if I got him. He meant you, huh?

"Anyway, he reached for his gun." His eyes turned dreamy now, as if in the throes of sexual ecstasy. "And I cleared my holster and fanned four shots into him and he went down. Yeah, died with his boots on. It was just fine."

"Four shots?" I said. "One of them missed."

"One out of four when you're fanning the hammer is pretty damn good."

"Get your gun belt and put it on," I said.

"We gonna shoot it out?" he said, chuckling to himself.

"Just put your belt on and shut up. I've got something to show you. Chick, get his gun and put it together. Get some shells for him, too. Let's go."

We went outside, with Chick prodding Montana with his gun. The snow had let up but was still coming down in large flakes, more falling and drifting than driving and swirling now. Gentle. Peaceful.

That's when we saw the large bearlike form walking through the snow.

"What the hell're you guys doing now?" said Dirk Donovan.

"Go home, Dirk," I said.

"I need him," said Donovan, his eyes squinting through the flakes.

"You can have him in a minute," I said.

"Alive."

"Sure are particular."

"Who's this asshole?" Montana asked.

"Your only hope of getting out of here alive," said Donovan.

"Stay out of it, Donovan," I said.

"Can't do that," he said. "You turned in Braden's kid and screwed everything up. Braden scheduled a press conference tomorrow afternoon. Word is he's going to withdraw. They're on my ass back East. I need the little black book you have."

"There's nothing in it of any interest to you. We were just trying to throw you a curve."

"Still want it."

I shrugged.

"What's this got to do with me?" asked Montana.

"Big money," said Dirk. "You refute their story. Take responsibility for everything. You'll never spend a minute inside. We'll guarantee it."

"Who's we?"

"The federal government."

"What do you mean? Who are you?"

"Can't tell you that."

"How do I know what you're telling me is straight?"

"Because he's a member of that famous international fraternal organization," said Chick. "The Central Ignorance Agency. But he can't help you today, Coy boy."

"He's going with me," said Donovan.

"I don't think so," I said.

"But I insist."

"No, Dirk," said Chick. "You can't have him. Now, I know that pisses you off, but I can't help it. And you're good. Real good. And you know there's nobody from Langley I'd rather be screwed over by, but I'm with Storme and you know what that means."

Donovan crossed his arms. He laughed. "Might have to be that way."

"Can't chance that," said Chick. He pointed the .380 at Dirk. "You're too good. Come on over here now, old buddy."

"That's a little bitty shooter, Chick," said Dirk. "Always liked small calibers, didn't you? I'm a big guy. Probably wouldn't be able to stop me from getting my gun out."

"Aw, come on, Dirk," Chick said. "Don't be that way. You've seen me shoot. Base of the throat. Hard to shoot when you're gargling blood. And you know he ain't worth it."

"You've got a point," said Dirk. "Hands on top of my head?"

"That'll do it. Fingers laced."

"You'll tell them I did my best if anybody asks?"

"Sure."

"What the hell is going on here?" asked Montana, as Donovan walked toward Chick.

"Big guy stuff," Chick said. "Don't worry yourself with it." Chick got behind the agent and, grabbing the collar of Dirk's jacket, pulled it halfway down the heavy man's arms, then reached inside Dirk's suitcoat and pulled out the Glock.

"That's the second time you've gotten the drop on me and taken my gun. I must be slipping."

Chick said, "No. Seen you work enough to know you wouldn't let it happen twice. Walking through the snow and hollering out. Tsk, tsk. A crummy performance. Never make it on Broadway. But anybody asks me I'll cover for you."

"Thanks."

"Anything for a buddy."

Montana was confused by the turn of events. Good. I was going to need every edge I could get.

"I've been practicing, Coy," I said. "Want you to see how good I'm getting." I pointed at his truck. "See the big O in COY on your license plate? That's about twenty yards from here, wouldn't you say?"

"Yeah sure. So what?"

"Think you could fan your wheel gun and put four shots into the circle?"

"Not fanning it," he said. "Nobody could do that. Maybe do it if I had time to aim."

I pulled off my coat. Facing the truck, I quickly reached and jerked the Browning free of the shoulder holster, pointed, and very deliberately squeezed off four rounds, punching dark holes that obliterated the circle. The noise of the gun rang in my ears. I turned and looked at him.

"Big deal," Montana said. "Took you all day to shoot."

"See, you don't pay attention. All four shots went where I

aimed. Not three out of four. All four went where I wanted them. Can do it every time. Fast doesn't mean anything. Accuracy. That's the key. A steady hand. A sure eye. And motivation to hit what you aim to hit."

"Might be a different story when somebody's shooting back."

"I don't think so, Coy. See, you killed my friend. You've been scaring his wife. My one true love has dumped me. This is not a good time for me. Lot of frustration. And I don't like you. Right now, I only want to do one thing and that's put a bullet in your brain. Now," I said, removing the clip from the pistol and taking out all the bullets except one. I reinserted the clip and shuffled the shell into the chamber. "Here's the way it's going to work. You get one bullet."

"One bullet?"

"That's right. One bullet. Twenty yards apart. A little different than you're used to. And you only get one shot. Better make it a good one, because I always hit what I aim at and I haven't decided where to put the bullet yet." I felt my jaw tighten. "But I'm going to get my chance because I don't think you've got the nerve to take me with one shot. Wonder which bullet missed Matt? I'm betting it's the first one."

His mouth was working now. "What about him?" he asked, nodding at Chick. "What's to keep him from shooting me?"

"He won't."

"How do I know that?"

"Because I said he won't. Tell him, Chick."

Chick didn't look happy. "I won't kill you, Montana," he said. "Not today."

"There you have it, Coy, old pard," I said. "Put a bullet in his gun, Chick, and put the gun in his holster."

Chick did so, then said, "If you get any ideas about shooting before Storme's ready, Montana, I'll put the whole clip in you."

"May I take my hands off my head now?" asked Dirk.

"Sure," Chick said.

"Go stand him behind his truck," I said. Chick walked Montana at gunpoint to the truck, then backed away, the .380 trained on him. I saw Montana looking at the license plate.

I faced him, the gun at my side.

"Don't do it, Montana," said Donovan. "You don't draw, Storme won't shoot. Not in cold blood, and Easton'll get you for sure if you get Storme. Sooner or later."

Montana looked hesitant.

"What's the matter, Montana?" I said. "Afraid? Thought you were the fastest gun in the West. Or is that just talk?"

His eyes narrowed. "Ain't afraid of you."

"Then let's get it done."

"You gonna holster your gun?"

"No. Gives you a chance to show how fast you are." The tension was giving me a headache. Relax, Storme.

"You think that's fair?" His voice sounded strained through the curtain of snow.

"Don't care about fair. Just *want* to shoot you. You going to pull that thing or run your mouth?"

His hand clenched, then relaxed.

The snow fell between us.

I raised the Browning. As I did, Montana's gun seemed to jump from the holster. I saw the powderflash of the cylinder then felt a sensation above my hip like being punched with the end of a baseball bat. It turned me sideways a quarter turn. I recovered and held the gun on Montana, sighting on his heart.

"Shot too soon," I said. "Different without backup, isn't it? One squeeze and it's all over for you. Where to put the bullet, though?" I started walking toward him. The leg didn't respond quite right and I shipped to one side. "Between the eyes? Through the throat? Maybe the heart? What if I just give you a disfiguring wound? Shoot you through the cheek? Take off an ear." I felt dampness seeping down my side. There was a heavy, expanding circle of pain in my left side. I tried not to think about it. "Or just blow out a kneecap."

I walked closer. Within ten feet now.

"No more line-dancing with the young fillies. Carry a cane for life. Limp everywhere."

He had his back against the truck, the gun hanging from his hand like a dead animal. I could see his chest heaving.

"No," I said, still advancing. "I've got it." I pointed the gun between his legs. "Right in the crotch. Make a gelding out of you. I tell you I got a hollow-point in the chamber? In like a pinhole out like a porthole."

Montana fell to his knees in the snow. "No!" he said, one arm out to me. "Please. Don't. Don't shoot me."

I stood over him. He was shaking from cold and fear. His lips were trembling. Snot ran from his nose. I put the barrel of the Browning against his forehead. "You shouldn't have done that to Matt, you son of a bitch," I said between gritted teeth.

"Don't do it, Wyatt," said Chick. "We got his confession on tape. This won't solve anything. Let it go. It ain't no good, man."

My breathing was labored now and there was a thudding heaviness in my left hip. The inside of my head was frosted with cobwebs. Static waves of pain crackled up my leg. I thought about Matt. I pointed the gun between his killer's legs and pulled the trigger. The gun cracked and a spray of dirt and snow erupted in a tiny volcano between Montana's knees.

He jumped in surprise and slumped sideways in the snow, snuffling and sobbing, untouched by the shot. I could smell the involuntary release of his bowels.

I watched him writhe pitifully in the snow.

"Missed," I said. "Never was any good up close."

My side throbbed with each heartbeat like a kinked garden hose and I felt light-headed. The white-powdered trees swirled around me.

I swayed and dropped to my knees on the cold, damp ground.

And the snow fell like feathers.

EPILOGUE

I was packing.

Leave my mountain behind.

Things were over. Done. However unfinished they might be.

Roy Orbison's haunting tenor filled the cabin. I stopped what I was doing and changed stations. Couldn't listen to him now.

"Wouldn't have worked out anyway." I surprised myself by speaking out loud. Nobody was listening. Loony.

I packed my bow, my Winchester 94 and the new pistol, and loaded them in the Bronco. Head for Missouri and whitetail deer and solitude. Different meadows. Different trails. Far from here. No snow there.

We turned the tape of our conversation with Coy Montana over to Detective Elliot. It was inadmissible as evidence, but it gave him enough to pursue it further. The gun Montana shot me with matched the riflings on the bullets that killed Matt Jenkins. Montana had foolishly kept the gun as a keepsake.

It had a notch in the handle. Only one.

The gunshot I received nipped me just above the hip and touched nothing but meat, leaving me with a temporary limp and a permanent scar. It was hard to sleep nights because of it. And because of other things. Two weeks had passed and I could get around without the cane. There was no parade in my honor. The governor didn't call and thank me. Neither did Sandy. But her half-brother came by a couple of times to clean up the cabin and do some odd jobs around it. Kid was going to be all right.

Congressman Braden had withdrawn from the Senate race. The media smelled blood and was circling the corpse. Republicans called for hearings into Michael Braden's desertion and fake death. Braden was avoiding the press. He was on borrowed time.

I sent Kelly Jenkins some of the cash I'd "confiscated" from Captain Marvel and company. She deserved it. I won't say how much. But I'm not cheap nor am I that philanthropic. It was a nice sum.

I heard a truck bumping up the grade. I looked out and saw a dented four-wheel-drive Blazer. The driver got out. It was the gofer from Channel Seven I'd paid to move my car out of Richie Caster's parking slot. I walked outside.

"Man, you live back up in here," he said. "Glad I got here before you left. Miss Collingsworth said she'd give me an extra fifty if I got up here before you left." He handed me a package and I hefted it. My Missouri address was on it.

"If you weren't here I was supposed to send it Fed Ex," he said. "Glad I caught you. Worth a hundred bucks to me."

He wished me a nice day and left. Drove through the mountain snow with a summer smile on his face. I don't remember what I said to him.

There was a letter attached to the outside of the package. "Read this first," it said. I peeled the envelope from the package and walked back into the cabin. Once inside, I laid the package on the table and sat down. Opened the letter.

Inside, in familiar handwriting, it said:

Dear Wyatt:

I've had time to think. About you. About us. Father just left. He's been playing Barnabas to your Paul.

So much has happened. Too much. You hurt me with Kelly Jenkins. I couldn't stand the thought of it. I was so angry it made me sick.

I remember something you said, the second time you asked to marry me. I said there had been other men and you said you didn't care (in fact you said something silly like "none that can bend horseshoes with their eyebrows" or some such thing). You never mentioned it again.

Mother knew about Father's indiscretion. He told her. At the end Mother had nothing left but her love for him. Her death was too much for him. He was overcome by it. Mother's love for him was unconditional. All these years I've been afraid to love like that.

I did come to rescue you the other night. Couldn't stand to think about something happening to you. I don't understand the way you live. It's frightening. Probably why you don't like to share it with me.

I have something for you. Inside the package. You'll know what to do. As always.

Sandy

I sat. Stared at the package. Starting to snow again. Had to leave soon or I would be stranded. Soon. I looked at the package some more.

I opened it.

Inside was a strange gift. In two pieces.

It was a broken arrow.